THE LEGACY OF WIZARDRY

Alodar gazed at the master wizard and read the truth of all that Handar had told him. "But is it certain that I alone must oppose this greatest of demons?" he asked.

Handar nodded silently.

Alodar filled his lungs with a slow rush of air. "It is not for this that I have quested," he said at last. "But I have offered my life already, and then merely for a queen. How can I sacrifice less for the fate of all our world?"

"It is as I knew you would say." Handar tossed Alodar the crystal of magic metal.

"But when and how should I use it?" Alodar asked. "Now, just before the attack, during the battle, or only if all seems irretrievably lost?"

Handar slowly shook his head. "That is for you, the archimage, to decide," he said softly.

Master of the Five Magics

LYNDON HARDY

A Del Rey Book

BALLANTINE BOOKS • NEW YORK

A Del Rey Book
Published by Ballantine Books

Library of Congress Catalog Card Number: 80-66556

ISBN 0-345-31157-4

Manufactured in the United States of America

First Edition: October 1980
Fourth Printing: February 1983

Cover art by Rowena Morrill

To my wife, Joan

CONTENTS

PART ONE: *The Thaumaturge*

PART TWO: *The Alchemist*

PART THREE: *The Magician*

PART FOUR: *The Sorcerer*

PART FIVE: *The Wizard*

THAUMATURGY

≈

The Principle of Sympathy — like produces like
The Principle of Contagion — once together, always
together

ALCHEMY

▽

The Doctrine of Signatures — the attributes without mirror
the powers within

MAGIC

○

The Maxim of Persistence — perfection is eternal

SORCERY

The Rule of Three — thrice spoken, once
fulfilled

WIZARDRY

Law of Ubiquity — flame permeates all
Law of Dichotomy — dominance or submission

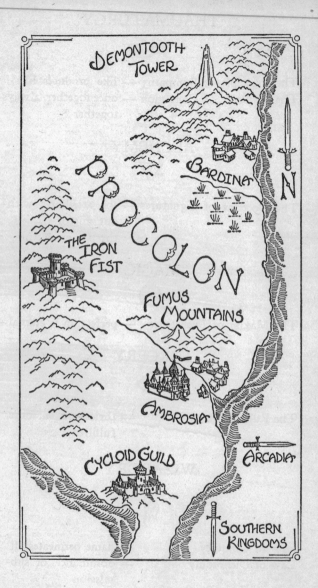

feelings with him. I am a journeyman at an honest craft and accept my lot. I desire no empty formality that stirs up the dying embers of the past."

He stopped and stared into the big man's eyes. "And I ask no more than what you should show any man who labors in our common defense, regardless of his station."

For a long moment their eyes remained locked, but finally the sergeant shrugged and turned to the group of men crouching within the archway into the keep. "To your positions, then," he ordered.

The men rose, and two edged out to the crenelations which framed a deep cut in the hills to the west. The third, the smallest of the three, climbed into a waist-high wicker basket which stood by the spinning disk.

Alodar stepped to the woven box, withdrew a chisel from one of the pockets in his cape, and hacked a fresh splinter from it. His cowl was thrown back over his shoulders, revealing a narrow face topped with fine yellow-brown hair. His nose and mouth were drawn with an economy of line, plain and straight, with nothing to mark him as either handsome or uncomely. Only his eyes removed him from the nondescript; they were bright and alive, darting like dragonflies, missing no detail of what happened around him. His face held the smoothness of youth, now marked only by two short furrows above his nose as he concentrated on the task before him.

Standing scarcely taller than the basket's occupant, he stepped back from the box, holding the scrap of wood at waist level, glanced again at the position of the sun, and began the incantation.

He spoke with skill; the words came quickly but with the sharpness necessary for success. His tone was even and the rhythm smooth. The two words of power sounded with a lack of distinction. They fitted unnoticed into the stream of improvised nonsense which surrounded them. In a moment he was done.

Alodar nodded a warning to the man-at-arms facing him and slowly began to raise the splinter upward. Simultaneously the basket lurched and cleared the stonework of the platform. The splinter rose with almost imperceptible slowness but the gondola with its passenger climbed at a rapid rate.

The big man returned to Alodar's side. "Can you not

go faster? They will spy him before he lines with the sun."

"No, sergeant," Alodar said, not turning to nod in reply but keeping his attention on the sliver he held in his hand. "This splinter is about one part in a thousand of the basket as a whole. For each palm I raise it, your man climbs another forty rods. Were I to move faster, we might use too much of the wheel's spin just in fighting the wind we would make with our haste. I do not yet wear the cape of a master, but I understand enough of thaumaturgy to do what is proper for this task."

The sergeant grunted and Alodar continued to raise the splinter upward. Several minutes passed and the basket rose to become but a speck in the sky.

"High enough," one of the men shouted while sighting through his sextant. Alodar glanced at the wheel. The crank now turned lazy circles about the axle with no hint of the blurring speed it had possessed moments ago. The sergeant followed his gaze and looked back at Alodar.

"If there is but little wind," Alodar explained, "there is enough spin left to keep the gondola properly positioned for some time. It takes far less energy to resist a sideward thrust than to fight the earth for height."

While he spoke, Alodar began to step in the direction of the hills. The platform far above moved in proportion. The two observers darted their instruments about, sighting first the sun, then the basket, and finally the crags themselves. Alodar made but two slow steps and part of another before one of the observers called him to stop.

"A little more forward now. Hold it an instant. Now to the left a palm. Freeze it in place," he directed as Alodar shifted the splinter back and forth.

Morwin jumped from his inactivity beside the slowly turning disk and ran through the archway to the chamber beyond. He fetched a tripod with a small clamp attached and returned to where Alodar stood with the splinter still at arm's length. After a few moments of adjustment, the clamp was in position to secure the scrap of wood firmly, and Alodar relinquished his grip. Massaging his now numb arm, he moved quickly to the edge of the bartizan to see the results of his effort.

He whisked a telescope out from his cape and sighted the basket. It now stood fixed firmly in the sky, suspended

4

directly in front of one of the sheer cliffs that was their target.

"Luck be with him soon," the sergeant muttered as he watched with his own glass. "If he does not find a ledge wide enough for the catapult within the hour, we will strike no blow for ourselves this day. And tomorrow may be too late for any scheme, sound or foolish, to prevent a breach."

Alodar turned from watching the rider scramble onto the face of the cliff and looked at the plain below.

"They will be in the bailey within two days for certain," the sergeant continued. "And even if help did appear, how could it get through all that?"

Alodar followed the sweep of the mailed arm, and the sick feeling returned to his empty stomach.

The gray hills in the west stretched from horizon to horizon, stark and unbroken except for the one deep and wide notch, like a missing tooth, directly facing him about half a mile distant. The walls on the right rose tall and sheer, unbroken monoliths, smooth and inaccessible. The slopes on the left were as steep but cracked with fissures, chimneys, and ledges, and upon these clambered the man Alodar had transported there. Between the two faces, a train of wagons and carts, piled with baggage and arrayed with no pattern, hid the floor of the pass from view. Alodar could make out a motley collection of tents rising in its midst, and from the pinnacles of each flew a blue and silver banner.

Much closer stood an orderly array of artillery, drawn out in a precise circle that Alodar knew completely surrounded the stronghold. With drilled exactness, their crews would load and fire in unison. The great bows of the ballistas hurled their rock hard and flat against the battered outer walls, while the mangonels sent theirs high and lofted to rain down on the foundation of the keep and the surrounding courtyard. Lighter but more accurate trebuchets blasted at the spots already weakened by the heavier siegecraft.

Nearer still, in more irregular array, many clusters of armed men crouched behind full-length shields shining angrily in the morning sun. The groups farther back used their protection, casually bobbing heads and torsos to see the battle's progress. Those closer, within range of the defenders' longbows, huddled in tight balls, exposing no arm or a leg as a target.

With each volley of the rockthrowers, the answering fire from the manchicolations and loopholes in the castle's walls would cease, and the men in the field would creep a little closer, their scaling ladders and belfries dragging behind them. From high on the keep, Alodar could see that, long before the clusters reached the outer wall, they would converge into a single continuous ring of attackers.

"Yes, it would take a large force to break through to us," he finally agreed, "but Iron Fist has never fallen to assault."

"It takes more than stone and iron to defend this mound," the sergeant said. "Muscle pulls tight the bowstrings and swings the broadswords, and at last muster we numbered fewer than two hundred fighting men. Two hundred for over half a mile of wall."

He shook his head with lips pulled into a tight line of disapproval. "A mere two hundred, because Vendora wanted to flaunt her might along the southern border. Almost every garrison in Procolon stripped to nothing, so that those petty border kingdoms think to stop their raids and return to bickering among themselves. Hah, I wonder if those raids seem so important to her now? Fully provisioned, we could withstand anything that Bandor could throw at us. As it is, only the great height and thickness of these walls have saved her crown and pretty neck this long."

"But her miscomputation was no worse than mine," Alodar said, spreading his palms outward. "How would anyone but a sorcerer surmise that one of her most faithful vassals would suddenly lose his reason and plunge through that gap in the west, just when she was here? The gates clanged shut on noble and craftsman alike who happened to be here, and none claim to have foreseen it."

"Yes, it is strange," the sergeant said. "The ferocity of the attack, the way he drives his men on with no regard for their exhaustion. I have heard it whispered about more than once at night that Bandor has lost not his reason but his will. Like a mere craftsman, he has been possessed."

6

Alodar blinked with surprise, but before he could reply he was interrupted by one of the observers.

"He has found a spot and is signaling for us to proceed."

"Sweetbalm, luck is with us today," the sergeant exclaimed, jumping his thoughts back to the task at hand. "Start bringing up the beams and lashings."

Alodar stepped to the stand and released the splinter from the clamp. Holding it at arm's length, he dropped his hand a fraction of an inch. The basket sank correspondingly, and the wheel again started to spin. He retraced his steps, and it shot across the sky to hover directly overhead. Finally, as he lowered the splinter, it settled gently onto the floor of the bartizan. Again the giant crank was a blur as the wheel spun, but it turned not nearly as fast as when Morwin had first propelled it.

Alodar rapidly recited another incantation, virtually indistinguishable from the first. When he was done, he flung the splinter high into the air with a dramatic gesture while the basket remained unperturbed on the ground.

The men-at-arms wasted no time in loading two large notched beams into the basket. Morwin against cranked up the wheel, and Alodar removed a fresh splinter and spoke the incantation. Moving with more haste than before, he brought the splinter directly to the clamp; the basket with its burden hurled from the castle to the cliffs. The sergeant directed some small corrections until the basket hovered directly below the ledge that the rider had found. Morwin moved the clamp and secured the splinter in the new position.

After the gondola was unloaded, the entire process was repeated many times, with each worker intent upon his tasks. Alodar broke the spell upon the return. Morwin rewound the crank and the men-at-arms packed a new load of beams, brands, or lashings. Another incantation and fixing of a splinter in the clamp and another bundle would be delivered to the ledge in the distance. Several hours later the men-at-arms were the passengers for the final two trips, and then the job was done.

Weary from the concentration, Alodar looked to the west. "How long will it take them to assemble it?" he asked.

"At least six hours. They must take care to tune it to

7

exactly the same tension it had here. Every shot will count, and they can waste none on range calibration," the sergeant responded, his voice now showing some excitement. "With just a bit more luck, Bandor's entire siege train will be smouldering ashes by nightfall."

They fell silent and waited, listening to time being marked off by the rhythmic crash of rock and swish of arrows below. Near dusk, Alodar sprang up from his vigil excitedly.

"Look, they are signaling that they are ready."

As he spoke, a flaming brand arched upwards from the ledge and down into the valley, disappearing into the silhouettes of the tents formed by the setting sunlight.

A minute passed with no discernable change in the campsite; but then as the second shot was being launched, the central tent became alive with flame.

"A hit, a direct hit on Bandor's tent," the sergeant shouted. "Look at it take hold of that dry canvas! It will spread to the others in no time at all. And look, here comes the next missile right on the mark as well."

A second tent burst into flame, and then a third. Even from the distance, Alodar could hear an alarm gong sound and the rising hubbub of voices.

"They are shifting targets now; good men." The sergeant banged his fist down on the wall. "Let us see how those wagons can stand up to a little heat."

The incendiaries began falling more rapidly as the crew on the ledge gained confidence in their engine, raking their fusillade back and forth across the pass, starting fires at random in the densely packed train. Alodar could see some of the blazes start up and then quickly be snuffed out; but for every one extinguished, two more sprouted elsewhere in the camp. In some places, the isolated pinpoints of light had converged into large walls of leaping flame, brilliant even against the setting sun.

Finally trumpets sounded from somewhere within the widening conflagration, and the siegecraft directly between the camp and the castle ceased their firing. Throwing arms and cranks were battened down, rocks tossed back upon supply wagons, and the engines began to withdraw. A frantic mob of men burst from the flame and confusion, like seeds from a flattened melon, and ran to meet them, alternately waving greater haste and pointing up into the cliffs from which came the rain of fire. Alodar heard the zing of arrows from the castle walls increase intensity as the defenders, unchallenged for the first time in days, vented their frustrations. The assault from the west ground to a halt.

"The range is too great for them to be accurate enough," the sergeant crowed. "They will never dislodge us from there. A few more hits will put the fire completely out of control. Let us see what kind of siege Bandor can conduct, demon driven or not, with no supplies and only this brushland to forage on."

Alodar watched intently as the mangonels were turned into a straight line, halfway between their previous positions and the enemy camp. A hint of hope soothed the rumble in his stomach as the first volley fell short of the ledge, crashing into the face of the cliff far below. His eyes swept back and forth across the panorama, up to the ledge, into the burning camp, and back to the engines and the growing mass of men surrounding them.

"But wait a moment," he said suddenly. "I see the logo of similarity on that cape down there. See, the tall one, next to the second mangonel. He is a master, just as Periac is. I fear that my craft will play a still larger role in the affairs of the day."

As they watched, the master thaumaturge directed the three running up behind him to dump the sacks they carried onto the ground. A pile of small stones discharged from each. Two more men lugged into position a huge cauldron and began filling it from a wagonload of jars that halted alongside.

"Lodestones," Alodar cried with sudden recognition. "Tracers. By the laws, let there be no marksman good enough for this task among them."

A small group of archers formed a single file; as they passed the cowled figure, he deftly chipped a fragment from each rock and gave it to one of the bowmen. After each had received his charge, he bound it to the shaft of an arrow and let fly at the catapult in the cliff above.

Alodar watched the ledge as the missiles hurled upwards. Most were wide of the mark, splintering against hard rock and falling back to the floor of the pass. Several minutes passed as volley after volley did no harm. But

9

finally one shot struck the frame of the catapult and held fast.

"Quickly!" Alodar shouted. "Signal them to remove the shaft before he can complete the incantation."

"But a single arrow does them no harm, journeyman. Let them use their time to continue firing while it is still light," the sergeant said. "You remain with your craft and I will manage mine."

"Get it removed or they will hurl nothing more today. See, they have the other stone in the acid already."

As he spoke, the master cracked one of the remaining untouched rocks in two and dropped one half into the cauldron steaming atop a hastily constructed fire. The brew frothed like storm-driven surf as three heavyset men slowly tipped the contents of the huge crucible onto a pile of artillery stones stacked at their feet. The crews from the siegecraft each retrieved one hot wet stone and loaded and cocked their engines. The thaumaturge held his hands high overhead. In one was the stone from which the chip now affixed to the catapult had been cleft; in the other was the remains of the one consumed in the acid bath. Alodar held his breath, knowing what was to come next.

A mailed figure astride the horse surveyed the ready engines and the waiting craftsman. He signaled the crews to fire and the projectiles sprang from their beds in unison. An instant later, with the missiles already rising high into the air, the thaumaturge brought the two small stones swiftly together.

The flying rocks wrenched out of their natural trajectories; like sunlight focused with a glass, they converged simultaneously on the ledge. The catapult exploded in a mass of ragged timber, splinters, and dust. The bombarding rock shattered into an avalanche of gravel against the cliff face and cascaded to the plain. The hills rocked with the violence of the impact and the shock threw Alodar nearly to his knees. Where once there had been form was now a shattered ruin of timber and flesh.

The scene was quiet, attacker and defender alike shaken by the force of the blow. Alodar looked back at the enemy camp and noticed only a few wisps of smoke where the fire had raged but moments before. Of course, the perfect source, he thought.

As the last rays of the sun faded, the detachment of artillery slowly returned to the besieging circle and both sides made ready for the cessation of action for the day. As elsewhere, the stunned silence continued for several minutes more up on the high keep. Finally the sergeant turned for the archway.

"In two days, for certain," he muttered..

"A waste of time, if you ask me, Alodar," Morwin said irritably as they stumbled along the passageway that evening. "How are we, in a single night, going to find something that has eluded the occupants of this fortress for probably three hundred years? And with a single torch yet? Why, I can barely make you out two feet before me, let alone some secret mark along these clammy walls. And you know Periac is probably pacing his quarters right now, wanting a full report on what happened today with the air gondola. Let's be done with this, I say."

"Not just yet, Morwin," Alodar said. "I admit it seems hopeless, but what are we to do? Just follow through our prescribed tasks until the inevitable happens?"

"Oh, by the laws, Alodar, I relish this entrapment as little as you. But I would rather save my strength for something useful tomorrow, rather than burning off my evening gruel sloshing through puddles in the dark, three full flights beneath the ground."

"But look, Morwin, there must be something to aid us here. Some clue to help us break the siege. Think about it. Why are these passages and chambers under the walls even here? The whole castle is laid out with such an economy of design, not a wasted stone anywhere. The perfect fortress, the men-at-arms say. The flanking towers project out just the right amount to cover walls of optimum height. Crenelations and loopholes are cut to maximize both protection and density of fire. The central keep is pocked with bartizans of all sizes for observation of missile launching. With all of that care, why honeycomb the thing with these subterranean caverns unless they too somehow play in the defense?"

"Well then, for what do the records of the builders say all of this is to be used? We use the chamber under the northeast tower on the first level as an area of discipline.

11

Perhaps this place was intended to be a grand dungeon?"

"With this layout, hardly. There aren't any small cells, just long corridors connecting large chambers, and no gates to impede one's access. And as to the builders, would that we could ask them. The sagas say only that when the scions of Procolon first pushed into these desolate western lands they found the Iron Fist open and unoccupied. The portcullis was up and the oaken doors of the gatehouse full ajar. Inside was nary a trace of man or beast or any sign that any had ever been here. Just mute stone in a silent wasteland. Vendora's forefathers used their luck well, granted. They garrisoned the place, and ever since it has protected Procolon's western flank with its grip of iron against the likes of a Bandor gone wild. But no one living knows more of this castle's secrets than even you or . . . Hold, I think we are under the keep again."

Alodar thrust his torch forward, staring into the blackness ahead. He could see the walls receding from him on both sides the gloom but could discern no other detail of their surroundings. He began to move cautiously to the left, one hand on moist stone, the other still advancing the torch in front.

"Look," he exclaimed, "a wall cresset, and with oil still in it." He touched his torch to the small pool in the lip of the rock and it sprang to life. He and Morwin again looked about them, now able to see to the opposite wall of the chamber.

"Cressets all around, Alodar," Morwin said. "At least here we will be able to see what we are stumbling over."

Alodar quickly circled the chamber, lighting the wall flames as he did so. When he was done, he moved towards the center to survey what the flickering light revealed. The chamber was large and circular, though not as huge as the massive keep which towered above it. The walls were smooth and damp, pieced with precision from many small stones and pierced by four dark archways evenly spaced around the periphery. The stone floor sloped downwards from all directions; in the very center stood a pool of dark water fed by the drippings from the walls. As he approached, Alodar thrust the handle of his torch into the still surface.

"Why, there is a well here, Morwin," he exclaimed.

"See, the depth is much greater than the slope of the floor would indicate. I wonder how deep it is?"

Suddenly a flicker of light in one of the passageways caught his eye. As he and Morwin turned, they heard the clank of arms and the stomp of many feet echoing down towards them.

In a moment, several men-at-arms tromped into the chamber, torches held high and swords drawn. "Halt, who's there?" the first called out belligerently as his eyes adjusted to the increased light.

"Alodar, journeyman, and Morwin, apprentice, to master thaumaturge Periac, in the service of fair queen Vendora," Alodar quickly responded as half a dozen more poured into the room.

"Then you serve me in most unusual ways, journeyman," a woman's voice answered him in turn, soft and distinctive amid the growing din.

Alodar turned from the approaching men to the new speaker, and his eyes widened in surprise.

"Caution, my fair lady," growled the tall, white-haired man who now entered and stood beside her. "I remember this name, Alodar, and I doubt his interests would truly serve your crown."

Vendora the queen smiled at Alodar and then turned to her advisor. "And what great threat does this journeyman harbor, lord Festil?" she asked. She brushed back the tumble of her golden blond hair with deliberate casualness. Her blue eyes, that mirrored the morning sea, sparkled above a small upturned nose and lips of apple red. Her smile radiated the promise of delight, and Alodar felt his pulse suddenly quicken. She wore men's clothing, leggings, tunic, and cape, but they did not hide the thrust of her ample figure. With a dramatic sweep, she thrust back the cape and stood arms akimbo, left fist above a small dagger, awaiting Festil's reply.

"You were too young a princess to take notice, my fair lady," Festil said. "But many were the council meetings in which your father pounded the table with rage, the blood bloating the veins of his neck, his face flushed red. And all because one headstrong vassal dared to stand fast to his opinions when unanimity with royal persuasion was obviously what discretion demanded."

Festil stopped and then pointed his red-gloved fist at

13

Alodar. His lips downturned with displeasure, pulling tight age-blotched skin across high-thrust cheeks on his narrow face. "No, my fair lady, this man's father put his interests before those of the crown. In the end, he refused to yield one time too often and received his just due. It was a matter of no lasting importance, but your sire demonstrated that he was indeed king. His lands confiscated and title revoked by royal decree, Alodun ended his days in common squalor, trying to enlist others in his effort to regain what was no longer rightfully his. I judge his son tracks you here seeking restitution, hoping the years would dim the memories of your father's faithful advisors. But I served your sire well, as I serve you now, and on his deathbed promised that I would ensure nothing be forgotten in matters of state."

Vendora dropped her arms to her sides and laughed. Her voice floated lightly like a wind-blown leaf, with no hint of the weight of the crown. "But if I were but a young princess, lord Festil," she said, "then the journeyman here could have been but a lad. How deep could such passion burn in a heart so young?"

She turned to Alodar, eyes widening, and he felt the royal demand for a reply. For an instant he paused. Festil's words stung, and the memories boiled out of their hiding places, fresh as when they were new. He had been young, yes. Too young to aid, but old enough to feel the helplessness when he saw the faces of cruel laughter and the sneers over shoulders of hastily turned backs. He remembered the image of his father, eyes finally dim and spirit broken. Not a single vassal had pledged to convince a stubborn monarch to return what he had so capriciously taken away. The impulse to lash out with words of his own welled up within him, but he clenched his fist into a tight ball and swallowed painfully.

It was so futile a struggle then, he thought. Could it be any different now? Was not the decision to cease resistance to the forces which overwhelmed him a good one? Renounce the claim to be a noble of Procolon and follow instead wherever fate might lead him. Ignore the feeling of incompleteness, of nagging dissatisfaction with each niche in life that he might try. Travel on to the next and the next, sampling and testing until he found the one that he could embrace with relaxing acceptance.

He looked into Vendora's eyes and spoke slowly. "As I have said, my fair lady, I am a journeyman thaumaturge. Not that my craft should matter. Since my father's death, I have been many things, goatherd, woodcutter, tavernhand. And it is true that I seek, but my presence here is not by plan of supplication. Rather I had hoped that these dungeons might finally yield something to aid us all."

"And what have you found?"

"Nothing, my lady, nothing yet," Alodar said turning his gaze from Vendora to answer the smaller woman similarly clad standing at her side. She too had her cowl thrown back revealing short auburn hair and eyes that danced darkly in the firelight. If she were by herself, men would turn to look, but next to Vendora her beauty would go unnoticed.

"Sweetbalm, of course nothing. Nothing as one with any sanity would expect," Festil exploded, brushing aside Alodar's presence with a wave of his hand. "May I state the case bluntly again, my fair lady? We will not extricate ourselves from this siege by following the whims of lady Aeriel here, no matter how good her intentions. This is a matter that can be settled only by arms, arms striking in unison to achieve the same objective. You must choose, and choose now before it is too late."

"My choice for life, merely to help us better fight a border skirmish. A weighty choice indeed, lord Festil," Vendora responded.

"It may well be your life, my fair lady. We are too undermanned to defend the walls properly. We must use every man and weapon we have with utmost efficiency. Yet we squander our time and resources in as many ways as we have lords within these walls. Andac launches a sally with no cover; Fendel crams all of his archers into the southwest tower, leaving the whole southwall unprotected; old Cranston detaches his men to the bidding of a mere craftsman with some mad gondola scheme. And why is this chaos so? Because each man strives to outdo the next in some feat of valor, some deed for the sagas, to make you swoon and choose him for your champion. Your beauty inspires great desire. Vendora, as perhaps no queen of Procolon did before, but thus far it has also created great turmoil in the realm as well."

Alodar watched as Vendora received Festil's words

15

with a slight smile, again brushing back her hair. She glanced about the room, testing what was being said, her smile broadening as she caught the reaction of each man in turn.

"My fair lady," Festil continued, pounding one fist down upon the other, "we need your choice now, not after each brave man here has gone singly to his fate in a vain attempt to impress you. Name the man and the petty bickering among our young scions will cease. Name the man and all here will follow him as we are sworn to do. Name the man so that we may fight as an army, rather than a horde of errant lords, each intent upon his own private quest."

"And so, rather than many small uncoordinated thrusts," Aeriel cut in, "we will unite and make one large one that will prove equally ineffective. You deprecate the sagas, Festil, but in your heart you cling to them still. One last hurrah and men of stout heart and unity of purpose rout the enemy against overwhelming odds and secure the Iron Fist once again. A noble tale, but one that we cannot make so. Our salvation, I think, lies outside the traditions of our forefathers."

"Had we the wisdom of our forefathers, we would not face the difficulties we have here now," Festil boomed, his voice echoing off the walls. "Had our queen chosen the hero of the realm last solstice, he would have the kingdom in good order by now. The states to the south would not risk his displeasure, and all of the border fortresses would be fully manned. Had we the champion now, he would have persuaded her to remain where she belongs in the safety of the palaces of Ambrosia. He certainly would have had the sense not to send her venturing unto the very borders with only a small party of retainers, more for show than for protection, no matter what the babbling of some court sorcerer. The mines in the Fumus Mountains may indeed be surrendering the last of their wealth, and the royal revenues thereby decreased. But to risk seeking alchemical formulas hidden here, merely on the word of enfeebled Kelric, is the height of imprudence. Why, Bandor merely had to wait until the portcullis clanged down and he nigh had Procolon handed to him on a platter."

"Enough, Festil," Vendora interjected softly but with

authority. "I grow weary of the same long-winded discourse between you and Aeriel whenever you get the opportunity. You have served my father well, and I value your council now. But I wonder how hard you would press were not your own son within these walls and vying with the rest for my favor. I will choose the hero of the realm when it suits me personally and not just the circumstances.

"And Aeriel, I weary also of this tramping about in the gloom. This chamber holds for us no better clue than the ones above, I fear. A thick iron slab on the floor of the topmost, a featureless pillar floor to ceiling in the second, and this pool of water here, with nothing else to catch the eyes. Let this journeyman continue his search and report to us anything unusual that he may find. We should now return to our chambers and contemplate how we shall conduct ourselves tomorrow."

With these words, Vendora turned and marched back into the passageway. The two men-at-arms nearest scrambled to pass in front and light the way ahead. The rest dutifully filed out behind. In a moment, Alodar and Morwin were again alone, surrounded only by the musty smell and echoes from the retreating party.

Morwin looked about the chamber, awaiting what they should do next, but Alodar stood fixed, deep in thought.

"What, speechless? A rare day for one so glib," Morwin finally said mockingly. "What affects you thus?"

Alodar was silent for a few moments more, then replied. "Your remark betrays a boy's heart still beating in that lanky frame of yours, Morwin."

"And what kind beats in yours, most august journeyman?"

"Oh, enough. Let us be off and do the queen's bidding."

17

CHAPTER TWO

Craftsman at War

THE next morning Alodar awoke with a stab of pain. He grabbed his side and blinked up into the predawn light. He heard the familiar noise of the courtyard: treading feet, clinking mail, and the barking of orders as the castle sprang to life to begin another day of defense. He squinted up at the figure standing at his side, fully armed from steel-tipped boots next to his now sore ribs to a head encased in mail.

"Up and present yourself, journeyman. You serve me and my men today. Their first barrage is but minutes away and I want you ready."

Alodar rose to sitting from the straw on the bailey floor, his head groggy from lack of sleep, and his heart heavy from the lack of success in his labors the night before.

"Come on, man, make your preparations. Wake your apprentice and get up on the high platform," the armed man persisted. "As soon as we ferret your master out of the keep, we will place him there as well. I fear we will have need of much healing today."

Alodar stood up and looked the man in the face. The features were familiar and the red surcoat confirmed his guess. "You are lord Feston, Festil's son," he said, "marshall of the west wall."

"Yes, today I am that," Feston replied curtly, staring back from deep-set eyes. He had his father's narrow face and high cheeks, but his brow jutted forward with rough angles, giving him the appearance of a perpetual squint. Beneath shaggy brows like woolly caterpillars, a large nose hooked down over a wide gash of a mouth pulled into a grim line. "Now see to your task," he said as he turned and in great haste sprinted off in the direction of the keep.

18

thrown open and archers within answering the volleys from the castle, shaft for shaft. Along the wall he heard additional screams as more missiles found their mark.

"Quickly, Morwin," he shouted. "Start filling the molds."

The next archer in the line, several crenels away, saw his stricken comrade and slowly began to crawl to him, well aware of the swish of arrows that now sailed with deadly regularity through the openings in the wall. When he arrived, he pinned the wounded man firmly, and Morwin, with one mighty heave, yanked the arrow free. The soldier cried with pain as he passed into unconsciousness, and the ragged hole in his arm disgorged a flood of deep red blood and bits of flesh.

Alodar blotted a bit of the blood onto a piece of cloth and tossed it into the small crucible he had ready, simmering nearby. He added some starch and said the incantation quickly, with no elaborate subterfuge of words. In a few moments the starch began to thicken into a gel and Alodar turned his attention to the wax, not bothering to check that the bloodflow was stopping as well.

"Which one is the coolest, Morwin?" he asked as he looked over the apprentice's growing collection of limbs, torsos, and heads that he dumped from small lead molds. The apprentice pointed to his left and then resumed filling the empty molds from the bubbling vat and lining the solidified forms in a row.

Alodar selected a waxen arm and twisted a deep gouge near the shoulder joint with his thumb. Returning to the archer, he broke the connection of the spell and then cut the mail and underjersey away from the wound. He stabbed the scraps of cloth and ringlets into the soft wax of the model and began a second incantation. When he was done, he held the limb over his small fire. Then working with steady strokes he slowly filled the gouge, returning the wax to its original smooth shape.

To all external appearances the man now seemed well; the blood had stopped and the wound was neatly closed. But from the furrowed and sweating brow Alodar knew that the pain was still there. The soldier would recover much more quickly than if unattended and with no risk of infection, but it would be some time before he again drew a bow.

"Thaumaturge, over here and hurry."

"On the second level, two men down."

"Quickly man, stop the bleeding."

Cries for Alodar's assistance rang out along the wall and from the platform underneath. He bundled up what gear he could carry and scurried toward the nearest call for help. He quickly patched up two men and moved off to a third, too intent upon his tasks to watch the progress of the approaching attack.

He attended three more on the second level in as many minutes and then climbed back up to Morwin for new supplies. As his head popped through the platform floor, he heard several ragged hurrahs and the sound of sword on shield. Down towards the flanking tower, he could see that two belfries had made contact with the wall. The blue-surcoated troops of Bandor poured from the openings onto the walkway and into the press of defenders converging upon them.

Two separate mêlées formed on the small confines of the narrow ledge. Alodar squinted at the swirls of activity but could not guess the outcome, since neither side could maneuver many men into striking position.

"By the laws, Alodar, look," Morwin shouted. Alodar ripped his gaze from the fighting to the wall immediately behind him. A third belfry thudded against the stone, and men began to jump out over the merlon onto the platform. Alodar quickly looked beyond the men to the gatehouse and then back over his shoulder to the south. No one else was near; all the men-at-arms along the wall had rushed to defend against the first two onslaughts.

Six men bounded onto the walkway, with swords drawn, and began to move towards Alodar and the ladder to the courtyard. Alodar looked wildly around the paraphernalia for some weapon to aid him. He saw the still reclining form of the first man he had tended. With a deep breath, he stooped and withdrew the unused sword from its scabbard.

The cold steel felt surprisingly heavy and unbalanced, and he clasped his left hand over his right around the thick hilt. He advanced one step and grimaced with the effort of remembering the meager instruction he had re-

22

ceived as a boy. The advancing men seemed to pay him no heed and rapidly closed upon the point of the blade he held before his chest.

As they met, the lead man raised his sword to strike, and Alodar jarred himself into action, pushing his own blade up with arms extended. The blow landed near the hilt and the edges grated along one another until the guards locked with a dull clank. Alodar felt his elbows begin to bend from the downward pressure and struggled to push them straight.

He drew his thoughts away from the others immediately behind and looked into the eyes staring back from a face ringed with mail. He saw the beginning of a smile as his arms trembled and bowed even more. With a sudden wrench, he twisted his sword free and danced aside as his opponent's blade flew past his shoulder to strike the ledge with a numbing clang. Alodar slashed down on the exposed arms and, though it did not break mail, the force of the blow pitched his adversary forward, sprawled at his feet. Hastily he glanced back upward at the other five who collapsed upon him.

"Stand aside, journeyman," he heard suddenly over his shoulder. Before he could react, he was knocked from his feet. In a blur he saw the red surcoat of Feston streak by and several more heads bob up through the platform opening.

Feston did not hesitate. Lunging low with the impetus of his initial charge, he speared the first man he encountered with the point of his sword. He raised his shield to ward off a blow from a second on the left and slammed his steel-capped knee into the groin of a third on the right. Freeing his sword, he slashed savagely down on the neck of the man as he stooped in reflex and then pirouetted to drive his blade into the face of the next. The blue surcoats hesitated and Feston sensed his advantage. Yelling loudly, he raised his sword overhead and, with swift right and left slashes, tore through their ranks. The men just exiting the belfry saw their comrades in front fall and hastily climbed back inside. The others on the platform, sensing the desertion behind them, turned and ran for the protection of the tower and shut the doors. Feston laughed a deep booming laugh as the followers

23

ran up with opportunity to strike only at Alodar's foe still sprawled on the walkway.

"Quickly, the rocker," Festil commanded as additional men rose to the top level, carrying barbed iron spikes and long coils of rope. The men spread out into two lines on either side of the belfry, uncoiling the rope as they went; while Feston strutted, guarding the doors, each line was tied to a spike driven into the belfry's frame. Then one group pulled the rope taut with a sudden jerk, rocking the tower a little to the side. As it swayed back the other team pulled in synchronization and added to the magnitude of the swing.

"And heave, and heave," Feston marked the cadence. With each thrust, the belfry rocked with greater amplitude upon its base.

Alodar picked himself up from his dazed sprawl and glanced over the wall to the ground below. "Of course, Morwin," he exclaimed. "The wheels move it forward and back. We could but push the belfry from the walls with a direct thrust but not topple it. But from the side, it sits firmly on the ground and cannot compensate for the motions we force upon it."

As he spoke, the top of the tower oscillated in wider and wider arcs. Finally it tipped over in a huge swing and continued on, to crash upon the hard ground, like the last tree logged from a forest. With a sharp wrenching growl, it splintered into several parts, throwing men, steel, and dust high into the air.

The defenders down the wall gave a shout and increased the vigor of their thrusts. The knots of men started to grow smaller as the attackers now began to inch back slowly under the intensified assault. A second shout went up as Alodar saw the other belfries also begin to rock, pushed by beams thrust through the archery loopholes one platform below. As with the first, each shove swayed the belfries more and more from a stable footing. Bandor's men gave back more ground to the press, casting anxious glances over their shoulders.

In a moment, a trumpet sounded on the plain, and the disciplined circles of blue and silver dissolved into masses of fleeing men. Swords, shields, and fallen comrades were abandoned in the rush, as if they stung to the touch. From the distance, Alodar saw the confusion as they raced for the belfries, leaping from the wall into the open doors as the towers tore free and began to pull away.

As the belfries withdrew, a third shout, the loudest of all, coursed along the wall. "We are thin," Feston yelled waving his sword above his head in defiance, "but not so thin that we cannot stand against a mere three belfries. Thus be the fate of whomever tries the walls of Iron Fist."

As quickly as they had come, the surviving siegecraft rumbled back to the precise line of mangonels and trebuchets. The scaling crews, who had never got a chance to plant their ladders, scurried alongside, shields on their backs to protect against the renewed rain of arrows from the wall. All was quiet for a moment; but once the formation was reestablished, the throwing engines resumed their bombardment.

The missiles again filled the air, but Alodar felt the tension of the morning dissolve away; the downward crash of rock seemed less potent a threat than enemy towers at the very edge of the wall. He looked about him and reassembled his gear. Ducking for cover during the volleys, he made his way methodically back and forth along the three levels of the walkway, repairing injury from the abortive thrust as he found it. Morale was high with the first success of the entire siege. The sergeant's dire prediction of the day before was nowhere to be heard. The men babbled away about the tower's great crash, and Feston's feat grew larger with each retelling. As Alodar trudged along, the day fell into the routine of the many that had preceeded it. The exchange of stone and arrow continued, but the men laughed and sang, choosing to ignore that the ring grew still tighter, and that on the morrow many more than three belfries would come.

Alodar worked his craft in reverie, wearily unmindful of the passage of time. With the setting of the sun, he and Morwin returned their gear to the cart and fell into line for their daily meal. His stomach growled, his muscles ached, and his fatigued mind had had enough of siege. As the ladle was pouring its watery contents into Alodar's bowl, he saw again the red surcoat bounding across the courtyard.

"Father, have you heard?" Feston boomed. "Hero of the day. Vendora herself pinned the ribbon on my sleeve. Ah, would that every day might present such opportunity.

25

Then there would be no doubt as to who is most worthy to be hero of the realm."

"Well done, my son," Festil replied, matching stride and pounding him firmly on the back as his group merged with Feston's. "Surely you distinguish yourself above all others here. If only the fair lady would choose now, there would be no other choice but you."

"Yes, a virtual demon of swiftness," one of the accompanying retinue broke in. "Seven men felled with but one mighty blade."

"Only seven?" Feston turned to stare at the praise-giver. "I distinctly remember nine."

"Oh, nine surely," the man quickly amended. "Nine men down and the tide of the attack turned. A tale for the sagas with no doubt."

The group marched for the northwest tower, cutting through the queue in which Alodar stood. The line parted in deference and reformed as a throng, lining the course of the men-at-arms. Alodar heard murmurs of admiration and girlish giggles as they passed through with purposeful tread and clink of mail.

"But you know, father, the competition runs keen for Vendora's hand." Feston laughed. "I was but the second man to challenge Bandor's vassals on the high wall. Some fool thaumaturge was there before me, somehow planning to stop the rush with but a single blade. I suppose to be fair, I should have given him his chance first."

"Yes, it would have served him right to take on such pretense as to be a man-at-arms," Festil replied. "These people have their uses, but they should also know the limits of proper behavior."

Alodar flung his half-filled bowl of swill to the ground, red flushing his cheeks, too fatigued to let the irritation pass by. "The defense of Iron Fist rests as heavily on our shoulders as it does upon you lofty lords," he blurted. "Without the thaumaturge, carpenter, and smith, these walls would have fallen long ago. Fault me not for picking up a sword when it was needed. It is far more than I have seen you do when the rubble was cleared or the horses fed."

The crowd fell abruptly silent, and Feston turned to see who accosted him. "Well, well, if it is not the budding hero?" he said. "And what would you have done with your great prowess at arms? Dispatched a dozen men to my nine or ten?"

"I claim no great skill at arms, my lord Feston," Alodar said slowly. "Thaumaturgy is my trade and I am here only by chance. I follow an itinerant master from settlement to outpost, earning what we can by applying our craft where it is needed. Had not the siege doors slammed shut, we would be long gone from this place and our paths never crossed. But we are here, all of us together, lord and man alike. And each of us, mason, carpenter, smith, tanner, and flockmaster, aids our common cause as best he can. I do not envy you your skill at arms, only question your judgment that its value far exceeds what I have to offer."

Feston advanced slowly back to stand directly in front of Alodar, eyes glaring down from his extra six inches of height. "Do I hear your right, most bold journeyman? Your trade of equal worth to a man-at-arms? If so, then tell me quickly now how much training have you received at the hands of warmaster Cedric in his sparring yard in Ambrosia? How many lives has your blade cut short? How many battles for Procolon have you won? How many great deeds in the sagas relate to the smith or carpenter? How many times has your like been hero of the day? Yes, perhaps even hero of the realm?"

Feston's supporters broke into laughter at his ridicule, and Alodar breathed deeply to maintain what composure he had left. "No, my lord, the sagas are silent indeed on what you speak," he said at last. "But mark you, suppose that lowly Alodar be born to the table of mighty lord Festil, and Feston scion to doomed Alodun. What then of my chance to be a hero, with blade paid for with gold, with training in arms from the likes of this Cedric, with soft bed and groaning board always provided for? And what then of yours, forced to survive as but you could, grabbing at whatever trade gave you enough coin to feed your belly and keep out the cold?"

Feston eyed Alodar's lean form, tilted his head back and drowned out even his chorus with his booming laugh. "Sweetbalm, might the blackest demons aid the house of Festil, were the likes of you born to be heir. Know you that I am marshall of the west wall, hero of the day, and the mirrors know what else, because I deserve it so

27

The blood of glory runs in my veins, and I will burn my name into as many pages of legend as I am able. I and men like me will chart the destiny of Procolon with as firm a grip of iron as this castle has upon the plain. And for that stewardship the men of this land sing grateful praise."

Before Alodar could reply, someone in the background shouted, "Hail Feston, hero of the day and savior of Iron Fist." The crowd took up a rhythmic chant, drowning out any chance of Alodar's being heard. Feston turned slowly around in a small circle, arms folded across his chest, and attempted a stern smile to acknowledge the accolade. Alodar looked at the throng as well and saw adoration on every shouting face. He spotted the first archer he had attended raising his good arm and yelling hoarsely, unmindful of who had saved his life. Even Morwin could not resist the hypnotic tug of the rhythm and shouted with the rest.

After a minute, Feston raised his arms to stop the cheers, and the courtyard fell silent, under his complete control. With even heavier sarcasm, he addressed Alodar again. "And what makes you aspire to rise above your station so, journeyman? Could it be that you hope by such a feat to turn the head of our fair lady away from true men-at-arms and upon your own heroic profile?"

To his own surprise, Alodar's cheeks flushed involuntarily as he thought of the beauty of the queen.

"Sweetbalm, my son," Festil's deep voice roared, "you have hit upon it. This shamed varlet's son seeks no less than Vendora herself and truly to be hero of the realm. You had best redouble your efforts tomorrow to stay in contention."

The crowd crowed with laughter in unison with the guffaws of the retainers, drowning out any of Alodar's sudden protestations. The noise echoed across the courtyard and seemed to him louder than any of the din of battle. He looked about for a sympathetic face; finding none, he lowered his eyes to wait until they tired of the sport. Eventually the noise began to subside, and the charge, "Feston, hero of the day," started again in its place. The men-at-arms resumed their pace towards the tower, and the crowd fell in behind, cheering them on. Alodar looked up and, seeing no eyes still upon him,

28

headed in the opposite direction across the courtyard, torn between the tugs of haste and decorum.

In a moment, he was alone. Seething in his own thoughts, he paced along the wall into the night. He struggled to submerge again the memories of hurt and frustration, but this time they would not go. He ran his hands through the many pockets of his cape, trying to concentrate on the contents he found there, enumerating the ways in which they aided him in his trade.

Had he fooled himself all this while, pretending that it did not matter? Accepting what deep inside he could not? Choosing to float and seek, when he should fight the current, no matter how swift? Is that why, regardless of what he had tried, it always seemed the same, empty, incomplete? With an uneasiness that was compelling, pushing him onward to yet another craft? If he was a lord's son, could he truly rest content until he was what fate has chosen for him to be?

He stopped and filled his lungs as the anger did not cool but boiled higher within him. By the laws, he was as much a man as Feston or any of his peers! If not by deed then by birth, every respect shown Feston was his by right as well. Enough of drifting; he would accept half rations as his lot no longer.

Alodar let his breath out slowly and threw his head back, eyes closed, trying with reason to divert from the path his emotions were taking him. But how? How could he grasp what had eluded his father's every effort and in the end crushed his spirit from him? Whenever Alodar had dared to consider it in the past, the answer had always been the same. First try reason, then plead, and finally beg as they tossed him out of each manor in which once he was welcome.

What would make the likes of a Feston meet him eye to eye, weigh courteously what he would say, force from the noble's memory whatever had befallen Alodar's house before? No, even better! Feston should meet him on bended knee in recompense for what has happened and with the deference such as that shown to the queen.

Alodar blinked his eyes open and jerked his head forward fully alert. The queen, he thought, a beauty who would be the fair prize of a quest from the sagas. A queen besieged, who had yet to select her hero of the realm. A queen naturally gracious to whomever might rescue her from the peril in which she was now ensnared. Title and estate restored would be the least of her favors. And the hero of the realm. For him they would be forced to bend their knees.

He looked up at the night sky, the tension suddenly gone, his lips curving into a slight smile as he savored the image forming in his mind.

He envisioned himself rounding the corner to the main throughfare that led to the palace gates. The roar of the crowd intensified and he patted his mount gently on the neck to soothe already jangled nerves. From the second and third stories which dotted the way, streamers and confetti rained down onto an already clogged street, and many a lesser building seemed on the verge of collapse from the humanity it carried.

Royal guardsmen paced slowly ahead trying to clear a way for the procession. Young girls sighed as he passed, batting eyes or gesturing outrageously to catch his attention.

"Alodar, Alodar the hero, Alodar the savior of the fair lady, Alodar of Procolon," the crowds shouted over and over without tiring, each small group trying to drown out the rest as he passed. And Alodar smiled and waved expansively. He glanced over his shoulder at his groomsmen who followed and saw them riding straight and tall, sharing in the fame that showered down on their leader and touching them as well.

Far too quickly the concourse was traveled and Alodar and his guard dismounted at the base of the wide gate that led to the house of the rulers of Procolon. The crowd momentarily fell silent and trumpets sounded from within with the voluntary of the queen. With regal slowness the gates parted and, five abreast, the nobility marched down the steps to meet the one who had saved the queen.

White-haired lord Festil was first. With a dramatic flourish of his cape he fell to one knee and bowed his head.

"Where you command, may you see fit to let me follow," he said. "Your deed will forever shine in my heart and in those who come after me."

He stepped back into line and Feston swore his allegiance in turn. In quick precision the barons of the outlands, the lords of the fortress towns, and the lesser nobles as well knelt and gave Alodar the accolade of the hero.

The trumpets blared again and Vendora appeared unaccompanied at the gateway. With a long gown trailing behind she gracefully glided down the steps to extend Alodar her hand. Alodar knelt before Vendora and kissed her offered hand and she immediately bade him rise.

The fantasies raced on as Alodar continued his pacing, unmindful of the time. Finally, as the moon rose against the gatehouse of the east, he broke out of his reverie as he saw Morwin's lazy shuffle coming his way.

"Ah, there you are, Alodar. Thinking of another scheme to get the attention of the lords on the morrow?"

Alodar wrinkled his brow and his eyes shot flame at the apprentice. "Listen, Morwin, I strive to break this ring of siege as much as anyone, but by the laws, I will no longer abide some popinjay taking more credit than is his due. I tell you this, the battle is not yet over and we shall see who is most deserving of the chant of the crowd and who the ridicule." He paused, recalling his newly found resolve. "And yes, the hand of the fair lady."

Without waiting for a reply, he stomped off to seek sleep in what remained of the night.

CHAPTER THREE

The Castle's Secret

THE next morning Alodar again was roused out of deep slumber, but this time the figure bending above him was shrouded in black cape and hood.

"Master Periac?" Alodar squinted through sleep-filled eyes. "I had almost given you up for lost in the underground chambers. We have not seen you for days."

"Yes, it is I," Periac said, pushing back his hood and

patting into place his ruffled black hair. His temples were bare; but, by judicious positioning, he was able to cover the bald spot on the top of his head. His watery, pale blue eyes straddled a nose too small for the blocky face, and his mouth was hidden top and bottom by white flecked hair.

"I have been busy with contemplation, Alodar, busy with contemplation. A well turned thought may save the fevered activities of many. In any event, I trust you have conducted yourself to credit our craft in my absence. A good reputation goes a long way towards unlocking the next door, as I have often instructed you. But there is no time for lecture now. We must go at once for audience with the queen."

Alodar immediately sat up, eyes wide awake. A chance for information, he thought. Information for the plan that I must soon put into shape.

"But Morwin and I are assigned to aid Feston's men on the west wall, master," he said with distaste, "and should prepare for the bombardment soon to begin."

"There is no time for that; it will wait. The queen summons and we will go. It is an opportunity, and we must use it as best we can for advantage. A queen's gratitude goes even further than reputation."

Alodar smiled and Periac's brows knit into a frown.

"Do not presume you know already the full value of what I instruct, Alodar," he said. "You are quick to learn, yes, and have experienced more of the craft than those who have spent twice the time as journeymen. The best that I have had, I truly admit. But the practice of thaumaturgy and living with profit from it can come only from patiently following what a master has to pass on to you."

"But have I not correctly performed whatever you have asked of me?" Alodar asked, rising to his feet. "And then eagerly pressed for more?"

"It is exactly that impatience of which I speak, Alodar," Periac said, stroking his goatee. "One evening's discussion on the weaker similarities of form, the next day a single trial with stream-rounded pebbles and a few acorns, and then you are done with it. Why, when I studied, I spent more than a year on that one subject alone. You seem less interested in learning thaumaturgy than in

32

just getting through it. But as I have often said, there is no great mystery revealed at the end. You become a master by solid progress, not by superficial dabbling or sudden revelation."

"I do not fault your methods, master," Alodar said. "The haste comes from beyond the boundaries of the craft. Look, when you were a journeyman, how sure were you to dedicate your life to the art?"

"Why, there was no question," Periac said. "My father and uncles were masters before me. From their hands I learned my trade. No other calling did I consider."

"And had I come to manhood a nobleman and a nobleman's son, then I think I would have felt the same," Alodar said. "Content with my lot, not questioning what else could be. But instead, I have raced through thaumaturgy as I have the rest, seeking the mystery that you say is not there, the feeling that this indeed is what I really am."

Periac stared at Alodar for a moment in silence. "You have the makings of a master in you, Alodar," he said. "But that feeling will come only when you are truly worthy of it."

He paused again, and then suddenly drew his cape around him. "But enough of this for now. The business of the moment is the audience with the queen."

Periac started for the keep in the center of the courtyard. As the barrage began, Alodar ran to catch up with his mentor.

Once inside the keep, they spiraled several times around the staircase along the inner wall before they arrived at the level of the queen. One of the two guards with crossed halberds at the doorway checked a list with his free hand and motioned them to enter.

Beyond the doorway, Alodar found himself in a large, quiet anteroom, with smooth stone walls hung with tapestries that damped the battle's din. Low benches and stools, covered with rich velvet and scattered about like a child's cast of jackstones, cluttered the entire floor. Two more men guarded a small archway draped with a thick curtain, and from time to time a page emerged and called out a name to the group sitting or pacing about. In response, one of the waiting men would spring up and fol-

33

low the page when he just as quickly disappeared. No one ever returned; presumably they all left after their conference by some other door. From time to time, additional messengers burst into the room and proceeded unchecked through the curtain, waving hastily scrawled notes on the progress of the fighting down below.

Time passed, and Alodar saw Periac settle into a comfortable introspection, staring off into space. He tried to imitate the master as best he could, but the anticipation made the time crawl. The shadow from the window to the east diminished to nothing, and the one from the west had grown nearly full length when finally the page motioned them to come forth.

As the guard pulled back the curtain and Periac stooped to enter, Alodar understood why he had been asked to attend. The inner room was tapestried like the first, but almost devoid of furnishings. In its very center stood a long, oaken table with seats for eight. Seven of the chairs were occupied by Vendora and her advisors, and behind each stood an attendant arrayed in the colors of his master. Periac took the seat at the foot of the table, and Alodar stood behind him, gripping the chair back in imitation of the others.

He looked down the length of the table at Vendora and saw that she wore a sea-blue dress deeply cut in front with a large aquamarine snuggled like a nesting egg in the cleavage of her breast. Her hair coiled in elaborate wavelets, framed by a sparkling tiara. In regal attire, she seemed impersonal and distant, less of a woman and more like a trophy to be placed on the mantle at the end of an adventure.

On her right sat lord Festil, arms folded across his chest and his back ramrod straight. To her left, lady Aeriel rose to speak, and Alodar noticed she wore the same clothing as when he had seen her before, tunic and leggings on a pleasing slender form, dagger at the waist, but on her right side rather than the left. Her hair was shoulder length and simply kept, and her cheeks were clear and fresh, covered with freckles scattered about like a sunburst through a willow tree. She glanced down at Periac and Alodar, and her dark eyes smiled encouragement as she began.

34

"We have solicited and heard diverse suggestions today, my lords, from commander to soldier alike, on how we might break the grip that tightens about us," she said. "But we must leave no possibility unexamined, and I have recommended to our fair lady that we hear also what the common craftsman has to offer for our cause."

"The hour grows late, my fair lady," interrupted Festil, "to waste our time in so fruitless a manner. Exactly what is it that you would perform for true men-at-arms, tradesman? How will your pox healing and wart removal gain us deliverance when sword and shield will not?"

"My lord Festil," Periac responded in a voice cool with deliberation, "judge the potency of my craft not merely by the practices you see about you. These wastelands are but one corner of the world. Here by tradition, for want of a better reason, thaumaturgy and the other arts play but a small part in warfare. But I assure you that in realms elsewhere, my craft has a bigger role in deciding affairs of state."

"Then how shall you dispose of our problem?" interjected the short and corpulent man on Periac's left. "Will you rip the earth apart and have Bandor's forces swallowed up whole? Or perhaps you can enchant each of our blades so that they can cut through his mail like a knife through butter?"

"My good lords," Periac said in the same rolling tones of salesmanship that Alodar had heard so many times before. "On one hand you belittle the scope of my skills and on the other you allude to the fantasies of the romances. My craft is neither trivial amusement nor total omnipotence. Like all things, its true worth lies between. And if we are to use thaumaturgy for our great gain, then we must all understand what its capabilities and limitations are. Understand them well, else why would the fair lady call me here?"

Periac paused and Alodar saw each man settle back into his chair, resigning himself to hearing the master out. "Thaumaturgy," Periac began, "is the most clear and straightforward of the five arts in its execution. Unlike alchemy, magic, and the rest, it requires no great erudition or dedication to effect its results. Here in Procolon we regard thaumaturgy as we do masonry or smithing.

With it we forge large works of metal or stone from small models in our shops. We increase the yields of whole fields while carefully tending only a part. We purge the body of plague and mend it whole again. But the true potency of thaumaturgy is limited only by the cleverness of the man who understands its basic concepts, the principles of sympathy and contagion."

"Sweetbalm, we are gathered here to plan our military strategy, not listen to an apprentice's first lecture," interrupted Festil.

"Let him speak, Festil," Aeriel cut him short. "Perhaps he is unaffected with the blindness that a feat of arms will somehow yet save us."

"Two principles," Periac continued, stroking his goatee. "Sympathy and contagion. The first simply stated is: like produces like. By manipulating objects in a simulation we can cause corresponding effects to occur on a different scale in time and distance. My gondola soars in the air in response to the movement of a small sliver."

"So then," challenged Festil again, "why not build a small model of Bandor's camp and smash it with your fist and save us the wounds and sorrow of tomorrow?"

"Because there is another important ingredient of any spell and that is a supply of energy, a force or power to do the work. It does no good to smash a model, unless I control the forces necessary to level the tents as well. Without a spinning flywheel to draw upon, the gondola would not lift in response to the rising splinter. Without the heat of the fire in Bandor's camp, the missiles launched at our catapult could not have been diverted to the mark. Practitioners of my craft seek ways to channel energy, but alas, we cannot create it.

"Not only is energy needed but, in most cases, much more than common sense might dictate. The coupling between the simulation and the actual is not perfect and there are always some losses. The more closely the two resemble one another, the better the connection and the less the energy waste. The best coupling is provided by things which were indeed once part of a single whole. Or as the principle of contagion states it· once together, always together. In principle, we could use any object for control of the gondola, but a small piece of it works

36

better than any foreign substance. And in like manner, a wound is most effectively sealed if a drop of blood is mixed with the gelling starch, and a bit of flesh with the molding wax.

"So, lord Festil, with the wave of my hand I cannot topple the belfries that will thunder towards us, for it would take too much energy. Nor can I, say, render any man invisible or pass through solid walls, for I cannot simulate these things. Nor yet can I strike at an enemy far away without something of him to bind in the spell. But I can apply my craft in the fair lady's service with as much imagination as I am able."

"And if thaumaturgy is so straightforward then, master Periac," Festil continued, his tone still hard and unconvinced, "what need have we of any of your services at all? Why cannot one here at the table perform the craft for the queen as well?"

"There is that little matter of the spells which bind the simulation and energy source together and then subsequently release them," Periac said. "To safeguard the means of our livelihood, we must naturally protect their nature, passing them on from master to journeyman but to no one outside of our craft.

"And as I have already said," Periac persisted before Festil could stop him again, "success is not merely a matter of rote application of the well proven. Rather it depends upon the skill of the master to see through surface distractions to the deeper similarities around him. To recognize subtle and time-worn connections that form the true basis of our art."

"You state so well the limitations of your craft, master Periac," Festil persisted, "that now I wonder if perhaps one of the other four might not serve us better in our plight."

"They have their shortcomings as well," Periac said. "For example, the formulas of alchemy have no guarantee of coming to the same result with each use. Only one time in hundreds does one end with a solvent that can dissolve more than the glass in which it was formed. The massive factories on Honeysuckle Street produce mostly waste, repeating and repeating the same steps in order to form some modest quantity of healing balm or sense-enhancing philtre."

"There is truth in what you speak," Aeriel said. "We are here because Kelric, the court sorcerer, entranced himself to find what great wealth might lie undiscovered in the kingdom. In his vision he saw Iron Fist and a formula of alchemy of great merit, one with high yield and hence potential for large profit. With it, the queen can hope to replace the wealth which used to come from the royal mines, now thrust as deeply into the mountains as men can go.'"

"But what details did he see?" Alodar blurted. "What did he say of the passageways and chambers underground?"

The fat man on Periac's left rose to protest the interruption, but Aeriel shot him a hard glance that settled him back in his seat. Alodar looked about the table and marveled at her control. Except for Festil, she clearly had the respect of the group and all deferred to her lead.

"No detail could he see," she said, "and the only words that came from his trance were that the Iron Fist must loosen its grip before the formula could be found. It may be that the castle will have to fall because we have yet discovered no grimoire in these mute walls."

"And as for sorcerers," Periac continued as if no interruption had occurred. "With one at court you know well the difficulty of dealing with them. Reclusive and obstinate their art must intrinsically pervert them from a decent relationship with their fellowmen. Why else do they deliberately play upon our fears of enchantment when we plead for some small illusion or prophecy?

"And magic is no better. The rituals performed in seclusion sometimes take several lifetimes. Except for such useless trinkets as the ceremonial dagger I see on lady Aeriel's side, it would take many a castle's treasure to afford what magicians have to offer. Their swords that never dull and mail that does not break are far better, true, than the alchemical salves which rot away, but who among you has ever seen the like?

"Finally, there is wizardry," Periac said, raising his hand and counting his fingers into his palm one by one.

"Yes, what of that?" the fat man said. "The talk of

the bailey floor is that Bandor is possessed by a devil and pushes this attack for no mortal cause."

"I cannot accept such groundless whisperings," Festil cut in. "Revolt against the crown has happened before. But traffic with demons, like a baseborn craftsman? No noble of Procolon would think of it."

"Judge not all of wizardry by the few poor examples we have seen among us," Periac replied. "The wizards we judge as wise know that their wills are of insufficient strength to dominate any but the simplest of imps. They travel with carnivals and the like, content with pushing their sprites through idle tricks as one would a trained mouse. Their lot is far better, however, than that of the foolish who have dared to struggle with true power and ended as the hoop-jumper for the demon instead. It is fortunate that their cruel masters soon tire of the bizarre acts they force upon them. The crumpled and abandoned shells whimpering for bread are better off as beggars than when they were the submissive slaves to powerful djinns.

"But it was not always thus," Periac said, sweeping his upraised index finger in Festil's direction. "The sagas of our past tell of men of great will and courage who struggled with the strongest demons and bent them to their bidding. The power they could thereby command made them much respected throughout many lands. No, my lord, you would not judge a wizard of long ago as a mere craftsman."

Festil scowled, but Periac turned his attention to the queen and continued. "But as to lord Bandor, I must say in truth that possession would be most unlikely. He conducts the siege with coherence and precision, not with the mad acts of contradiction that a fiend would force upon him."

"For a master of a single art," Vendora said, "you seem well versed in the rest as well."

Periac smiled and tipped his head with a slight bow. "What I have said is the depth of my knowledge, my fair lady. Each craftsman guards with pride what is his own and deals reluctantly with the others. For more, you must consult with the proper practitioners. But, to the point, there are none of them here to aid you, only I. And to escape Bandor's trap, I can indeed be of service."

Alodar tightened his grip on the chair and the lords about the table leaned forward in anticipation. Periac saw the increased interest and paused to heighten the effect.

"If Iron Fist is to fall, and I see no way that we can prevent it," he said at last, "then we can save much bloodshed by raising the white flag."

"Never," thundered Festil pounding his fist on the table. "This stronghold has never fallen and it shall not fall now. Or if indeed we cannot hold, we will defend the walls to the last man for the honor of our fair lady."

"I think, my lord," Periac said, "that our fair lady's honor is better preserved by subterfuge than by singing sword. If we surrender, you men-at-arms will become captives, yes. But we lowly tradesmen might be allowed to go our way after performing for our captors some of the same services we have done for you. The queen can slip out with us and then return to Ambrosia unharmed."

"And do you not think that every cart that leaves this place will be searched from axle to highpost once the fair lady is found missing in the keep?" Festil said. "And how could anyone miss her beauty, no matter what maid's dress you cast her in? Her doom would be sealed on the spot, once such a scheme was exposed."

"Her beauty is renowned, yes," Periac said, rubbing his hands together with deliberate slowness. "But with my craft we could alter that. A small simulation, a wax head, and then in an instant it would be over. A bulbous nose, thrusting chin, slanting brow, and pox on the cheeks. No one would choose to look at her. And then once safely away, we can restore her countenance to what it was before."

"You mean to apply a disguise," Vendora said, "as if I were an actress playing the part of an old crone?"

"I do not speak of makeup, my fair lady," Periac said. "The face I would give you would be as real as the one you have now. The sores would ooze real pus and no putty or paint would stick to a searcher's hand. They could not detect it."

"Then how surely can you undo what you have done, master Periac?" Vendora said with the softness missing from her voice.

Periac rubbed his hands together more forcefully. "I am a skilled practitioner, my fair lady. My eye is still good, my hand firm and my memory sharp. I doubt that anyone would notice a significant difference when we were done."

All eyes turned to the queen to await her response. She touched her hand to her cheek and then back to smooth her hair. Alodar held his breath trying to imagine the same gold dusted to dirty brown atop a pock-marked and misshapen face, painful to see. He thought of his resolve of the night before and how strong it might be if Periac's transformation were indeed so.

Suddenly, before the answer could form on Vendora's lips, another page burst into the room, blood streaming from his nose and ears. "The south wall," he gasped. "Scaling ladders, too many of them. We could not hold. Flee, my fair lady. Flee as best you can."

"Quickly, my fair lady, this way." Festil bolted from the table and motioned to the rear exit from the chamber. "The rest of you, to the bailey floor. Secure the keep from the intruders."

The assemblage exploded for the doorways like pieces of shattered glass. The advisors scrambled by Alodar, and he hesitated as he watched Festil usher Vendora and Aeriel out the other way. In an instant he made his decision. As the curtains swished shut, he rushed after the departing queen.

He sprang into the passageway beyond the conference room and saw the three descending a long spiral staircase like the one he had climbed in the morning, but narrower and with no windows to the outside. As they disappeared from view, Alodar plunged down the stairs. Down and down he sped, just able to catch sight of Vendora's flowing gown around the curve. He glanced over his shoulder and saw Periac about the same distance behind, racing after.

More openings whizzed by on the inside, but the outside curve remained featureless and unbroken. Only an occasional torch on the wall prevented total darkness. Around and around the stairs wound, until Alodar completely lost his sense of direction.

Finally the staircase ended and joined a level walkway

that continued to curve about the keep. Alodar increased his speed and closed on those in the lead. He raced around nearly half the circumference and then saw a flash of copper from the top of Aeriel's head as she disappeared into a square-cut hole in the stone floor. He ran to the opening and peered inside, motioning Periac to hurry and catch up. A second staircase spiraled into a room below, where Festil was busily straining at a large lever hinged on the wall, while Aeriel and Vendora descended.

"Why, it's the first chamber," Alodar exclaimed. "The one with the iron slab on the floor."

Festil looked up, unable to budge the giant lever from where he found it. "Quickly, man," he said. "Help me here so that we can seal them out."

Periac caught up with Alodar and together they descended into the room. All three tugged at the lever, and slowly it began to move. Alodar glanced back up at the opening through which they had come and saw a giant stone slab, held against the ceiling on metal tracks, sliding in response. It rumbled across the opening and thudded into place, sealing off the entrance from above.

Festil and Periac collapsed to the ground, holding their sides and panting from the exertion. The two women leaned against the walls, chests heaving, unable to speak. Alodar glanced about the chamber he had visited two nights before and saw no change. A square-cut slab of iron, rusted red from the dampness, sat in the center of a featureless floor. The circle of round walls had no structure except for indentations for the lighting oil and the four archways that radiated to the castle's corner towers. Only the lever which closed the exit to the keep seemed to serve any purpose.

Alodar moved about the room, glancing into the long dark tunnels radiating from it. Three were pitch black, giving no clue as to what lay beyond. But as he looked into the fourth, he saw a procession of many torches and heard the jingle of mail. Even in the distance, he could recognize Feston's bright surcoat reflecting the torchlight.

Soon Feston and the group he brought with him were in the chamber and fanning out to explore the entrances to the other passageways. "My fair lady," he said, "thank the amulets that you are safe and not in Bandor's grasp. We may yet win praise for the sagas on this day."

Vendora pushed herself from the wall and straightened to a free standing position, brushing down the disarray of her gown and readjusting the aquamarine to its proper position.

"How stand our forces now, lord Feston?" she gasped, still gulping air between her words.

"Not well, my fair lady," Feston replied, "but not so badly that there is not hope still. The battle rages fiercely on the bailey above, and I think in the end it will be to no avail. But we have secured the lower levels under each tower, just as you have done with the keep, and we find no sign of Bandor's forces here to peril us. The bulk of our defenders are left above, alas, to fend as best they can, and we could not prevent some craftsmen coming down into these fortifications along with men-at-arms. But we have secured most of the food and I think, judging from these walls, lack not for water. It will be a long while before Bandor can begin to hope of reaching us."

"With the queen so neatly bundled up," Aeriel interrupted, "why should he even care? Do you propose no more than to await our fate just as we have done for the last forty-three days? I am not trained in matters of war as you are, my lords," she said, "but it seems to me that these chambers and passageways serve a better purpose than to pass the time. I think aloud and without deliberation, but do not these walls and interconnectings at least give us an element of surprise? When Bandor eventually takes full command of the castle above, he will find the five entrances to us, and probably can do no more than station guards at all positions to await what we would do next. He must split his forces into fifths, and we can concentrate ours to strike at one—and at a time of our own choosing."

"Necessity imparts sharpness to your thoughts, lady Aeriel," Festil said while rising slowly to stand besides his son. "Quite surely I believe you have hit upon the intent of the castle's original design. If the walls were to fall, the towers would still have to be taken; then with underground communication, each could aid the others so that all might stand. But on balance, my son's plan seems a

43

good one. We have not the towers, but only the chambers underneath them. In addition, the blood of Bandor's vassals now runs hot with victory and lust for rape and plunder. Our salvation may be a surprise thrust, as you say, but I think it wise to sit until our captor's zeal cools in the careless boredom of guard duty before we try."

"Well enough, lord Festil," Vendora said softly. "We need time to assess our situation. Lord Feston, continue to conduct yourself as you have. I appoint you commander of whatever forces remain. See that order is established and the entrances to these dungeons well guarded."

As she spoke, the queen looked around the high and windowless walls of the chamber and reached behind her for a cloak that was not there.

"Here, my fair lady," Feston said dramatically, releasing the clasp of the cape of the man who stood near and whirling it about her. She clutched it eagerly and drew it tight while her eyes darted again about the room.

Alodar and the others caught her mood and somberly shifted about as the reality of their plight began to sink in. They were safe for now, true, but in the long run what did that matter? A desperate attempt to break out was the best they could devise. Their lives were at stake and no glimmer of hope could credibly present itself.

No glimmer, unless indeed the castle possessed one more secret defense to aid them. And if he could find it and thereby save the queen, ah, who would be the hero then? Oppressed by their trap as were the others, but grimly determined, he headed into one of the passageways to search again for some clue.

Alodar flicked back his cape and sat to rest on the rust-encrusted slab in the center of the chamber. He glanced over to the wall where Vendora huddled in the cape Feston had given her two days before. Her shoulders stooped and her hair lay tangled and matted against her brow. She listened half attentively as Feston squatted easily at her side, telling her small talk of the four guard detachments under the towers.

Alodar sighed. Their band was so small and their fates so intertwined that the formalities of rank had begun to give way. But he did not want to approach the queen himself until he had some positive news of discovery to present to her. He dug his gouge into the soft red rust beneath him for perhaps the tenth time and left another shallow furrow beside the others. The fresh cut revealed nothing new, only rust deeper still. Perhaps the whole slab was rotted through and would soon turn to dust.

"Marking off the hours, journeyman?" a voice asked over his shoulder, and Alodar turned to see Aeriel taking a place beside him. The dagger at her side clanked against the slab and Alodar glanced down at the bare blade and stubby hilt.

"Are you left-handed?" he asked as she followed his gaze downward.

"No." Aeriel laughed. "It is but my nature. The fair lady insists that I wear the badge of office as do the others of her court, and so I must. And were the blade of any value I would carry it properly; but it is only a useless symbol, so I display it accordingly."

"A magic dagger and of no value," Alodar said, raising his eyebrows in disbelief.

"Costly enough in coin or barter," Aeriel said. "Enough so that a craftsman could never hope to own one. Yet not so dear that the nobility would be likewise denied. It is the perfect token for one to declare that he is wealthy. But for its utility as a weapon—here, judge for yourself."

Aeriel withdrew the dagger from the loop at her waist and passed the hilt to Alodar. He wrapped his hand around it and immediately pursed his lips in surprise.

An electric tingling pulsed through his fingers and shot up his arm. He felt goosebumps pop out on his chest and back. For a moment his eyes watered and his tongue felt dry.

"It is magic, there is no doubt," Aeriel said. "What else gives one such a feeling? Though you do get somewhat used to it after a while."

Alodar nodded and tightened his grip on the hilt. His fingers and thumb slipped smoothly into small indentations in the grip, and the pommel snuggled comfortably against the base of his palm. The dagger felt like a natural extension of his arm, as if custom tooled to fit his hand and no other.

He reached out with his index finger to test the point

which looked surprisingly blunt and frowned in puzzlement when he made contact with the cold gray metal.

"Yes, that is why it is so absurd," Aeriel said. "And the edge of the blade is the same. Impossibly dull and unyielding to any grinder's stone."

"Cannot the magicians give it an edge as well?" Alodar asked as he handed the dagger back, releasing his grip reluctantly. "With a feel like that one almost would be tempted to take on a swordsman."

"As I understand it, the ritual is set," Aeriel said. "Any change destroys the symmetry of the whole. Either one accepts a perfect hilt with a blade of no value or a dagger with no magical properties at all. And of course, if such a dirk as this could cut, the magicians' price would preclude it from the baubles of the nobility."

"You speak most strangely of your peers, my lady," Alodar said with the beginnings of a smile.

"I did not reach the council of the queen by adhering to what convention would expect of me, Alodar," she said. "Had I thought and acted as the rest of Vendora's childhood friends, then now I would be no more than a lady-in-waiting, concerned with pretty needlework, rather than affairs of state. Let the likes of a Festil be guided by tradition, rather than what each situation uniquely demands. I will not be frightened by an idea, just because it has not been previously recorded in the sagas.

"And as proof of that," she continued, returning Alodar's smile, "please call me Aeriel. There is no need for ceremony for one who seems to work so diligently in our cause. I could not but notice that you react to our situation in a different way than most everyone. Rather than moping about when free from a turn at guard, you have been examining each mortar joint with that small glass of yours. Do you still carry out the queen's commands of now so long ago?"

"Yes, I still look for a key," Alodar said. "But as yet I have found none. I am beginning to think that there is nothing in the passageways to aid us. The answer must lie in one of these three chambers under the keep. So I visit each in turn, hoping for some inspiration."

"And which is next?"

"The second level, the one with the pillar."

"Good, let me go with you."

Alodar blinked, but then quickly nodded his agreement. The two left unnoticed out one of the passageways to the towers. They trudged along in silence for awhile, and then Alodar decided to make the best of his opportunity.

"How fares the queen under our duress?" he said.

"Alas, she lets her fate weigh heavily on her shoulders. As you can see, she broods too much to conduct herself as her station requires she should."

"But if somehow we are indeed rescued?"

"Ah, she would return to her former self in an instant, full of glory. And ample gratitude for the man who saves her."

"Regardless of station?" asked Alodar.

"Yes, regardless." Aeriel laughed. "I see the queen interests all men in the same way."

Suddenly, before he could continue, the ground shook with a long rolling wave; the torch lights blew wildly and flickered dim. The narrow passageway roared with the sound of crashing stone, and the shock, muted and stretched by the thick walls, echoed for several moments.

Aeriel reached for Alodar's arm. In the quiet that followed, he muttered, "The second one today. It only can mean that they are toppling the towers, one by one. Either our remaining defenders above give them difficulty or they seek to level Iron Fist on some mad craze. It is well that they have not yet discovered any entrances to these chambers."

Aeriel released her grip and breathed deeply. "Come, she said. "We were going to the second level."

They reached the tower in a short while. Descending through a hole in the floor, they climbed down to the next landing. Retracing their steps one level down, they returned to a chamber under the keep. It was deserted and built similarly to the ones above and below, except that instead of a slab or water pool, a massive stone column ran from floor to ceiling.

"It certainly is not needed to support the vault," Alodar said. "The other two chambers have the same span and the ceiling runs free from wall to wall. Yet strength is somehow the essence of that column. Look at it, not a seam anywhere, a monolith of granite. It could withstand

47

the blows of many a mangonel and give up not a single chip from the shock."

"If it does not support, is it indeed even secure?" Aeriel asked.

"Yes, the base penetrates below floor level. From the look of it, it also projects up into the ceiling as well."

Alodar stepped back to survey the column but found himself instead watching Aeriel as she inspected the stonework. Her eyes darted first to the ceiling, then to the floor, and finally scanned the length slowly for any crack or seam. She looked back at Alodar when she was done, and her eyes widened as she realized what his focus of attention had been.

"Excuse my boldness, but you are most pleasing fair," Alodar said without thinking.

"Oh enough, Alodar." Aeriel raised her hand as a slight color came to her cheeks. "I have seen the effect of the queen on too many men not to know what truly constitutes beauty. Let us concentrate on our search."

Alodar nodded and motioned to the archway, suddenly pleased with himself for what he had said and the reaction it had caused. Without another word, they left the chamber and returned to the flanking tower. As they began to climb down to the bottommost level, the ground shook again like a blanket snapped taut on a newly made bed, and the rumble echoed about them so that neither could speak. As the reverberations died, a man-at-arms poked his head through the opening to the level above.

"Lady Aeriel, come quickly to the queen's bidding," he shouted down. "A strange occurrence in the central chamber."

Alodar and Aeriel quickly reversed direction, following the man back to the queen. Everyone of their small band was there, filling the room, and all heads looked anxiously upwards towards the huge vault of the ceiling. Vendora was where Alodar had seen her last, but now she stood propped against Feston, leaning heavily on the arm he wrapped around her.

A sudden streak of motion caught Alodar's eye. He turned his head upward to see several large drops of opaque liquid ooze out between two of the massive stones. They fell and spattered against the rusty slab at the chamber's center and added to the messy orange slurry of their predecessors.

He frowned in concentration. Nothing from thaumaturgy certainly, he thought. But what had Periac told him of the other arts? What would seep through what no mason could chisel in a week?

"Solvent!" he yelled as the answer struck him. "And it looks high grade. Everyone out! The ceiling is going to collapse. That is how the towers were toppled. They are dissolving the mortar between the stones."

No one moved. All were transfixed by the slowly increasing tempo of the drip and the widening pool on the chamber floor. Before Alodar could say more, the giant keystone in the center of the vault began to slide slowly down and away from the rock which surrounded it. It gathered speed; with a cascade of liquid on every side, it fell away entirely, into their midst. With a resounding crash, it hit the slab and sprayed liquid and splinters of rock in all directions. The crowd screamed and sprang alive, bolting for the passageways, shouldering one another aside in their haste.

Alodar and Aeriel moved to one side to let them pass, their eyes on the queen across the chamber. Feston, with his grip still on Vendora's arm, spun her towards the nearest exit and pushed her ahead. Periac recovered his balance from a brushing blow and plunged after the queen. Festil immediately followed, almost catching the thaumaturge's cape with his long running stride.

Alodar looked again at the ceiling. Through the new opening, Bandor's men were lowering a rope ladder and several were making ready to descend. He glanced over his shoulder into the passageway from which he had just entered and then hesitated no longer. Grabbing Aeriel's hand, he raced across the room, avoiding the many small pools of solvent which were now working on the seams in the floor. As he passed the slab, his eyes was caught by its now shining brilliance. The bath had cleaned away the rust and a good portion of the iron as well.

He stopped suddenly and looked again. The shine was not from the iron alone.

"Look, Aeriel," he exclaimed. "In the center of the iron, a disk of copper! It is not a solid iron slab, after all.

49

Beneath the rust is this circle of copper in a yoke of iron. A circle at each level. The copper here, the column below, and a well at the bottom of it all."

Three circles of the same diameter! One above the other. In a flash the castle's secret came to him. He looked again at the rope ladder. Two men were already gently swinging on it. He grabbed Aeriel again and ran off after the others. He had the answer. If there was only enough time to use it.

CHAPTER FOUR

The Hero's Reward

THE passageway blurred by and Alodar glanced back over his shoulder. Bandor's men were already in the tunnel after him. He increased his speed; the drawn swords shining in the torchlight gave his legs urgency even beyond what he had felt two days before when the outer walls had fallen. He squeezed Aeriel's hand tighter, and they rapidly closed on Vendora and the others up ahead.

They caught the queen just as they entered the small room under the corner tower. The panicked flight momentarily stopped in a mass confusion of waving arms and shouted directions.

"Up, up to the surface. It is our only chance," yelled Festil as he tumbled Periac down from the stairs and started to climb.

"No, no father," Feston boomed louder still. "See the stonework. We must go down." As he spoke, he yanked Vendora out of the way of dripping liquid that began to ooze from the ceiling and pushed her through the opening in the floor.

Everyone clambered after. As Alodar brought up at

the rear, he saw the small group disappear into the passageway that led back under the keep.

"We will make our stand around the pillar," Festil shouted back to the three soldiers who now ran with him. They drew their swords as they raced, and Aeriel instinctively started to follow.

Alodar grabbed her by the arm and held her back. "Our only chance lies below," he said. "Let us hope that Feston and the others can hold them off until the spell is finished."

He plunged down to the bottom level, pulling Aeriel with him. The staircase seemed to spiral for an eternity and his heartbeat almost drowned out the clank of mail and shouts of the chase that now filtered down after them.

Finally at the bottom, he raced for the central chamber, scarcely noticing the diminishing noise as the hunters chose to pursue the quarry one level above. In a moment they reached their destination and saw the serene pool at the center. Alodar looked rapidly about. They were alone.

"Quickly, Aeriel," he said, "your ring. No, no the unadorned one. Gold is not the best choice and we must at least make the shape as similar as we can."

Aeriel slipped one of the rings from her finger and, with a puzzled expression, handed it to Alodar. Without pausing for explanation, he fumbled in a pouch at his waist and withdrew a small collection of coins.

"At least the copper will be right," he said as he quickly tried matching the coins one by one to the shape of the ring. "Ah, this one jams in properly. Now fill the cup with the water from the well."

Aeriel took the cup he whisked from his cape and dipped it in the pool. "What spell do you cast here, Alodar? I see that the coin in the ring is like the copper disk in the iron collar we saw bared above. But their intent I still cannot fathom."

"The cool water of the well will shrink the metals slightly," he replied, "and because they are different, the copper disk will slip free."

"But what can we use for the energy source? There is naught here but stone and water," Aeriel said, waving her arms about the empty chamber.

51

"You listened to master Periac well," Alodar said, "but no source is needed for this spell. Rather, we need a sink to absorb the heat we extract from the hunks of metal two levels above. And the water in the well will serve that purpose for us. Now stand close to me, for in truth I know not all that will happen."

Alodar glanced quickly into the four passageways, but no figures fleeing or pursuing showed in them, and he began the binding. When he was done, he thrust the ring holding the coin into the numbing cold of the water and held it motionless. Simultaneously the stillness of the pool was broken by the eruption of tiny bubbles all across its surface.

Alodar held the ring firmly, though his fingers began to ache with the cold. The simmer of the pool changed into a boil, growing more vigorous by the second, and the first wisps of steam crept upward into the already dripping air.

Alodar looked anxiously back and forth between the now scalding well and the placid ring. Was it cold enough? Was there enough water in the well?

The feeling left his hand and the opaqueness of the steam engulfed them; so the passageways were blotted from view and the oil lights in the wall became dim and diffuse.

Finally as the fog closed in, the copper coin dropped clear of the ring and gently fell to the bottom of the cup.

"Look to the ceiling," Alodar shouted as he tore his eyes from what he held. Brushing aside the vapor, they could dimly see the round keystone at the center of the vault tremble and begin to move. It slipped down a foot and then another, increasing speed with each moment and heading unerringly for the well in the chamber's floor.

"Why, it is not a stone at all," Aeriel exclaimed. "Look, it is getting longer and longer like a giant column."

"The column from the second level," Alodar explained, "held in place by a copper cap in the yoke of iron."

He could say no more before the granite cylinder fell into the concentric hole in the floor, missing the edge all around by mere inches. With a sharp crack like a giant bullwhip, it hit the water's surface and drove the liquid downward. Aeriel stumbled to her knees from the intensity of the blow, and Alodar fell awkwardly over her, both flailing and grabbing for their ears in pain.

Small geysers shot from the well around the edges of the column as it continued its plunge, moving more slowly as it pushed the resistance before it. The din of the contact echoed about, and Alodar felt dazed from the onslaught. The cacophony continued unabated for minutes; but through his cupped hands, Alodar could hear another sound slowly increasing in intensity, the rumble of stone on stone.

He looked about for the source of the noise and, as the copper top of the column slid from view into the well, he spotted motion in the northeast passageway.

"The whole floor," he exclaimed, "the whole floor moves as one unit. No wonder we could never spot a break in the stone. There isn't any."

"What has happened, Alodar?" Aeriel asked weakly, still on her knees from the shock. "What did the column do in the well?"

"It was a giant water ram, Aeriel. A giant ram that moved the whole passageway floor upwards a good three feet. We are seeing what no one has witnessed since Iron Fist was constructed hundreds of years ago. By the laws, let us hope we also see our way out of this trap. Look at that gap," he continued excitedly as he approached the raised floorway. "Stone a foot thick but still a slot beneath the bottom and the level of the cobbling here in the chamber."

As he got nearer, he lit a candle and thrust it into the newly made opening. "Stairs," he exclaimed. Before Aeriel could protest, he huddled down and disappeared from view.

The passage was narrow and confining, and Alodar had to stoop and bow in his shoulders as he made his way downwards. He held the candle in front as far as he could, but the darkness extended farther than the feeble light could reach. He paused and tried to concentrate on whether to continue or return to the chamber and announce his discovery. Each heartbeat relentlessly ticked away the time they had left, and the fall of the cylinder would surely bring Bandor's vassals on the run.

Aeriel's scream made his decision for him. Alodar quickly spun about and retraced the few steps he had made into the gloom. As he surfaced, Aeriel ran toward him, pointing frantically down the passageway that lay atop the newly discovered stairs. Alodar turned and squinted down the long length of stone archway that led to the corner tower. His already rapid pulse quickened as he saw in the distance the wave of torches and the glint of armor. At least six of Bandor's men were on the bottom level, babbling wildly about the raised flooring and pointing down at the newly discovered prey under the keep.

Alodar grabbed Aeriel by the hand and turned to descend again into the darkness. He took a step and hesitated. "The queen," he said. "Where is the queen? It is no good unless we can also save the fair lady."

He ran back to the center of the chamber and sighted down the two passageways he could not see from the edge. The first was empty, but in the second he saw rapid movement towards him. His heart leaped with his good fortune.

"It is the queen, Aeriel," he shouted, motioning her towards him. "Feston is still with her, and I can see Periac and Festil close behind."

He moved his head from side to side, trying to see behind the four fleeing figures. He sucked in his breath. "More of Bandor's men hot on their trail," he cried.

He glanced back into the passageway with the raised floor. The men there had begun to move towards the chamber, though not with the speed of those pursuing Vendora and the others. Angry shouts and the rapid tread of feet sounded from behind, and Alodar whirled about, his worst fears realized. Enemies converged on them from all four corners.

Alodar felt his muscles tense and his breathing turn to shallow gasps. Run, run, take the only chance that you have, his body said. But he steeled himself and held his ground, eyeing each tunnel in turn, trying to estimate which group would reach him first. Time lost all meaning while he waited; it seemed an eon later when Feston and Vendora burst through with their pursuers hard at their heels.

"Where are the other men-at-arms?" Alodar scouted as

Periac and Festil followed the first two into the center of the room.

"They stood their ground nobly to defend the queen," Festil gasped, waving aside Alodar's question as irrelevant to his own plight.

"Then follow me," Alodar commanded and he led Aeriel into the passageway. He did not pause to re-kindle a candle, but caught the rhythm of the steps and descended as rapidly as he could in the blackness, pulling Aeriel after him. He could hear the voices of the other four following close behind.

They descended for more than a flight, and then Alodar stumbled as the ground suddenly became level and the tunnel widened. The others tumbled over him. As they flailed to disentangle, a dim light filtered down from above.

"Down here," a voice shouted, and Alodar heard the cautious tread of steel on the cold stone. His eyes began to adjust to the dimness, and he extended his hand against the floor. Immediately he felt an indentation and, sweeping his arm to the side, he discovered another. With an extended finger, he touched smooth and straight edges on either side of the depressions but found they extended forward farther than he could reach. Grooves, he thought, long narrow grooves cut into the stone floor. He cautiously pressed forward and saw a shape gradually taking form in the dimness.

The light brightened with each clinking step, and Alodar recognized what was before him. "A wagon," he exclaimed. "Some sort of wagon with wheels that are guided by the grooves cut into the floor."

He puzzled over the flat frame, unadorned except for the two central pillars that supported giant two-handed cranks; but as the light grew brighter and the sounds closer, he flung himself up onto the platform. In blind imitation the rest followed.

Feston was the last; as he leaped aboard with a sure-footed bound, the tunnel behind them blazed forth with light. Bandor's men packed into the narrow confines three abreast, holding torches high and staring down at Alodar and the others. The stairs sounded with rapid footfalls as more and more poured in after them.

Pushed from behind, the first three charged with swords

drawn and bore down on the small party. Feston drew his own blade and stood in a crouch at the platform's edge, awaiting their rush. The three jostled for position and the first momentarily lowered his guard. Festil lashed out with his boot and caught the man on the chin, sending him sprawling.

The wagon lurched with the recoil, and Alodar saw the cranks turn lazy circles about their axles. In a flash, he realized their intent. While Feston parried the blows of the other two, he leaped up to the nearest post.

"Man the other one," he shouted as he cranked the handles before him. They responded slowly to his effort; but with each inch that he pulled and pushed, he felt the car begin to move underneath them. He saw the two men lunge at Feston again, but the warrior deftly leaned back, and the blows cut air. One of the two stumbled and fell, surprised by the motion that the retreating wagon gave to his target.

Alodar felt the pumping ease as the car gained speed. Then, as Periac rose to join him on the other pillar, they jumped away from their foes. An angry shout roared from the pursuers and they lunged forward after the car, trampling over the two who lay sprawled in front of them.

Alodar readjusted his stance and pushed all the harder, beginning to feel the wind made by their progress whistle over his back and around to tickle his face. The vanguard of Bandor's men kept pace for awhile, but then he saw them start to fall behind. The soldiers perceived the outcome of the race as well, and hurled their torches towards him in rage. He ducked the first two as they sailed harmlessly overhead and kicked the third from the platform, barely loosing the rhythm of his methodical strokes.

With a sudden lurch, the car made a sharp curve and cut off the men-at-arms from view. They increased speed still more. and the voice of pursuit lessened as they flew on. The only sound was the muffled scrape of the wheels against their precisely chiseled guides.

Alodar cranked on. He had escaped and at the same time saved the queen.

The small crew remained silent, oppressed by the pitch blackness that gave them no hint as to their path or destination. Alodar felt odd, facing backwards to the direction of motion, but determinedly kept at his task. After many minutes, Periac sagged to the platform floor, gasping for breath, his energy spent, and Alodar felt the crank-arm's resistance stiffen. His arms ached and began to tremble from the effort, but he gritted his teeth and continued. His thoughts soared with what he had done. Beyond his wildest expectations, he had accomplished everything. He was alive and well, free of the tragedy of Iron Fist, free to think again of the future, to mold his own destiny. And that destiny now was far more exciting than what a thaumaturge might dream of attaining even two months ago. He was not merely Alodar the journeyman, but Alodar, savior of the queen.

After much more cranking, the resistance began to increase, and Alodar felt a gradual tilting of the platform on which they rode. They were slowly rising, he thought, but no more could he tell in the blackness. He pushed harder still against the handles, but the slope increased faster and the speed slackened.

Slower and slower moved the cart in the darkness. The wind no longer whistled about them, and each revolution of the arms was a fresh agony. Suddenly the front of the platform clanged and latched against a metal abutment, sending Alodar sprawling and filling the tunnel with noise. Simultaneously he felt fresh air blow by his face and looked forward to see a stone slab hinging up before them and starlight beyond.

The party clambered forward through the opening and into the cool night air. They walked on coarse grass and looked down a gentle slope into rolling farmland. In the distance, a scattering of candlelight hinted at man-made structures, and the air carried the odor of animals corraled close by. A gibbous moon, high in the sky, cast faint shadows, but none could look at it without squinting, so black had been the passageway.

"Why, we have covered a good fifteen miles," Festil exclaimed. "These are the farms on the last ridge that bounds the wastelands to the west. We are indeed well away from Bandor and his threat."

"Yes, and by what strange means were we conveyed here?" Feston wondered. "I have not seen the likes of it

57

in any battlecraft before. The builders of Iron Fist, whoever they were, provided her extremely well."

"As well as you have provided the queen, Feston," Vendora said, raising and stretching her hands high overhead, deeply drinking the fresh air. "If only we had what we set out for, our adventure would be complete. But for the moment, I would settle for a comb for my hair. Aeriel, have you one about you?"

"No, my fair lady," Aeriel responded. "I do not. But mark you, did not Kelric say that we would not find what we sought until Iron Fist lost its grip? That it did in most emphatic fashion. Perhaps our search is indeed not yet over."

Alodar pondered Aeriel's words, then returned to the opening in the slope and squinted into the darkness at the car. He withdrew and relit the candle from his cape and began a close inspection.

He did not have to look far. This time there was no subterfuge or deception. There, in the flat platform between the two cranking pillars, was a small square of metal, hinged at one side and with a finger grip on the other. Alodar bent down and swung the door open, his light illuminating a tightly bound parchment, hard and cracked with age.

"Look here," he shouted, running quickly back to the others. "You spoke of alchemy formulas. Do they not record them in grimoires of about this size?"

All faces turned as he advanced, and Feston reached out and grabbed the bundle from him. With a quick flourish, he ripped the cord and outer covering from the package and began to thumb through the bound parchment within.

"Hold the candle closer," he commanded before Alodar could protest. "Sweetbalm, is that what you seek, my fair lady? The ink is faint, but I can see the beginnings still. Powders, ointments, philtres, elixirs, amulets, and fetishes. Formulas of high yield, none less than eighty-five parts in a hundred."

"Eighty-five!" exclaimed Vendora. "Why Feston, you have done it all. A sweeping rescue and a treasure besides. With a yield of eighty-five, we undercut the costs of them all. The royal products will sweep the competition from the field, and my coffers will be fed by a much-needed new source."

"You speak most glowingly, my fair lady," Feston said. "Can I interpret your praise to mean that you at last see fit to choose the hero of the realm?"

Vendora's smile stiffened and she drew herself erect. "Do not presume too much, lord Feston. You have done me great service here these past few days, but not so much that my senses depart me."

Feston's heavy brows furrowed, and Vendora laughed at his discomfort. "Do not fret, my warrior. Know that I look upon you with much favor. I wish you to journey with me to court, be known as a royal suitor, and stand by me as you have done here. If in time I grow used to the roughness of your features, then perhaps I will indeed honor you with my hand."

"Wait a moment, my fair lady," Aeriel said. "Alodar, the journeyman thaumaturge, did apply his mind and skills with marvelous imagination to our cause. It is to him that we owe our good fortune."

Vendora frowned, paused, and then pulled her face into a smile as she turned to Alodar. "Indeed I thank you all for my deliverance," she said. "Your steadfastness in propelling the car was most dedicated."

"That was but a minor part of it," Aeriel persisted. "He fathomed the castle's secret. He discovered the passageway out. Why he even found you the grimoire."

"May I remind the fair lady," Festil cut in, "that many of the more restless vassals of your crown will interpret the fall of Iron Fist as a sign of weakness. Without the house of the red surcoat standing at your side, you may be hard pressed to deal with them, Bandor, and the border kingdoms to the south, all at the same time."

Vendora looked at Alodar and then back to Feston. Her eyes narrows in thought. She stared at the sword at the warrior's side and then studied Alodar's cape-draped form.

"Oh well enough, Aeriel," she said at last. "I am sure that the thaumaturge did exercise his art most exceedingly fine. He and his master may henceforth speak of royal favor when they lure customers to their craft. But I cannot see how his acts compare with the feats of lord

Feston or the comforts he gave me. What indeed can you profit by pressing his suit upon me so?"

Aeriel opened her mouth to speak again, looking first at Vendora and then to Alodar. She hesitated a moment, but finally snapped it shut. Vendora nodded approval at her apparent acquiesence and returned her attention to the grimoire that Feston now held before her.

Alodar flung his candle aside and stepped forward, his eyes starting to smoulder, but Aeriel placed her hand on his arm. He shot her a sidelong glance, then halted when her fingers squeezed more tightly.

"My fair lady, there is no more business to conduct here," Festil said quickly as he saw Alodar pause. "We must start immediately for Ambrosia. Each hour we save will limit the time Bandor has to consolidate his victory. Let us descend this slope and appropriate a quicker means of transport from the first farm we encounter."

Vendora looked up from the grimoire and into Alodar's eyes. "It is settled then," she said. "A royal endorsement for the thaumaturges and status as suitor for lord Feston. Ample largess for deeds well done."

Alodar sucked in a deep breath and opened his mouth; but before he could speak, Aeriel covered his lips. Vendora smiled and looked around the group, from Periac standing silently near the car to Festil already ten yards down the slope. She nodded her agreement to the old man's suggestion, placed her hand on Feston's offered arm, and started to descend the incline. She paced ten slow steps and then looked back over her shoulder at Aeriel.

"In a moment, my fair lady," Aeriel said as she cautiously lowered her hand from Alodar's mouth while still maintaining her grip on his arm.

The two stood silently, not moving, watching the queen draw away from them. Several minutes passed, and she and the two lords gradually shrank to dim outlines, fading into their surroundings.

"By the laws!" Alodar exploded. "What feat must one accomplish to be held worthy in this kingdom? Can she not grasp what I have done?"

Aeriel again raised her finger to his lips. "It will avail you no good, Alodar," she said. "The queen is clever enough to know how her actions influence the safety of the crown. And the circumstances here prevent her from giving her reward in a just manner. So long as Festil and his son feel they have some claim, she can bestow it on no other."

She turned and looked down the hillside. "But at least I know who is the true hero of the day," she continued softly as she released his arm and then suddenly clasped her hands behind his neck. Alodar's eyes widened in surprise and he felt her lips pressing his as she drew against him.

After a moment she dropped her arms and started to step back, but Alodar put his hand behind her. She stopped when she felt the gentle pressure and smiled, watching him intently.

"You indeed behave most unlike a lady-in-waiting," he said huskily after a long pause. He drew another deep breath and the emotions churned within him like the hot acid in the thaumaturge's cauldron. The exhilaration of freedom, Vendora's beauty, the grim determination of his resolve, the anger of yet another injustice, and now the warm presence of Aeriel in his arms, all tumbled in confusion, and he could not sort them out.

"And you are most unlike the tradition-bound noble or the meekly accepting craftsman, Alodar," she said. "You have dared to seek as did no other and because of it you have saved us all."

He smiled and pulled her towards him, and she again reached her arms to ring his neck.

Yes, he had saved the queen, his thoughts raced. Had not Feston been along for the final dash, then all would have followed. Title restored, respect of the peerage and hero of the realm.

Suddenly he stopped his gentle tugging and frowned as the realization of what he was doing hit him. The queen and hero of the realm—or Aeriel and whatever that future might bring? She has judged him by what he had done, rather than by his station. He could treat her in return with no less fairness.

But would not the surprising passion that boiled for the moment cool as suddenly? He was driven to the queen by what had smouldered for years. How could a chance encounter stand against it?

He looked at Aeriel, trying to clear his confusion, and then lowered his head.

"What is it, Alodar?" Aeriel laughed, continuing to come forward.

"I am resolved, my lady," he said thickly after a moment. "I strive for no less than does lord Feston."

Aeriel's lips curved in the beginning of another smile, but then she looked deeply into Alodar's eyes as he raised his gaze to meet hers. For several minutes they did not speak. Finally she reached and pulled his arm from around her.

"I see," she said crisply. "Forgive me for thinking your aspirations to be so low."

"My lady," Alodar replied, "forgive me that your presence confuses me greatly. But I will not have peace until my birthright is restored. And that I see accomplished only if I am hero of the realm. For that end did I labor and almost succeed. And I cannot with honor accept your favor, so long as that is my quest."

Aeriel took one step back and studied Alodar at arm's length. "Had I not seen what you have done," she said, "I would not credit the chance of such ambition." She sighed and looked in the direction in which Vendora had disappeared. "But if that is your goal, then may the random factors align in your favor." With a whirl she suddenly turned and raced down the hillside without looking back.

Alodar stood dumbfounded, watching her go. It all had happened so quickly. He had held excitement in his arms and then deliberately pushed it away. But with each passing second the lure of Aeriel's image lessened and the anger, temporarily diverted, gathered strength.

Total success—and now, nothing! His deeds completely discounted in favor of a strong arm and flashing sword. Great spells worthy of a master judged of lesser worth than the formulas of alchemy. Despite what he had done, the warrior still stood first in the minds of men; and apparently no thaumaturge could displace him.

Alodar watched Aeriel fade from view like the others. When she was gone, he stood motionless, continuing to look down the empty hillside. After several minutes, Periac approached Alodar and threw his arm about him.

"Come, my journeyman," he said. "Never mind the twisted thoughts of the nobility. You have done credit to your craft tonight, and we have been amply rewarded. We can call ourselves thaumaturges to the queen; Vendora herself has given us leave. No more mending pots or keeping the frost from winter fruit for a single night's meal in the backward outlands. Let us also travel to Ambrosia and ply out craft where the coin is gold, not copper."

Alodar blinked as he remembered his master's presence, but then shook him off and looked down at his feet. Not by thaumaturgy could he accomplish his quest! With his face pulled into a tight grimace, he kicked in frustration at the grimoire's outer wrappings, lying where Feston had tossed them. They leaped high into the air; catching a breeze, they began to float gently down to earth some ten feet away. Alodar absently watched them settle while he tried to calm his thoughts, and then suddenly focused his attention. A sparkle in the moonlight caught his eye.

He ran to the parchment scraps as they touched the ground and hastily scavenged them. "Look here, master Periac," he exclaimed. "More deception still. The grimoire alone does not contain all of the formulas we have found tonight. Another is scrawled on the inside of the coverings. See it glow in the feeble light."

"Waste not your thoughts on such distractions," Periac said with a wave of one hand while he began stroking his goatee with the other. "Find yourself a spot of comfort and I will give you some instruction. We will pass the time constructively until dawn to see if there are any survivors and Morwin among them. And then to Ambrosia to better our fortune."

Alodar looked down at the scraps in his hand and clinched his teeth. It was only one formula against a whole book's worth, but he had started with less two months ago. His pulse calmed as he settled his mind to it.

"No, master," he said firmly. "I have had a brief taste of my destiny. I cannot rest until I savor it full swallow. If it is with sword and formula that one wins the fair lady, then on that road I will travel."

With a flourish, he loosened the tie at his neck and dropped his cape to his feet. "I am a thaumaturge no more."

Periac's mouth opened in disbelief, but Alodar stood before him in silence, jaws set and fists clenched until the knuckles showed white.

"To cast aside the time you have spent with me is folly," Periac said at last. "And to dabble with the likes of alchemy is greater folly still. Come, study with me so that you learn enough of one art to become a master."

"My life now has purpose," Alodar replied with determination, "as it has never had before. I thank you for the knowledge you have given me and hope my service has been ample payment in return. And I will journey with you to Ambrosia, yes, but then I follow this scrap wherever it leads me."

Periac looked at Alodar for a long moment, then raised his hands and dropped them to his sides. "Very well, my insatiable one," he said. "Explore what Honeysuckle Street has to offer."

He paused and then continued with deliberate slowness. "And when you decide instead to be a true craftsman, seek out my door. For a while it may remain open for you."

Alodar's eyes narrowed, but he did not speak. With a sigh he settled to the ground to await the dawn.

PART TWO

The Alchemist

CHAPTER FIVE

Honeysuckle Street

A stream of muddy liquid spilled from the lip of the overhead vat and into the first crucible in the row. Alodar stepped back against the rough timber wall to avoid the spatter and forced open his eyes, tearing from the caustic haze. The man in front of him tugged on a chain that looped a ring in the bottom of the oaken container; with a low-pitched squeak, the vat rumbled forward along wooden rails. The workman shuffled alongside and then yanked the chain over his shoulder. The high bucket pivoted on pins near its rim and delivered a dose of its contents to the next crucible in line.

Alodar watched in silence as the workman proceeded down the row, chin on his chest and shoulders slumped, like an old horse pacing the same rut around a grindstone. He squinted past the worker, down the line of crucibles riding above small blue-white flames, and saw that they spanned the breadth of the building, some three hundred feet, wall to wall. To his right, six more rows with overhead tracks ran parallel to the first, each one fitted with hundreds of identical stations, lines of graduated beakers, and funnel-mouthed flasks, all filled with dancing liquids or incandescent powders.

Beyond these, the majority of the area was partitioned by a maze of tiny cubicles barely chest high. In the ones nearest, he could see caped figures hunched over cluttered workbenches of dirty glassware and leather bound books. On a raised platform jutting from the rear wall, he saw piles of dull white stone, applelike fruits, cattails and rushes, and other materials he could not identify. Beside each, a worker pounded and strained the substances into powder, pulp, or liquid, and thrust the products into the tracked vats stationed nearby. The thud of the hammers and groan of the presses bounced off the ceilings and walls, producing mushy echoes that masked all but the sharpest of sound.

Alodar followed the track around the entire periphery of the building, down the windowless rear wall, across the row of silos that formed the western facade, back along the front with its many doors, and finally overhead as it merged into a complex of switches which fed the seven rows of waiting containers. As the first worker reached the end, Alodar saw a second pull his vat onto the same track and begin to drop measured doses of a coarse gray powder into the simmering crucibles. One row over, a third lifted a beaker from its tripod and held it up to the light cascading from the high windows in the east. He shook his head and poured the milky contents into a trough running the length of the bench, then moved on to the next.

"That last one was clouded only the slightest," a voice behind Alodar suddenly yelled out as the inspection continued. "How can I show a profit if you dump every flask just because it isn't crystal clear?"

The man replaced an empty beaker on its tripod and looked in Alodar's direction. "I fear I am too liberal as it is, Basil," he called back. "With only the merest trace, the chance of skunkwater is most high. We are lucky you have not contaminated half of the work cubicles from what we have processed already this morning."

"I have given it only to the old ones," Basil shot back. "The way they dawdle, it would be a small loss in any event. Now see that the yield is greater; if the light shines through, however faint, then it is worth the risk. We must have one of three if any volume is to result when we are done."

Alodar turned to face the speaker and looked into large eyes, wide-set on a smooth round face. Heavy cheeks sagged on either side of a slash of a mouth; thick lips pulled down at the corners into a perpetual look of disapproval. Shoulder-length hair, held stiffly in place by an aromatic pomade, brushed against a flared silk collar of deep purple. The rest of the tunic shimmered golden-yellow, embroidered with intricate designs and hanging free on a stocky form. Alodar looked down to see stumpy calves dropping into fur-lined boots trimmed with silver.

"Are you the proprietor?" he asked. "I have come in from the street and wish to discuss a proposition to our mutual benefit."

Basil quickly ran his eyes up and down Alodar's roughly clothed form. "Another one with a formula, are you?" he said. "It seems a grimoire lay hidden under every rock in the countryside, just awaiting yesterday's dawn for discovery. Ever since the rumor of the royal shop tooling up for a new run hit the street, there has been no end of it. But no matter, I will watch your demonstration for the usual fees."

Basil turned back towards the cubicles and motioned for Alodar to follow. "What will you need?" he continued. "Anthanors and the rest go by the time, the ingredients by what is consumed."

Alodar matched the short man's stride and tightened his grip on the parchment scrap in the pocket of his new cape. The lack of his thaumaturgical gear made it feel strangely light, and he was continually glancing down at its brown plainness to see that his shoulders were still covered.

"Tell me more of these fees," he said as they reached the cubicles and began to wind their way into their midst. "I am from the outlands to the west and unfamiliar with the practices of alchemy in Ambrosia."

"From the west!" Basil said in mock surprise. "It makes the story so much more plausible. If the queen found her fortune in the fall of Iron Fist, why not a common craftsman as well? But to your question, I am a merchant and it is only fair that I receive just payment for use of what is mine. You wish to show me some alchemy. Very well, do so as your formula directs. But be prepared to render in double proportion for what is consumed in the process."

"Double proportion," Alodar said. "Why should there be any cost at all? I propose to share with you whatever my formula might bring. That will be your compensation, not a few pieces of copper for a single execution."

"Yes, double proportion," Basil said with a wave of his arm. "I manage a profit only because, like the rest, I perform my formulas on the largest of scales. A hundred times I boil the murky muds of mangrove swamps with the gray clays from the barbaric north, so that I may get fifty crucibles filled with syrup of extraction. And to those fifty I add the fleshy skin of the cactus, so the sweetness

68

may be pulled away in seventeen, leaving clear liquid to be decanted here."

Alodar followed Basil's arm to the nearest workbench and saw a figure huddling under a cape studded with the inverted triangle logo of the alchemist. A bony hand reached out from the folds and carefully poured the liquid from a beaker into a funnel filled with what looked like coral-red flower petals. With a scratchy pen, the alchemist slowly copied strange glyphs from an open grimoire on a clean sheet of paper and then crumpled and cast it into a flame when he was done. For a moment the liquid seemed lost in the crevasses between the petals, but then a drop of light pink formed at the bottom of the funnel's stem and fell into a flask below. Several more drops followed the first, and then a small stream of color trickled free. Almost as quickly, a smell of stifling sweetness filled Alodar's lungs, and he coughed violently in surprise.

"It is always that way when it is fresh," Basil said. "Diluted and aged, you do not notice. But I am lucky at that. Out of seventeen, I expect maybe three flasks of honeysuckle oil. Three flasks out of a hundred for spices, perfumes, and as ingredient for a dozen formulas more. Can you not imagine the waste and expense if I tried the steps one at a time all the way through? No, the only way is to perform all the identical operations at once with a minimum of effort. A demonstration is the epitome of extravagance. Double the cost for disrupting the production line is only fair; be thankful triple is not the rate instead."

"But why a charge at all?" Alodar persisted. "As I have said, I am prepared to share in whatever gain might accrue."

"So say they all," Basil responded. "And after the formula fails four times running, what have I then? Only pleading for one more try for which the random factors will surely align. And if not, then for the next. No, I insist that the demonstration pay for itself."

"And if one does not have the payment," Alodar asked, "how then do you ever find new formulas of merit?"

Basil's eyes widened and his lips curved upwards into a toothy smile. "Why you agree as did the last two yesterday," he said, "the ones now pulping up on the platform to the right. All they had to offer was their labor, which I accepted. In six months they will have paid in full for their little fantasy and be able to leave free men. Is not that right, Eldan?" Basil turned and pounded the back of the alchemist watching the last of the pink liquid fall from the petals, now bleached white.

The craftsman slowly removed the funnel from the neck of the flask and dropped its contents into a bin at his side. Without saying a word he pivoted and held the flask out for Basil's inspection. As his cape fell away, Alodar saw wrists cuffed in iron and held rigidly apart by a two-foot length of dark black bar. The alchemist's eyes stared straight ahead, unblinking. The left side of his face was splotched a deep green, and the flesh of his nose hung limp like a deflated balloon on the plane of his cheeks.

"Now, Eldan here," Basil continued as he accepted the flask, "could have fared better. I offered him a regular wage. But he preferred to be independent, tinkering in his own shop down the street, taking risks beyond the call of prudence. There are others like him still out there, obtaining loans from me to purchase ingredients for wilder and more unproven schemes. And finally when they can borrow no more on their names, they offer their labor instead as payment.

"For Eldan," Basil said as he pounded the alchemist a second time, "it is ten years served and only ten more to go. Of course, the splash of dye and the cartilage rot are to be expected. And we have had to add a few restraints to ensure he keeps to his work cubicle."

Basil passed his hand in front of Eldan's eyes and then snapped his fingers. A long moment passed and then the alchemist jerked his head and blinked. "Finally the honeysuckle does slow one down," Basil said. "In a year or so more he will be good enough only to pull the vats around the circle."

Basil paused and his smile was smug. "I own this factory outright, have part interest in two more, and even mine one of the richest veins left in the Fumus Mountains. It is not bad progress for a humble apothecary who once carried blocks of peat from the bogs for a few coppers. I used to jump to the alchemists' beck and call; now they jump to mine."

Basil snapped his fingers again and Alodar waited for the delayed reaction. "Well," Basil said, "let us see what you need and strike a bargain. There is no point

70

in trying any of the others. The rates the length of the street are all the same."

"I have no gold," Alodar said.

"Then your labor," Basil replied. "Fear not that you may later reconsider. I have the means to ensure that I receive payment in full."

Alodar gripped the formula tighter as he saw Eldan's face finally twitch. He coughed again from the lingering smell of the oil of honeysuckle and wiped another tear from his eye. He looked at the manacles on Eldan's wrists and a cold chill ran down his spine.

"I will have to think about it," he said finally and turned for the door to the street. Even outside, he could hear Basil's deep laugh echoing after.

The air suddenly crackled, and Alodar leaped up onto the counter as a glowing blue globe bounced through the doorway. With a swiftness the eye could hardly follow, it darted to and fro, careening off the walls, floor, and ceiling. It sped by his face and, as he pulled back, he felt the hair rise from his head and stand on end, tracking the passage.

"By the laws," a high voice sounded from the room beyond, "you would think not an amulet in this place worked. What rotten luck. Nine batches in a row, and every one of them producing ball lightning instead of the elixir. Well, this is the last of the baneberry. It had better work, Saxton, old boy, or it's a diet of caraway for quite a spell."

Alodar watched the dancing ball slowly shrink in size and activity, and then finally expire among the dusty glassware of the alembic in the far corner. He swung down on the other side of the counter, advanced to the doorway, and peered into the workroom behind.

Light from the setting sun cascaded through highset windows down upon a massive disarray. The wall on the left was shelved floor to ceiling, and all available space was crammed with row upon row of bottles and vials of many shapes. Most were empty and uncorked, long cobwebs linking them together and filling their interiors with ladders of dust. But here and there, neat little collections sparkled with deeply colored liquids or glowing powders.

The wall on the right was also shelved, but stacked

with a tumble of small boxes. Alodar could see a label on each, but in a script that he did not recognize. Most of the containers were of rough-hewn wood, but an occasional one had sides of shiny steel, clasped shut with a strong lock and chained to a nearby support. Crucibles, aludels, and curcubits competed for space on the floor, leaving only a small winding path from where Alodar stood to a workbench on the far wall. There, beneath a bookshelf sagging with almanacs and grimoires, huddled a robed figure intent upon his task. The fiery heat of an anthanor colored his plump cheeks red, and large beads of sweat formed upon the folds of his neck. He stoked the furnace and pumped the bellows, oblivious to Alodar's presence.

"Alchemist Saxton?" Alodar called to the man. "Are you alchemist Saxton, the one with the powder of deep sleep?"

Saxton turned to look briefly at the interruption, waving his hand back towards the doorway. "In the outer room, the second display case. It is ten coppers a vial; leave it on the counter."

"No, no. I have come to see you about another matter," Alodar said. "I understand from the street that you work independent of the factories and need a novice to help you in your craft."

"Yes, that I do," Saxton answered without looking up from the anthanor. "One with enough stomach to stand by his job once I have taught him. But leave me for a moment, I have a formula to complete."

Alodar watched as the alchemist withdrew a crucible glowing red hot from the furnace door and set it down to sizzle on the workbench.

"Well, no lightning this time," Saxton said, running one hand across his bald pate and then wiping it against his robe. His smile split his round face like a wedge removed from an orange, and his small, close-set eyes nearly disappeared into the folds of his cheek.

"One more step," he said, "and we may yet line our purse this month." He waddled down the workbench, withdrew one of the grimoires from the shelf overhead, and rapidly thumbed to the desired page.

"Bloodroot," he mumbled and ambled around the clutter on the floor to face the wall of boxes. After staring for several moments, he reached on tiptoe and pulled one container from its resting place. He extracted a large red bulb and returned to the workbench, placing it in the middle of a stack of clean parchment.

"And now the activation," he said as he withdrew a quill from a nearby bottle and deftly drew a complex symbol on the sheet beneath the root. As the ink dried, he stared at the strange glyph and grunted satisfaction.

"About the novice," Alodar interjected.

Saxton's eyebrows jumped and he turned to look at his intruder. "Still here? Then you are either brave or foolhardy. This last step could make the dancing ball look like a toy, and it only has six chances in ten of going right."

"I wish to learn of alchemy," Alodar replied, "but do not care for the way a factory offers to teach it. I have heard that there are risks and am willing to accept them."

"Very well, then, we will see the fiber of which you are made." Saxton shrugged, returned to the bench, diced the bloodroot into a fine powder, and added it to the crucible now already cool. He looked warily back at Alodar and threw the inscribed parchment into the anthanor.

"All is ready for the final formula," he said as he began to write upon the next page in the stack. His pen rapidly flicked out line after line of intricate symbols, pausing only occasionally to dart back to the well for more ink. In an instant, the page was covered, and Saxton set it aside to begin a second. He filled half of another and then paused a moment with his pen poised high.

"The last symbol," he said as he glanced at the crucible. With a flourish, he added a few more scratches to the paper. Alodar heard a sudden bubbling and turned to watch a thick froth come over the top of the little stone dish and descend to add its stain to the richly covered bench.

"By the signatures," Saxton exclaimed. "Chance is with us today. No explosion to test you with. Instead, more than two whole gills of the finest nerve elixir north of the isthmus."

Before Alodar could interrupt again, the alchemist scurried to the wall on the left and removed a rack of small corked vials, covered with dust like the rest.

"Here, if you want to be a novice, make yourself useful. Dust them off and label and fill them properly. And when you are done, place a sign on the door that we have

73

nerve elixir here, freshly brewed and only two gold brandels at that. The factories may be able to undercut us on the sweetbalm, itching powders, and the like, but they would never risk trying for nerve elixir."

The alchemist set the vials down, ran his hands across his smooth brow, and began a small shuffling dance among the paraphernalia around the workbench. He kicked up the dust with several energetic stomps and then suddenly stopped and looked Alodar squarely in the face.

"You are too old to seek seriously the robe of a beginning novice," he said with a frown. He pursed his lips and stood a moment in thought.

"And so, let us see this wonderful formula then." He smiled at last. "Though I warn you, some deluded soul comes here with such a tale fortnightly, and I have yet to see one worth the effort to look upon it."

"You do not speak of fees," Alodar said.

"No, no, that is not my way," Saxton answered. "If you have spent your good money on a hastily scrawled piece of nonsense, I will tell you so."

Alodar hesitated a moment, then removed the old scraps from his cape and handed the first across to Saxton's outstretched hand. "I come to you, alchemist Saxton, because I have inquired carefully and the street gives you the reputation of an honest man. Nevertheless, my first efforts at bargaining have filled my thoughts with caution. Permit me to reveal only the first part of the formula for my own protection."

"Oh, a powder for the street talk. Here, let me see it," Saxton said, ripping the scrap from Alodar's grasp. "Know that I could have been as the rest. Only the safe formulas, high yield potions of low potency. The long lines of pipes and valves and the endless belts of the pretty bottles that the ladies like so much. But what does that get you? A steady and frugal return and a chain to your workbench for all of your days. Ah, I could have been that but I am not. A fetish for all such bookwork. I have more daring and will stake my whole stock on the one chance for a truly remarkable philtre. If it goes awry and burns me to a crisp, what of it? If it produces only skinrot, I can start again. But my lad, oh ho, suppose I succeed. What then of those who stand in their neat stalls, performing the same step as each indentical vial comes down the line? Why, with the right potion, one could be rich for life, selling drops here and there for a baron's ransom when the need struck."

Saxton stopped as the glyphs on Alodar's scrap finally penetrated his consciousness. "Great amulets, my lad, where came you upon this?"

"From the fall of Iron Fist, alchemist, from the same trove that produced Vendora's new grimoire. Can I assume that you are interested?"

"An elixir of boils on the royal shops." Saxton waved him off. "They push polluted swill through their pipes no less than do the likes of Basil the apothecary. But enough of that. The formula interests me indeed. What is your proposition?"

"What is yours?" Alodar replied warily.

Saxton ran his hand over his head. "Well, you could proceed as you originally stated," he said. "I will accept you as a novice. In the course of time, you will learn enough to activate the formula with no assistance. The craft is broad and the knowledge diverse, however. Much more than what is specifically needed would be thrust your way, and you would have to wait patiently until you understood the signatures of the final ingredient before attempting the mixing. I estimate that in perhaps seven years you would know enough to try."

"I seek not mastery of all of alchemy," Alodar said. "Just the meaning of these scraps in my hand."

"Wait," Saxton said as he raised his open palm. "I have not finished with my proposal. You could study as a novice and have all in seven years. Or we can work together on this specific formula, sharing equally in the labor for perhaps six months and then equally in the rewards as well."

"I put forth nothing but the formula and the effort for its preparation?" Alodar asked.

"And I nothing but my knowledge and equal toil as well," Saxton replied.

"I sought no better arrangement when I saw Basil this morning," Alodar said, breaking into a smile and showing Saxton the rest of his scraps. "See then all. It is with you I would rather strike a bargain."

"And in truth, we are not totally clear of the apothecary's grasp," Saxton said as he quickly shuffled through the pieces of parchment. "From time to time I have had to borrow from him when my luck ran sour. Even now I owe him a sack of brandels a half year hence or my services for a full twelve months thereafter. And as I scan the formula here I see that the ingredients go quite beyond what one can expect to find in my little shop. Pennyroyal, gold thread, dried salamander, camphor, and sandalwood are the stock in trade of any alchemist on the street. But the others, a dead man's candle, root of shrieking mandrake, midnight dew collected under a moon eclipsed. Not standard items and it will take much to procure them. Yes, we may have to deal with Basil before we are finished, I fear."

"Is it a risk you are willing to take?" Alodar asked.

"It is your risk too," Saxton said. "You would take it, even if we did not have to barter with him again. My present agreement binds any novices I may have as well. If we fail to earn enough to make payment on time, then you also will pull vats and carry beakers from mixing line to workbench cubicle. The juices that stain your skin and the vapors that rot it away will surround you for a year. Even for such a short time you will not escape unscathed."

Alodar frowned and stood a moment in silence. Eldan's image was still too fresh and he shuddered at the thought. "What product does the formula produce?" he asked. "For what magnitude of reward do I take the risk of this bondage?"

"Oh the rewards are great enough," Saxton said with a smile. "This formula is for an ointment, no less than a caloric shield, allowing one to endure great temperature that would otherwise be fatal."

Alodar's frown deepened. "I can fathom no use for that," he said. "I was hoping for something more dramatic and powerful."

"It is powerful enough," Saxton said. "Powerful enough for the Fumus Mountains."

"How can such an ointment aid in the mineshafts which everyone declares to be delivering their last?"

"Those tunnels are not the working of man," Saxton replied, "but natural fumaroles and fissures in ancient volcanoes which have smouldered since before the first sagas. And in their walls we have found hundreds of perfect crystals of emerald, aquamarine, beryl and other fine gems. With a few chips of the chisel, they fall free into the pouch, more like collecting wild mushrooms than wrenching soft metals from their tightly clutching ores. And the deeper we have gone, the larger have become the stones. Last year a topaz the size of a robin's egg came from Basil's mine next to the queen's."

"Then they are hardly playing out," Alodar said. "Great treasures might be at lower levels still."

"But it is the heat," Saxton explained, "that is bringing collection to an end. Near the surface, where the cool air mixes with the humid blast from below, one can stay as he will, although with discomfort. At depths where gem quality stones were first found, a miner worked his full day, if properly attired. But all such levels have been discovered and searched many times over until there is no more treasure. Now all that remains are mad dashes by the daring into passageways which burn to the touch, to retrieve one stone and then hastily return.

"Why do you think I risk neck and limb to make elixir to calm one's nerves, to keep cool-headed in time of peril? No less than three lords have announced that they will venture beyond where any have dared and bring back jewels to fill the treasure chests of the queen. Yes, ever since she returned from the west with that rough Feston in tow, Ambrosia has been seized with a fever for noble deeds to attract her attention. Every lordling seems convinced that a brave quest that returns much fortune will turn Vendora's head before she settles on the red surcoat by default. And the jewels of the Fumus Mountains would top any feat in bravery and reward by far. We will be amply paid for an ointment which makes possible such a success."

Alodar's frown turned to a broad grin, and he pounded the older man on the shoulder. "I knew I was on the right track," he exclaimed. "Yes, yes, of course, the jewels of the Fumus Mountains. But why settle for a stack of gold coin when the greater reward is ours for the taking? Do not plan to sell the ointment when it is finished but smooth it on my limbs instead. I will brave the heat and darkness and bring back the jewels for us to share. Gems enough for you to dole out a few at a time to keep you in expensive pleasure, and yet enough for me to overflow Vendora's royal coffers. With wealth from your al-chemy and the lays of the bards for what I will have done, how could any other have better chance for the hand of the fair lady?"

Saxton blinked at Alodar's outburst and looked cau-tiously into his gleaming eyes. "It is not certain," he said, "and risks are still present. The ingredients are so dear that we can not afford great quantities. Only a modest chance will we have of success; one cannot guarantee certainty in this craft. And even if we do succeed, know that the ointment will reduce the heatflow to your body but not completely stop it. There may be no gems worth the taking except at depths for which even the protec-tion is insufficient."

"You stated you are willing to risk all on one chance," Alodar said. "For my quest, so am I."

"And finally if you do stagger to the surface laden with wealth," Saxton persisted, "do you think that others will stand by and let you remove it? How well can you wield your sword to protect the fruits of our labor?"

"I received modest training as a small boy," Alodar said. "But I am willing to undertake more, if that is what is needed."

"Oh, by the laws, you have my interest and know it," Saxton said as he looked again at the scraps in his hand. "The parchment smells old, the script looks ancient. If any formula is to make my fortune, then why not this? But the effort will be a great one, and many hours must we toil before it is done. Even to get one vial at the end, it looks as if we must start with no less than a thousand of the first step; and as you see, I am ill-equipped to perform repetition with much efficiency. But yes, I think you must become a warrior as well. I have a distant cousin who instructs sons of the nobles somewhere across the expanse of Ambrosia. Cedric is his name, and perhaps he would teach a novice alchemist as well."

"I have heard of him," Alodar said. "His skill was praised in the bailey of Iron Fist."

"Very well then," Saxton said, "we will proceed as follows. You spend your days with the soldier's toys while I continue my usual routine with mine. After all we must still earn the coin that keeps our minds alert and heart's blood pumping. During the hours of darkness, we will work to produce the caloric shield. Hopefully, by the time the ointment is ready, you will have sufficient skill to protect whatever treasure is found as well."

Saxton stopped and looked out through the high windows. "Tomorrow you can seek out Cedric," he said. "But by the looks of the shadows we may as well begin now the first evening's labor. Let me see, I said we must prepare to activate the first step a thousand times. That would mean we need no less than twice that number of spider eyes all neatly cut free and dipped in honey. You begin with them while I start to set up the rest."

"Spider eyes," Alodar groaned, "and two thousand. But that could take months all by itself."

"Persistence," Saxton said, raising his index finger. "Persistence is the primary attribute of the alchemist."

Alodar looked up at the sun high overhead and yawned. He had wielded the tiny scalpel for the better part of the night and getting proper directions had taken most of the morning. But at last he was headed out of the winding alleys of the craftsmen and into the heart of Ambrosia.

The street ahead widened, and well worn cobbles replaced the mud underfoot. Painted storefronts mixed with rough clapboard. In the distance Alodar saw inns, taverns, and liveries rising above the smaller structures.

As he continued, the street crowded with beggars and merchants with pushcarts, badgering the patrons who ventured forth for business before noon. Hawkers standing on balconies added their voices to the melodious background clop of horse-drawn coaches. The aroma of freshly baked meat pies on storefront shelves blended with the smells of human exertion as he pushed his way through the thickening swarm.

Alodar pressed on, and the shops gave way to private dwellings and finally to expansive mansions, high-walled with gates closed to the street. He no longer blended in with the traffic but stood out against the glint of mail and sheen of silk that passed him by. Near the river which split the city, Alodar stopped and banged a heavy knocker against a door of iron.

"I wish an audience with warmaster Cedric," he said to

the anonymous eyes which peered through a small slit in the door.

"Have you an appointment?" the voice behind the eyes asked. "Warmaster Cedric is presently giving private drill and has two more pupils after noon today."

"I wish to engage him in like manner," Alodar said, "and am here to arrange terms and times. Perhaps he can see me for but a moment."

The impersonal voice exploded in a hearty laugh. "And I see by your attire that you must be the scion of some lord in Vendora's court itself. By all means enter. My master needs a diversion this morning and I think he will be most amused by the value you place upon his craft."

The door swung open and Alodar saw two figures clashing long staves against one another in the large courtyard. Vine-covered walls ran around the periphery, meeting either side of a two-story structure at the far end. Large wooden racks of precisely hung clubs, swords, and maces hid all but one small doorway, and the windows above were crowded by cabinets of daggers, crossed halberts, and double-headed axeblades secured to the wall. Circles and squares of dusty chalk divided the hard clay ground into the pattern of an often-patched quilt, and in the arena nearest the building the two men struggled. Alodar's irritation over the servant's manner vanished as he advanced to meet them with a rapid stride.

"No, no, no," the taller of the two growled. "If he thrusts with both hands equally extended, push your staff perpendicular to it. If you do not, he will slide around your guard and drive home like this." With these words he dropped his left hand from his stick and, swinging with his right, soundly thumped it against the ribcage of his opponent. The second man yelped with surprise and tripped to the ground in a tangle of arms and legs.

"Enough for today, Dartilon." The victor dismissed the other with a flourish. He smoothed back into place short, silvery hair and twirled the end of his waxed moustache into sharpness. His eyes were an unblinking steel blue and his cheeks axeblade flat about lips drawn into a firm thin line. The skin on his bare arms and legs showed the crisscross of many scars and blotches of age but stretched tight like a drumhead across his thickboned frame.

The fallen man scurried away into the house at the

courtyard's end, rubbing his side, and Alodar seized the opportunity to speak. "Warmaster Cedric, have you room on your calendar for yet another? I cannot pay as well as some, but I will be an attentive pupil and learn well what you may teach."

"My fee is a gold brandel per lesson," Cedric rasped. "Does your eagerness extend that far?"

"A gold brandel, no," Alodar said. "At least not at once. Not until I receive return on my formula."

"Alchemy," Cedric snorted. "Hardly a stable undertaking on which to depend. I have a cousin, Saxton, who practices the craft in some little shed out on Honeysuckle Street. He toils alone from sun to sun and all of his hard labor keeps him no more than days away from beggary. I prefer to instruct one whose purse always jingles, regardless of the luck of each morning's brew."

"It is from Saxton, in fact, that I come," Alodar said. "And surely you had rather someone asking to learn than some lord's son sent because it is the fashion?"

"I take the rich men's gold because they thrust it upon me. If they wish me to ride on past laurels instead of upon the horse of the commander, then it is only just that I do so. Time with you only deprives me of coin for my purse. Be gone with your ideals so we can both spend our time more profitably."

"I come on no idle whim, warmaster Cedric," Alodar persisted. "I am determined to learn the craft of fighting and seek to learn it from him who teaches best."

"Determination, my scars." Cedric waved aside Alodar's words. "Determination until you feel the first true stab of pain and realize that it is not some glorious game for the sagas."

With these words, Cedric suddenly lashed out with his staff and knocked Alodar's feet from under him. Alodar's eyes blazed, but he understood the intent and choked down his cry of protest. He slowly rose, rubbing his shin. Through clenched teeth he said, "Such a blow I can stand, warmaster."

"Indeed so," mocked Cedric and he flicked out and tripped Alodar to the ground once more. Alodar grimaced from the shock to flesh already growing sore, but scrambled upright, reaching out wildly for the end of the stick which now quivered tantalizingly in front of his face. As he extended his arms, it whizzed through the air with lightning swiftness and pounded his stomach with three quick thrusts. Alodar involuntarily doubled up, grasping his hands to his middle, helpless to ward off a series of blows which now rained down upon his unprotected head.

In an instant the barrage stopped, and he huddled, licking blood, ears ringing, barely able to understand Cedric's words.

"What now of that determination, lad? Do you still want to be the mighty warrior?"

Alodar struggled to his feet a third time, still clutching his stomach and squinting to see through eyes beginning to puff shut. "If this is the way you instruct, let me have the other staff and continue," he spat out. "By the laws, yes, I am determined."

Cedric lowered his weapon and intently studied the figure Alodar cut before him. "Yes, let us test it fairly," he said as he scooped up the second staff and tossed it in Alodar's direction.

As Alodar reached for it, the master's stick sprang to life, whirling, thrusting and pushing with lightning speed. Alodar, numbed as he was, could only imitate a stance he had practiced as a boy and thrust his staff horizontally forward. Cedric whipped his erect and cracked Alodar upon the top of the head and then each shin. Alodar shifted his stick vertically to ward off the blows, and Cedric replied with lunges to both sides, methodically hitting shoulders, arms, thighs, and calves. In desperation, Alodar released his left hand and swung his staff in a slow arc towards Cedric's dancing body. Cedric smiled and cracked Alodar's knuckles. The stick dropped once more to the ground.

Now defenseless, the barrage increased in intensity and Alodar huddled, hands over his head in helplessness. As the shower of pain continued, Alodar curled up smaller still, saying not a word but tightening his lips as each blow again hit his swollen knuckles and the puffing welts forming on his back. Finally Cedric tired of the sport and stopped the pummeling. "And the determination, now?" he taunted.

"As before," Alodar croaked, struggling to rise on quivering legs. "Let us go at it again."

Cedric dropped his staff and stood a long time in silence. At last he said, "You are either addlepated or burn with desire, my lad. What indeed pushes you so?"

Alodar managed to pull himself erect and return the older man's stare. "I wish to prove myself worthy," he said. "Lord Feston spoke highly of the value of your teaching and his reputation at arms is great."

"Sweetbalm for reputations. More come from circumstances than from merit. Ambrosia is babbling even now about how this Feston, one of my former lordlings, bettered fifteen men on the walls of Iron Fist. Fifteen men surely all like yourself. Yanked from some town or field, dressed in leather and told that they were now warriors. Why, with any training at all, one could hack away among the likes until his arm grew tired, with no threat upon his own person. But true skill in arms is not measured by such petty reputation. It is by trial in which yours is not the only sword that bites deep. And such skill is achieved at no little cost. Can what you seek be worth the agony of this morning and the days to follow?"

"Yes," Alodar answered simply, holding fists tight against his sides, determined not to collapse until the interview was over.

"Valdo, tend his wounds with sweetbalm." Cedric turned suddenly and beckoned to the servant still at the gate. "And fit him sparring gear for the morrow."

"Sparring gear?" Alodar asked. "For tomorrow?"

"Yes," Cedric said. "My pupils need practice against the lesser skilled order to build confidence and polish their technique. They would never dream of testing themselves against one another, and you can serve their needs admirably. And if you watch while I instruct, you may learn enough to fend against them. Can your determination take day after full day of that?"

"It can," Alodar said. "It will have to."

Cedric gave Alodar one last look. "A hero and a fool," he muttered and walked out of the courtyard.

CHAPTER SIX

Luck of the Potionmakers

ALODAR pushed the cork into the last flask and sat down on the small stool beside the workbench. He shook his head to clear the numbness and looked through fatigued eyes at the two rows of transparent liquid that barely covered the bottoms of their containers. Only sixty-three, he thought, sixty-three small flasks to represent the results of over five months of labor.

Saxton placed a fleshy palm on Alodar's shoulder and rose on his tiptoes in a back arching stretch. "Well done, my lad," he yawned. "You have been an apt pupil and we have accomplished much. Four steps completed and six more to try. If all the rest go right half of the time, then we have about three chances in four of producing the ointment. And with fewer repetitions to run at each stage, we will progress all the more swiftly."

"From such speed we can well benefit," Alodar said. "The monotony of repetition bothers me less than the time remaining before we must make good the loan from Basil."

"There is an additional matter for concern," Saxton said. "I have traded what useful stock I could for ingredients to get this far but can continue in the same manner no longer. The sixth step requires peat tar dug in darkness and Basil virtually monopolizes the entire supply. Either we deal with him or attempt instead to use a substitute."

"I would rather not give him further claim upon our futures when we have come this far on our own," Alodar said.

"Nor would I," Saxton replied. "I have escaped the snare in which he has entrapped others by bartering but

84

modestly and then only when I had no other choice."

He stopped and ran his hand over his head, his eyes frowning in thought. "And by the laws," he said, "we may as well try. There is more danger if we substitute in a formula this potent, but if we do not, we increase our risk as well. Let us look in the almanac and see what signatures must be provided."

Saxton reached up on the shelf and pulled down one of a matched set of volumes placed in a neat line amid his jumble of assorted grimoires.

"Yes, peat tar, here it is," he said. " 'Thick, sticky black liquid with pungent odor.' Well, the thickness and stickyness are well enough understood. Almost all of the more complex formulas that have many diverse ingredients need some substance to bind them together. The other properties are a little more ambiguous, depending upon the final objective. For transfigurations, black provides the animal's coat, for invisibility, the quenching of light, and so on. Ah, this is the entry. For heat-shielding, black gives the dissipativeness of empty space. Let us see, for the pungent odor there are likewise many interpretations but they all seem to deal with repulsion. In our case, yes, here it is. For shielding ointments, the odor repels heat."

Saxton slammed the book shut and replaced it on the shelf. He closed his eyes, folded his arms across his chest and rocked back and forth on his heels.

"Sap from the maple tree," he said at last. "I have some here. And if somehow we could use the powder of distaste with it, the signature should be close enough to work."

"You have the powder as well," Alodar said. "I came across it while looking for more of the syrup of narcissus."

"But as you said, we can ill afford the labor," Saxton replied. "The powder binds but poorly with any other substance. It would float on the surface of the maple sap like oil on water. We would have to force each grain into the liquid one at a time and hold it there until it was soaked through and would stay. And for each of our flasks we need hundreds of grains. Your task with the spider eyes was a small effort by comparison."

"Does the soaking require an activation," Alodar said, "or merely the effort to bring it about?"

"There would be no alchemy in the preparation,"

Saxton said. "That would follow when we had the peat tar substitute ready for use."

"Then I have the solution," Alodar said excitedly. "What you describe is but a perfect application of thaumaturgy. We can hold one grain in a bead of sap and, with a simple spellbinding, the others will follow."

Saxton wrinkled his nose and frowned. "I have no need for another craft," he said, "and certainly not for another craftsman. Besides no thaumaturge would accept an invitation to my shop even if I were to extend one."

"I can do what has to be done," Alodar said. "Let us pour out the sap and I will show you."

Saxton looked at Alodar a long time, then shrugged his shoulders and pointed to one of the shelves. Alodar slid off the stool and retrieved a glazed jug with a stopper crusted with mold and hardened streams of sap running down the sides like candlewax about a bottle. He decanted a generous amount into a large shallow pan and, sucking on a glass tube, extracted a droplet to place in a vial nearby. He found the powder of distaste and grabbed a pinch between thumb and forefinger. Like a cook spicing a stew, he sprinked the dark black powder over the open dish. Then, with a pair of tongs, he extracted a final grain from the small square tin.

He looked at the anthanor flame burning nearby and spoke the words he had not used for the long months he had labored at his new craft. Then, with a sudden motion, he plunged the tongs into the vial and turned to watch the surface of the pan. The powder disappeared from view, sinking into the darkness of the sap and leaving sluggish ripples in its wake.

Saxton crept closer, his squinting frown replaced by eyes wide with curiosity. He looked at the uncluttered surface of the liquid in the pan and then to the tongs in the vial. "The quarter part of an hour should be enough," he said quietly as he studied the mixture.

Some time later, Alodar released the connection and pulled the empty forceps from the small vial. The grains of powder remained where they were, floating in suspension. "We are ready with the substitute peat tar," he said with a smile.

Saxton grunted at Alodar's success and motioned him aside. He picked up the first of the stoppered flasks and carried it across the room to a ring above a small smoking flame. The soot immediately began to blacken the bottom of the glassware and send wisps of carbon up the sides. Saxton removed the cork and added to the clear solution some of the impregnated sap, using a large bulbed pipette. Then as he watched the liquid simmer, he began to copy a parchment scrap onto clean paper.

"By the signatures, why must the good formulas all be such a bother?" he wondered. "Ten steps in this one, each with no more than an even chance of proceeding correctly. Ten steps, by the laws. One thousand setups for the first, so we get about five hundred successes. Five hundred successes so we can have step two go right in about two hundred and fifty. Here we are at the fifth and must try it no less than the full sixty-three times just so we have two chances of having the final activation succeed. Were the stakes not so high, I would be tempted to make one lot and be done with it. Would that these formulas could be multiplied as are those of a cook without a corresponding decrease in their potency."

Before Alodar could reply, Saxton had completed all but the final symbol and raised his pen-hand high. All was ready, and Alodar tensed as the quill descended to the paper.

The room suddenly exploded in light, and Alodar's eyes pulsed with pain. He blinked once and then twice more. All was strangely dark except for a dull glow in the direction of the flask, which remained even when his lids were closed. Saxton lurched against him, and both fell to the floor in a crash of splintering boxes and the tinkle of broken glass.

"Hellfire," Saxton coughed. "We have to get out."

Alodar opened his mouth to reply but quickly shut it again, gagging on a thick, stinging vapor which burned the linings of his throat. He raised one hand to cover his nose and felt a trickle of fresh blood on his palm. He stood upright, crunching glass, and flailed blindly with his free hand until he found Saxton's arm. The doorway should be behind them. As he pulled the alchemist to his feet, he began to grope towards the exit.

More glass clattered as they staggered together, stumbling against the gear scattered about the floor. Alodar banged his shins against a heavy iron bar across their path and fell to his knees. He rose and limped forward, free hand in front reaching for a familar object. He took three more steps and then stopped, feeling the blank wall that separated the workroom from the front of the shop. He reached back, placed Saxton's hand on his shoulder, and began inching to the doorway on the right. His lips started to quiver behind his guarding hand and he fought to hold back the growing demand for air.

Each cautious blind step seemed to be his last, but he pushed on for another until he felt the jamb of the door. He could hold breath no longer and bolted into the front room, ricocheting into the walkway beside the counter. Saxton scurried behind, and together they crashed forward, ripping the latch from its guide, and out into the street.

Alodar stumbled for the last time and sprawled on the sidewalk planking. He took a tentative breath; although it was tainted with the smell from the workroom, it filled his lungs with air. He rolled over and looked at the sky. The dull glow was still there, but fainter now, and the dim outline of the moon began to form beside it. He turned to his side and deduced that the mass beside him must be Saxton, painting rapidly, but alive as well.

"Cut short your stay at Cedric's tomorrow," the alchemist rasped. "We will journey to the apothecary and barter for what we need. So Basil has all the supply of peat tar. It is well worth whatever price."

Alodar ducked behind his shield and the padded club whizzed over his head. Unarmed grappling, staves, broadsword and shield, and now the mace, he thought. The months of monotonous execution of the first steps of the formula had given him time to observe Cedric well. Well enough that Alodar was beginning to be a true match for Dartilon and the others like him.

His opponent staggered as he halted the rush of his missed blow, and Alodar seized the opportunity to strike. He thrust his shield diagonally across his body, blocking Dartilon's arm at the top of its backswing. Reaching out with his own mace, he swung it in a wide arc, catching the young lord squarely on the back of his unprotected head. Dartilon sagged to the ground, momentarily dazed by the blow.

"Enough," he said weakly. "I am tired from the festivities at my father's manor last night. Enough for today. When I am fully awake and fresh, we shall see who can better handle the club."

Alodar said nothing as Dartilon rose and retired to the dressing quarters. His left arm ached from holding the heavy shield through three successive combats, but he did not mind the discomfort.

"Well enough, Alodar," Cedric's voice rasped behind him. "Rest a bit in the shade of the courtyard wall. You will find progress faster if you do not try to master it all in a single day."

"I think I can make it worthwhile for another match," Alodar said as he turned and saw Cedric heading for the shadow. "And I do not rest easy so long as there is more to learn."

Cedric sat down on a small bench pushed against the vine-covered wall. "And when you have learned all that I have to teach you, what then do you expect?"

"As I have said, warmaster," Alodar replied, "the respect which is my due."

Cedric pulled his lips into a tight line and slowly shook his head. "Come," he said, "there is no one else to instruct for the next hour. But there is more that I can teach you than the crash of the mace."

Alodar dropped the shield and joined Cedric on the bench. He looked the older man in the face and raised an eyebrow expectantly.

"I was lowly born," Cedric said, "and sought the glory of the sagas with my sword. Long hours and numbing pain I endured perfecting my craft. Fatigue and aching soreness were my only companions. I have seen few in my lifetime whose dedication matched that of my youth."

Cedric stopped and his lips curved into a slight smile as he looked at Alodar setting beside him. "But no matter for dedication and training," he said at last. "The border wars of Vendora's father provided many opportunities for me to show my mettle, and by luck, skill, and reckless abandon I made my name known throughout Procolon and the neighboring kingdoms. From warrior, sergeant, captain, to commander I increased my glory fighting thirty years for the king, and when I thought I had enough to compel the respect from any man, be he lord or no, I came finally to the royal courts of Ambrosia."

Cedric threw back his head and closed his eyes. "I remember it well," he said. "A courteous audience, a gold medallion, a flush of balls and parties, and then, when the novelty of my presence faded, the postern gate. Retired with honor so the proclamation said, but not so much that I could pound a lord on the back or join him in a cup of wine. The craftsmen of the street might sing my praises, but so long as I was not a part of the faction with the ear of the king, then it did not matter.

"I became a bodyguard of a minor noble and observed from his retinue the workings of the court. I saw the whispered conversations, the hints of special knowledge, the alliances, the coercions, the allegiances that shifted with each interpretation of the actions of the king. It took me some while to understand the rules of the games at court, and once I learned I did not care to play. Better they pay me soft gold for their son's instruction than I pay them for an occasional bow or polite greeting.

"You speak of respect, and I tell you it is not for deeds but for influence. Have the favor of the ruler or the conviction of others that you do, and respect will follow. And no feat of arms, regardless how closely it resembles a tale from the sagas, will have the value of a simple bribe to an appointment herald of some high placed noble."

"It is not only by arms that I plan my assault," Alodar said. "I intend to use the result of Saxton's alchemy as well."

Cedric pushed Alodar's words aside with a wave of his arm. "How can that serve any better?" he said. "Practice at arms at least returns with increased skill the investment of time you give to it. Random dabbling on the Street might yield nothing at all."

"Of the five arts, alchemy is indeed unique in its uncertainty," Alodar admitted. "Using exactly the same ingredients in the same formulas does not necessarily produce identical results. The next to final step for nerve elixir, for example, produces ball lightning instead four times out of ten."

"Unpredictable outcomes that make useless such experimentation," Cedric rasped.

"No, they are indeed related," Alodar replied. "With nerve elixir, we stabilize our erratic impulses to fly and jerk uncontrollably in just the same way the crackling forces of the ball lightning are aligned and held in check. And although the chance outcome inhibits methodical investigation, the fundamental doctrine of alchemy does give some indication on how to proceed."

"And what is that?" Cedric asked.

"The doctrine of signatures," Alodar said, warming to the task of displaying his new-found knowledge. "Or as it is simply stated: 'the attributes without mirror the powers within.' Beeswax is an obvious choice for use in a formula that transmutes lead to gold. Its ability to polish helps to create the metallic sheen of the final product. Vulture feathers play a role in the production of rugs of levitation and so on."

"If it is so clear then," Cedric persisted, "why all of this talk of trade secrets, new formulas, and profit margins?"

"It is true that if cost and time were not factors, an alchemist could devise a formula to produce almost any product desired, a powder of immobilization, an amulet of unbounded luck, or an ointment of true invisibility. Indeed the alchemist's logo is a triangle impossibly balanced on a single point to show how the laws which govern thaumaturgy are easily transcended. To work his craft, he would consult his almanacs of the properties and brew together the right combination of powers to achieve the effect. But, alas, nature works in perverse ways. The more potent the product, the longer the progress must be, and the smaller is the chance of a successful outcome. The experimentation of alchemy is that of finding the shortcut, the formula with fewer steps, cheaper ingredients and a higher chance of producing the result. A grimoire with formulas of high yield is a treasure indeed."

"Then perhaps I do waste my time toiling with sword and shield," Cedric said. "I would be better off on Honeysuckle Street tearing apart their shops and acquiring these formulas for my own use."

"I think that a grimoire by itself would do you no great good, warmaster," Alodar replied. "Knowledge of three

91

things is needed to activate a formula successfully, and the grimoire will contain only two: the ingredients, and how to prepare and mix them. It will even describe the complex string of symbols for each step of the formula to be copied fresh for the reaction actually to take place. But what is missing are the additional symbols which must be drawn to activate the ingredients to release their power into the brew. And the symbols of activation are closely guarded by the master alchemist. Though I work closely with Saxton on a product of mutual benefit, he reveals to me only a few of the signs which form the heritage of his craft."

"It would seem that the persuasion of pain might reveal what is missing," Cedric said. "And then one could in a trice have what has taken years to find."

"For one formula, perhaps," Alodar said, "but the varying repertory of even a modestly successful alchemist runs to thousands of formulas and activations."

"Yes, but as I have noticed," Cedric said, "nothing these brewers produce seems to last for long."

"It is true," Alodar admitted, "that the virtue of the powders and elixirs does fade quickly; and the more potent the effect, the sooner it is gone. Only true magic can be permanent; magical armor is proof against all blows forever. But the toil of magicians is not easily come by."

"Vendora could make good use of more than one such shirt of mail," Cedric said. "Bandor still runs wild in the west and several of the neighboring barons have joined him in his rebellion. It is no longer a simple matter of one recalcitrant lord."

"I have not heard," Alodar said. "Between my efforts here and in Saxton's shop, I have had time for little else. But how could Bandor attract any to his cause? It was even rumored that his madness was no less than demon driven."

"According to Kelric, the court sorcerer, it is no rumor at all. In his trance of all seeing, he finds no mind of man stoking the fires of revolt. Some of the nobility still refuse to believe it of one of their own. But what in truth pushes Bandor and how he persuades others is of little matter. The west acts in concert against the queen and she must respond. Even now the armies speed homeward from their

92

idle swordwaving in the south so that they can bite real flesh in true defense of her crown."

"Then the sooner I am proficient, the sooner I can aid," Alodar said.

"And the alçhemy?" Cedric asked. "Do you labor at night as hard as you do here by day?"

"As hard," Alodar said, "although the effort by itself will not be sufficient. We must travel this noon to Basil's mines in the Fumus Mountains to barter for more ingredients for our craft."

"Well, your enthusiasm does arouse curiosity, Alodar," Cedric said. "Perhaps enough that I will visit my cousin one of these days to see first hand what all this fuss is about."

Alodar started to smile but Cedric cut him short. "Look, young Solidar arrives early for his instruction. You wish not to waste your time with rest; then swing your mace in challenge. I will wait here and then instruct him when he is sufficiently limber."

"By the amulets, Rendrac, not so fast," Saxton said. "You know every turn in the passageways and the torchlight is sufficient. But this heat addles my brain and I must concentrate to keep from tripping over the rubble directly underfoot. I cannot be looking ahead twenty feet to follow which side tunnel you duck into."

"You said you had urgent business with Basil," Rendrac growled back, his deep voice echoing off the tunnel walls. "He will not be out of the mine before nightfall and so I lead you to him. But know that I am hired not merely to run errands for whomever might ask. Be thankful that my own work takes me close by and accept the pace with which I choose to reach him."

Alodar squinted at their guide and saw only a hulking silhouette against the flickering torchlight. The form hunched over to avoid a descending ceiling, burying his head between boulder-like shoulders that brushed the narrowing walls on either side.

He followed Saxton through the constriction and then around a sharp corner into a dazzle of light. He blinked his eyes and looked out a large jagged hole in the smooth stone wall that admitted a flood of afternoon sun.

"A gas bubble popped through here," Rendrac grunted as Alodar moved to the opening to look outside. "We connected through to the passageway we just traversed because it was convenient."

Shielding his eyes with his hand, Alodar looked down the gentle slope of the mountain, barren of plant life and strewn with dark basaltic rocks, streamlined from their molten passage through the air and pockmarked from the gases which bubbled from them as they cooled. Standing on tiptoe, he looked to the left and saw in the distance the snakelike walls which wound their coils around the city of Ambrosia. He exhaled the heavy sulphurous vapors of the interior and for the first time noticed the detail of the tunnels in which he and Saxton had stumbled for the better part of an hour.

Like the boulders outside, the walls were smooth and firm, melted and scoured by the hot vapors that forced their way upward through not quite solid rock. He stepped back and looked down the passageway from which they had come and saw it heave and fall and then twist from sight, like a gigantic wormhole that wandered randomly through loose-packed earth. He ran his hand along the glassy wall and felt an occasional indentation that caught his fingertip or snagged his palm.

"Matrix for the gemstones," Rendrac said. "Some of the first ones found. But all such have been taken out ages ago." Rendrac waved his arm about the chamber and then ran his hand down stubble-pocked cheeks. His hair was cropped short and unkempt, sprouting from his head like coarse grass, woven by the wind. Cruel, dark eyes capped square jaws that merged into the sinews of a stumpy neck fully as wide as the head it supported. A thin, sweat-soaked tunic covered a barrel-like chest above thighs as big around as a smaller man's waist.

Banging his sword against the stone wall as he turned, he motioned them forward and started down the passageway on the otherside of the opening. Saxton took a deep breath, coughed, and then pushed Alodar ahead, placing a hand on his shoulder as he scrambled by. The tunnel dipped down a steep slope and the air immediately turned oven hot. Alodar dug in his heels to control his descent and felt his throat prickle from the irritants that he scooped in with each shallow breath.

Downward they descended at a cruel pace, and Saxton's hand on Alodar's shoulder became an aching wetness that gave fresh irritation with each step. His tunic clung, and his eyes stung from the salt deposited by the steady trickle from his sweating brow. He felt a weakness soak into his body, and his arms flopped limply at his sides, far wearier than they had been after a full day in Cedric's courtyard.

"Enough, we will see him another day," Saxton croaked at last, but Rendrac did not reply. He continued on for another thirty feet and pointed to a dim opening to his left. Alodar and Saxton stumbled forward and looked inside.

"Rendrac," a voice called out of the side passageway. "It took you long enough to arrive! No one will try any further. They claim that imps are popping through the torch flames in much greater numbers, and that the petty tricks destroy what little concentration they have for their tasks. And not only the simple imps but sprites as big as a fist, and through common flame at that. I explained that some sulphur must have been burnt accidentally, but they would not listen. I think that your logic may well succeed where mine does not."

"I was delayed by the two who came with me, Basil," Rendrac said as he ducked into the passage. "I will take care of the others in but a moment. A few broken limbs and a jarred brain or two, and they will know what they must do."

"But remember what you are about," Basil warned. "They are of no use if they cannot still swing the chisel and carry the pouch. The last two you persuaded were able to crawl down the mountainside free men because I could no longer profit from their effort."

"I will be careful," Rendrac growled as he moved past Basil. "So long as they do what I say, then their pain will be but little."

Basil turned and frowned for a moment as Rendrac disappeared into the gloom, but then shrugged his shoulders and continued forward.

"Why, Saxton," he said as he approached and saw the alchemist standing in the torchlight. "What ever could compel you to seek me here? I thought you far too lazy

95

for such exertion. Are you so anxious to repay the brandels that you cannot wait yet another day?"

"You judge me correctly," Saxton gasped. "It is not for your repayment that I would endure such as this. But the brandels I do not have and the days remaining before they are due are precious few; I must use them efficiently."

"An extension, then." Basil suddenly broke into a toothy smile. "Ah, Saxton, you have made my afternoon. Each time in the past you have somehow come through and settled your contract. Each time I have looked forward to the day I would have your labor all the more. An extension, yes, I can arrange it. Say another month against two years of service rather than one."

"It is not for an extension," Saxton continued weakly as he ran his hand over his head. "By the laws, Basil, cannot we proceed upwards and talk as we go? If we do not, then you will soon have to carry me instead."

Basil waved Saxton's words aside. "It is only your first time and you are not used to it," he said. "It is the lower levels which really test one's mettle. If you descend deep enough, the tunnels run together; no one can say that they belong to me, the queen, or some other. Yet we do not squabble over what is found there. It is just reward for anyone who has the fortitude to brave the heat and return with a prize. Of course, if they depart and return by way of the passageways which are clearly mine, then I receive my fair share.

"But of your visit, tell me more. Despite the nonsense about the imps, I feel quite generous today since my other endeavors go well. Look at my waist and what do you see? Yes, it is no less than a magic dagger, the same that is strutted about the royal court. The nobles are not the only ones with sufficient wealth to own such blades. I have no less than eleven more; an even dozen purchased from Lectonil, the master magician of the Cycloid Guild. An even dozen free and clear. He was anxious to sell and gave better terms the more I would take. The profit I will make from resale of the rest will more than pay for the one I wear here. So tell me of your desires and with a light heart I will listen."

"We need more ingredients," Alodar said, "and wish to barter for time and terms."

"Most aggressive for a novice," Basil said. "Especially for one who is bound by the agreement as well. But is this correct, Saxton?" He rubbed his hands together and broadened his smile. "Do you need more, when I am yet to receive payment for the first?"

"It is as Alodar says," Saxton replied. "We work his formula and need additional ingredients. Dead-man's candle, midnight dew, peat tar and the rest. I have a list of it here."

Basil took the offered piece of parchment and then looked for the first time in Alodar's direction. "You saw me in my factory in Ambrosia some time ago," he said. He glanced at the list and then furrowed his brow in thought.

"I find this hard to believe of you, Saxton," he said at last. "You have eluded me the longest because you have been so careful with your agreements. I cannot see one of your training swept up in the hopeless dreams which blow in from the Street."

"Look at the list," Saxton persisted. "What I choose to blend is no concern of the apothecary. State your terms and let us be done."

Basil's frown deepened and he rubbed his chin. "You have not yet worked off your existing debt," he said. "Yet, for the first time, you are willing to borrow even more and for a formula not of your own making. Tell me what you are about, Saxton, and then once I understand, perhaps the arrangement will be easier."

"Your terms," Saxton said, and Alodar felt the alchemist sag his other hand on his shoulder as well.

"But these are not inexpensive ingredients," Basil said. "Why for the shrieking mandrake alone, to root them out I must use trained dogs with wax plugging their ears. And the peat tar is dug underneath light-tight sheds. The sparkle of a single star would destroy it all."

"Terms, your terms," Saxton said as he collapsed his full weight down upon Alodar's support.

"Very well," Basil replied with a sudden edge to his voice. "Keep your petty secrets, but remember well when you crawl back in less than a month's time that it was not I who was inflexible on alternatives." He stopped and twisted his face in thought. "Twenty years of service for

97

both you and the novice against three hundred brandels on our agreed upon date," he said at last. "Is your formula so precious that you will risk terms such as those?"

"Twenty years is not a fair price," Saxton said. "It should be five at the most and we would agree to that most reluctantly."

"I care not to waste my time in bargaining. Twenty years is the only price," Basil snapped back. "I have waited too long for this opportunity."

"Then perhaps, Alodar, we can reconsider," Saxton said. "It is not the first time I have abandoned a formula before completion. You have taken to the craft well and there will be more opportunity to make our fortune."

"Accepted," Alodar said, ignoring the alchemist's argument. "I would rather deal with this apothecary no further, but if this is our only choice, then we will take it. If we succeed with the formula, the cost for the peat tar and the rest will be unimportant."

"You accept?" Basil said. "Twenty years and less than a month's time?"

For a moment there was silence and Alodar looked over his shoulder at the alchemist. "Accepted," Saxton said weakly with a wave of his hand. "It is as the novice states. If we succeed, then it will not matter.

"To the shed on the mountainside then," Basil said slowly as his frown of puzzlement returned. "We will seal the agreement there and arrange the details for the delivery of the ingredients to your shop."

Basil turned and headed upwards. Saxton shuffled by Alodar to follow. "Twenty years," the alchemist muttered as he passed. "Would we fare even as well as Eldan in such a time?"

"We quest, do we not?" Alodar replied. "The potential of such adversity spurs us onwards to our goal."

"Yes," Saxton said, "but the next step could fail all sixty-three times, regardless of our motivation."

CHAPTER SEVEN

The Random Factors Align

ALODAR dumped a bucket of oily water into the gutter and slumped to the planked curbing. He kneaded the tired muscles in his neck and looked up into the early evening sky. It seems bright enough now, he thought as he saw the disk of the moon balanced like a platter above the roofline across the street. He hoped Saxton's decision to wait three days until it was full was the right one. Even foregoing all time at Cedric's and spending two full weeks working the formula, there was little time to spare.

Alodar stretched his arms over his head and frowned. It was well enough for Saxton to propose a few days rest to uncoil his knotted muscles in some tavern, but it had only given Alodar pause for the first time in months to consider deeply the path he had chosen.

All of this effort for only four samples. Four small vials, filled with what looked like motley collections of tiny colored beads. But when held to the eye, each globule was a many-faceted crystal, able to withstand great stresses without breaking, stresses from grinding forces or searing heat. Surely one tube would produce the ointment for which they had struggled. Four chances to soften the crystals into a thick gel; then for each that succeeded, one additional procedure to make the ointment safe for contact with bare skin. With four vials, they could expect the contents of two to transmute properly, and then one of them to be rendered harmless as well.

Two steps but with only four samples remaining. Alodar pursed his lips and shook his head. When they had six stages to go and sixty-three chances, Saxton's caution in the mines had seemed hard to understand. But now the outcomes could be enumerated on one's fingers and the boldness of their pledge seemed a much greater folly.

Each result was random. If the last step failed on the first attempt, then there would be one chance in two that all this work would have gone for nothing. Or if none of the four vials liquified in the way they wished, then Basil's factory, not wealth and glory, would be the final reality.

Alodar closed his eyes and tried to recall Vendora's beauty, to taste again his anger at Feston's ridicule, to feel the prickly bitterness at Festil's blind rejection. But the images of half a year ago were blurred and fuzzy, the hunger and pain at Iron Fist buried far beneath the numbness that rode on top of his thoughts.

Was it so important, he puzzled. Could he not instead steal away in the night, perhaps to the kingdoms to the south or even to Arcadia across the sea? Cedric did not seem to value greatly the opinion of those who buzzed about the royal court. Was such respect worth the risk he ran to gain it?

Alodar breathed deeply and then let the air out through his nostrils. No, there was first the question of honor. Saxton was enmeshed in this as deeply as he, and they must share the peril as well as the potential for great gain.

A sudden crash from the interior of the shop broke Alodar out of his reverie and he sprang to his feet. For a moment there was silence, and then he heard the crunch of glass grinding underfoot. He kicked the bucket out of his way and dashed into the storefront, looking for the sword and shield Cedric had lent him for practice. As he stooped and thrust his hand through the enarmes, a massive figure loomed in the workroom doorway.

"Rendrac!" Alodar shouted as the form came forward into the candlelight. "What cause have you to be in the confines of Saxton's shop?"

"No bar did you have on the workroom rear door and Basil is most curious about your formula," Rendrac said. "He will reward me well when I tell him something of it."

Alodar raised his swordpoint in front of his chest. "You will learn nothing of it here tonight," he said slowly. "Be gone and return only if we need more ingredients from your master."

Rendrac smiled and stepped forward, fingering the hilt of the sword at his side. "And I leave when it suits my own purpose," he growled. "Not the whim of a mere novice."

Alodar took a deep breath and tightened the grip on his blade. His heart began to race and his eyes widened as he looked up at the giant coming towards him. He ran through his mind his sparring yard training and set his jaw in a determined line. It must come to a true test sooner or later, he thought, and defending the four vials was as worthy a cause as any.

Rendrac completed one slow step and stopped, eyeing the distance between them. "Come forward, little man," he said. "Come forward and show your mettle."

Alodar looked at the angle of Rendrac's sword arm across his body and tilted his shield upward. The man would slash down rather than across, he thought, as he slowly slid his own blade toward the side.

"You learn nothing of alchemy while you stand frozen," he spat back into Rendrac's smile. "To search the shop you must first win the right to do so."

"Very well," Rendrac growled. "If you are alive or dead, I will find out what I wish. To me it does not matter."

Then, with the swiftness of a much smaller man, he drew his sword and dashed it down towards Alodar's unprotected head. Alodar whipped his shield upwards and received the blow with a numbing jar. A shock ran through his arm; his elbow buckled from the contact. Involuntarily he stepped backwards, banging the heel of his boot against the wall. He peeked over the top of his shield and saw Rendrac's sword arm again raised above him. He took a deep breath and stiffened his body in anticipation for the next downward slash.

The blow rocked his shield and skittered away. Alodar staggered and huddled lower to the ground. He thrust tentatively to the side, but quickly withdrew his arm. His reach was too short. He would have to extend beyond cover even to prick Rendrac's skin. He scowled and gritted his teeth as Rendrac's arm flew upwards for the third time.

"When you have finished with him, prepare to take on another," a voice rang out suddenly from the doorway to the street. Rendrac halted in midswing and glanced in the direction of the challenger. He looked back quickly at

Alodar, then thrust the countertop candle towards the door with his free hand.

The flame flickered from the motion, then held steady and cast its light across the entrance. Rendrac grunted in recognition and pointed his blade in challenge. "I am no weaklimbed and untutored pupil, old man," he said. "You would fare no better than the novice."

"You will not slip past my guard with words, Rendrac. I am willing to cross swords with one of your petty reputation, if you are with one such as mine. Use your sword or put it away. It is one or the other."

Rendrac flexed his fingers on his swordgrip and paused in thought. Alodar frowned at his hesitation, and then turned and squinted across the countertop.

"Cedric!" he said. "Why are you here?"

"I have not seen you at practice for two weeks now," Cedric replied, "and, as I have said, your activities with my cousin have piqued my curiosity. It seems that I arrive at a most fortunate time."

Alodar lowered his eyes and dropped his shield to his side. "You must think I am no great credit to your teaching, warmaster," he said.

"A big man is not often bettered by a little one, no matter how talented the latter," Cedric said. "And you cannot expect six months' training to make up the difference between you. Raising your sword against this Rendrac would have cost you your life and proved nothing. But I am more of a match in size. Let him decide if he wishes to measure which of us has the greater skill as well."

"As I have said," Rendrac growled, "you will find me more a match than your fledgling pupils."

"That I judge to be true, Rendrac," Cedric replied slowly. "But then you will find me more than you have yet encountered as well. In my life I have fought a dozen of your bulk and I suspect I will learn little from another. But the choice is yours. Sheath your sword and walk out unscathed. Or come forward with it drawn and afterwards we will remove your body."

They all stood silent for several minutes, but finally Rendrac scowled, thrust his sword back into its scabbard, and stomped around the counter. Cedric stepped into the shop and motioned to the doorway. Rendrac pulled in his cape and shot a last glance back around the room.

His eyes danced to avoid Cedric's; when he looked in Alodar's direction, he saw the beginning of a smile. His scowl tightened and he waved his fist threateningly. "The next time, you may not have a protector," he growled.

Alodar opened his mouth to reply, but stopped when he heard loud voices suddenly spilling in from the street.

"But do you not see, Saxton, that the risks you take are unnecessary. I have to demand twenty years because, as I understand it now, no fair return will I get for the brandels I have lavished already upon your venture. But as a partner I can do much to ensure the success of all."

Two stout figures suddenly jostled to enter the doorway, and Alodar saw Saxton guided through by Basil's silk-covered arm. Basil's cheeks flushed red from the exertion of supporting the sagging weight at his side and Saxton's were redder still from his visit to the tavern.

"Rendrac," Basil said as his eyes adjusted to the candle-light. "What are you doing here?"

"No less than what you attempt with a jug of wine," he snapped back.

Basil looked to Alodar, then Cedric, and finally frowned at Rendrac's words. "We will speak of this later," he said at last.

"Why such attention?" Saxton cried gleefully as he sagged to the floor. "There has not been such activity in my shop since twelve years ago when I thought I had stumbled on to a philtre of longevity."

"Oh, be quiet, you fool," Basil said, "else I add the cost of the wine to what you already owe. Come along, Rendrac. The night is wasted here, and we should be off to attend other matters."

"Poor Basil," Saxton chortled as he sat with his hands folded over his stomach. "It is too much to bear, is it not? Someone else on the street is to make a profit from the Fumus Mountains and you cannot let it be."

Basil stopped in the doorway and turned to look down on the alchemist. "What about the Mountains?" he asked slowly. "What does your formula have to do with the mines?"

"You may as well know," Saxton laughed. "There is nothing else to purchase. We will be done in three days time and then it will not matter. Yes, Basil, it is the Fumus Mountains and the jewels of the lower depths. We

103

shall get them, Alodar and I, while sweat stains your fine garments as you watch us pass by."

"A new tunnel," Basil said as he bent down beside Saxton and grabbed the folds of his soiled robe. "Some sort of acid that will eat through to the hidden passageway that runs high and cool."

"No, far better," Saxton giggled as he tried to brush Basil's hands aside. "A caloric shield that will make the depths accessible for exploration. I wager that you will be repaid with a topaz far larger than a robin's egg."

"Then the partnership," Basil said excitedly. "It is as I have promised. Forget the debt for the ingredients. Share with me the plunder from the bowels of the volcano and I will release you from the agreement to which you are bound."

"The wine loosens my tongue," Saxton said, "but some sense I still retain. It is Alodar and I who have shared this formula in good faith. It is only right that we reap all of the reward from it as well."

"A novice of a few months," Basil said. "How important could such a loyalty be? I have worked the Street for years and in truth am a member of your craft as much as one whose robe bears the inverted triangle. What cause can you have to deny me so?"

Saxton slowly shook his head. Then with surprising strength, he wrenched Basil's hands free from his robe. "I remember too well the stare of Eldan and the others," he said, suddenly sober. "Too many fine craftsmen have I seen you sweep into your factories and too many poor useless hulks have I seen you push into the alley on the other side. No Basil, I will not share with you the fruits of my labor."

Basil stared for a moment into Saxton's unflinching eyes and then slowly rose. He smoothed his tunic and adjusted the magic dagger at his side.

"Very well," he said at last. "If you choose to play by the letter of our contract, then so will I. You have assured your repayment by gold or by the future labor of your back and brain. But that assurance is good only so long as you possess sound faculties upon the date they are due. If I judge that you endeavor beyond the usual risks of the craft and jeopardize the value I may receive, then I can rightfully ask for a guarantee of sounder value. And adventure into the Fumus Mountains does qualify certainly as an undertaking of high peril. Your labor is no longer sufficient bond, Saxton. What can you offer in its place?"

"Why nothing else, as you well know," Saxton said, rising uncertainly to his feet. "And I have never heard of such a condition binding an alchemist so."

"The clause is there," Basil snapped. "Before, I have not had cause to use it. But if you have no assurance for your loan, then by right I can call it due immediately."

He stopped and twisted his face into a forced smile. "You are wrong when you think you have five days more, alchemist," he said. "It is in fact less than one. Have three hundred brandels in my hand by the next dawn or prepare to be measured instead for the restraints of the factory. I think I will put you next to Eldan's stall, so that each day you can watch and know full well what you will become."

"Your investment is well protected, Basil." Cedric broke his silence and reached into his cape. "Here is a pouch with ten brandels. In two days time I will arrange to have the rest. Take it as token and follow your hireling out into the street. I shall be the guarantee that the obligation is met."

Basil turned and looked up into Cedric's stern face. His smile vanished. For a moment he was silent as he studied the unblinking eyes and felt the gold in his hand. "You have a reputation as a warrior, Cedric," he said at last, "not as a merchant. I can not be sure that your promise is any better than the rest." With a flourish, he tossed back the pouch. "I need not accept this," he said. "Dawn is within my rights, and even the queen herself would have to agree to it."

Cedric took a step forward, but Saxton moved between him and the apothecary. The alchemist glanced out of the shop into the moonlit sky. "Your offer is well appreciated, cousin," he said. "But Basil's twisting of words does no more than to force us to hasten our work. The moon is not quite full, but enough so that probably it will little matter. Be gone, Basil. If it is by the first rays of the sun that we must stuff your purse, then so it will be. Return to your factory and await there your disappointment."

"Yes I will go," Basil snarled, "but to the first rays of

dawn, and then no longer. Mark you, Saxton, even six hundred brandels a minute late would not be enough. You pay in the dark or cough on honeysuckle for a full score of years to follow."

The apothecary turned abruptly and stomped out of the shop with Rendrac close on his heel. Saxton steadied himself against the door frame as he watched them disappear down the street. Finally he ran his hand over his head and looked back into the interior.

"And good night to you, Cedric," he said. "Alodar and I will not need your help further and we have much we must do."

Cedric grunted and stepped to the doorway. As he left, he turned and looked back into the store. "Next time, hold your shieldhand yet higher," he said, "and prepare to thrust under rather than around the side."

Alodar started to reply, but Saxton waved his arm towards the workroom. "Find me the pills which will clear my head," he said. "The next eight hours will decide it all."

Alodar looked up at the moon well into the sky, and then down to the square opening at his feet. Saxton's bald head popped through, and he extended his hand to help the alchemist up the last few rungs. Saxton stopped his climb and waved away the aid.

"In a moment, Alodar," he panted. "It may be easy enough for you to climb to the roof of the shop a dozen times, but for one of my dignity, it is a different matter."

"The moon is almost to its zenith," Alodar said. "If we do not begin soon, there will be no time for the mountains before the sun follows it into the sky."

"As I already have taught," Saxton replied, "the purity of the ingredients materially affects the chance of success. The more the moon rises, the less the air pollutes the passage of its cool light. We must make haste, but not so much that what chances we have are thereby compromised."

He stopped and looked upward. "But a few degrees more should be satisfactory," he said. "Make ready the lens and the filter."

Alodar turned back to the apparatus at his feet and lifted the large lens from its case. He placed it in the semicircular base for the support stand and snapped the confining ring shut. He sighted through the thick glass at the two closely set panes placed some two feet behind and rotated the optical axis into line. Stepping over the gear they had hurriedly brought up from the workroom, he found the bulbous flask and pulled the cork. The odor of baneberry tickled his nose, and he carefully decanted the deep blue liquid into the narrow space between the two vertical sheets of glass.

Alodar walked back behind the lens and dragged the huge mirror into place. He sighted into the sky where the moon would be in the next few minutes and tilted the reflector to catch the light and bounce it horizontally. A parallel beam, he thought, converged by the lens, filtered by the baneberry and finally focused on the flask at the end of the line. How much more complex than the simple spells of thaumaturgy.

He pushed the gear into final adjustment and stood back to watch Saxton finish his preparations. "I am ready," he said as the alchemist pulled a long flexible hose from an earthen jar and inserted it into the mouth of the flask.

"As am I," Saxton replied. "When the moon's light strikes the mirror squarely, I will invert the jar and the limestone will fall into the oil of vitriol. The gas from the reaction, the blue moonlight and the granules we have placed in solution will interact and if we are lucky form the ointment."

Alodar nodded and stooped to sight the moon through a small hole in the back of the mirror. The bright edge crept into view and then the whole disk dazzled his eye with brightness.

"It aligns perfectly now," he shouted suddenly as he turned to watch the light streak through the apparatus and hit the flask with a dull blue glow.

Saxton inverted the jar and the first cautious bubbles burbled to the surface of the solution. The alchemist snatched a pad of parchment, activated the ingredients and scratched out the formula. As the final glyph formed, Alodar caught his breath, awaiting the reaction. He looked at the flask, hoping to see the clear liquid instantly haze into a translucent gel.

Several minutes passed but nothing happened. Saxton

107

rocked nervously back and forth on his heels and ran his hand over his head. Alodar squinted at the glassware trying to see some change in the solution, a slowing of the bubbles' rush to the surface indicating a transformation.

"Have you placed the flask at the precise focus?" Saxton asked. "With the moon not full we need all of the intensity we can muster."

"It is the lens, Saxton," Alodar replied. "With such a size you cannot expect it to bend the rays that strike the edge with the same precision as those near the axis. I have placed the flask so that the circle of confusion is smallest. Any better is beyond the grinder's art."

"Then it is the brew which is bad," Saxton said. "Toss it aside and we will try another. Three chances will be as good as four since I have only enough salamander skin left for the two success we expect. The rest I already have used in barter."

He looked at the solution bubbling as if no formula had been activated. "Yes, let us dispose of it," he said. "Who can say what perversion of the desired result will occur if we let it interact any longer. Or if nothing is to happen, then it will surely spoil."

Alodar stared down the line from the mirror which first caught the moonlight to the flask which finally received its filtered rays. He passed his hand in front of the solution and saw the pale blue spot on his palm the size of a brandel. He frowned and thought of his training as a journeyman.

"Yes, that will work," he exclaimed as the idea struck him. "Saxton, do not yet disturb the brew. There is more that can be done. Quickly now, help me find the small glass we used to aid in removing the eyes of the spiders."

Alodar ran to the ladder and descended into the workroom below. He began rummaging through the tools of the trade, tossing the gear aside like an excited dog digging after a small rodent.

Saxton shuffled to the opening and peered inside. "Not more thaumaturgy," he said. "Remember what happened the last time you mixed the two crafts together."

"Here it is," Alodar said, ignoring the command. "Now with another small mirror and a sample from the flask, it will be done." He quickly scooped up an armful of stands and clamps, and staggered back up the ladder to the bubbling flask. Pinching the gas tube with his fingers he decanted some of the fluid into a vial and then fastened it to the stand he positioned nearby. He ran back to the first mirror, adjusted it slightly and then inserted the edge of the second into the path of the light. A slender beam separated from the rest and darted across the rooftop to engulf the vial in brilliance.

"We risk enough, Alodar," Saxton said. "Let us try the next batch instead and take our chances within the confines of the art."

"But a moment," Alodar said. "I do not mix the crafts so much as use them in complement to one another. You need intensity and by no skill of alchemy can you make lenses perform better than the grinder has designed them. But the key is the light, not the glass which bends it."

Alodar did not wait for a reply but performed his spellbinding and then thrust the hand lens into the second beam's path. He slid it rapidly back and forth and brought the rays into a precise focus on the vial.

"The small glass converges with far more perfection," he explained, "and by thaumatugy we can force the larger to do so as well. Look now to the flask and observe how we fare."

"A sparkling brilliance," Saxton gasped, and Alodar turned to see the large tube of light converge into a tight point deep in the center of the solution.

Several moments passed in silence, then suddenly the liquid wavered before their eyes. The next bubble out of the tube dimmed from view and the one just leaving the surface left a small crater in its wake.

"It gels," Saxton shouted. "My lad, we have ointment on the first try. Yes, of course, we must have sufficient intensity or the ingredients will not interact. But no matter how you did it, let us set up for the second while the luck still points our way."

Alodar caught Saxton's excitement and hurriedly adjusted the equipment. He fixed the small glass in a clamp and then stood by the first mirror, keeping the moon directly in line as it crested in the sky. In a few moments Saxton had disengaged the first container filled with the glowing ointment and replaced it with a second. He tossed the spent gas generator aside and thrust the tube from

109

another while casting anxious glances at the shimmering brew.

He finished the final glyph and almost instantly the clear solution thickened into the transluscent cream. Saxton's eyes widened in wonder. He ran his hand over his head and then gently stroked the side of the flask.

"Two in a row," he exclaimed. "The random factors align, Alodar, I can feel it." He cast the second gas generator aside. Holding the flask high, he dance around the rooftop in exultation. Alodar smiled and started to break the thaumaturgical connection.

Saxton looked at the container he had set aside and then the two standing ready still filled with clear solution. He stopped his celebration, frowned at the knot of brightness where the last flask had been and stared back at the battered chest with small labeled drawers standing nearby.

"Powdered skin of salamander, less than three brandels more," he muttered and then his face recovered its smile.

"No, Alodar, leave the gear as it is," he said. "Run quickly instead into the city and get from Cedric the gold he offered as loan."

"Back to Ambrosia," Alodar said puzzled. "But, Saxton, whatever for? I am as happy as you that the first two produced the ointment, for we can dearly use the time. In less than four hours the moon will set, and sunrise will be but little after. Let us perform the last step twice as you planned and proceed on to the Fumus Mountains."

"But do you not see," Saxton ran on excitedly. "The random factors align. The transition was so dramatic, so emphatic. We are not dealing with chance. All of our trails will succeed tonight, I can feel it. We need not settle for two vials of the ointment when four are ours for the taking. If we double the supply of the skin of the salamander, there will be enough to perform the final step on all four. For a few brandels more we can secure what we need from the royal shop at the head of the Street. Go to Cedric's and maximize our good fortune."

"But sunrise," Alodar protested. "There will not be time enough for it all."

"We quest, do we not?" Saxton chortled, waving his index finger at Alodar's scowl. "And with the factors aligned, how can there be failure? I will complete the formula for the two flasks we have prepared while you are gone; when you return two more will be ready to process as well. Away. You may as well secure the powder as stand idly by while I exercise my craft."

Alodar looked down into the silent street and then toward the heart of the city. "Very well," he said, "I will go. But if the moon gets close to the horizon and I have not returned, follow me with whatever you have of value. We will meet and save time in taking the road north to the mountains."

"The random factors," Saxton said as if he did not hear. "They align and, by the laws, with a formula of great importance. Yes, hurry along, lad. Tonight, we can do no wrong."

Cedric wrapped his cape tighter and cursed at the bite of the cool breeze. "Alchemy," he snorted. "Only for such a craft would one have cause to tramp about the streets in the middle of the night."

"As I have explained, warmaster," Alodar said as he hurried to match the longer stride, "you need not accompany me to the dwelling of this seneschal. I can rouse him as I did you. Even if his irritation makes all ten brandels the price for the powdered skin, I will not begrudge it." He looked at the moon already uncomfortably low in the western sky. "Haste is far more important."

"If I did not come," Cedric rasped, "dawn would find you pounding at his gate."

Cedric stopped and turned off the street at the next open gateway. Buzzing voices and loud laughter from a dozen sources floated over the wall, and a caped figure staggered against Alodar and lurched into the night. He blinked at the torchlight when he entered the courtyard and stumbled past two more sprawling forms snoring in his way. The area was scattered with small clumps of richly dressed men nodding dutifully at each other's words and waving empty cups at the wine stewards wandering by. In a corner, a dark-haired girl tossed her veils to the rhythm of her small finger cymbals, but no one noticed.

"You come late to lord Dartilac's festivity," a man in servant's livery said into Cedric's ear, "And it is not so

111

light that I can recognize you as one of his peers from the court. I do not mean to offend, but have you brought the invitation affixed with his seal?"

"This is my invitation," Cedric said. He slowly tumbled the ten brandels from their small pouch. "I must speak with his lordship on a matter which I am sure he will find to his interest. Can you not arrange for such a moment?"

The servant scurried to retrieve the coins and stood up with his face in a smile. He beckoned them to follow and started to weave his way across the courtyard. Against the wall to which they headed, Alodar saw a blond-headed man of middle age holding a goblet in one hand and poking the chest of his listener with the other. The lines of the face twisted in frustration and the blank expression on the recipient of the argument forced each jab to be harder than the last. As Alodar and Cedric approached, the servant coughed and the conversation abruptly halted.

"Lord Dartilac," Cedric said without waiting. "I am the one who teaches your son, Dartilon, the use of arms."

Dartilac set his glass on a bench nearby and frowned. "I pay you well and on time," he said. "I see no reason to call upon me here and at such a time."

"What you say is most proper," Cedric said, "but, as you know, I instruct the sons of many of the lords and learn much that might not otherwise be common knowledge. Lord Cartilon, for example. His son I taught this very day."

Dartilac picked up his glass and took a cautious sip. "And what news do you have about the house of Cartilon?" he asked slowly.

"As you know," Cedric said, "the queen is most appreciative of the loan of your seneschal to aid in the activations of her formulas from Iron Fist. And Cartilon has in the past always aligned his house with yours, careful to say to all how you aid the flow of coin so necessary in these times of increased peril."

"And now," Dartilac repeated, "what news do you bring?"

Cedric smiled back into the lord's knitting brows. "Nothing other than what your own speculations might give you," he said. "But first a small boon, my lord, as a token of the good faith in which we deal. Your seal on a

112

writ against the royal stores for powder of salamander skin, a few drams, no more. I am sure your steward would honor it, since he knows who ultimately decides his welfare and keep."

"Salamander skin," Dartilac said. "Do you jest? What you know is of little value if such is the price you place on it."

"I need it before dawn and that makes it more dear," Cedric replied. "With your seal I can obtain it from your man as I could no other way."

Dartilac rubbed his chin while he studied Cedric's unblinking face. After a moment he grunted and snapped his fingers overhead. The servant reappeared and dipped his head in a small bow. "My seal on a writ to the royal factory of alchemy," Dartilac said, "to be drawn immediately but to a maximum of three brandels and no more."

The servant frowned questioningly but Dartilac waved him away. "And now what of Cartilon?" he said.

"The army returns from the south," Cedric said. "What will be Vendora's first concern, to pay them their due or to see that they are properly led?"

"Leadership, of course," Dartilac said. "It is true that her vassals have already provided their yearly aid to the crown to which they are shown and further provision must come from her own purse. But with a strong man at the head, they will rally to her needs and point to the west; their pay can come later."

"And between the lords who aid with ready coin and those who assist with sword, for whom would she show more favor?"

"But both are needed as she knows full well," Dartilac said. "Leadership may be her first concern but she would not turn her thoughts from those who support the crown in so generous a manner."

"In a situation such as this," Cedric repeated, "who would she favor?"

"Arms," Dartilac growled. "Under the present conditions she would tend to arms." His frown deepened and he stopped in thought.

"But surely Cartilon would not shift into Feston's camp without much reflection and consultation," he said at last. "He has been steadfast in our course to resist the influence

113

of the rough outlanders. Old Festil may have been a favorite of Vendora's father, but Cartilon sees as well as any that Feston dangles on a string. Why even now my staunch friend labors to influence lady Aeriel to add her voice to ours. And he is here tonight somewhere across the yard, partaking of my hospitality as do others of the same persuasion."

"Thought and consideration," Cedric said. "I would judge that all of the intimates of the court spend a good part of their time in such profitable fashion. To be a member of a faction swinging into ascendency is a temptation. And even if one were himself steadfast, it would behoove him to reassess critically the loyalties of every man that he thought stood behind him."

"But Cartilon," Dartilac said.

"I instructed his son this very day," Cedric said.

Dartilac grabbed his chin and gazed past Alodar's shoulder. "It is a matter to look into," the lord muttered behind his hand.

Cedric stood silent, and Alodar saw the pensiveness grow on Dartilac's face. While he pondered, the servant returned and thrust a folded parchment in Cedric's direction. The warmaster nodded and motioned Alodar to accept it.

"Value given and just value received," Cedric said. Without waiting for a reply, he turned and started for the exit.

"You train many of the scions, did you say?" Dartilac shouted after him. "Perhaps there is more in your future than a few drams of salamander."

Cedric continued to the gate and nodded once over his shoulder. He ducked through the opening and Alodar followed. In the street, the warrior walked in silence, his lips pulled into a grim line.

"I see that your way is far more effective than my pounding," Alodar said. "It is fortunate that you learned something of Cartilon's leanings in time to be of such advantage."

"Think over carefully what I said," Cedric replied. "Cartilon's son said no more than that Dartilac was having yet another festivity." He stopped and grabbed Alodar by the shoulders. "I learned the rules but did not choose to play," he rasped. "And I do not care to begin even

114

now. Finish this foolishness with Saxton and be done with alchemy. I expect you back in my sparring yard on the morrow."

Alodar started to speak, but stopped when he saw the bottom edge of the moon's disk shorn away by the line of Dartilac's roof. He tore free of Cedric's grasp and spun around to look to the east, squinting into the lights of the city and trying to detect the glow that preceded dawn.

"I shall repay you with honor, warmaster," he said at last. "But for now, my quest comes before all else." He grabbed the writ firmly and plunged down the road. Sprinting around a corner, he raced back to Honeysuckle Street.

CHAPTER EIGHT

Moltenrock Treasure

ALODAR panted up to Saxton's storefront too out of breath to shout his return. He entered and swung around the counter and into the workroom. As he dashed through the doorway, he stubbed his toe on a plank jutting in the way and his eyes widened in surprise. The shelves and cabinets lay tumbled to the floor in a vast clutter. Alodar stepped cautiously through the rubble, knee high in splintered wood and broken glass. The air stank of a mixture of odors from ruptured containers and he could not see a familiar sight in the confusion.

He walked slowly forward, scanning the floor, each step accompanied by the pop and crack of additional small destruction. The large cabinet from the south wall blocked his path. As he surveyed a way around, he saw a single pudgy hand thrust from underneath its heavy oaken boards.

Alodar quickly stooped and heaved the box off the

115

fallen alchemist, who lay face down in the tangle on the floor.

"Saxton," he shouted as he rolled the brown-robed figure over. "What happened? What happened here? Are you whole or hurt?"

Saxton stirred slightly and opened his eyes to the noise. He frowned and focused with difficulty, small trickles of blood oozing from his mouth and the many small cuts on his face.

"Alodar," he stumbled out softly. "Alodar, by the laws, it worked. It worked not once but twice. As I said, the random factors aligned and both of the flasks produced safe ointment. The chance of an alchemist's lifetime and I had it succeed twice."

"But what happened here, Saxton?" Alodar persisted.

"Rendrac," Saxton said, and then he began to cough uncontrollably, throwing up great quantities of clotted blood. Alodar looked quickly about and spied a pottery jug still unbroken on a high shelf. He fetched it and, cradling the alchemist's head, gave him a small drink of water.

"Yes, Alodar," Saxton continued after a moment. "The luck of a lifetime is often balanced in this perverse world. The factors aligned, but Rendrac could not give us the slightest chance of success thereafter. While you journeyed to Cedric's, he returned here just as the contents of the second flask transmuted into a form safe to the touch. I thrust them into the clutter as he entered, but this body was not meant to withstand the warrior's pain. He pummeled me as well as the shop, and finally I had to tell him where they were."

"You did as well as you were able, Saxton," Alodar said as he looked about the room. Anger began to boil. "I will pursue and give Rendrac his due. We shall recover the ointment yet and your treasure as well."

"It is too late for that, my lad," Saxton said, beginning to breathe with difficulty. "I have studied the inner organs of animals enough to guess what has happened to me. I am not to partake of any of the jewels of the mountains."

He stopped, and a deep sigh rattled through his lungs. "But then neither will Basil have his way," he continued. "Two successes with a caloric shield! It is enough for any alchemist."

"Sweetbalm, or perhaps thaumaturgy," Alodar said. "We have quested, Saxton, you and I. Do not falter when the goal is in sight."

"All the balms were destroyed in the mess." Saxton waved one arm in a feeble arc over his head. "Think no more of me. Flee instead while you can. Basil will receive enough from Rendrac's trip into the heart of the mountains to care little for the service of a novice."

"Rendrac braves the heat?" Alodar asked.

"Yes, he anointed himself with the full contents of one flask as I looked on helplessly," Saxton replied. "When he was done, he resembled less a man than a silver demon, the coating did shine so. And the second batch he crushed underfoot and rubbed its precious salve into the muck he already had made. The other two flasks on the roof were destroyed as well, I fear, when he tossed all the gear to the earth in his rage to find the ointment."

Saxton resumed his coughing. As Alodar offered him another sip of water, he waved it aside. He hacked on for several moments more and then, in one giant convulsion, arched his back with a final gasp. He fell limp into Alodar's arms, staring at the ceiling with unblinking eyes and saying no more.

For a moment Alodar held him in silence and then lowered him gently to the door. He stood up and ran his eyes aimlessly around the clutter. He remembered Saxton as he had first seen him preparing the nerve elixir, struggling with his craft but free of the doom which finally claimed him.

It was the formula, the quest that had turned him from what he had done so well. Had Alodar not come to his door, he would be tinkering here still, not breathing his last trying to defend a treasure he probably did not know how to spend.

Alodar slowly let out his breath and looked out the window into the night. "But by the laws, it is done," he said. "There is nothing in my knowledge of the crafts to bring him back."

He pulled the small packet of salamander skin out of a pocket and tossed it into the clutter. And now that the alchemist has finished, what of the novice? What Saxton had said was true enough. If Alodar disappeared now, Basil would see little profit in tracking him down. And so little time remained before dawn that the chance of finding gemstones to redeem his future was impossibly small.

Alodar wiggled his head and tried to shake out the fatigue. But if he were honor bound to aid Saxton in life, then the vengeance was his as well, he thought. No matter that safety lay in the opposite direction from the mountains. He must track Rendrac there, regardless of the consequences. And the fair lady—a treasure for her he must have as well.

He gave Saxton one final pat and rose with his jaw set in a determined line. "Rest easy, alchemist," he said. "Rest easy for I will continue on." He paused and then pulled his face into a bittersweet smile. "We quest, do we not?"

He shook his head to clear the feelings and, for the third time, surveyed the wreckage scattered about. As he scanned from wall to wall, the torchlight reflected into his eyes from the shards of glass and plates of metal on the floor. Then he caught a glimmer subtly different from the rest, silvery and opalescent, from a small bead in the midst of the litter.

"The ointment, surely," Alodar said half aloud. "Perhaps Saxton's second flask will serve its purpose as well as the first." He stooped and extended his gloved index finger into the small drop. It parted sluggishly and formed a pool around his fingertip, dense like mercury but affinitive like water.

Alodar put forward his other hand and gently stroked the drop up the side of his finger. The ointment followed, leaving a thin layer of shimmering silver. Heartened, he quickly worked the rest of the salve onto his hand, kneading it around to fill all the cracks and crevices of the glove. When he was done, his entire hand was covered; when rotated in the torchlight, it gave off a soft silvery glow.

Alodar looked around the floor, carefully righting equipment and pushing aside the rubble as he went. He found a second small bead and then another; with each he repeated the same slow process of transferring it to his body. In an hour, both his arms were covered; in another two, his legs and the front of his torso. He rummaged through the wreckage, found a sliver of a mirror, and then carefully covered his back with a small stick and the droplets he found nearby. As he discovered more and more of the ointment, the search for the rest took longer. The moon touched the horizon as he finished his face and eyes.

One part of his mind cried for haste, to strike out after Rendrac before his headstart became too great, before all the time was wasted in preparation. But the balance argued caution, and he continued his methodical search and application. He had begun to despair of finding yet more salve when he discovered a bead in the corner, evidently arched high over the intervening floor by Rendrac's shattering stomp.

He deftly scooped up the globule and rolled it around his palm, hesitating as he watched it skitter about. Saxton had said nothing about the internal effects, but what he must do was a logical necessity. Shrugging his shoulders, he popped the droplet into his mouth and began to swish it around. His tongue glazed and his lungs acquired that tickly feeling he had had as a sick child. He exhaled forcefully and felt his nasal passages coat up as well.

He held his hands before his eyes, turning them from side to side, watching for telltale signs of spots with no protection. The stuff was spread too thin, he suspected. How could such a meager layer protect him from the heat of the mountain?

He stepped into the rubble and flipped open a small strongbox. Reaching inside, he scooped up the handful of coins that remained. Four coppers—all that was left of Saxton's wealth. Barely enough for the rental of a horse to take him to the Fumus Mountains.

Alodar raced his mount into the midst of the torchlights and jumped from the saddle. The horse stomped forward into the circle of miners taking their morning meal. On his left, Alodar recognized the circular hole where the gas bubble had burst through the mountainside. At his feet were picks, torches, iron strapped chests, and piles of small leather pouches, mixed with the pockmarked rock littering the gently sloping hillside. Straight ahead, rising from a silken mattress spread over the rough ground, was Basil the apothecary. Alodar glanced at the pale glow forming in the east and quickly drew his sword.

"You come a trifle early to pay your debt, novice," Basil said as he recognized the intruder. "And in so theat-

119

rical a manner. I am a reasonable man and would have allowed you the hour remaining."

"Rendrac—where is he?" Alodar snapped. "He has an obligation to pay to Saxton as well."

"The alchemist is no longer bound," Basil said. "I do not fault a man if he changes his mind, so long as his last decision is the correct one. And having Rendrac coated in the caloric shield is payment enough for what Saxton owed. I do not mind assuming whatever risk resides in the depths of the mountain. Full share is far better than a part."

He stopped and shredded a piece of parchment into the air. "See, the contract is concluded," he said.

"If the ointment was satisfaction enough," Alodar spat, "then why did you direct Rendrac to take his life as well?"

Basil knitted his brow. "Saxton's life," he said, puzzled. "I know not of what you speak. I would not order Rendrac to such an extreme measure, for what could it profit me to do so? Saxton dead is of no value whatsoever. Alive he either repays in goods or with labor. No, I may covet the products of his craft but I have no use for his life."'

Alodar stared into Basil's eyes and hesitated. It might be true, he thought. Basil's control over Rendrac did not seem absolute. He tightened the grip on his sword and looked quickly around the group of miners slowly creeping back to form a circle around the two. He glanced into the opening into the mountainside and made up his mind.

"Then where is Rendrac?" he asked. "It is he that I will deal with first."

Basil looked to either side and signaled for his men to converge even closer. "He is already into the mountain," he said, "but that should be no concern of yours. Saxton was freed of his contract, but unless you have the brandels then *you* are still bound to my will. Put down your sword and submit. I will even let you stay and see with us what Rendrac brings from the depths below."

Alodar cast quick glances to either side and took one step backward. "It is not quite dawn. Until then I am still a free man."

"An exercise in futility," Basil said as he motioned his men forward. "If you do not have payment now, how can you hope to within the hour?"

120

"I will discuss it with Rendrac." Alodar suddenly turned and scrambled up the lip of the opening. He tumbled over into the passageway and spun around with his sword still pointing forward. Two miners appeared over the edge and then hesitated as Alodar flicked his blade back and forth in challenge.

"Oh, let him go." Basil laughed. "He will return soon enough, begging for water. Or if not, Rendrac will spot the body on his way out and we will dispose of it later."

Alodar did not bother to reply, but turned and headed into the bowels of the mountain. He followed what seemed to be the same tunnel he had traversed before, torchlit and sharply sloping downwards. He raced past the side passage in which he had bartered with Basil, and the line of torches led him onward for three hundred paces more. He ripped the last source of light from the wall and dipped through a small opening into the blackness that extended beyond.

The path tumbled and pitched as he slowly progressed, occasionally opening up to impressive heights and then narrowing down to slits to be traversed on hands and knees. But each step led him generally downward; and with each, Alodar felt the increasing discomfort of stillness and heat.

Suddenly the pathway opened wide into a larger tunnel that sloped even more forcefully into the mountain's interior. Alodar looked up at the roof, fully three times his height and could see bright spots of light from cracks that led to the surface. He held his torch to the floor, illuminating the smooth and hardened rock that had confined an ancient upward thrust of heat-laden gas.

Alodar looked down the direction of the tunnel's path and saw a dull glow in the receding blackness. He thrust his torch forward and picked up a small dot of light far ahead. He watched for a second to make sure it moved, then ran to follow, his footfalls echoing loudly down the passageway.

Apparently alerted by the noise, the bearer of the light stopped and waited for Alodar to get closer. The dot resolved into a torch, its light reflected from the gleaming ointment of Rendrac the warrior.

"Sweetbalm. you are indeed a nuisance." Rendrac's voice resounded through the cavern. "But, I see, a dim-witted one at that. If you come no more protected than that dull sheen indicates, I need worry about you only a few steps further."

"The ointment protects me as well as it does you," Alodar shot back. "I feel only a little discomfort and could survive with even less if I had to."

Rendrac responded with a booming laugh. "Oh could you now, novice? How well do you think you are protected now? Try your spittle on the rock before you answer."

Alodar wrinkled his brow, but complied. To his surprise, his saliva hissed and foamed and in an instant was gone.

"Yes," Rendrac continued, "the meager ointment you have protects you well enough now. But if you have any sense, you would turn back to save your flesh from baking."

Rendrac whipped his free hand about with a flourish and then placed it firmly against the wall. A blur of fine mist spewed from the contact in much the same way as the spittle had from the rock. "The ointment also evaporates in response to the heat," Rendrac continued. "I am well anointed and presently feel not even your discomfort. I shall be able to descend much farther into the depths of the mountain, but that thin coating of yours will be gone in a trice."

Rendrac laughed again and turned to continue his downward march with an easy stride, small tendrils of vapor rising from where his boots touched the hot rockbed.

Alodar breathed deeply in defiance and then immediately regretted the act, coughing back the harsh volcanic gases into the humid air. He pressed forward after Rendrac, dimly aware of pinpoints of heat in his boots where the nails joined the heels to the soles.

Downward they went, following the tunnel's gentle turns, shining torches high to illuminate the smooth and featureless walls. Alodar stepped rapidly, trying to keep up with Rendrac's easy gait. Concentrating on closing the gap, he struggled to shut out the growing discomfort and feeling that his strength and clearheadedness were ebbing away.

They trudged on in silence for many minutes, Alodar

some ten yards behind and unable to draw closer. The walls echoed the methodical rhythm of their step as they placed feet firmly against the downward slope of the tunnel. The cavern of smooth and unweathered rock loomed high and wide about them, majestic in its size. Like the intestine of some giant monster, it undulated forward into the very center of the mountain.

As they continued, Alodar suddenly caught another gleam of light reflected back from his torch.

Before he could act Rendrac cried out in recognition. "The first one! By the staves, it alone makes the whole journey worthwhile," he said. He stopped, reached on tiptoe to the tunnel's high wall, and deftly wrested a gem from the matrix which held it.

"A topaz of at least thirty carats," Rendrac exclaimed as he dropped it into a silvery pouch hung at his side and resumed his pace. Almost immediately, he shouted again, "More sparkles. Just look at them! Sapphires, emerald's, aquamarines, bulging from the walls like the warts on the face of a crone. I doubt if a pickaxe is even needed for them." In a hastened effort, he began wrenching the jewels from the bedrock, excitedly advancing further into the depths for still bigger stones that blinked back his torchlight.

Alodar exerted himself to plunge after, now that Rendrac was slowed with his gathering, but his limbs responded sluggishly to his will. Small pains began to shoot through his lips; when he held them apart, the interior of his mouth ached for them to be shut again. Eyes darting about, he spied a small stone that Rendrac had missed and hastily reached out to snare it. With a start, he dropped it to the cavern floor, fingers stinging from the hasty contact. He spread his hands as he had done before he left Ambrosia. The opalescent shine was still there, but now barely noticeable against the fabric background that it covered.

Alodar turned to pursue Rendrac with plodding steps, each one an effort that barely kept pace with his adversary's slower meander back and forth across the tunnel's breadth. He saw Rendrac stop, pant, and catch himself as he almost wiped his brow. Alodar's own eyes watered and ached, and each breath brought fresh pain when he inhaled.

123

They rounded a sharp corner, and Alodar noticed that he could see farther ahead than the sphere of light provided by his torch. In the distance, a bright red glow filled the cavern floor, and the reflections bounced back and forth off the walls. Beneath the sharp echo of Rendrac's boots, he heard what sounded like a creamy ointment bubbling in a cauldron.

Rendrac looked at the soft background lighting, back to Alodar's torch, and then extinguished his own. He tied shut the third small pouch crammed to overflowing at his waist. With a grin, he snapped open a large sack that hung to the floor. Picking the jewels from the walls and dropping them inside, he continued onward.

They drew nearer the glowing redness until it filled the tunnel with its light. Alodar extinguished his own torch and let it hang at his side, no longer needing it to show his way. With a dull realization, he saw that the glow came from a pond of molten rock lapping the floor some hundred yards ahead. The liquid nearest them was placid, but farther on Alodar squinted into a violent frothing of reds and yellows that shot brilliant sprays to the very top of the cavern, melting rock where it struck and tumbling giant stones into its midst. Further back, the tunnel roof glowed amber as it blended into the level of the lava. They could advance no further.

"The biggest prizes yet," Rendrac called out, panting down to the very lip of the lake of lava. There in a crystalized border around the pool, like the icing on a cake, massive gems sparkled in the glow. The smaller stones were the size of cherries and the largest as big as a man's fist. Rendrac lowered his pouch to the ground with its mouth gaping open and shoveled the jewels inside. Like a garden keeper removing autumn leaves, he methodically moved around the edge of the lake, raking in the treasure.

He finished stuffing his sack and bound it shut as Alodar came closer, wobbling on each step, his eyes glazed into an unblinking stare. Rendrac opened a second bag; holding it low to the ground, he tried batting the larger gems into the folds with his gloved fingers. His eyes raced over the jewels strewn about, disdaining those which were less than a baron's ransom. He looked out over the pool, stopped his collection, and hesitated.

"It will be enough," he said. "I need not test the ointment that far." Returning to the first sack, he wrapped the drawstrings around his wrist and then slowly pulled it over his shoulder. He staggered slightly as the heavy weight thumped against his back, grasped the second bag firmly, and started to return in Alodar's direction.

This would be his chance, Alodar thought dumbly. With painful slowness he forced his hand down to the scabbard at his side and winced as he tightened his grip on the hilt.

Rendrac saw the motion and laughed. Without a word, he stopped, slowly balancing his weight on one foot and then kicking out with the other at Alodar's stomach. Alodar saw the boot rising but his reactions were too dulled to respond. With his sword only six inches from the scabbard, he felt the blow strike home. As he crashed to the tunnel floor, Rendrac swept by, leaving him to regain his breath and scramble to his feet alone.

Alodar sloughed aside the effects of the kick, but his palms and the soles of his feet felt burned, and the rest of his body ached with protest from the heat. He tried to lick the roof of his mouth with his tongue, but it lay flaccid and no moisture would come. He should have been disappointed that Rendrac was gone, but the heat dulled his will to care. He looked dimly forward to where the large jewels had been and saw no more. Only the smaller gems that the warrior had left lay scattered about the edge of the undulating pool of lava.

Like an enchanted harvester, he stiffly lumbered forward and dropped a dozen small stones into the pouch at his side. He looked uncomprehendingly at the wealth at his feet, back up the passageway, and then across the sea of molten rock.

As he scanned the bright red liquid, he saw what Rendrac had chosen not to investigate, a small dark speck bobbing in the fiery waves. He squinted his eyes against the light to see what it was.

"A chest," he gasped. "Much smaller than the largest of the jewels, but a chest nonetheless." He hesitated as he watched the small box bob on the slowly rolling surface, trying to remember why he was there.

He looked again at the chest. It might be the means

for his freedom—and the treasure for the fair lady. The quests were still intertwined.

He hesitated for another moment, trying to anticipate the shock of contact, but his thoughts fused together in a sludge. He shrugged his shoulders and took a first step towards the very edge of the pool and then another.

The pain coursed through his palms and he felt the burning sensation creep down the nape of his neck and onto his back. He tried to shut his mind to the protests of his body and plod on to the edge. He concentrated only on raising one foot and extending it in front of the other. His supporting leg trembled with each step. His gait became a simple shuffle, each pace bringing him only inches closer to his goal. Finally he stood by the edge of the pool, feeling the angry waves of heat rise and bake his chest and thighs. He hesitated and then reached down into the lava to retrieve the small container from where it floated.

His hand screamed anew, not only skin but muscle and bone feeling the energy penetrate deep. Waves of heat pulsated up his arm and into his body. His flesh seemed to sear and his vital fluids boil as the feeling ripped through him. Alodar somehow ignored the pain and, clasping the small box as firmly as he could, he rose to stand erect.

The pain throbbed for several minutes more, and then was replaced by a deep numbness that ran the length of his arm. There was nothing left to stay for, he thought finally, and he turned and started to climb the tunnel to safety.

With great effort, he placed one foot up the incline and then followed with the other. Far more slowly than he had descended, he struggled upward. His consciousness slid nearly away as visions of Iron Fist, Saxton's shop, Cedric's courtyard, Aeriel and the angry red walls hallucinated before him. To the small amount of reason that remained, it seemed that retreating from the heat should bring relief, but nothing seemed to change.

On and on he staggered, focusing only on the floor, not knowing if each step would be his last, and dimly not even caring. One weaving stride followed another up the passageway, and Alodar could not think clearly enough to recognize any of the natural features he had passed on the way down. After a countless number of steps, he began to realize that his torch was again of use and the fiery lava no longer lighted his way.

Some time later the pain lessened as he climbed, but he could not take heart, so weary were his limbs and lungs from the punishment they had received. His breath was forced, and every muscle throbbed from its abuse. Eventually the slope became less steep, but Alodar did not notice as he continued to plod onward. He saw the light flickering along the wall and he followed the guide-posts upward. Finally he looked forward and blinked at a large patch of rosy blue directly ahead, beckoning to him with whiffs of fresh air.

Alodar threw one leg over the lip of the opening and pulled himself out of the tunnel. Sliding down the outside of the slope, he tumbled into an exhausted heap in the midst of Basil's camp.

He looked slowly about and saw Basil on his knees in front of two large chests with their lids thrown open. The apothecary brought his hands upwards, filled with gems, and then let the jewels spill through his fingers. About ten paces behind, Rendrac stood, holding a large pole horizontally across his chest and pushing back the excited miners straining for a glimpse of the treasure.

"You return," Basil said looking up from his play. "By the laws, you return." He looked quickly about the camp and then to the horizon. He turned back to Alodar with a smile. "Yes, you return," he said, "just in time to begin your lifetime of service."

Alodar sighed wearily and looked up into the first rays reaching over the horizon. "My contract is not yet completed," he said as he set the small chest aside and fumbled into the pouch at his waist. He grabbed a few of the small stones and flung them across the ground. "With these gems, you are more than paid in full." He looked down at the chest and reached into the bag again. "And a fee for the rest since it is by your tunnels I obtained the treasure that is totally mine."

Basil looked at the small jewels scattered at his feet and then down at Alodar's side. "Well said, novice," he replied. "You as well as your master Saxton have a spirit I would love to break. But I am not a man for grudges. Give me that interesting item you extracted from the depths and you leave a free man, with whatever remains in your pouch, as well."

"You have already been paid," Alodar said. "You have no just claim to anything more."

Basil looked quickly about the camp. "Perhaps I do not," he admitted, "but then Rendrac is not so principled as I. His impulses cannot always be controlled, although when he apologizes to me with small gifts such as these, all is forgiven." He again ran his hands through the chests and motioned Rendrac forward with a wave. "Take the small chest," he ordered. "The treasure from the depths. I want it all."

"Well enough," Rendrac growled, stepping forward. "Let us see what this novice can do without a protector standing at his side." With a frown of irritation, he wiggled both arms stiffly in a shimmer of opalescence in the rays of the rising sun. He grimaced and reached up to pull at his cheek, frowning with the effort.

Alodar struggled to his feet and tried to force his senses alert. He looked at the giant striding forward and he sighed with his fatigue. "Cedric says that you will not win unless you think that you can," he muttered, but other thoughts brushed his concentration aside. For months he had received less than a good night's sleep, and in the past day none at all. Whatever energy he had left seemed boiled away in the depths of the mountain. His arms and legs were no more than dead limbs on a burnt-out tree, hollowed to the core. And Rendrac had pummeled him into the corner of Saxton's shop with ease when he was fresh and alert. What chance had he now? But it was for vengeance he had come, and it must be seen through to the end.

Alodar drew his sword and tensed, ready as he could be. He breathed the sweet air deeply, trying to force life back into his tired limbs as Rendrac unsheathed his blade and slowly swung his arm back for the initial blow.

Alodar dully watched the tip of the sword as it cut through the air in the backward swing and then reversed direction to begin its journey forward. He turned to the side and presented his own sword as guard, wincing in anticipation of the shock of contact. He blinked once, but the blow did not come.

In disbelief, Alodar looked to Rendrac's face and then

back to the weapon still in midswing. As Alodar watched, it slowed to a crawl and then stopped motionless.

Almost simultaneously, the big man uttered a weak yelp, and his free hand slowly rose with a spasm of effort from his waist to a mouth held rigidly open under eyes filled with fear. For a second, nothing happened and then, like a silver statue, Rendrac toppled to the ground with a loud clang.

Alodar moved to the prostrate form, its limbs still in the rigid position they had held when erect. He reached out and touched the hand that held the blade and felt a deep coldness, rock-hard and smooth. Alodar struck down with his own sword, pommel first, onto an outstretched rigid arm. The now inert form rang from the contact.

"The ointment," Alodar murmured. "It was meant to be used sparingly and burnt off. Rendrac was too greedy and applied too much. And now it has degraded with age and entrapped him."

Basil's jaw dropped in stunned disbelief, but he recovered and turned to the miners cautiously pressing closer behind. "After him," the apothecary shouted. "His blade can touch but one or two, and we will have his treasure to add to our own as well."

The miners hesitated, and Alodar saw his opportunity. With his last burst of energy, he sprinted forward and tipped over the chests at Basil's feet, sending a cascade of brilliant jewels rolling down the hillside.

The advancing miners paused, then spun around in pursuit of the treasure as it tumbled by. In a moment, they were racing pell-mell after the speeding stones as they fell. Basil hesitated a moment more, eyeing first Alodar and then the gems cascading away.

"Stop, you wretches!" he yelled at last. "Unhand what is rightly the property of Basil the apothecary." The men paid him no heed and raced onward, stooping and picking up the gems as they went.

"Stop, I say!" Basil called out as he pursued, pulling the magic dagger from his belt and waving it high in the air. With a vicious swing, he whacked at the neck of the slowest moving henchman as he stooped, and kicked out at another as he halted to consider which path downward to follow.

In an instant Alodar was alone, with only dim shouts

and an occasional cry to break the stillness. He sat wearily down at last to collect his thoughts and decide what to do next.

The sounds grew fainter, and he decided that Basil and the others would not soon return to bother him. He looked about and retrieved from the hillside the small chest he had found and gently cradled it in his hands.

The deeper he went, the bigger had been the gemstones; and this was the deepest of all. Jewels for a royal diadem had been strewn about the cavern floor. What greater treasure must be resting within the confines of this small box? Visions of perfectly cut diamonds bigger than oranges danced in his mind. With a wrench of his knife, he popped open the lid.

He peered inside, and his heart sank in disappointment. Instead of breathtaking jewels, he saw instead two black spheres of volcanic basalt. Six months of effort, backbreaking labor and great risk to his life from the hazards of the formula, the snares of Basil's factories, and finally the furnaces in the center of the mountain; and what did he have to show for it? A few jewels in his pouch and two machined hunks of common rock.

He had pictured himself questing for the fair lady like a hero from the sagas. His deed of daring was to win great treasure and sweep him in front of all others that sought her hand!

He sighed and set the chest to the ground. With his chin slumped he sat inert and unmoving and let the sun climb silently into the sky.

The inn room door creaked open to Alodar's knock, and he looked into the face of Periac, the master thaumaturge.

"Alodar, you have returned," Periac exclaimed. "Come in, come in. You are just in time for an evening's instruction. We will continue from where we left off on the hills that bordered Iron Fist."

Alodar looked wearily around the small bare room and headed for the stool in the corner. "A meal and a night's rest first, master, for which I will fairly pay," he said. "And it is not for knowledge of thaumaturgy that I seek you out."

As Alodar slumped down, Periac reached out to brush

130

the dust off the table with a sweep of his arm. "But I fare quite well in the city," he said. "There is much pot mending and cistern excavation to be done and word of an honest craftsman soon gets around. I can well use a journeyman and you would find your stomach far better filled than when we worked the outlands. I doubt your start with alchemy has fared as well."

Alodar reached for the pouch at his side and placed it on the table. "I have learned a few of the simpler activations and formulas," he replied. "Saxton was most trusting with his craft when we had a rare idle moment together. It is true that I still know more of thaumaturgy. But as for the fruits of my effort, what do you think of these?"

With a flourish, he tipped the sack. A sapphire, a tourmaline, and two rubies clattered onto the table.

Periac's eyes widened and he stroked his goatee in thought. "In truth," he said at last, "you have always impressed me as a clever lad. Perhaps your skill does better reside with another craft."

Alodar waved his hand over the table. "It may well be impressive," he said, "but not enough to turn the head of the fair lady. Here, take one ruby. It is yours for the favors I ask of you. Seek out the shop of the alchemist and use the second to see that he has a decent burial. The sapphire I would have you carry to Cedric the warmaster, in compensation for my not continuing instruction at his hand."

He glanced down at the table and put the tourmaline back into the pouch. "The last I will save," he said, "for I suppose tomorrow I must eat as well. But the true reason for why I am here, master, is because of your knowledge of other than the craft of which you are master." Without waiting for reply, Alodar reached again to his waist and brought forth the small chest. He flipped back the lid and held it forward for Periac's inspection, his eyebrows rising in expectation.

"They are magic," the thaumaturge said without hesitation. "Magic spheres of fine construction."

"Magic," Alodar echoed, squinting at the container. Gingerly he grasped one of the spheres with his gloved hand and found that he could not extract it, so smooth was its surface polish. He removed his glove and tried again with his bare hand. An electric tingling suddenly

131

pulsed through his fingers, and immediately he was reminded of the feeling when he handled Aeriel's dagger. Exerting all the force he could muster to prevent it from slipping away, he slowly pried out one of the orbs and turned it quickly over to gaze at it in his palm.

It was black, totally black, the deepest black Alodar had ever seen. In an indescribable way, it sang of perfection, a sphere of such precision that no mere lathesman could ever hope to duplicate it. His hand vibrated from holding the orb, and somehow he was acutely aware that it contained great power.

Alodar returned the sphere to its resting place and examined its companion in the same way. It was identical to the first, except that a thin line neatly circumscribed it, dividing it into two perfectly equal hemispheres.

Alodar had never seen such handicraft in his life, but there could be no doubt. "Magic," he mumbled as his spirits returned. "Magic spheres somehow placed in a pool of molten lava.

"But what more of them can you tell?" he continued. "Of what use can they be? Surely they have more utility than ornamentation."

"They are incompletely formed," Periac said. "The ritual that has created them is not yet complete. And when it is finished, I cannot fathom what will be their virtue, but to their possessor they will convey great power indeed."

"Power," Alodar muttered and then paused in thought. "At Iron Fist I applied my wits and was bested by skill in arms," he said at last. "In Ambrosia, I learned those skills, but in the end Rendrac's brute force carried back the treasure for the queen. It is raw power I must have to win the day; wits and training are not yet enough.

"Power," he repeated, lightly juggling the small chest in his hand. "My quest leaves me little choice but what I have here. Yes, there can be no other way about it. Either I am defeated or strike to unlock the secret of the spheres and hope it gives me what I will need to win the fair lady."

He popped out of his introspection and looked into Periac's face. "But how can I learn of magic?" he said. "Basil the apothecary did mention dealing with a Lectonil to the south. Perhaps in his guild I will find what I must know."

"He would be as good as any," Periac said. "But from him or any other magician you would learn little. Judge not the manner of instruction of the other crafts from what you know of the nature of thaumaturgy." He glanced at the gems still on the table and stroked his goatee. "And perhaps of alchemy as well. Magicians are a secretive lot, far removed from the dealings of nobles and common men alike. They pass on their rituals only to the initiates and acolytes who pledge lifetimes to their secluded service."

He shook his head and spread his arms wide. "You have experienced the workings of two crafts, Alodar," he said. "Is it not enough? If alchemy is not to your liking, then return to my instruction. To delve now into magic will only compound your folly."

Alodar snapped shut the chest and returned it to his pocket. "Perhaps you are right, master," he said, "and someday I might indeed return to your teachings." He paused and his eyes widened. "But power!" he said. "It is worth giving the random factors another chance to align. Yes, by all means, master, let me profit one more day from your instruction. But tomorrow I will travel south to ferret out the spheres' meaning. Ferret out their meaning in a palace of magicians."

PART THREE

The Magician

CHAPTER NINE

The Palace of the Cycloid Guild

ALODAR gently lowered the card onto the others and held his breath. The flimsy structure did not collapse and he reached for the next one in the deck. A child's pastime, he muttered to himself. What possible bearing could it have on determining his merit. He frowned at the tower already three tiers high and tried to, decide the best place to start the next level.

"Enough, there is no need to proceed further," a harsh voice sounded from across the table.

Alodar blinked out of his concentration and looked up just in time to see a robed arm sweep across and tumble the construction away. "But I had not reached my limit," he said. "Even as a boy, I was able to form a fourth story before it crashed to the ground."

"There was more to the directions than just building a house of cards," the man facing him said. "After three blacks in a row, then a red must follow. And at no time can your elbow touch the table unless you place your free hand to your forehead as well."

"I ignored the details in the depth of my concentration," Alodar replied. "Though in truth, master Lectonil, I do not see how they can matter."

"They are important because they illustrate my point," Lectonil said, stabbing his index finger down against the deck. His hair was white and covered his head like a fuzzy bush growing on top of a rocky mound. Deep-set wrinkles furrowed his broad face with age and his eyes always frowned, regardless of what he said. He wore a black robe covered with a pattern of many tiny silver rings, the logo of the magician.

"What you were attempting was not magic, but a ritual

nonetheless," he continued. "And it is by ritual that all magical objects are made." His frown deepened and he examined Alodar's expression critically as he spoke. "These rituals must be performed with utmost precision. Utmost precision or else they will fail. One hasty step or sloppy motion and all the labor that went before is instantly undone. A ring already priceless can become no more than the one in the nose of a bull."

"I was most careful as I proceeded," Alodar said.

"Yes, to construct a house of cards, each one must be precisely placed," Lectonil said pulling his lips into a grim smile. "But you must satisfy the boundary conditions as well."

Alodar did not reply, but glanced around the small bare hut and then quickly through the single window to the landscape beyond. The terrain sloped uphill, much steeper than the Fumus Mountains. Except for one well-worn path, the rough ground was untouched by the mark of man. The summer green of hearty shrubs stood out brightly in the midday sun, but farther back vague shadows shimmered and faded like reflections in an agitated pond. Except for this single shack, the entire palace was hidden behind that curtain. Periac was right about the secrecy of the magicians. A hard hour's climb from the village in the valley below, admission to the grounds only when accompanied by someone who knew the way through the shimmering veil, and acceptance on a permanent basis that depended upon satisfying arcane criteria hidden by these tests.

Alodar looked again at the dancing images, some soaring high like runs of rope dangling in the air. Others hugged the ground like giant slugs. The larger structures must be buildings, he thought, and the smaller blobs people moving between. He squinted and tried to discern some detail, but nothing resolved in the blur.

"Precision is the essence of magic," Lectonil continued, waving his arm towards the window. "Even for the most menial of tasks, one must have sufficient control. But you have fared well in the preliminary tests of the others. And my exercise with the cards shows your hand to be steady and your mind quick enough, despite the error at the end." He studied Alodar and his eyes narrowed. "Quick enough to execute properly a long and complex list of instructions, once you have learned to follow exactly the direction of a master magician."

"Do you mean that I am admitted as an intitiate?" Alodar asked.

Lectonil raised his hand palm forward. "Our roster of initiates is complete," he said, "and until one advances to an acolyte, the Guild is reluctant to accept more. I offer you now the position of a neophyte only."

"If I have aptitude, as your examination has indicated." Alodar asked, "then cannot I somehow profit from your instruction nonetheless?"

"My day is quite full with research and direction as it is," Lectonil said. "I have no time to waste on one not of my persuasion."

Alodar wrinkled his brow in puzzlement but Lectonil continued. "Of that I make no secret," he said. "Beliac opposes me openly in the council. He proposes new lines of investigation, new experimentation with rituals as yet untried. They might hold the glitter of excitement for the younger masters and some of the acolytes but they present much peril as well. We have prospered over the centuries with objects of great tradition and modest embellishments carefully researched. What need do we have for radical dissipation of our resources on tinkering that may produce no return at all? Had Beliac shown the proper respect when he received his black robe, I might have nurtured him along. But immediately he attacked my ways; no heed did he pay to my station. With each passing year his boldness grew as he subverted more to his cause. Such is not a proper way for a master to act. He should have pride in his Guild, of which I am the senior member."

He spat. "Beliac! How can he be so blind to what I have accomplished, the reputation I have established through years of carefully planned research? I would not doubt he is demon possessed, so destructive is the direction in which he tries to convince us to go. Yes, demon possessed. If it can happen to some uncultured outland baron, then why not a learned master magician as well?"

Lectonil's cheeks flushed and his eyes glowered. "And so I show my favor only on those who side with respect and tradition," he said at last. "Respect, tradition and what is proper as well for the future of the Guild. How you would align in the matter I cannot tell from tests such as these. I must wait and observe your actions over a period of much longer time."

"But if I perform my tasks and do not get involved in such abstract affairs," Alodar persisted, "what then of my chance to learn the craft as well? Without such opportunity, my best course may be to seek admission with other magicians farther to the south."

"The border is troubled," Lectonil said. "You would have a difficult time in passing through."

"Nevertheless, it is an option to consider."

Lectonil scowled and looked down at the cards scattered about. "Oh very well," he said, with a wave of his arm. "My need for someone not encumbered with study is pressing. Work for a few months as I instruct and then if you prove worthy, I will elucidate some of the art as a suitable reward."

Alodar hesitated for a moment, trying to decide whether to speak of the two spheres he carried with him. Perhaps they would interest Lectonil enough so that he would cooporate to mutual benefit. Both Periac and Saxton had been quite open with instruction; if the magician saw an advantage, then he might also teach.

Alodar looked intently at Lectonil's uncompromising features and then to the shimmering curtain which hid the palace from view. He thought of the cryptic tests and how little he had learned from questioning the villagers in the valley below. Finally he frowned and moved his hand away from the pouch at his side.

"Is a few months two or three?" he asked at last.

"Oh, it may as well be two," Lectonil growled. "We will discuss it in more detail later. For the moment, follow me through the curtain. I will see that you are properly robed and lodgings assigned. If you make haste, you will be in time to witness a part of one of the major rituals, which emphasizes the importance of what I have said here." He stopped and gritted his teeth. "And were it not for Beliac, I would be there as well."

Alodar ran his hands down the sides of the long brown robe. How strange, he thought for the fifth time in as many minutes, that there are no pockets. The acolytes and magicians he could understand, but even the covering of the neophyte was as uncluttered as the rest.

He shouldered his way through a wide doorway with the rest of the crowd and searched the stands rising from either side for seats still empty in the rapidly filling stadium. He saw a row of brown in the midst of the motley colors of the onlookers and climbed to join it.

"A new man," a voice called out as he neared the group. "Welcome to the neophytes of the Cycloid Guild. I am Hypeton and these are your fellow strugglers for truth."

Introductions bounced around as Alodar found a place on the rough bench. He looked about the structure and reestablished his bearings. To his rear, the air oscillated in the curtain and he followed the shimmering overhead, squinting briefly into the disk of the moon. Rather than a perfect circle of light, it appeared like a large drop of silvery oil undulating on the surface of water and casting diffuse rays in all directions. His eyes tracked across the sky; in the direction behind other buildings of the Guild, he could see the protective veil again bend to earth. The large rectangular stadium floor was walled in on all four sides with many doors around the periphery, but only on the two longer ones did the seating rise into the air.

"You join us at a most propitious time, Alodar," Hypeton continued, pushing back the shock of brown hair which tumbled down his brow. "Did you note the closeness of the evening stars to the rim of the moon yesterday eve? They will certainly occult tonight, the six hundred and twenty-fifth day since the last total eclipse. It is the perfect time for a fifth striking and we are lucky to see one in our lifetimes."

Alodar started to question the meaning of Hypeton's statement but remained quiet as three trumpet blasts from below silenced the crowd in anticipation. From an opening low in the wall opposite, a slow procession began to make its way onto the stadium's floor. In the front, three heralds, long trumpets thrust ahead, marched in step with the drummer a dozen paces behind. Following them, twenty white-robed initiates pulled a large wheeled cage. As it came into view the crowd murmured with excitement.

Alodar stared into the cage to see a green-scaled beast, winged and resting on powerful thighs, a long forked tongue whipping idly between rows of large, serrated teeth. Saucerlike eyes sat unblinking atop the flat snout, and the whole head oscillated from side to side in response to a snakelike rhythm which coursed up the long, sinewy neck. The wings stayed tucked close to the body in the confines of the cage, but Alodar could see many folds of thick, leathery membrane that contrasted sharply with the rough scaling of the rest of the body.

"Is that a wyvern?" Alodar exclaimed. "Never in my travels to the west or even in Ambrosia itself have I seen the like."

"A wyvern it is, Alodar, one of two that we have here," Hypeton answered. "Old Lectonil was able to hatch them some fifty years ago when the lesser moons of the blood star lined with ours."

Alodar returned his attention to the procession as more and more marchers filed onto the broad floor. Seven golden-haired women, bare breasts bobbing in unison with each step, preceded a large brass gong hung from a man-high frame. Gray-robed acolytes carrying huge, two-handled, golden keys followed a second caged wyvern, this one blindfolded and sitting docile in its narrow cage. Finally, silence engulfed the crowd as the master magicians of the Guild, robed in deepest black with circular logos of silver, brought up the rear.

"Only four are needed for this ritual," Hypeton explained, "and, by the laws, you can imagine the fighting that must have gone on in the council chamber for which of the fourteen it would be. I see that Lectonil is missing and Beliac too. The masters must have been so polarized that they could only agree on the neutrals like Mentenon there. A solid searcher so they say, but no great flashes of intuition or daring to try new theorems. But look, they are nearly ready."

Alodar watched as the first of the four black-robed men mounted on a tripod a small telescope handed to him by one of the initiates and began to sight the moon and its companion stars of the evening. He raised one arm and extended his index finger to command attention. Alodar stole a quick glance skyward. As the first of the two flitting stars passed behind the wobbling moon he saw the black-sleeved arm fall with a sudden flourish. Almost simultaneously, a second magician inverted an hourglass, and the seven women joined hands and began to sing a soft, harmonious chorus.

The sands ran for several minutes, and all stood transfixed on the stadium floor. When the last grain fell, the third magician started gesticulating wildly, conducting the other performers in their tasks in a complicated rhythm. The drums pounded in a seemingly random cadence, and candles sprang to life at what Alodar judged to be the cardinal points of the compass. The blindfold of the second wyvern was pulled aside, and the beast added a deep bass moaning to the high chorus as it saw its caged mate.

The gong rang once more, and the chorus stopped. The second magician produced another sand glass; when it emptied, the wyvern's eyes quickly were covered again. As its wailing stopped, acrobats exploded from the entrance tunnel and did a complex series of flips and tumbles that ended in the formation of a human pyramid three men high, in the center of the floor.

The fourth magician suddenly awakened from his inactivity and motioned to the stocky acolyte nearby who staggered forward with an anvil of gleaming gold. Alodar squinted to follow the detail as the magician removed a ring from his left hand and placed it on the flat metal head. A second acolyte handed him a hammer. As the gong sounded, a third and final time, he deftly tapped the small band of metal.

In the silence that now filled the stadium, Alodar heard a small grunt from the blow and then a babble as all the participants suddenly relaxed and began talking at once.

"Enough, it has proceeded well," the magician commanded the assembly as he picked up the ring and thrust it back onto his hand. The entire group dropped their various props to their sides and, in an unplanned confusion, jockeyed back to exit the way they had come.

"Is that all?" Alodar asked, puzzled, as he and the others also began to exit from the stands. "I do not understand the intent of the performance."

"As I have said, Alodar, it was a rare event indeed," Hypeton responded. "A striking of the rough outer edge from a ring of transportal. Only one more striking to finish the inner and it will be complete."

"Then why not spend a few more minutes and be done

with it?" Alodar asked. "Surely such a pageant is assembled at great expense."

"Yes, would that it were true, Alodar," Hypeton said. "But the strikings can be accomplished only when the rituals of magic make it so. The next and last cannot be done for yet thirty years. As you say, the expense is enormous. Each man on the stadium floor received much rigorous training to perfect the part he had to play so that the ritual could proceed correctly. That training, that dedication to the goal, is such that only a guild of magicians could attempt it. No small wonder that rings of transportal and their like fetch the entire treasuries of kingdoms when they are completed."

"But how fare you in the meanwhile?" Alodar persisted. "How can even a guild survive to make such wonders?"

"A question that cuts close to our very own keep, Alodar." Hypeton laughed. "Though I only repeat the rumors that circulate among the neophytes, the Cycloid Guild is in the most part living off gold from the sale of magic armor some three hundred years ago. But to this legacy is added the smaller sums that come from easily made lesser items and the admission charges to the town dwellers to see the rituals. And the Guild lives in fashion to make it a self-contained community, independent of the principalities that rise and fall about it. Why, you are here today because you will serve a function of that community, so that itinerant laborers or city-dwelling craftsmen need not be consulted."

"Then, since I serve a goal common to all," Alodar said, "might I easily approach one of the magicians to consult on a small conundrum that has drawn me here?"

"By the laws, no," Hypeton said. "A magician hardly speaks with civility to his peers, barely tolerates the intrusions of acolytes into his thought, and instructs initiates only because he must. A neophyte addresses a black robe only because he has been spoken to. If you desire such company, study the rudimentary texts they give to each of us and try for the initiate's robe yourself. If you are truly skillful with the equations and postulates, you may have a black robe of your own in thirty years and can then riddle your conundrum as you see fit."

143

"But Lectonil himself said he would give me instruction in two months time in partial payment for my tasks," Alodar said.

"So the masters say to all prospective neophytes they interview in the shack outside the curtain that surrounds us." Hypeton laughed. "There is much mundane work to be done in the Guild, and they dangle a promise if they must. Why, I have been here three years and know no more of the construction of rituals than the day I arrived. But the food and bed are fair enough exchange for the work that I do. And if I eventually tire of it and leave, then they will find another."

"Is there no other way, then, that one can satisfy even the smallest curiosity about magic?" Alodar asked.

"By the angles, no, Alodar," Hypeton said. "And take me seriously now, for I jest no more. The secrets of this Guild, like any other, are closely guarded and much ill fortune befalls him who tries to discover them in other than the prescribed way. I remember well the printer two years ago who somehow whisked away to his chamber a box of organization so that he would no longer have to sort his type by hand after each day's press. A harmless enough ambition and an item easily enough made by the scores. Alas, when they ran the ritual of presence, the box glowed red hot and shook the air with a mournful wail for all to hear. They took him from the neophyte towers and, before the central library, showed him his reflection in a mirror of inversion as we all watched. A most gruesome sight, Alodar, his heart still pumping and entrails hanging out for all to see, surrounding the features and skin trapped inside."

"The ritual of presence?" Alodar said.

"Yes, Lectonil and his followers want to perform it once a fortnight to keep the Guild secure. Beliac argues it wastes our time and resources, and yearly is sufficient, if at all. But between the poles of both, it is yet often enough. You will feel it when it is run; hair stands on end and skin pimples with cold. Warning enough to leave magic to the Guild and concentrate only on the tasks they have given you."

Alodar's thoughts raced. The magic spheres were too valuable to entrust to some hiding place outside of the

144

grounds of the Guild. They represented all that he had of importance in his quest for the fair lady. But to leave them in his new quarters to await the next ritual of presence was greater folly still. He must find out their intent and be away quickly, no matter how interesting the knowledge he might gain here proved to be.

"I will regard master Lectonil as a man of his word," he said at last, "and follow explicitly what he says for a full two months. But at the end of that time, he will be reminded of his end of the bargain."

"Then do not judge him too sharply by his reply," Hypeton said. "You will find the others are no better."

The sky dimmed in sunset and Alodar started down the ladder. The torches were already lit, but he could do no more work by the feeble light. He reached the bottom and looked along the broad expanse of the building. Still clutching the brush, he ran the back of his hand across his brow. Some four hundred feet of wall, and after three days it was still only half painted. And this on top of digging a quarter mile of trench and cleaning more than three score dirty pens.

He heard footfalls on the cobblestone steps and then the gentle swish of a robe against the grass. He dropped the brush into the bucket and turned just as Lectonil approached from behind.

"You make good progress, neophyte," the magician said. "In a few more days the south facade will be done. In another week perhaps the north as well. I am pleased by the even thickness you have applied with precision."

"Pleased enough to begin the instruction?" Alodar asked. "You said that for certain this night you would be unencumbered."

Lectonil stopped and frowned. "Another session with an acolyte," he said with a wave of his hand. "It was scheduled late this afternoon. Perhaps when the south wall is done, or better yet, when the north is completed as well."

Alodar wiped his hands with an oily rag and dropped it to the ground. "How can I be sure that in another two weeks time the answer will not be the same?" he asked slowly. "I took you at your word when I entered the Guild, master, and did not question when you put me off for one excuse or another. But the delays have persisted for thirty days more. For three months now I have served in good faith, mucking the stables, digging trenches in the hard clay, and patching the walls with paint. It is time enough that you make good what you have promised. I give you the benefit of the doubt no longer."

Lectonil's eyes narrowed and his voice tinged with hardness. "You speak at great odds with your station, neophyte," he said. "And I will instruct you when it is a convenience to me, not when you happen to beckon."

"It is knowledge of a specialized type that I seek," Alodar said. "The demands on your time would not be great."

"No matter if it were but the number of beats in a dance of divergence," Lectonil said. "I would reveal it only when you deserved to know, be it in another two months or perhaps even two years hence. There is no cause to treat you differently from any other. You receive a fine bed and ample meals for your efforts. I doubt you would be rewarded as well for the same labor in the town at the foot of the mountain."

"It is not for bread and board that I sought out the Guild," Alodar said. "It was the lure of magic that made me come. I explained quite clearly my aspirations when you interviewed me in the hut a quarter year ago. And as clearly, you did agree to aid in its achievement."

"I understand full well your desires," Lectonil snapped, "but the frustrations you feel when they are not instantly fulfilled are your own struggle. They are not the concern of a master magician."

"Then what of your word?" Alodar asked. "One receives in kind what he deals out to others. If you do not honor the rights of a neophyte then how can you expect him to deal fairly with yours. It is a temptation of many, I would imagine, to seek by stealth what you will not give freely."

"Do not speak of a magician's word to a mere neophyte," Lectonil said, his eyes suddenly flaming. "Such a concept has no meaning. And do not threaten what you cannot deliver. It will avail you no better than the pestering you are employing with increasing frequency."

"It can avail me no worse." Alodar growled back.

Lectonil started to reply, but then paused for a moment in thought. His brows furrowed, and he pulled his face into a grim smile. "Yes, if it will stop your irritations, it is worth it," he said at last. "And the example would be most instructive to the others. If it is by stealth that you propose to learn the secrets of the Guild, then by all means I give you my leave. Whatever you can discover by your own devices is yours for the taking. Not a single fact will I begrudge; no retribution will be exacted. But be prepared to accept as well the consequences of your actions when you tamper with the safeguards that have protected those secrets for so long and so well. Mark you, you will fare far better with a paintbrush and awaiting instruction when it is my pleasure."

Before Alodar could reply, the magician stomped back onto the walkway and disappeared into the night. Alodar waited motionless until he could hear footfalls no longer and then he exhaled slowly.

He smoothed the covercloth over his gear and then stood up abruptly. Lectonil had given him leave, permission to find out on his own whatever he could. He looked across the courtyard to the hall of the initiates and, in a flash, made up his mind.

Alodar spent the evening hours in hasty preparation. Near midnight he returned to the courtyard. The night air blew cool and clear as he walked the spacious grounds that were deserted by the workers of the day. His heels sounded sharply on the cobbled walk that ran in a long, gentle arc out from the hall of administration past the towering library and then to the gates of the magicians' private quarters.

Smaller pathways diverged gracefully from the main thoroughfare and led to other structures along the way. Except for the stadium, none was so grand in size as the hall of magicians, but each was worthy of any of Procolon's lords. Off to the left was the house of the wyverns and other exotic animals, a low stack of jutting terraces made as much of glass as of stone, and displaying for all the animate treasures within.

Further back and barely visble stood a cluster of small towers, each topped in unique fashion, some with crenelations and some with gently curving bands of silvery metal meeting at the apex. The space allotted each neophyte was small but still a finer appointment than any Alodar had known before.

To the immediate right was the square block of the initiates, white and windowless, but covered on all four walls with the deep gashes of immense calligraphy. Out of sight behind, lay the quarters of the acolytes, in back of them the cubicles of instruction, and beyond that the stadium of major rituals.

To the left stood the library, a tall slender pyramid covered with a mosaic of fiery red jewels, glowing of their own inner light. Four windows, tiny as viewed from the ground, covered each side near the apex; but for them, the walls were as unbroken as those of the hall of the initiates.

He looked back along the way he had come. The hall of administration covered fully half his view; unlike the beauty of the rest, it was a jumble of towers, blocks, and ramps. Brick butted against marble, graceful columns supported rough hewn beams, tiered archways of metal looked like scaffolding for new construction. The collage showed the haphazard growth of centuries as the Guild expanded and needed more space to provide for the increasing demands for self-sufficiency. Alodar had explored only a small fraction of the passageways inside but he had found a kitchen, a tannery, a carpenter's shop, a soap works, a small bath, and three testing rooms in which one demonstrated his qualifications for advancement in the Guild.

Alodar resumed his deliberate tread on the cobbled arc. These grounds could swallow the likes of Iron Fist a full ten times over, yet no solid wall ran along the periphery to protect what was within. Who would be foolish enough to brave the magical traps and delusions that served in their stead? Who indeed, he thought grimly, as he stood finally before the sealed doors of the hall of the initiates.

The vast grounds were empty and silent as Alodar stood before the portal. He took one breath and firmly pressed the small disk which glowed dully at his left, just as he had seen the initiates do during the day. Soundlessly, the smooth slab before him parted and revealed an alcove not much better lit than the starry sky.

Cautiously, he entered and the door slid shut behind him. Alodar turned as the air rustled with the closure but he saw no second disk to indicate his way back out. He faced forward and advanced two small steps. Either side of the alcove was featureless, but the walls radiated away from him so that, some ten feet distant, he faced not one but four more doors.

A simple expedient, Alodar thought. Only one of the doors leads any farther. The other three probably are trapped and three out of four would-be intruders are disposed of without the use of magic.

Alodar approached the one on the far left, hinged and handled with gilt and covered with velvet, tufted with small stones of jet. He listened intently but could hear nothing and advanced to the second.

The next, unlike the first, was made of rough hewn beams, splintery to touch and with fixtures of crudely beaten iron. Alodar placed his ear gingerly against the surface. After a moment of deep concentration, he heard distant voices from the other side.

The third door was of stone, but with a giant blue steel bolt that held it firmly into the frame that contained it.

The last door gleamed of glass, smooth and cold to the touch and dimly reflecting Alodar's figure as he squinted through it. Deep black lay beyond, shadow on shadow, with no form.

He stepped back and pondered his choice. He did not know enough of the ritual and symbology to make the correct guess. Some other clue must guide him. After a moment's thought, he withdrew a small, telescoping rule from the knapsack he had fashioned to hang under his pocketless robe. He carefully laid it at the foot of the first door and ran his fingertips along the stone floor. The masonry lay flat and true, like all of the construction at the Guild, with not a single crack or niche to disturb the gliding motion of his hand.

The area before the wooden door was the same; but in front of the third, a narrow gap at one end of the rule widened to a barely perceptible depression in the middle and then returned to true on the other side. This alcove was originally made with great craftsmanship, but since its construction it had served as the footpath for countless initiates. This was the one that he must take.

149

He straightened up, secured his rule, and pulled back the blue steel bolt.

Nothing happened immediately in response; to Alodar's gentle touch the thick slab swung gently inward on its hinges. Alodar blinked as he gazed down a small tunnelway into a well-lighted cross passage. He waited a moment to accustom his eyes and saw two white robes stroll leisurely by in the brightness beyond. A third shuffled by in the other direction, arms heavily laden with thick scrolls of cracking parchment.

There, not twenty feet in front of Alodar, unobscured by any visible impediment lay the goal of the night's venture. He smoothed down the spare neophyte's robe he had bleached with the aid of some of Saxton's teachings and slowly began to traverse the narrow passageway. He took a first step and then another, and the lightness grew correspondingly nearer. Suddenly another white robe poked his head into the tunnel and headed in Alodar's direction. Alodar turned sideways and averted his gaze. The newcomer paid him no heed but sped past and on outwards to the promenade.

Encouraged, Alodar resumed his cautious pacing of the distance to the hallway. He covered fifteen feet more and nothing happened. Then, just as the exit was within tantalizing reach, a brace of bells began ringing rapidly in the recesses of the ceiling. Metal grated loudly against stone, and he looked over his shoulder to see a heavy steel portcullis descend to block the entranceway behind him. He whipped back to look at the ceiling directly ahead and saw a second barrier begin to fall. Without thinking, he sprang forward, hurling himself low into the rapidly diminishing opening, arms out straight and stomach sucked tightly against his spine.

With a swoosh, he slid across the polished stone into the cross passageway, just as the steel shafts jostled his feet out of the way. Alodar stood up and confronted three initiates startled by the sudden appearance and the din of the bells. Alodar took advantage of their hesitation, spun about, and sprinted down the hallway.

"An intruder!" somebody shouted behind him. "Stop the man! He has tripped the watcher in the west entrance." A chorus of footfalls began to echo Alodar's own.

150

As he sped past the openings to cubicles, more inquisitive heads poked out into the passage.

Alodar looked forward and saw the hallway turn to the left some twenty feet ahead. He increased his speed towards the corner, hoping to perform some evasive maneuver while he was momentarily out of sight. As he approached and prepared to dart to the left, the sound of more bells added to the din. Alodar wasted no time in speculation but flattened himself for a second slide.

Another portcullis banged down as he dove, this time catching his robe on its sharp spikes. With a savage effort, he wrenched himself free as his pursuers slammed into the ironwork and thrust their arms through at his retreating form.

Alodar took but three steps before a third set of bells added to the chorus of the others and he saw yet another barrier begin to fall some twenty feet ahead. He looked hurriedly to the left and right and saw that a single side door was his only remaining exit. He ran through the entrance into a small cubicle, furnished simply with a bed and writing desk, but marked by no windows or other openings.

Alodar reached into his knapsack and withdrew a small bag filled with powder. He looked around the room, stacked the chair upon the bedframe, and climbed up the wobbly structure. Outside he could hear the gateworks being raised and the pursuers yelling out his location to others who came to join in the hunt.

Swaying on the chairbottom, he stretched to full height and chiseled away at the mortar between the corner ceiling tiles. He crammed the bag into the small hole, inserted and lit a fuse, and jumped to the ground as three white-robed figures rushed into the room. Alodar quickly fell to the floor and ducked under the table. The initiates stooped to follow.

"The game is over," one cried as he pulled on one of Alodar's legs. "What great sport. The masters have not had someone to punish publicly in some time. I do hope they choose an entertaining ritual."

The ceiling exploded and Alodar's assailants were hurled to the ground in a tumble of tiles, mortar, and stone. Alodar scrambled out and back up onto the bed.

He saw blue sky above; the overlying stone had fallen with the tile. Without pausing, he leaped upwards, arms outstretched, and caught the edge of a block which still remained. Before those below could recover, he pulled himself up and onto the roof.

He ran rapidly to the edge and leaped off to the ground. No one yet was coming to investigate the explosion, nor had an initiate popped out of the hall in pursuit. Alodar waited long enough to regain his sense of direction and then sped back towards the neophytes' quarters.

Just read a few scrolls to find out about magic spheres and be on my way, he thought as he ran. Perhaps something more passive, such as waiting for Lectonil, was not such a bad choice after all.

CHAPTER TEN

Barter and the Beauty

"BUT with all due respect, sage Beliac," the acolyte said, "let not the length of my tenure here color your decision. I have the proficiencies of a man many years my senior. Indeed I can produce a wand of ebony in but a fortnight, one of jet in two. I know by memory the rituals for fourteen talismans. I have mastered not only central, diagonal and symmetric but adjacent orthogonal magic squares as well. Listen and I will tell you of the method for producing a helmet of a thousand blows. First swing a pendulum with a bob of solid gold over the egg of a turtle as it hatches in the noonday sun. Next paint the claw of a roc—"

"Enough of the classroom recitation, Duncan." The magician waved him to cease as Alodar leaned forward to hear the quieter and slower tones. "It takes far more than rote to win the robe of black, as you well know."

Alodar stretched on tiptoes to get his head above the wall and catch the words. Two full weeks had passed since his adventure in the hall of the initiates, but nothing had happened as a consequence.

Still, another frontal assault might be suicidal without more data. Eavesdropping certainly was not the way of the sagas, but for the moment it was the only path open. Beliac and his acolyte had met in this grove often at this hour. The piece of eggshell placed in the grass behind them had the right shape to focus the sound, and the alchemical coating made the reflectivity nearly perfect. With the spellbinding of thaumaturgy, nearly all of what they said came his way, even though the grove was some fifty feet distant.

The small stand of trees was between the library and the hall of the acolytes, and the maze of open study cubicles nearby was ideal cover. From his hiding place, Alodar squinted at the magician and tried to catch his facial expression as he spoke. His hair was jet black and combed in long, straight strokes back from his forehead. Deep-set eyes and a narrow nose seemed buried in a forest of heavy eyebrows, thick moustache, and long curly beard. The effect was intended to convey the dignity of age, but the smooth, wrinkle-less skin betrayed Beliac to be one of the youngest masters of the Guild.

Duncan was younger still, perhaps five years older than Alodar, but with a hairline already receding to the top of his head. His eyes were close set, and his face carried a pained look, as if life were always treating him unfairly. His gray robe hung askew on his shoulders, dipping to one side and twisted into disarray.

"But most gracious sage," the acolyte continued, "I have studied the record of investiture of Valeron when he secured the silver ring for his own. There is no question of his that I cannot now answer. The apex of the library should not be denied me just because I have been an initiate only three years and an acolyte but two."

"The key ring to the apex is not lightly granted, Duncan," Beliac said. "We must have sufficient judgment and wisdom to use properly the rituals and theorems that are enscrolled there. It would not do for one unseasoned to have access to such power. And why the rush? Look at the pace of the neophytes. Some linger on for decades before even attempting the examination for initiates. Indeed, some are content with the simpler tasks and never strive for what is beyond their immediate grasp. We have some two score acolytes in the Guild at present; yet only a dozen or so have the potential to be magicians. Only the best will don the robe of black, when we deem them truly ready."

"But I am ready, venerable sage," Duncan said. "There is no new ritual that I could master were I to wait even a fortnight more. Time would only be a burden."

"Would it now, my acolyte? Then ponder the solution to the following proposition. A coven of ice demons appears from the black rocks in the valley below. They flash through the air to our very gates and, though the air shimmers and distorts as always, they slide through in a heartbeat. With convulsive power they begin to thunder our buildings down in mighty ruin. What defense do you propose?"

"Most surely my sage, I would make ready our supply of djinn bottles and lamps and instruct all at the level of acolyte or greater to fashion more as quickly as they are able."

"A divergence of djinn bottles," Beliac shouted. "I said ice demons. The like that confines an imp or figenella would not secure the devils of which I speak. Such an answer is insufficient. What else could you suggest?"

Duncan was silent for a long moment before answering. "Nothing more is in my learning, sage, but then I assert that no answer need be given. You propose what cannot come to pass, as if to ask how to move the stone of infinite weight. Except for a stray gremlin here and there, demons of power spark through our world no more. Common flame is insufficient to bridge the gap so that they can appear of their own volition. Contact with the demon world is mediated by fire. Without something exotic burning, the barrier is too great for the powerful to overcome. Small wonder that I do not recall an answer to such a problem in the recital of those who have preceded me."

"You wriggle out of the proposition too easily, Duncan," Beliac said. "I seek to see how you respond when the answer is not in the recitals you have so carefully memorized. But there is some truth in what you say. There are few wizards of note in Procolon, and the ones to the south

154

act most reclusive of late, though it is the time of year they usually stage the battle for the kings. But this year they have announced no such display. Perhaps they are too engrossed in what happens in the west with two barons themselves possessed."

"Two? I have heard of Bandor and no other."

"Another peer to his north was somehow seized as well, or so say the lesser sorcerers. Kelric has not confirmed it, but I wonder if his power has not slipped to such an extent that he refuses even to try."

"But if there are indeed two, then the fair lady's problem is solved," Duncan said. "The demons will turn their puppets against one another in the same fashion as the wizards direct their slaves in the south. Either both will be destroyed or the devils will tire of their game and retire whence they came."

"Such has not yet happened," Beliac replied. "The west of Procolon rises in coherent revolt as before, and with a unity of purpose they struggle against the queen who now besieges them. Indeed, Vendora has called throughout the kingdoms for a wizard brave enough to attempt an exorcism to come forward. Clearly she must defeat not only the discontents of the west but the devils which propel them as well."

"Among the acolytes, we hear much talk from the south that the several kingdoms view Vendora's trouble as an opportunity," Duncan said. "If they were also to act now in concert, there is little resource left that she can call to her aid."

"Perhaps only Arcadia across the sea or even the barbaric tribes to the north, if they could be convinced to fight," Beliac agreed. "All else is pressed into the struggle to the west. But such mundane happenings should not concern us. Our safeguards are good, despite what Lectonil will say. Which prince rules the valley and the townsmen does not matter. But enough of affairs outside our walls. Come now, what do you say to the problem?"

"I see I give you no direct satisfaction, O sage," Duncan replied. "But let me press on to another perhaps more practical reason to consider my petition now. The council stands sorely divided between those who support your august views and those who fawn behind Lectonil's robe. It is no secret among the acolytes how many issues of great import are laid aside to another day with seven votes yes and seven more nay. A fifteenth magician would bring great changes in the state of affairs in short time."

Beliac paused for a moment and then spoke with care. "And what would your persuasions be, were you indeed to get the privilege of the black, acolyte Duncan? Where do you stand on the issues that so dearly concern the council these days?"

"Why most assuredly with you, inspiring sage," Duncan answered. "I like not the constraints to which Lectonil wishes us bound. Many times have I heard you argue the need for expanding the number of acolytes, diversifying their skills, experimenting with new rituals and the rest. And on such a course I would see the Guild steered as well."

"Yet the manner in which you approach the craft is more like that of Lectonil than mine," Beliac said. "He would much favor one who found comfort in memorizing what has gone before, rather than daring what is new. Why have you not approached him instead with your proposition?"

Duncan bit his lip and lowered his eyes. "Please do not take offense, my sage," he said, "but in truth I did approach him with the same offer. 'I need no help from outside the council,' he snapped. 'A change of one vote and it will be over.' "

The acolyte paused, but when Beliac did not immediately reply, he rushed on. "But my method of learning is a superficiality. I am at ease with your leanings as well as any other. When I have the robe of black, such things will little matter."

"I see you have studied more than just the magician's craft, Duncan," Beliac said. "And I am much conerned about the issues of which you speak. The occurrence two weeks ago will be pivotal in the next council meeting. Lectionil will make sure of it. He will demand the ritual of presence be performed immediately. And since I am opposed to such waste on principle, I will resist him this time as well. But he will paint a dark picture of the threat to the Guild, the danger of so many uninitiated roaming at freedom within the palace grounds. Though he knows full well how safely we are protected, it will cause one or two of the more neutral to pause and consider it."

156

Beliac stopped and touched his fingers to his lips. "He has kept to his chambers since the incident," he muttered. "I would not doubt that somehow he put a neophyte up to the whole thing."

He was silent for a moment, and then his eyes narrowed. "Long ago, I visited his quarters. Topmost in the towers and the largest besides. Thick woven rugs, the newest sheets, and the freshest fruits in his bowl. And why should he have the lightest load of instruction and be the one to call our council to order? I am more the magician and it is only the accident of birth that he is older. If there is to be order in the Guild, then the trappings of senior master should belong to me. But enough of such discourse. I will ponder what you have said. It is not a decision given easily in a single evening."

"As you wish, my sage," Duncan said with sudden hope in his voice. "I ask only that you consider my petition with care."

Alodar watched the two men depart, Duncan skipping rapidly toward the hall of acolytes and Beliac, chin on chest, pacing slowly past to the magicians' quarters beyond.

Alodar looked down from the third story window onto the swatch of grass in front of the hall of administration. He smiled as he detected the bits of eggshell scattered about in the turf. On the carpet spread in the middle of his array Lectonil sat with his back erect, facing another magician in the same formal pose. Behind each, arms akimbo, stood four acolytes in a row. Looping around to enclose them all was a complete circle of initiates of both Guilds. To the side, objects of their craft peeked from a disarray of crates.

"Then it is concluded, Trodicar," Lectonil said. "The gong of shattering resonance and the well-tempered djinn bottles for the boots of varied prints and the amulet of blinding light. But the everlasting candles we will save for another time."

"Oh, very well," Lectonil's counterpart replied, starting to rise. "By what means are the rituals to be exchanged?"

"By the usual method of the wax-sealed book, two copies, freshly illuminated."

"When we dealt with Beliac, he gave us three,"

Trodicar said. "Two for the masters' immediate use and another for the library."

"No wonder his research drains our treasury so," Lectonil growled. "Half of his gold must be consumed by extravagance. But I assumed you would request no less and am prepared to deal as generously as he. Mark you, an additional copy to replace one lost to the hazards of the trail will not be forthcoming."

"It is fair enough." Trodicar nodded and the conference suddenly broke into an informal activity of exchange and packing. In a few minutes, the group split into two and moved in opposite directions. Lectonil and his followers passed from Alodar's view into the hall entrance below. Shortly thereafter, Trodicar's retinue strung out into a single line that wove across the sward and then through the curtain of distortion. The last initiate passed into the dimness, pulling at the donkey with their provisions. High on the backpack Alodar saw the corners of the recently bartered books protruding through the topmost flap.

His eyes widened with excitement. Books of magic moving away from the protective devices of the Guild!

He looked out to the shimmering view. It was well that he had taken every excuse to visit the town. He had been guided through the curtain enough times that he should be able to make the transit alone.

Alodar waited a few minutes more until everyone was out of sight and then quickly sprinted down the stairs. He raced outside the hall, across the swatch of grass, and into the haze. Rocks, shrubs, and the pathway ahead distorted in dizzying shapes that flickered from one glance to the next. Trunks waved back and forth, leaves expanded to giant size and contracted to pinheads, while rocks oscillated like soft gelatins. In a dozen steps, he was completely surrounded by the distortions, unable to tell by sight from whence he had come or the direction of the true pathway ahead. He glanced behind to see the towers of the hall of administration seemingly sway in the breeze, soaring to the sky and then drooping like a waxen model left in the hot sun.

Closing his eyes and concentrating, Alodar paced off a dozen more steps and then turned abruptly to his right. After several minutes of dead reckoning, aided only by minimal clues from the texture underfoot, his boot sounded against a large flat stone. The edge of the chasm, if the talk among the neophytes was accurate, was a deep cut wrapping around the Guild within the interior of the curtain. With his eyes still closed, he gingerly pushed one foot forward and felt the narrow beam which must span the gap. Arms outstretched for balance, he stepped off the six steps and felt with relief the firm contact with the stone on the other side.

He opened his eyes and saw the diffuse light grow dimmer still, as if the sun had suddenly sunk towards the horizon. The scrubby chaparral shriveled away to isolated clumps of gnarled and bare branches, and a single needle-like spire wavered above a rolling landscape. Alodar blinked, trying to remember if he had seen such a scene when he was guided before, but the image shimmered away.

He stepped forward six steps and then turned to his left. After a score more paces, he spun back to the right and continued down the slope. Twigs and small branches pulled at his robe, but when he peeked in the direction of the tugs, the grotesque shapes only added to the confusion. He stumbled over the small stones which littered the way and finally banged his toes against the sharp point of a flat rock directly in his path.

He mentally ran through the sequence from the beginning to make sure of the correct path and then started down the branch to the left. After several more minutes of concentration he broke through to the still air of the outside world.

Alodar sighed with relief at his accomplishment but had no time to stop and savor it. He ran to the edge of the trail and looked over the side. The pathway switched back several times below him. On the second bend he saw the guildsmen pulling their beasts of burden. Downhill, the trail cut back in a wide arc that nearly circumscribed the hill before reversing direction.

Without waiting further, Alodar lifted a fist-sized rock and hurled it down at the donkey lumbering along. The first shot missed the target and the trail completely. The second was a lucky hit directly on the animal's haunch. The donkey reared upright, wrenching the rein from his handler. Another hit on the lower neck was enough to terrify the beast into bolting down the trail with the magician and his acolytes racing behind.

Alodar quickly turned and began to scramble through the bush to the other side of the hill. His feet slipped on small rubble. Several times he had to grasp at a nearby shrub to keep his balance. Pulling and tugging his way, he pursued a rough arc through the chaparral while the magicians zigzagged on the looping path below. Several minutes passed in a frenzy of exertion, and then Alodar stopped and looked down the slope. If he hurried now, he could meet the beast on the long switchback and have a chance at the books before the pursuers could come around.

He took a deep breath and charged down the hillside, hitting the rough ground on a dead run. He leaped over the small barriers that lay in his way and zigged and zagged down the incline. His legs seemed to acquire a will of their own, hurling one foot in front of the other and dragging his upper body behind. He caromed forward with only enough control to twist and dodge the larger shrubs and rocks that swept by in a blur. Struggling for balance, he flailed his arms wildly in the air, more than once almost carried away by the avalanche of small stones he started with his pounding tread.

In a final burst of speed, he jarred onto the pathway, feet skittering across the ground towards the edge of the cliff. As he ran forward, the donkey rounded the curve and galloped directly ahead down the trail. Alodar slowed and stepped to one side, reaching out to grasp the pack lashings as the beast ran by.

Stabbing pain shot through his arms as he was stretched by the contact, but he gripped the harness firmly and was swept from his feet and dragged along. Trusting his grip to his left hand, he released his right and fumbled for the books peeking out of the top of the pack. With a savage motion, he wrenched one free and tumbled to the ground, rolling off the trail and cascading down the edge of the cliff.

Brush and rock slowed his descent, whacking at his limbs and ribs as he spun. In a dizzying moment, he lay still at the bottom of a little ravine, groggy and with blood trickling from a battered nose, but still clutching the magic book of the Guild. Up on the trail he heard the excited cries of the initiates as they ran past, calling for the animal to stop.

Alodar lay still, not so much to ensure that the magicians were gone as to let his body rest from the beating it had taken.

A long time later as dusk began to fall, he slowly sat up, wincing from the soreness in his back and legs. With a hand trembling from the effort, he cautiously broke the seal on the small clasp which bound the book shut. He breathed deeply and cracked the volume open to the middle.

The pages fell flat with a sudden puff of black smoke. As Alodar fanned the haze aside, he saw that the parchment contained not writings on magic but blankness from top to bottom. He quickly cut to another page and the opening was accompanied by the same explosion and absence of content. He spent the next hour trying to part the leaves in various ways, slowly, from the top, with eyes closed, behind his back, but always with the same result. When he was done the book was empty, ready and fresh for the first word to be written in it.

Alodar tossed the useless volume aside in disgust and began to climb slowly back up the cliffside. "Safeguarded still," he muttered. "I have yet to find the way."

"This way, Alodar," Hypeton called as he wove his way through the clutter of low benches and tables in the dark and musty room. Alodar followed, barely able to keep sight of the swirling brown of the robe in front as he avoided the outstretched arms and legs in his way.

He saw their target at last, a small round table in the far corner, already occupied by two figures huddled over the light of a single feeble candle.

"Ah, my night vision deceives me not," Hypeton said with satisfaction as he sat down. "The best bench in the house, I wager."

Alodar sat down in the one spot remaining and squinted into the gloom at the two others, white-robed but hooded as he.

"But we are much too formal," Hypeton continued, throwing back his cowl and reaching up to do the same to the figure at his left. The hood fell in a cascade of golden curls shining brightly in the light of the candle. "And yes,

I was right, it is you, Cynthia, and your companion must be Camphonel, is it not?"

"Enough of your light manner, Hypeton," the bare headed girl responded in a throaty voice. "It is barely tolerable back at the Guild. I care not to have it pursue me when we take leave to visit the village."

"Ah, Cynthia, as gruff as always," Hypeton said. "How is it that your heart does not mirror the perfection of your skin? It would be most wondrous if it were so."

"Which new one do you bring with you tonight, Hypeton?" Cynthia asked, ignoring the question. "Did the last one finally tire of the same parade of taverns and houses, week after week?"

"I am Alodar, the neophyte," Alodar said. "Are you also of the Cycloid Guild?"

"Indeed I am," Cynthia answered. "Perhaps you have already seen me in the course of your sojourn there."

Alodar squinted at the face across the table with eyes not yet accustomed to the darkness. The chin was square with a harsh line that contrasted sharply with the softness of the cascading curls. The nose and lips were a trifle too large for the thin, oblong face but the eyes were alive, returning with confidence Alodar's measured look. Men who did not know her would judge her plain, he thought, but those who did would feel a strong allure. Recognition sprang to him as he traced down the outline of her figure now hidden by the robe.

"Indeed, the ritual of the ring," Cynthia said simply. "But I see that the folds of your cloak hide something interesting as well. Here, let me see your hands."

She extended her arms across the table and Alodar placed his hands in hers.

"Your hands are scarred," she said. "What manner of labor do you perform for the Guild?"

"The same as always given to the newest of the neophytes," Alodar answered. "The marks are there because I have practiced at arms."

"Not only practiced, I see," Cynthia said, running her hands along Alodar's forearm, fingertips gently rippling over the token from some of Cedric's instruction. She looked deeply into Alodar's eyes.

"You must tell me sometime of the adventures that gave you these," she said. "A tale of arms would be a

162

most welcome change from those of magic, which is our steady diet."

Alodar opened his mouth to speak but hesitated, enjoying the pleasure of her contact. He tried to picture Vendora and compare her beauty, but the image was faded as if seen through the magician's curtain. He struggled to remember her as she looked in the dungeon of Iron Fist when they first met or later in the keep just as the walls finally fell. The queen was a stunning beauty, but how exactly her face was different from Cynthia's he could not tell. He sighed at the blankness and almost instinctively began to withdraw his arm.

Cynthia turned her hand over and playfully stroked the back against his. To his surprise, he felt a small nodule of hardness in the middle of the smooth skin.

"It appears the work of the initiate is also not only of the mind," he said.

"That is the mark of all who advance beyond the level of the neophyte," Cynthia replied. "When they stoked the branding iron with the small disk into the furnace on the day of my initiation ritual, I fainted dead away. When I awoke, my hand was bandaged and I was cloaked in the robe of white, free to roam the hall of the initiates. Several weeks later, only the little circle of scar tissue remained."

"And what true significance does it have?" Alodar asked.

"Who can tell?" Cynthia said. "So much of the initiation ritual is merely tradition from years gone by. I have no call to be reminded of it in my instruction since."

Before the conversation could continue, the murmuring of the crowd began to rise in anticipation and Alodar turned to view the small stage at the other end of the room. The curtain behind parted and a minstrel walked forward. He strummed a chord on his strings and waited for silence before beginning.

"The lava ran hot, fierce and glowing.
The fumes alone scurried the lesser men back,
But to the queen he had pledged the gems
So into the tunnels stomped mighty Rendrac.

"Knee deep in liquid fire he struggled
To the very heart of the smoking mountain;

163

In a sparkling pool of rich treasure
He stuffed his pack from the cascading fountain."

Alodar blinked in amazement as the ballad droned on. It was all there in traditional saga form. The brave hero setting out alone against overwhelming odds. By his mighty prowess he secured a treasure for his queen but, alas, perished in the deed. A hundred years from now more verses and embellishments would be added so that the true event could not be fathomed by the wisest from the telling.

The crowd showed its approval at the conclusion and then buzzed with the gossip the ballad had evoked.

"They say that his mentor truly reaps the benefits of his great labor." Camphonel spoke for the first time. "He rode into Ambrosia in magnificent style, tossing small gems like pebbles into the crowd. To the queen he presented a necklace of huge stones, with an emerald nearly fist size for the pendant. Vendora postponed her betrothal to some other outland lordling, and now Basil is in her company everywhere. But she craftily does not choose him over the other. Instead, she delights in their daily struggle for her favor."

Not one suitor but two! Alodar looked down at his brown robe and sighed softly. He shook his head and focused his attention on the conversation still bouncing around him.

"A lack of definition on the politics to the north!" Hypeton swore. "Their ways degenerate further with each passing year. Thanks be to the permutations that keep the Guild out of such pettiness."

"Your ear is as sensitive as your tongue, Hypeton," Cynthia said. "The Guild deals with struggles of power as much as any principality. Why the entire esplanade is talking of nothing else. The next council meeting is an extraordinary one called by Lectonil. It will be the real test between his faction and that of Beliac."

"And how do you see the outcome?" Alodar asked.

"The talk is mainly fueled by rumor, with no substance one way or the other," Cynthia replied, "but I think that Beliac feels the pressure of time to be against his ideas. He seeks to get votes by other means than those of cold logic. Else why would he beseech me to show certain favors to one of the less committed masters? Why, I wager that if a means of persuasion were presented to him, he might even traffic a neophyte."

"Of course," Alodar said. He quickly slid from the bench and headed through the night back to the tower of the neophytes.

CHAPTER ELEVEN

The Unfettered Dragon

ALODAR pushed aside the twig and peered out at the acolyte standing at rigid attention in the hot sun. He reached down to the small wax figure at his side and deftly drew the lips apart in a ghoulish grin. Duncan's features responded in kind, although his cheeks trembled from the strain of trying to break the grip which held him.

Alodar looked down the path and saw Beliac's slow approach to the library's entrance, his chin deep on his chest and every step reluctant.

As the magician passed, Alodar removed the cork from the flask and grimaced at the foul odor which arose from it. With a sweeping motion, he tipped his head back and downed its contents, feeling a raw, rasping sting all the way down to his stomach. His throat would be monstrously sore for a week afterwards, he knew, but Saxton's craft was never particularly concerned about the after-effects of its potent brews.

Beliac drew abreast of the immobile acolyte and Alodar pursed his lips to speak.

"Good riddance, pompous windbag," Duncan seemed to say. "I hope they see fit to take back the robe of black as well as denounce your ideas." The voice was high and sluggish, Alodar thought, but no one would doubt that well indeed.

Beliac stopped his pacing and looked up in disbelief. "Well move along," Alodar projected. "You may as well get it over with."

"See here, acolyte," Beliac replied. "The affairs of the chamber are no concern of yours, in spite of what you have surmised from our previous converse. And mark you well, regardless of what happens there, I will emerge with the unbroken circle on my robe still, more than a match for any acolyte in the Guild, no matter how lofty an opinion he holds of himself. None of your station dare address me thus."

"And in truth you are correct, O sage," Alodar said in his own voice as he stepped from his hiding place and out onto the walkway. "By a combination of the arts of thaumaturgy and alchemy, I made appear what was not so. Acolyte Duncan, of course, never of his own free will would make such statements."

"Then it is you, neophyte, who will feel the wrath of my punishment when I have time to deal with the matter," Beliac snapped in reply. "What is your name and station within the Guild?"

"My demonstration was for a most pointed purpose," Alodar persisted. "I believe that you have a need for the control of another's voice and posture within the very next hour. That I can offer to you."

Beliac's eyes brightened with comprehension. "Ah, what you say is true, most clever lad. Quickly now, inform me of the ritual by which this is done and I will reward you in due proportion."

"As I have said," Alodar replied. "It is not of magic, but the other arts. I must be present to perform, else it cannot become so."

"A neophyte in the apex. Unthinkable!" Beliac growled. "Give me the ritual or face my wrath on the spot."

"My presence or nothing," Alodar said coldly looking into the angered eyes of the magician. "Decide now or let the opportunity slip from your grasp."

Beliac was silent for a long moment and then flung his arm in hasty beckoning. "Very well, come along. We will deal with your lack of respect later."

Alodar returned quickly to the bush, ran his fingers

over the waxen eyes and laid the doll out on the ground. He bounded back beside Beliac, not even bothering to check Duncan's apparently slumbering form nearby.

Beliac extended the ring on his left hand and aligned its intricate design of miniature planes and cubes into a mating indentation in the slab in front of them. A moment passed with Beliac's hand rigidly extended forward, but there was no motion in the slab.

"Oh by the postulates, calm yourself man," Beliac muttered to himself. "It will not do for one of Lectonil's lackeys to see me so agitated that I cannot work the outer door." He took a deep breath and then another and pressed his ring more firmly into the slot. The rock parted at a line that Alodar had not detected, and they stepped into a small alcove.

"Here, since you are uninitiated, you must wear a talisman to calm the watcher." Beliac shoved his ring into another slot to his left. A small drawer extended from the wall and Beliac withdrew an ornate chain of gold braid and placed it about Alodar's neck. He then used the ring a third time to part the door at the rear of the alcove, and they entered the library proper.

Alodar's eyes darted greedily about as they passed down the center aisle towards a stairwell in the very center of the large square. Unlike the subdivision into many small rooming cubicles of the hall of the initiates, no intervening construction blocked his view.

The entire floor was covered with neat rows of desks and study benches, most occupied by figures robed in white and gray. From all four of the gently sloping walls, shelf after shelf of books, scrolls, and manuscripts cantilevered out into the study area. Alodar gazed up the spiral of the stairs to where they finally disappeared in a small ceiling area crowded by the four wall planes that converged to it. At regular distances along the flight upwards, catwalks radiated outwards from the wall and ran unsupported from below to join the spiral. At each level a second walkway circumscribed the interior and gave access to still more shelves of magical knowledge.

Alodar smiled with satisfaction. This was where he must search for an explanation of the power of the spheres.

They reached the stairwell, Beliac pressed his hand to the base of the banister, and they began to climb. Alodar's brown robe caught the attention of many who studied below, but Beliac's one of black silenced any questions. The long ascent was uneventful; no clanging bells or slamming barricades added to the sound of their tread.

"I would think the library to be more highly guarded than the hall of the initiates," Alodar said as they climbed. "Yet it would seem a knife in your ribs in exchange for your ring would imperil all the secrets here."

"The magic in my ring encompasses more than just the parting of the slab, neophyte," Beliac replied with a slight wheeze. "That ring was formed as part of the same ritual that exchanged my gray robe for black. Off my hand it is powerless, worth only the few brandels of silver of which it is made. It works for me and me alone, as do the thirteen carried by the other magicians of the Guild."

"Then that same knife might prompt you to use the ring to gain my entrance, just as you have done of your own free will. The result would be the same."

"As I said, neophyte, a ring most magical," Beliac continued. "It is attuned to me and to me alone, but in a state of mind of reasonable tranquility. If I am stressed, it will not work and fear for my life would render it useless. You saw how I had to calm my slight anger to effect our passage. No, there is no way into the library save by the will of a master magician. But enough of my craft. At the moment, I am more concerned with yours.

"When we enter I shall greet first the one you are to control. Let him be until we are to vote on the elevation of Duncan to the black robe, and then have him vote yes. Can you indeed effect this?"

"If within the next hour, before my powers for voice casting subside, yes," Alodar answered. "And I will need in addition something from his body. A hair perhaps will be the easiest to secure."

"Hmmm, yes," Beliac said, touching his fingers to his lips. "That I can arrange. Be ready for it when the opportunity arises. But, hold, we are at the portal to the apex."

Beliac stopped and placed his ring against the ceiling and an opening formed as it had on the ground level. Following the magician's lead, Alodar rose the last few steps and entered the top of the pyramid.

Unlike the giant room below, the apex was windowed,

but the openings did little to alleviate the cramped feeling of the four walls sloping to a point overhead. A large, U-shaped table filled the room. Wedged between it and the wall behind sat the other thirteen magicians of the Guild.

"What illogic is this?" Lectonil's voice boomed against the walls. "Beliac does try all patience to bring a neophyte into the council chamber." He looked at Alodar and his eyes widened in recognition. "And one such as this will fill your ears with lies when we discuss what transpired in the hall of initiates. Take him out before his words taint our reason."

Beliac waved his speaker to silence and moved to the wall not blocked by the table. He turned to the left and squeezed behind the seated magicians, motioning Alodar to follow.

"Well, what explanation do you have for this?" Lecontil persisted. "I have monitored the work of this man before. He has no need to be concerned with things magical." He looked Alodar in the eye. "And I seriously doubt that his motivations are for the good of the secrets of the Guild."

Beliac ignored the challenge, and turned instead to the magician next to the empty seat. "Why, Fulmbar," he said, "you look in fine spirits for this council. Does it perhaps foreshadow that you have reconsidered your change in stand? No, do not answer now. Save your surprise for the vote. I first must deal with master Lectonil, as vocal as ever."

Beliac took the empty seat and glared across the table to his adversary on the other side of the room. "I brought the neophyte to induce just such an outcry as you have made, Lectonil. It betokens the illogical panic in your thought, the fear of losing some prerogatives of your station by the slightest liberalization of our rules and conduct. His presence here is in no way connected with what happened in the hall of initiates."

Lectonil frowned at Beliac's words but then rapidly recovered. "We are all well aware of the way you twist the most innocent statements to your own purposes," he said. "A neophyte should be denied access to the apex, not because of illogical fear but firm deduction of what the consequences might be. Now if you have done with your theatrics, send the man back to his duties and let us consider the business at hand."

"He remains for the purpose that I have called him here," Beliac said. "I will not be badgered by your stern words."

"By the laws!" Lectonil's face grew red with rage. "Your statement summarizes the entire basis of your thinking. Loose and careless with no respect for your seniors. Do you not know that this Guild was founded and flourished on rigor? Rigor in postulate and proof, not a wave of the hand, an approximate result, a truncated expression. If we follow such thinking, we follow it to our doom, Beliac, and so long as I can balance the diagonals of a square, I shall fight with pride to have such thought purged from the consideration of our council."

"The times have changed, old man," Beliac responded unruffled by the heat of Lectonil's words. "Such rigidity might have worked in centuries past when kingdoms were large and their treasures vast. We could afford to invest all our efforts in monumental magic, knowing that there would be some buyer for the goods when we had finished. But look at our transactions recently. We labored hard to produce ink of purity in lots greater than a gill. But what has happened? The liquid lies unused in some storeroom. No alchemist comes forward with sufficient gold to claim it. We spend a goodly share of our endowment yearly just to supply your two precious wyverns with the meats that keep their scales tight and well fitting. And to what purpose? So that we may in thirty years have a ring of transportal. What monarch can possibly afford what it has taken us to produce it? And yes, more to the point, look at our annual outlays. Will the Guild even be here in thirty years to complete the ritual?"

"It is your sloppy ways and little dabblings that squander our endowment," Lectonil said. "And with them you somehow hope to change the course of centuries. But have you not the depth of thought to see that it cannot be? The Maxim of Persistence still guides, Beliac. As you have apparently forgotten, simply stated, it says 'perfection is eternal.' Perfection, Beliac, perfection. Not some convenient approximation. If we do not use the proper steps and follow them exactly, we will become nothing more than expensive alchemists with gold rings

170

that turn to tin if you rub them but once. The everlasting quality of our work will be but myth for the sagas."

"I am as well versed in the fundamental laws as you, Lectonil," Beliac replied. "In fact, judging from the relative number of monographs the two of us have circulated in the last year, I would say I am more in tune with the true meaning of our law than you. At your zenith you may have discovered some interesting rituals, but I fear you are now far past your prime in productivity and in judgment."

"If I may interject a few words, most august masters," one of the other magicians interrupted. "Master Lectonil, I fear you disparage young Beliac here greatly. He does not compose the ritual elements into magic squares, it is true, but his constructions in three dimensions are made with equal rigor and have produced new objects and lines of research undreamed of just ten years ago."

"Undreamed of and unwanted," Lectonil snapped. "Of what use are twelve elements that seem to fit together into a dodecahedron whole if the result is only a ring that ties one's bootstraps?"

"Now you are most unfair." Beliac shouted for the first time. "That ritual was merely the first example. I dare say that the first square produced results no more inspiring. The field is young but in time we will have objects that are totally outside the reach of such well traveled avenues as square construction, be they trimagic, panmagic or symmetric."

"Masters, if you please," another rumbled. "Our ears tire of such discourse. We are here at master Lectonil's calling to decide on the petition to elevate acolyte Duncan to the status of master magician, and we need not hide behind philosophical rhetoric. We can all count. If the majority backs master Beliac's petition, then future councils no longer will be evenly divided. If we vote the proposition down, it indicates clearly that master Beliac no longer can muster sufficient strength to cause deadlock. In either case, the work of the Guild will proceed."

"The first issue before us, master Zinted," Lectonil said, "is the presence of the neophyte. He must be removed and then Beliac must be censured for jeopardizing the secrets of the Guild."

"By the traces, Lectonil," Beliac said, "we have said

171

nothing to compromise our heritage and methods. Look I prove it to you."

Beliac turned to Alodar and continued his explanation. "As you may have gathered from our discourse, the making of a magical object is a matter of performing a ritual, a ritual that is perfect in some well defined sense. Possible ritual elements, the ringing of a bell, drawing of a bow and so on all have different rutualistic attributes and numerical values. In our research, we strive to arrange and order these elements in such a way that a perfect sequence is obtained. Such sequences produce objects indeed most magical.

"One such mechanism of arrangement and a successful one, I freely admit, is to order the elements in a square in such a way that certain of the numerical values of their attributes sum in the same way whether considered horizontally, vertically or diagonally. Once these conditions are satisfied, one performs the ritual, taking the elements in sequence row by row.

"Now I have told you much more than you could deduce from what we have said and I will add one thing more. Pluck a hair from master Fulmbar's crown. There, you have performed the first step in a ritual of no mean potency. How do you proceed now?"

"Why I have no idea," Alodar responded as he drew his hand into the folds of his robe and planted the hair into a second wax doll he had strapped to his waist. "You have told me some principles but with no instruction on the values of the elements or how to assemble them, I cannot proceed."

"As is obvious to any with clear wit in this room; he knows less than what one could pick up through idle gossip in the neophyte's tower. I further submit that our decision on Duncan will be common knowledge in the esplanade within the hour in any case. No secret has been revealed by what transpires here, so let us proceed. Besides, master Lectonil, do you wish me time to change further the minds of our assemblage here or do you prefer to have our collective decision recorded so the Guild may proceed?"

"You are ready for the vote on Duncan now, and did not bring this neophyte because of my stand on the ritual of presence?" Lectonil asked.

"As I said, the neophyte is here merely to illustrate my position," Beliac replied. "It is to be Duncan first, and if there is no deadlock, then the rest will naturally follow."

Lectonil twisted his face further but at last waved his arm to begin and said no more. The magician on his left stood and formally stated the resolution before them. At its conclusion, he cast his negative vote and sat down. The counting began to move around the table. Alodar quickly muttered the incantation while the eyes and ears of the assemblage were on each speaker. He broke the small vial of caustic soda from his underbelt into the oil of vitriol and felt the heat begin to rise in his hand. He looked about, but cramped and shielded by Beliac's chair, no one paid him any heed.

Beliac rose and voted, and Alodar began to manipulate the little waxen image. Fulmbar seemed unsteady and awkward as he stood, but the strangeness was lost in the murmur of disbelief that followed his vote.

"What manner of substitution is this?" Lectonil shouted out above the rest. "You have wavered from time to time surely, Fulmbar, but you assured me not an hour ago that your vote was switched to be mine. It is for that reason alone that I called for the extraordinary session."

"I have indicated my choice and say no more," Alodar projected through Fulmbar as he made the magician slump back down onto his chair. The magician in the seat immediately adjacent sprang up and cast his affirmative vote, apparently to insure that Fulmbar would have no change of heart. In a moment the vote was finished, once again a seven to seven tie.

"Well, well," Beliac chuckled. "It appears, master Lectonil, that we are back to more individual sessions of persuasion. I suggest that you not call the council to session unless you are more sure that a productive decision will result. Until then, it seems our time will be better spent on research, instruction, and meetings at the usual hours. I wish, however, that you remain a moment, master Fulmbar, so that I may thank you for your enlightened change of heart."

With no further words, the magicians rose and filed to the exit in the center of the room. Lectonil left last, glaring at his opponent and frowning at the placid figure of Fulmbar at his side.

"And now, neophyte," Beliac said, "we must secure master Fulmbar away out of the reaches of Lectonil until I can devise a means of persuading yet another vote."

"And once we have done that," Alodar said, "then might we discuss the matter of the reward for the service I have provided you?"

Beliac eyed Alodar coldly. "I think that to continue living would be reward enough for your impertinence," he said.

Alodar opened the outer door to the neophyte tower and felt the refreshing coolness of the evening air. Marching Fulmbar slowly to Beliac's quarters had taken a good hour. Releasing Duncan in his patron's custody and then arguing with the magician had consumed another, though for his own part, Alodar did not feel anxious to press his case. He had learned more than he had hoped from his exploit and saw no point in trying to pry out more.

After he was dismissed from Beliac's presence, Alodar had returned to his lodging and napped into nightfall to melt away the tensions of the afternoon. Now refreshed, he walked slowly along the esplanade. Beliac had bought only a little time with the stratagem, he mused, and sooner or later must own up to what was done to another magician of the Guild. He would be busy enough not to make good any threats for the immediate future. The problem rather was how to gain access to the contents of the library, knowing now what the security measures were.

As Alodar passed the house of the exotic, a sudden flicker of movement caught his eye; as he turned, he heard the crack of glass under a heavy tread. He paused for a second. Then a woman's high scream of terror filled the air. Instinctively, Alodar sprang for the entrance, his brown robe flowing behind.

With a sudden shove, he rocked the huge double doors back on their hinges. The long corridor which transversed the ground floor ran before him, and slowly stomping away from him down the passageway was a huge, green-scaled dragon.

174

A second scream echoed down the corridor, and Alodar saw, beyond the wyvern's shifting back, the golden curls of Cynthia the initiate. She stood transfixed at the hallway's end, back and palms outstretched against the unyielding wall, looking with terror at the beast which lumbered towards her.

"Hold your courage," Alodar shouted through a throat still sore from the potion and broke into a run after the two-legged dragon. He reached quickly down to his side for a sword that was not there. "Curse these robes," he muttered as he ran.

In an instant he was up to the giant tail that gently swished back and forth with each step. Having no other weapon, he stomped the heel of his boot down upon the rigid spine of scales. The wyvern did not react but continued his steady plodding gait. Alodar steadied himself against a wall and then leapt with both feet upon his target. This time the tail twitched spasmodically, knocking him to the ground into a scatter of broken glass.

Alodar quickly scrambled up and dusted his hands against his robe, ignoring the blood which began to ooze out of many small cuts. He hastily looked about and saw that all of the glass partitions into the various cages had been broken. Here and there, small creatures scurried in the wreckage.

In the opening to the left Alodar saw that two jagged daggers of glass still stood in a shattered frame. He lashed out quickly with his boot and snapped one at the base. Fingering it gingerly, he caught up with the advancing dragon and jabbed it with his makeshift weapon. The point skittered along the scales, but Alodar felt sudden pain in his hands as the edges caught and cut his flesh.

Grimacing, he tightened his grip, feeling blood pour out onto his palms and the hurt intensify in its sharpness. The beast was almost upon Cynthia, lowering its head and extending its forked tongue expectantly, when Alodar lunged again, this time with the full force of his body behind the blow.

The tip caught between two scales and the shaft snapped a few inches from the point. Alodar fell forward upon the beast's back, frantically rolling to one side to avoid being impaled on his own point, and clattering to

175

the floor. The wyvern yelped; distracted, it turned to see what annoyed him.

"To the side passage," Alodar shouted, righting himself and gritting his teeth as he placed his free hand against the wall. "Move, I say," he yelled again. In desperation, he flung the remains of the glass in Cynthia's direction.

The initiate instinctively moved to one side to dodge the missile, jarring herself out of her petrification. She quickly ran into one of the arms of the cross corridor, while Alodar scrambled backwards from the head that was turning to examine him. He ducked into one of the cages and looked from side to side for another weapon. To the left, he saw Cynthia peering in at him through another broken window. He was in one of the cages at the corner of the tee, with viewing from two directions.

As the dragon extended its head into the cage, Alodar hopped out to join the initiate, staining her robe deep crimson as he threw his arms about her.

"This way," he yelled as he pushed against Cynthia's stiffening form. "We have to get some distance so we can search for a weapon."

The two began to run down the passageway, and the wyvern withdrew his head from the empty cage and turned around the corner. It saw its quarry sprinting away and ruffled its wings in annoyance, scarping the walls which confined it. It hooted after them and quickened its pace in pursuit.

Alodar felt the air grow warm as the call of the dragon echoed down the passageway. He turned a puzzled glance to Cynthia, who gasped out as they ran, "It is getting angry and firing up. We will not have a tradesman's chance if it gets within three strides."

Alodar turned to see how close the wyvern pursued and was surprised at the way the deliberate lumber had been replaced by a fast rocking pace.

"It is gaining on us," he shouted to Cynthia, pushing her from behind with his bloody hand until she nearly stumbled. "Look there, a staircase to the second level. Perhaps it does not know how to climb them."

Alodar spun Cynthia to the side, grabbing her arm to begin pulling her up the stairs. As they disappeared around the corner, the passageway flashed to the brightness of day as a cloud of flame rolled past, furnace-hot.

They reached a landing half a flight up as the dragon appeared at the foot below. It snaked its head halfway up the well, the raspy and pimpled tongue flicking out a foot more beyond. It roared in anger as it caught sight of its prey disappearing. As the echo trailed off, another fireball coursed up the stairs.

The shock of the heat flashed memories of the Fumus Mountains through Alodar's mind, and Cynthia shrieked from the blistering bath. The sphere of flame crashed against the landing wall and burst into smaller globes, which ricocheted towards them.

"Your robe, pull in your robe," Alodar shouted as the balls of fire danced by. One caught Cynthia's hem. Almost instantly, the garment burst in a new shower of incandescence.

Alodar looked over the railing and saw the wyvern slip and stumble as it tried to place one of its broad feet on the narrow risers. It unfurled its wings and banged against the walls; with one powerful downstroke, it levitated a few feet off the ground and onto the third step.

Alodar turned back to Cynthia, who stood on the floor above, frantically beating her hands against the ends of the robe which encircled her in flames. He bounded up and knocked her to the ground, sending her rolling down a hallway more spacious than the ones below. The flames sputtered for a moment; but as soon as she stopped, they sprang to life again. He ran to her. Ignoring the throbbing in his hands, he grabbed her disintegrating hem. With a mighty spasm, he yanked his arms apart, splitting the robe from bottom to top, and flung it away from them.

The wyvern careened to the first landing and Alodar pulled Cynthia to her feet, as naked as the day of the stadium ritual. As they resumed their flight, Alodar caught sight of a familiar glowing disk in the wall on the left.

"What is that?" he shouted, pointing as they ran.

"The initiate viewing room," Cynthia responded as she saw the small circle.

Alodar thought back to his previous encounter with such a disk. In a flash, their method of escape struck him. The timing would have to be perfect, but they had no other choice. "Then into it," he directed. "Let us find our safety there."

Cynthia responded to the command and firmly pushed the small button. The door smoothly parted and the two ran into a small anteroom that appeared to open onto a spacious balcony. Alodar took three rapid steps into the middle of the chamber. He stopped and faced the door through which they had entered.

"Let us go to the balcony and beyond." Cynthia tugged at his arm in a wave of fresh panic. "The wyvern will catch up with us in a moment."

As she spoke, the dragon glided up to the door and furled its wings, hitting the floor with a dull thud. Alodar grabbed Cynthia by the hand; with a whipping motion, he propelled her stumbling through the door to the balcony. He looked back into the hallway at the approaching beast. He waited an instant longer and then ran after Cynthia, but took only two more steps before a brace of bells began sounding in alarm.

In an instant, iron bars crashed to the floor ahead, cutting off his escape, and he turned to face the beast. The only other exit was blocked by the bulk of the wyvern, folding up its wings and stooping to enter. But as it extended its neck into the room, long tongue flicking expectantly, the second barrier began to fall into place from the jamb of the door. The heavy iron bars hit the floor with a thud and the lowermost crossbrace caught the dragon directly behind the head, driving it to the ground.

The wyvern let out a cry of anger and a large belch of fire that sent Alodar springing to the wall. With a frantic tug, the beast tried withdrawing its head out into the passageway, but the expanse of skull behind the large, opalescent eyes cracked against the stout iron bar.

Alodar scrambled to his feet and cautiously felt his way around the periphery of the room towards the dragon. The wyvern eyed his motion in anger and, between spasmodic struggles against its trap, sent volleys of fire into the chamber to consume its adversary.

In a moment Alodar was at the wall which held the exterior doorway and out of the angle of fire from the wyvern. He quickly dismantled a rod from which a small decorative tapestry hung and advanced on the beast from the side. His hands pained him enormously and he felt

178

giddy from the loss of blood, but he performed his task with determination.

Alodar leaned wearily against the wall with the bloody, brain-spattered bar hanging limply in his hand. How many blows it had taken he could not recall, but only a pulp of bone and flesh remained of the wyvern's head, and the great body lay silent, to flame no more.

The portcullis that led to the balcony raised back into place, and Cynthia cautiously came into the room.

Alodar motioned her to him. "It is all over," he said. "All that remains is to repair our wounds and forget what has happened." He reached down, grabbed the small tapestry, and flung it about her shoulders. "Come to my cubicle," he said. "I have a small amount of sweetbalm that will help those burns of yours."

Cynthia nodded her assent and the two found their way out of the building without looking back.

In an hour, Alodar was arching his back and smiling with contentment. The sweetbalm had anesthetized his pain, and the wine from the larder blurred the recent memories and the horror of what might have been. Cynthia lounged easily in the chair beside him, sipping from her glass and staring deeply at Alodar over the rim.

"Why do you think such vandalism occurred?" he said.

"For certain, I cannot tell," she responded. "I know however that the initiates loyal to Beliac were abuzz with activity. I suspect they feared that if Lectonil could almost change Fulmbar's vote, he might succeed with others. They struck to discredit him as best they could on such short notice. The maintenance of the wyverns has been a source of contention between the groups for many years. One running loose and slaughtering a few unlucky passers-by certainly would harm Lectonil's position."

Cynthia shuddered and drew the folds of one of Alodar's brown robes tighter about her.

"A most complete speculation," he said. "What points you to it?"

"I was not in the house by chance, but by direction of one of Beliac's acolytes. I had ignored his advances some years back and thought no more of the matter, but apparently he did not see it the same. Had you not come along when you did, I fear that double purpose would have been served by the mayhem."

"Then do you think to embrace Lectonil's position and seek protection from him? It seems to me that the entire Guild soon will be divided into the two camps."

"And doing increased violence to one another," Cynthia said. "A year ago they were content with finding flaws in the other's conjectures and theorems, but I think that day will not return. As for Lectonil, what he could offer is most limited. Few of the acolytes and initiates harken to his standard. Even the likes of Duncan casts his fortune elsewhere. For myself, I intend to leave the Guild on the morrow and wait in the village until it is settled. There is none here to whom I am attached. None that could protect me well. None that I can in truth call a man."

Cynthia lowered her glass and extended her hand to rub against Alodar's as she had done in the tavern. "None save one." She smiled and moved towards him. Alodar set down his wine and looked up as she stood before him. With a shrug, she dropped his robe from her shoulders and beckoned him to rise to meet her.

Instinctively he rose, pulse quickening. Again he tried to focus on Vendora, compare her beauty and position to Cynthia's and find her the winner. But Vendora was miles and months away. He sighed and all images vanished from his mind.

Alodar woke when the first rays of dawn filtered through the blinds into the room. Cynthia breathed in a deep slumber beside him, still in the euphoria of the sweetbalm. Idly, he fingered her curls which lay on the pillow beside his head.

What course now? Cynthia was enough woman for any man, beautiful and full-figured, intelligent, and a self-confident initiate in the magical arts. He had saved her life, and the little skill in arms he possessed stood to her in exciting contrast to the scholarly attitudes of her peers. He could seek out Periac, resume his trade in thaumaturgy, or better yet combine it with alchemy and provide services most unique. And would such a life be so bad? Could the secret of the spheres really mean more than that?

Alodar sighed and shook his head. No, he would soon tire of thaumaturgy, and with alchemy it would only take longer. At least his quest offered a definite goal and excitement. Alodar the hero, Alodar the savior of the fair lady!

His mind again of single purpose, Alodar quietly began to pace the room. His visit to the library with Beliac had shown him how he could enter. The problem that remained was that of moving freely inside without triggering the watchbells.

He puzzled over the ease with which the initiates and their superiors passed through the protected hallways, while he was instantly recognized as an outsider. They made no special motions, nor did they touch marked panels in the wall. In fact, Cynthia without a stitch was easily hurled past a barrier while he was trapped behind.

If it was nothing of action or what one carried, what indeed set the magic user as different from the rest of the workers of the Guild? Alodar stopped and pondered a few moments more. Only one thing marked the initiates, he realized in a flash of excitement—the small scar on the back of the wrist. Alodar walked to the bedside and grasped Cynthia's hand. He gingerly fingered the pad of flesh that indicated her station. The tissue was thick and told him nothing, but he knew what he must do.

He woke her gently and explained his request. She gave her consent. "If our paths are not to intertwine," she said, "then it is my parting gift for the brave warrior." She looked deeply at Alodar and smiled. "Perhaps in the village below I can find another."

A small dab of sweetbalm at the nostrils returned her to slumber, and Alodar grasped her hand firmly in his left while he opened his small knife with his right. Carefully, he began to cut around the base of the scar. Although tiny rivulets of blood obscured his vision, he heard the satisfying scrape of metal on metal.

He continued to cut for a full half circle; then with a pair of tweezers, he pulled the secret from its hiding place. Alodar wiped the object clean and stared at a small, unadorned disk of gold. The ritual of the branding was merely a ruse so that the initiates might not even know how they moved past the barriers so easily. The

181

thin disk looked innocuous enough, but it would be his safe passage on the floor of the library.

He dabbed sweetbalm onto the small wound he had made and saw it instantly close. If Cynthia went directly to the village as she planned, then the loss of the disk might go undetected until Alodar was long removed from the Guild and back on the road to Ambrosia. He let her arm fall and then hastily finished the rest of the preparations for his entry.

CHAPTER TWELVE

The Improvised Ritual

ALODAR stretched to tiptoe in the darkness and groped with both hands against the sloping library walls. His right brushed against one of the decorative nodules that randomly dotted the sides. He put his foot onto the projection at knee level and pulled himself up. He was off and climbing.

With his left hand, he reached out for another purchase and lifted himself three feet more. His feet wobbled against the narrow projections, and his hands felt slippery from the effort to scale the steep incline. Upwards he struggled, ten feet and then another ten, switching back and forth laterally across the face of the slope as he climbed.

After thirty feet, he stopped and cautiously adjusted the straps that held the pack to his back. The next handhold was only a foot above his head but far to his left, outside of comfortable reach. Alodar extended his hand, rocking all of his weight onto his left foot and stretching as far as he dared, but a good nine inches separated him from the grip. He looked back down to the esplanade and felt the first twinge of the instinctive reaction to his height.

He frowned tightly and shut his view of the hard cobblestones out of his mind. Moving his right hand close to his body for additional thrust, he sprang upwards and outwards towards the grip.

The momentum of his jump carried him past the target, and his hand closed on empty air. As he began to slide downwards, he lashed out again, catching the nodule as it seemed to rush upwards into his hand. He felt the tug of his body loosen his fingers, not yet set in their tenuous grip, and he reached about with his feet frantically for the perch they had just left. His right foot felt resistance and he thrust savagely against it to stop the downward motion.

In an instant, Alodar's hand grip was secure, but he was diagonally stretched across the face of the pyramid, holding on with opposite arm and leg fully extended. Slowly he worked his right arm upwards until he could clasp his hands together. Then, abandoning his foothold and pulling so that his arms trembled, he raised his head until the nodule he gripped was at eye level. Carefully, he extended his leg outwards to the left and then smiled with satisfaction when he felt another gemstone beneath his heel.

Other nodules were randomly scattered nearby; in a few minutes, Alodar was resting for a second time, but some ten feet higher than before. Only thirty feet remained until the top, and the grips seemed closer spaced than below. Exercising increased caution as he moved higher, he gained the level of the apex in another half hour.

Alodar peered in through the square opening and saw the back of a heavy tapestry blocking out the wind and starlight. He reached into his pack and withdrew the small disk of metal that he had received from Cynthia and clasped it firmly in his left hand. No grillwork or shutters barred his entrance. Pushing his arm in front, he squirmed through the window and thrust the curtain aside.

He dropped to the floor silently and stood frozen for a moment more. No bells sounded in alarm at his presence. Alodar waited a full minute and then another. Nothing stirred and only his own breathing broke the absolute quiet. Cautiously he lit a small candle and looked about in the flickering light. The room was as he had seen it before, cramped and unfurnished except for the U-shaped table that crowded about its periphery.

Alodar slowly moved to the portal in the floor that led to the library proper, expecting at each step to trigger the watchbells. He grasped the latch and pulled the door open, staring into the blackness below.

The candlelight showed the first rungs of the staircase that spiraled downwards to the floor, but Alodar did not place his foot on the first tempting step. The magicians let the lower orders into the library and then left them unattended. Something kept them from using the stairway. Indeed, Beliac had pressed his ring against the banister before they had started their climb.

Uncoiling the rope from his pack, he secured it to one of the legs of the massive table and let the other end fly downward into the darkness. He grasped the rope awkwardly, not trusting to remove the golden disk from his palm. Slowly, he let himself down hand over hand in the midst of the spiral, gradually loosing his sense of height in the blackness. Methodically, he descended a foot at a time, unmindful of how far he had traveled and how far yet to go.

His reverie was suddenly broken by the sharp contact of solid stone beneath his feet. He released his grasp of the rope and stood upright in exultation. He had gained the library floor.

Alodar relit the candle and let his eyes grow accustomed to its meager light. All about the four walls books, scrolls, and manuscripts were neatly stacked, beckoning with the secrets of the magicians. He quickly scanned the vast arrays of knowledge and saw in the north corner scrolls tossed in a disarray uncharacteristic of the order of the rest. He walked over to the pile and lifted the first one from the heap.

"Helices and spirals, tier four; Heptagons, tier three; Hexagonal symmetries and tiles, tier fourteen," he read aloud softly. "The index, precisely what I need."

He shuffled through the coiled manuscripts until he found the one that alluded to his metal spheres. "Tier seven," he mumbled and counted off the cases from where he stood. Several minutes later, after carefully scrutinizing titles in the dimness, he found what he sought and wrenched the book from its place on the shelf.

Cracking it in the middle, he held the exposed pages to the light and mouthed what he read.

"The two spheres of Dandelin are tangent to the ellipse at points one and two respectively and touch the cone along parallel circles. If we join the point of presence to the points of tangency and also the line connecting with the vertex, these lines will all lie entirely on the surface of the cone."

Alodar snapped the book shut, set it back in the rack, and exhaled a deep sigh. The secret of the spheres would not be a single night's work, he reasoned sadly. Time would have to be spent with some fundamentals before he could even begin to understand what he needed to know. The general education that took an initiate through acolyte to magician would not be necessary; he could focus on only those things necessary. Still, the walls of the library would have to be scaled many times before he was through with his task.

Moving with considerably less haste back to the index tier, Alodar began to search for the first reference text of the beginning initiate.

"And Cynthia disappeared without a trace as well," Hypeton babbled on. "She has been missing nearly a month, yet both sides avow no knowledge of her, but accuse instead the other of misdeed. The tension virtually pulls the Guild asunder."

Alodar nodded sleepily in reply and pulled closed his entrance curtain as the other neophyte departed. He worked with dedicated effort by day so no attention would be drawn to him, but even more diligently at night as he delved into the secret of the spheres. The ascent was by now a mere routine and most of the evening could be spent in study. Still, the intensity with which he concentrated and the strain of anticipated discovery took their toll as surely as the labors of the day. At least tonight would be the last, Alodar thought slowly, his weariness suppressing even the excitement of the occasion. He knew enough now about this one facet of magic to start the ritual that would release the power of the spheres. He shouldered his pack and looked about the cubicle. The paraphernalia for the evening and everything that he would need for a hasty journey were packed and ready.

If all went well, the sun would find him free of the Guild and on the road north back to Ambrosia.

He crossed the courtyard quickly and soon was at the base of the library, grasping for his first handhold with a grip made familiar from much practice. In scarcely ten minutes he was at the top and through the curtains into the deserted council chamber.

Alodar lit his small candle as before, but this time did not move to the doorway in the center of the floor. Instead he carefully spread a silken scarf along the surface of the table and removed from his pack the small box which contained his treasure. He opened the lid and felt immediately the aura of power that coursed up from his fingertips to permeate his entire body.

He removed the scraps of parchment that contained his notes from the previous evenings of study. Everything he needed should be here; but if not, he could descend to the floor below and consult with the texts.

He scanned the notes twice quickly and then began the ritual. Placing copper rings on each of his fingers, he grasped a small incense coffer with his left hand and immersed it in the flame of his candle with his right. The perfume began to well upwards into the small confines of the room; in a minute, it was almost overpowering with its sweetness.

Alodar stood immobile as the smell penetrated his nostrils and filled his lungs. Concentrating not to cough, he counted heartbeats to one hundred thirty-seven and then struck a small triangle hung from a tiny frame with the copper ring on his index finger. The chime sounded shrilly and, rather than dying away, rang in resonance with the structure of the ritual as it began to take shape.

Alodar listened only half attentively as he pondered the step to perform next. But as he thought, he gradually grew aware of a slight tingling that crept along the base of his scalp. His skin prickled as if scraped by a dull razor and a slight twitch tugged at his left eye. At first it was only an annoyance to be shut out of his concentration, but the feeling grew in intensity and began to move over his head and down his neck to the rest of his body. He shuddered involuntarily and felt a chill in his arms and legs. The triangle still hummed, but rather than diminishing as it should, the tone deepened and grew in power. The heavy table began to hum, and echoes bounced back and forth off the sloping walls. Alodar raised his hands to his ears as the sound suddenly increased to deafening proportions and the small band of metal grew red hot from the force with which it vibrated through the air.

Something was obviously wrong. Alodar thought slowly, his mind dimmed by the fury of the noise. Some other ritual was being enacted and interfering with his magic here.

Before he could think more, the doorway in the floor suddenly flew open, bathing the chamber with light from the library below.

Lectonil leaped up into the council room, and two other magicians panted after. "As I suspected," he said, "Beliac's deceit with the Guild is most complete. Despite his protests, he traffics our secrets even to the neophytes who would support him.

"Bring them forward," he motioned to the black-robed followers. "Let Beliac bite on the fact that it is the ritual of presence that has led us to the last of his crew of traitors."

The shrieking stopped and Alodar felt his thoughts clear in a rush. He immediately dropped the triangle to the floor with a clatter and reached to scoop up his spheres.

"Hold, neophyte, it is enough," Lectonil commanded and clapped his gloved hands together. A bolt of jagged yellow jumped from his palms and shot towards Alodar with a blinding flash. Before Alodar could respond, he felt his arms thrust apart and backwards and his whole body suddenly lifted and slammed into the wall. As a sharp explosive report echoed around the small chamber, his breath rushed out and his vision clouded from the force of the blow.

"Trifle not with a master magician, neophyte." Lectonil glared at him. "Especially one with the gloves of thunder."

Alodar opened his mouth to speak; but before he could, Beliac's voice rumbled forth from the stairway.

"And to what purpose do you rouse me from my studies, Lectonil?" he asked. "The protocols must be observed, I insist. There is no basis for council meeting without the notice of two full days to bring all rituals in progress to a satisfactory halt. Your prattle about the danger to the remaining wyvern can surely wait a fortnight."

"It is for a far more serious matter than the safety of a dragon that we are here, Beliac," Lectonil replied. "We convene tonight to judge the most serious charge of treason. Look, we have even caught your neophyte in the practice of ritual. Such disregard for the traditions cannot be condoned, regardless of the ends you think they serve."

Beliac looked across the room to where Alodar lay and then stared at the two spheres still sitting in the small box on the table. "I know not in what foul practice this neophyte engages," he said, "but it is without my council or direction. I have had no discourse with him since he was in this chamber over a month ago. I say as you that he should be punished for his deeds. Bring forth the mirror of inversion and let us be done with it. His crime is none of mine."

"Ah, but it is, Beliac," Lectonil persisted. "I would not have acted so precipitously this night had I not first solved the riddle of that last meeting when your follower was present. Bring in the other one and let us confront them," he said turning to the doorway.

Duncan was abruptly pushed into the chamber, a look of bewilderment on his face. Following him came another black-robed magician.

"Fulmbar," Beliac said in surprise as his peer entered.

"Yes, Beliac," the magician replied with hate dripping from his voice. "With the aid of Lectonil's acolytes, I am free at last of your bondage of this past month. And I have told them all of your conduct the last time I sat in this chamber. It is true I would have voted against you that day, but in the past I supported you as the issue merited. And had you stood by the honor of the master, I might have followed your cause yet again. But your deeds with the neophyte have cleared my indecision and firmed my resolve. I anxiously await the council vote on the form of your de-elevation."

"But wait," Beliac interrupted, with a shade of panic beginning to tinge his voice. "I acted in the desperation of the moment and no ritual magic was used in what I did. A minor transgression worthy of small censure at the most."

"Enough of the pleading, Beliac." Lectonil waved the protest aside as the rest of the magicians began to file in. "The case against you is tight. Your neophyte was caught in mid-ritual, working your will. Tell us now what you had planned, else your punishment will be all the harder."

"But . . ." Beliac's eyes rapidly searched the faces of his peers for signs of sympathy. "I know nothing of the dabbling in which this neophyte engages."

"Very well, then," Lectonil said. "Perhaps the neophyte himself will not be so guarded. What do you say about your deed tonight?"

"I work with the pair of spheres before you," Alodar answered, as he slowly rose to his feet. "The one is smooth and the other circumscribed by one great circle."

The assembled magicians followed Alodar's extended hand to the table. "Could they be spheres of protection?" one of them gasped. "Most rare and valuable objects indeed. The work of an eon before they were truly formed and ready."

"By the laws, Beliac, this is most undisciplined! The uninitiated should not traffic with such potencies. He might start one to activate before he knows what he is doing."

"As for example, by striking a triangle of discord," Alodar said, holding out the small instrument he had used minutes before.

Lectonil's mouth dropped when he saw what was in Alodar's hand. He reached out to touch the first sphere and then quickly withdrew with an involuntary yelp.

"They have started," he said, eyes suddenly wide. "Quickly man, how long have you been at this? We must know how much time remains."

Alodar frowned in puzzlement over the magician's sudden concern. He reviewed the steps that remained and the significance of each.

"But of course," he said aloud at last. "The power within the spheres has already been disturbed from their mold. Either we run the spells to completion or they will explode of their own volition with cataclysmic force."

Several of the magicians broke their ranks behind Beliac and began to jostle one another for position in the doorway.

Lectonil retreated a step in hesitation and then called after the fleeing members of the guild.

"Wait," he said shakily. "We must stay and resolve what to do. We cannot abandon the spheres. Their release will damage our chambers beyond repair and perhaps our heritage below as well. The ritual must be worked to completion."

"Then stay and work it yourself," the magician closest to the door yelled out. "It is you who burns most with the fire to confront Beliac with his deeds."

Lectonil backed another step from the table, but then stopped.

"Hold your positions," he commanded with more composure. "We can handle the situation with but little danger to ourselves. Bring forward the acolyte. He should know enough to complete what must be done."

Two of Lectonil's followers thrust Duncan forward to face the master.

Lectonil's face parted in a cruel smile. "So you wish the status of the magician, do you, Duncan?" he asked. "Then you can show your proficiency to us by completing the ritual of Cantor on these spheres. Surely you have memorized what is to be done."

Duncan's eyes darted to Beliac and back to Lectonil. "I have studied it, master," he said. "But the events of this evening jumble my thoughts. I recall it not. I have had no time to prepare. Please, we know not how much time is left; let us flee."

"Then for you it will be the mirror," Lectonil cut him short. "Unless you search your memory and are successful in the recall."

"But I cannot," Duncan protested falling to his knees in frantic supplication.

"Each minute you waste is one less to complete what is to be done," Lectonil said harshly. "Be about it, man, or you doom yourself surely."

Duncan eyed the pack leaning next to where Alodar stood. With trembling hands, he opened the top flap and began to extract the necessary equipment.

"And the time?" Lectonil addressed Alodar again. "How long ago did you start?"

Alodar drew his tongue across a mouth suddenly dry as the impact of the situation sank in. "A full five minutes," he said. "At least that much before the wailing stopped me from going further."

"Quickly, the glasses." Lectonil gestured and one of the magicians opened a drawer in the table. "That leaves twenty remaining." He watched as a sandclock of the appropriate size was set beside Duncan.

"Now we proceed with caution as follows," Lectonil said "Repair to our chambers until the crisis is past. Guard Beliac until the issue here is resolved. I will remain on the stairwell, watching these two as they proceed. If all goes well, you can rejoin me here. If I judge that insufficient time remains, I will incapacitate them with the gloves of thunder and retreat out of harm's way before the explosion tears the apex asunder. In either case, we will deal with Beliac's treason then."

The magicians mumbled their acquiescence and began to file out of the chamber. Alodar's eyes jumped from Lectonil to Beliac and back, hoping to see an opportunity. Beliac also watched the magicians file out. Suddenly, when four were already on the stair, he bolted forward and shouldered his way in front of those remaining.

"Magicians loyal to the new ways, follow me," he shouted. "We are outnumbered, but they will feel our sting before we are done."

Lectonil turned to the startled black robes who remained. "After them," he shouted. "Subdue them and repair to the chambers as planned."

The magicians pounded down the stairs after the ones who fled. Lectonil looked at Duncan and Alodar and then backed down the stairs until he stood only waist high in the room. As he took his place, a blue flash reflected upwards through the opening, followed by a rolling boom and an anguished scream. In an instant, the walls rocked and vibrated with an answering spasm of subsonic rhythm.

"A gem of blue blindness and the oscillator of life," Lectonil muttered. "It seems that both sides armed themselves well for our confrontation. But no matter, acolyte, tend to your duty."

Another flash burst upwards. Duncan jarred loose from his panic and began to work the magic with the gear from Alodar's pack. With eyes half closed, he rattled off the next steps of the ritual and executed them quickly. The

191

triangle sang again, three beehive hitches were woven together, feet stomped in a complicated rhythm. Alodar watched fascinated as the acolyte, immersed in his recall, jerked his hands faster with each step, blurring them together in his haste.

As Duncan worked, the chamber rocked and rumbled with the attacks and parries that flew about the library below. Lectonil steadied himself in the stairwell and occasionally glanced down the spiral, frowning at the uncertainty of the outcome.

"And that is one," Duncan said explosively. As he spoke, he held out the uninscribed sphere triumphantly in his hand. The sphere was no longer opaque rock, but danced in a rainbow of refracted light that radiated through its interior. In the very center, Alodar saw a tiny and perfect human hand suspended.

"The shielding hand," Lectonil said, mounting again into the chamber. "Here, let me have it while you finish the other."

As Alodar saw Lectonil stretch his right hand forward, he sprang from the chamber wall and over the table into the magician's open arms. The force carried both to the floor. As they fell, Alodar grappled for the old man's hands to force them apart.

"Quickly, Duncan, quickly," he gasped. "Help me subdue him while I pin his arms. Then you can finish the other and we will be away before they return."

The floor rolled with another crash. Duncan hesitated and took one step around the periphery of the table, then paused. His face froze in renewed terror as he caught sight of the sand which yet remained to fall.

"Help me!" Alodar yelled. "There is no time to waste."

Duncan put his hand on the tabletop, but his eyes remained fixed on the falling sand. With a shudder, he suddenly turned and climbed up onto the windowsill from which Alodar had originally entered the room. In an instant he was gone, completed sphere in his pocket, climbing hand over hand down the face of the pyramid.

As Duncan fled, Alodar summoned new strength; with a powerful whirl, he spun Lectonil around striking his head with a crack against the floor. The magician remained silent, and Alodar scrambled to his feet.

He shielded his eyes from another flash and steadied

himself from the rumble that followed. Almost half of the sand was gone.

There was still time to run. But if he did his entire quest would have been for nothing. He was no match for Duncan in rattling off the ritual by rote, but somehow he had to perform it on the second sphere.

He climbed back over the table and relit the incense; the ritual was begun. Alodar rang the triangle and this time it quieted at the proper time. Fumbling with his sketchy notes, he slowly began to lay out the twine on the table, covering and looping the strings in a way that would form a knot like a beehive. With the last tuck in place, he pulled the ends tight. The coils shrank into a lopsided triangle.

Steeling himself against the impulses that tried to make his hands shake, he undid the mess and again methodically went through the steps that formed the knot. He pulled the ends and the loops slid shut with beautiful symmetry. Encouraged, he began another and quickly laid a second by the first.

"The three knots define the plane in which the bees move to pollinate," he muttered to distract himself from his pounding heart as he began the third. "Three knots to form the plane to cleave the sphere." He stopped and hesitated. "Such a step makes sense for the first sphere, but what of the second with the fine line already dividing it in two?" Alodar frowned and concentrated on the lore which he had studied the past month. With the line already breaking the symmetry, the three points were redundant; they would lie in the plane already formed. He could proceed as before and the result would still be the immovable hand.

Alodar stopped completely and glanced up at the glass. If he continued, there was probably still enough time to complete the ritual as Duncan had done. A shielding hand in a sphere of protection was a king's ransom indeed. But the second sphere was different and somehow the ritual should be different as well. Perhaps a power far greater would be his if he acted with decision. But his notes would not help. He would have to get the reference from the library floor.

Alodar gauged the sand remaining and jumped over the table a third time. The floor shook and another scream exploded up from the doorway. Four minutes, he thought. If he could be back in four minutes, then he would still have a chance.

He grabbed the balustrades with both hands and bounded downward, six steps at a time. He closed his eyes to slits to block out the bursts of light and ignored the bells which immediately began to chime. Against the brightness, he could just barely see the black robes dancing to and fro among the benches to dodge and launch their magical blows.

In one corner he saw gloves like Lectonil's clap together and a yellow bolt arch out to shatter soundlessly against some invisible barrier in the way. Beyond the transparent wall, two magicians huddled, rapidly working their craft. Elsewhere the black forms grappled arm to arm, ladders of energy streaking outward from the ring of one to strike the gemstone of another, filling the air with a sharp pungency from the discharge.

Alodar reached the floor without a challenge and quickly ran for the tier that contained the reference he needed.

"The neophyte," someone yelled behind him. He dove forward and rolled as the yellow flash lashed out over his head and hit the tier in front, ripping scrolls apart and sending small scraps fluttering to the floor. Alodar crawled to his left and overturned a table as a second bolt followed the first, crashing into the protesting beams he flung in the way. A moment passed and no third shaft came. Inching up on his knees, he saw his attackers facing another direction and warding off the thrust of a dagger which seemed to dart through the air of its own volition.

Alodar scrambled back to the tier and with both arms spread the jumble of manuscripts. His hand closed on a familiar form; and with a feeling of sudden triumph, he grasped the other handle of the scroll he sought.

He bounded to his feet and ran back to the staircase, ducking and dodging the blasts of magic power that came his way. He thrust the scroll into his belt and started up the incline, both hands pulling him forward. He circled around a third of the distance, not pausing to look back but thinking only of the sand that remained in the glass. Suddenly he tripped and lurched forward, shins banging against the steps ahead. He wriggled his feet frantically, but they remained steadfast to the step on which he had just landed.

"The all-holding glue of Deckadin," he heard above him and looked up to see Fulmbar slowly descending in his direction. "It is well I decided to take a vantage point up here," the magician said, "although I did not suspect to have my trap sprung so quickly."

The room rocked with another rumble and the stairs groaned in protest. Alodar's legs wrenched violently with the wave of power but he remained firmly rooted still.

"The sphere!" he yelled. "Release me so that I can finish the ritual, or we are all lost."

"I am a master magician, neophyte," Fulmbar snapped back. "I will not be guiled by a trick so transparent. Lectonil has the matter well in hand, else I would see him bolt down these stairs to signal us to safety. You will hold your position until I summon aid."

Before Alodar could speak again, Fulmbar's eyes suddenly widened and he threw his hands upwards. Alodar instinctively ducked and felt cold metal fly by and brush over his back. He looked forward to see Fulmbar suddenly enmeshed in a net of fine silver wire that clung to him tightly and pulled him down.

"The net of the perfect catch," Fulmbar shrieked as he tore at the mesh, while it propelled him stumbling down the stairwell. The magician lurched against Alodar and dug a hand into his arm as he stumbled past. Alodar was twisted around by the grip, and then pulled backward onto the hard steps as his feet remained firmly locked into place. Fulmbar continued down the stairs and Alodar felt nails cut deep as the grip slipped up his arm. Using his free hand, Alodar tore at the fingers which held him, grasping at a beaded bracelet around the magician's wrist. With a final scream, Fulmbar relinquished his hold and fell with a rush, bounding headfirst on each step as he went. The bracelet snapped in Alodar's fingers; simultaneously his boots popped free.

Another bolt of yellow sizzled up after Alodar as he rose to climb, but he paid it no heed. The building shook with the biggest explosion yet, and he saw a gaping hole torn in the north wall, creating a shower of brick and gleaming red stones.

His lungs heaving, Alodar reached the apex and closed

and locked the heavy door in the floor. He looked quickly at the remaining sphere which now glowed red hot with a line of fiery yellow around it.

He unrolled the scroll and began to scan rapidly down the contents. The entire ritual fitted into a fifth-order magic square, and the tying of knots occupied the center cell. Replacing the three knots by two changed the value from five to nineteen and the square no longer balanced its sums.

Alodar hurried over the bulk of the text which dealt with the shielding hand and its variations. Near the end of the roll he found what he wanted, a footnote on transforming the squares so that they became panmagic, summing the same on all diagonals as well as by row and column. Quickly he worked the equations to produce the four non-equivalent variations. The third was the one he sought; the first two elements were the same as the ritual he had started, but the rest were permuted and the central value was nineteen.

Alodar drew a deep breath and plunged into the ritual. He poured a ring of fine powder around the box containing the sphere, lit it in a flash of smoke, and nodded with satisfaction as the globe began to spin. He clapped his hands together thrice, then slammed the lid of the box shut, wincing from the burn to his fingertips. "Another knot next," he growled and began weaving together four short pieces of colored twine.

The steps followed one another rapidly and Alodar lost track of the time in his concentration to perform each one with precision. He would have no chance to go back and try again if all was not done correctly. Finally he approached the end and beat out the syncopated rhythm that had been third in the standard ritual. He lifted the small flute to his lips and started the slow count to thirty that would signify completion.

Now with only one step remaining, Alodar's eyes darted to the glass, to see the last of the sand begin its fall to the lower chamber. He filled his lungs to blow before the final particles hit but checked himself with the knowledge that it would do no good. The blast of the pure note must come when it was needed, not before.

Sweat broke out on his forehead as he watched the trickle slow and a hole grow in the smooth surface and begin to widen to the edge of the glass. Five counts to go, and the sand continued its relentless fall.

Only a layer seemingly one grain thick coated the neck of the tube; then, with one coordinated wave, it rolled downward through the opening. Four counts remained—three—two. Alodar grimaced from the expected impact of the explosion to come. Then, as the final grains hit the mound beneath, he blew a piercing note that filled the small chamber with sound.

The echoes faded quickly, and Alodar's shoulders slumped with relief in the silence. The ritual was perfectly and precisely completed. The power had been released and transformed. It would now last forever. Alodar waited a minute more in the luxury of the quietness; then he thrust the orb into his pack and scrambled up onto the windowledge. Seeing the product of his labor must wait; escape from the warring factions of the Guild had to come first.

In an instant he was clambering down the wall and across the esplanade, dodging between the initiates and acolytes who stood gaping at the pyramid as it roared and shook from the battle inside. Shortly thereafter, beyond the bounds of the Guild, Alodar looked backward through the protective distortion in the morning sunlight. Even through the shimmering, he could see a huge towering plume of flame where the library had once stood.

On the trail northward beyond the village, Alodar turned from the path and paused to catch his breath. He squinted back the way he had come but saw no dustcloud of pursuit. He reached in his pack for the sphere, now quite cold, and brought it to eye level. The opaque darkness was gone; in its place gleamed a sparkling transparency. But unlike the one Duncan had taken, the center of this sphere held a single eye, lidded closed. It was tiny, like the shielding hand, delicately sculptured with fine detail. Small wrinkles wove across the lid and minute spikelike hairs curled in a precise line along the bottom edge.

Alodar blinked in surprise and quickly spun the sphere around, looking for one of the magical symbols he had expected to see. He shook the orb violently, as if to rearrange the contents, but the closed eye did not change.

Duncan had escaped with a hand of protection, and

what king would not give a treasure to be safe from any mortal blow? At the very least, Alodar had expected a magical object of equal value. But all he had to show for outwitting the safeguards of the Guild was yet another mystery. He was no nearer his rightful heritage or his true place in life than the day before the gates of Iron Fist slammed shut. In bitter disappointment, he thrust the sphere back into his pack and scowled at the ground.

He rested for a few minutes in silence, and then sat erect and looked up the trail. It would return him to Ambrosia. But what did he have to show the queen to turn her head from the others? A mere bauble that could have been fashioned by a jeweler. The eye did not even provide an imitation of magic. Nothing of what he had read in the library told of magical eyes, either closed or staring full open. Such a logo would be more appropriate to charm of the sorcerer than the impersonal ritual of the magician.

Alodar blinked at what he had just thought. He stopped and withdrew the sphere a second time from his pack. He brought it to eye level and stared, frowning into its interior. Surprised at what impulse directed his actions, he sat unmoving, concentrating on the tiny eye. For several minutes nothing happened; then he felt the weak tendrils of strange shadows rising from the depths of his mind.

His eyes blurred out of focus, and a hazy image formed in his thoughts. As if stroked by a gentle feather, fleeting snatches of a distant scene were pushed into place, and he saw a barren landscape, dominated by a single thrusting crag. Stunted and gnarled shrubs fought a strong wind to retain their meager leaves, and the sun hung low in the sky. Alodar felt himself drawn inside the huge monolith, into a tomblike cavern carved from the solid rock. In the very center was a coffin sealed with a thick glass lid.

The landscape was the same as that in the vision when he passed through the curtain. He gasped as the shock of recognition dissolved the scene, like a stone thrown into a reflecting pond. He looked quickly about and saw only the empty trail and the hills which contained the magicians' Guild.

Alodar struggled for several minutes more, but the feeling did not return. He lowered the sphere to his side and focused on the horizon. "Sorcery," he mused, "sorcery. Of the five arts it is the one concerned with expanding the limits of the mind to see in time and space. And what I just experienced can be related to nothing else."

He savored the sensations of the sphere while they were still fresh and then sprang to his feet. The disappointment of only a few moments before washed away in a wave of new enthusiasm. Well, why not? With only a piece of parchment he had plunged into alchemy; with two hunks of rock, he had braved the magicians' Guild. Perhaps in sorcery and with the eye, he would finally find what he sought. The quest would go on.

PART FOUR

The Sorcerer

Chapter Thirteen

Illusions of the Court

"Here, take the bauble back," Cedric rasped as he tossed the ruby in Alodar's direction. "You cannot clear your conscience with a bribe, nor will I accept it in lieu of your toil. When we left Dartilac's more than a season ago, I instructed you to be here in my courtyard the morning after. Instead some thaumaturge appeared nearly a week later with the stone offered as an apology."

"Periac," Alodar said as he glanced around the familiar vine-covered walls of Cedric's field of instruction. Like a warrior being reviewed, he stood before the warmaster while Cedric paced back and forth. "I must seek him out as well when we are finished. Does he still room at the inn where I saw him last?"

"I have not kept a record of your appointments." Cedric frowned at the interruption. "But for a fact, he is in Ambrosia no longer. Two days ago he saw me again, asking if I had news of you. Then he departed for the north. 'The milk has soured,' he said. 'The people in the capital have become panicked into hoarding their gold, rather than spending it on the likes of my craft.' Panicked indeed! The city is like a bubble of marsh gas, awaiting a spark. Vendora holds a royal ball tonight to foster the image of nonchalance. And her visit to Arcadia is broadcast to be only a formality of state, but everyone knows she sails tomorrow in desperate search for aid."

"Tomorrow," Alodar said. "But why must she go at all? And what of her court? Does sorcerer Kelric follow her as well?"

"It is as she feared," Cedric answered. "The kingdoms to the south have ceased their bickering long enough to coalesce their armies into one. This morning they have crossed the border, so the sorcerers say; nothing stands between them and Ambrosia. And no mere ambassador can she send across the sea to plead her cause. King Elsinor remembers all too well how he personally had to beg on bended knee for aid in suppressing a rebellion of his own. He expects the fair lady and no one less to argue for the return of the favor. As for Kelric, I imagine he sails with the rest. The barge is big enough for half her household, although not as seaworthy as many a smaller craft."

"Then I must seek him quickly," Alodar said, "before it is too late."

Cedric stopped and looked up and down Alodar's rough clothing, wrinkled and dirty after his journey from the south. "With your appearance and unpolished manner, you will fare no better than I," he said. "It is time for a man to be measured by what he can do, but they cling still to the trappings of blind tradition."

Alodar opened his mouth to reply but Cedric cut him short. "Too old," he spat. "They said I was too old for command. Why even now, I am worth three of their young sons, wet-eared boys who have been no more than nicked by cold steel." He crashed his fist into an open palm. "It was not my age, but that I still refuse to play by their rules. What difference does it make if it is Feston or Basil that I would follow, so long as my sword swings swift and true? But since I would not declare, neither side will have me. And so one less arm is raised in Procolon's cause."

"Lady Aeriel would know your worth," Alodar said. "I am sure she puts the true interests of the queen above the favor seeking."

"I have not dealt with her directly," Cedric replied. "But if she is a member of the court, then she will be no different."

"You speak with contempt of those who prejudge by pattern and rote," Alodar said. "I would not think you would so measure the lady. In any event, if the queen sails tomorrow, and Kelric with her, it is to Aeriel that I will appeal for a berth."

Cedric did not reply but again looked up and down Alodar's shabby clothing.

Alodar followed his gaze and then nodded. "I agree

203

that I must know something of the ways of the court. It is why I am here. You taught me well at Dartilac's. With a little more instruction, I am sure I will pass through the palace hallways like the rest. And if you will not accept the ruby for payment, then all I can offer is the high opinion of the teacher which is generated by the deeds of the well-taught pupil."

Cedric's eyes narrowed and he studied Alodar for a long time in silence. "It is true that you do not seek the position of a commander," he said at last. "Perhaps this lady can get you placed in a lowly group such as Quantos' marines. Some position that is not significant enough to require commitment to either side."

Cedric resumed his pacing, twisting his moustache into sharpness and looking over Alodar's head to the walls beyond. "I had hoped to wait until you were fully trained," he muttered after a moment, "but the events force it to be now." He shrugged, slapped his hip with decision, and then motioned to the bench nearby. "Come, Alodar, there is a matter of much importance of which we must speak."

They sat down facing one another and Cedric placed his hand on Alodar's shoulder. "I admit to some truth in what they say. On cold mornings my knees are stiff and my eyes no longer follow the tip of the fastest blades. I am still very much the master, but I know that someday I must pass my heritage on to another."

Cedric stopped and gently rocked Alodar back and forth. "You will never become a great warrior," he said. "With more training you will grow into someone not to be dismissed lightly. But you are too small and slow to hack your way through a screaming hoard or stand toe to toe with a thick-muscled giant. No matter how hard you try, I do not see you someday beating your chest in triumph on the top of a pile of bloodied foes."

Alodar's lips parted but Cedric raised his other hand for silence. "But you have spirit. Despite the meager abilities at your command, you track your goals like a hero from the sagas. And it is that drive that attracted my attention to you; it is that dedication which commands my respect and motivates me to aid you as I can." Cedric paused and looked deeply into Alodar's eyes. "I see my own burning youth in your quest, Alodar. Even though my joints grow stiff, through your pursuit I live again.

"And so, if by the random factors I am to remain behind when the fair lady chances across the sea, then I choose to send my spirit with you rather than some other dewy-cheeked warrior, no matter how skillful." Cedric unstrapped his sword and placed it across Alodar's knees. "Take this," he commanded, "but remember when it is drawn, it must defend not one reputation but two."

Alodar blinked at Cedric's words and tentatively reached out to touch the hilt in his lap. He looked back into the warmaster's eyes, saw the intensity of the feelings, and then tightened his grip. "I will wear it in honor," he said softly.

Cedric was silent for a moment longer, then slapped Alodar on the arm and sprang up from the bench. "Enough of this chatter," he rasped in his usual manner. "There is little time and much to be done. I will tell you the etiquette of the court, and the ruby will provide what you must wear. Then, if your tongue is quick enough, you can try to convince this lady Aeriel to secure you an appointment with Quantos of the royal marines."

Alodar wriggled his toes in the soft fur that lined his new calfskin boots. He glanced down at his silken tunic and smiled at the subtle pattern of silver thread which ran through the cloth. Around him mingled the nobles of the court, and nothing marked his raiment from theirs. The tailor had been right, he thought, the small ruby was twice again enough to purchase a wardrobe equal to any here.

Alodar looked around the large room and saw everyone crowded into the periphery. The center was clear, and the sheen on the parquet floor reflected brightly the light of the chandeliers overhead. Decorative columns with flowery capitals and fluted shafts were spaced with precision along all four walls; between them, frescos and tapestries blazed with heroic deeds from the sagas. On the far wall next to ceiling-high double doors, a small ensemble of musicians tuned their instruments, adding to the low drone of conversation. The mood was somber; the room resonated with the gentle hum of smoke-sedated bees, rather than the vigor of a swarming hive that one would expect at a royal ball.

Alodar scanned the assemblage for familiar faces from Iron Fist or Cedric's sparring yard and, here and there, he thought he recognized some lordling. The entire titled class within a day's ride of Ambrosia must be here, he thought. It was no wonder that the bribe to the footman to gain entrance had cost as much as the clothes on his back.

The buzzing around him rose slightly, and Alodar looked to the doors that connected the ballroom to the hallway beyond. Without fanfare, a tall, black-headed man entered the room with a military stride, and Alodar recognized him instantly.

"Look, it is lord Feston," someone to Alodar's right stage-whispered to her companion. "He can hardly control the agitation that disfigures his already uncomely face."

"Well enough that he is so discomforted," a second voice responded. "Perhaps he will then acknowledge the existence of other ladies besides the queen."

Alodar shut out the conversation and concentrated on Feston as the man moved about the room, acknowledging the greetings thrown his way. A year ago, Alodar would have been cowed. But today he noticed the way Feston moved his right hand to rest on the hilt of his sword, how he exposed his thigh when he gestured upward and away. His left foot was forward; he would swing from the side, rather than overhead. A contest between them tomorrow might have the same end but it certainly would not be decided by a single thrust.

Feston had not completed a half circuit of the room when a footman dressed as richly as anyone present skipped into the crowd, blowing a light tune on a flute. Behind him, with a dazzling beauty on each arm, came the massive bulk of Basil the apothecary. A gasp rose from the assemblage as he triumphantly advanced through the doorway, covered from head to toe in what appeared to be a robe of woven gold.

"My good company," he boomed across the hall. "What pleasure it gives me to see all of you so splendidly arrayed for the entertainment of our queen." As he spoke, he idly flicked his fingers in a rhythmic pattern, causing a random clicking sound to emanate from his palm. A small stone dropped from his grip in a glittering flash, and the ladies scrambled to retrieve it. In an instant, one held it aloft.

"Keep it, my dear," Basil said. "It is but a small sapphire. Have it set in a ring."

As he spoke, Alodar saw a flash of red hair as several more of the court crowded into the room.

"My lady Aeriel," Basil said, whirling about. "I see another fine setting for one of these stones." With a sudden flick of the wrist, he tossed a second gem in Aeriel's direction and it fell in a smooth arc down the front of her dress. Her cheeks momentarily flushed and the crowd tittered at her discomfort.

Alodar looked at Aeriel and his pulse quickened. He could not help a small smile of pleasant anticipation as he thought how his quest gave him reason to seek her company again.

Heralds at the door blew two stacatto blasts and Alodar jogged his attention back to the entrance. With unrushed dignity, Vendora entered the room in a gown of deepest red. He looked at her cold beauty and exhaled slowly. Vendora took two small steps into the corridor of people that opened for her and then stopped and looked back through the doorway. With a laugh, she motioned forward with her hand, and another figure entered the ballroom. The murmuring increased as Vendora spoke gaily to the assemblage, and Alodar's jaw dropped in disbelief.

"Lord Feston, apothecary Basil, and my distinguished company," Vendora said lightly. "As you well know, I have had much difficulty in choosing a consort between my two suitors. Can you imagine the difficulty in my decision, now that I have not two but three." She laughed again and waved an elaborate flourish. "I present to you," she said, "the distinguished magician of the Cycloid Guild, Duncan, the all-protecting."

From across the room, Alodar shook his head at the news. Feston had profited from his deeds at Iron Fist. Basil from his alchemy; and now even his magic sphere had been used for benefit of another. Although Duncan left the Guild only shortly before Alodar he must have been able to gain immediate access to the queen with the power that now glittered in a small cage of spun gold hanging from his waist.

"Perhaps later," Vendora continued, "Duncan will be so kind as to demonstrate for us the miraculous object he brings to the throne of Procolon. But for the moment, let us forget other depressing matters of state and revel instead in some entertainments."

Vendora moved to a more central position and Feston, Duncan, and Basil jockeyed for position immediately behind. The rest of the crowd crushed together in back of the three suitors and fell silent in anticipation. After a long moment, a robed figure, stooped with age, ambled slowly through the doorway. Alodar's brows rose as he saw the faded eye logos on the frayed robe, startlingly out of place in the finery about it.

Lectonil had been old but had carried his age with dignity, his back straight and his tread sure and firm. In contrast, the figure in front of Alodar shuffled uncertainly forward, dragging one leg behind as he advanced. His fingers were stiffly spread and curled like the talons of a bird, and rheumy eyes squinted from a face that sagged with loose and wrinkled flesh. The head was narrow and long, as if slightly flattened out of shape by a blacksmith's vice. A few long and straggly hairs hung to the shoulders from above the ears, and a slight ridge ran the length of the completely bald crown.

"The logo is the mark of the sorcerer," someone behind Alodar muttered. "What risk the queen takes to expose herself so."

"It is only Kelric, the seer of the court," a second voice answered. "He served Vendora's father and long ago used up his ability to enchant, so they say. He has little more than illusions left, and I wager that is what he performs for us tonight."

Kelric shuffled to the very center of the room and bowed stiffly to the queen. Without preamble, he began to sing a long, melodious song in an unfamiliar tongue. Alodar listened intently; with his trained ear, he tried to pick out words of power from the deception which surrounded them. The chant droned on, and he furrowed his brow in puzzlement as the melody caressed his ears. Far better than any thaumaturge, he thought. Every word seems to have substance and contain real meaning.

Each sound obeyed an intricate logic in following the one that preceded, and Alodar found himself almost dozing with the gentle rhythm that flowed through the room. He began to sense a pattern as verse followed verse in a repeat of what had been said just moments before. Then, as a third repetition coursed through his head, he felt an overwhelming compulsion to look the sorcerer in the eye. As he yielded, his eyes locked instantly on Kelric's, now wild and glowing owl-like in a stare that seemed to bore into his innermost being.

The scene around the old man blurred for an instant and then snapped back into focus, but somehow not so sharply as before. Alodar felt himself idly wondering what was different. Before he could complete the thought, the sorcerer vanished in a column of green flame that rose from the floor and splashed against the ceiling.

Like a fountain, the flickering flames caressed the beams which spanned the room, then arched outwards and fell towards the floor. As each globule neared the ground, it exploded in a small blossom of flame that winked out of sight. Gradually the column changed color, progressing through the rainbow from green to yellow to orange to furnace red. Then, with a sudden rush, the base of the column rose from the floor, crashed against the ceiling, and sent a dazzling cascade of sparks down onto the onlookers. Alodar winced with the expectation of fiery contact, but the globules seemed to melt away as they touched with feathery lightness.

A small ripple of applause broke forth from those around the queen as every spark but the last died away. The surviving point of light grew as it fell, subtly transforming from a bright speck of flame to a tiny opalescent sphere. As it floated downward, it grew fist-sized, then as large as a barrel, and at last enlongated to the shape of a giant egg. The shell touched the floor with a gentle tap, then cracked asunder. From the two ragged halves, a scaly reptilian form suddenly appeared, arching its neck and flicking its forked tongue in the direction of the queen.

The crowd involuntarily gasped as the monster grew in stature, belching fire as it stretched skyward. Alodar stepped backward and reached for Cedric's sword at his side. The wyvern at the guild had been monstrous, but it did not compare with the giant he saw now uncoiling before his eyes. With scales gleaming in the candlelight, it darted its tongue menacingly out across the room, seeming to reach directly for Alodar over the heads of those who stood in between.

Out of the corner of his eye, Alodar saw others flinch as he did and then, when the giant mouth opened and billowed out a ball of flame, the room erupted with screams of alarm.

Alodar threw his arm over his face to ward off the fiery breath and drew his blade chest high to slash at the dancing ribbon of tongue. But the heat and sting did not come, only the soft feathery caress that had accompanied the fireworks before. Looking to the center of the room, he saw the dragon now start to shrink in size, imploding to a small replica of its former self, hardly a foot high. Then, without pause, it began to whirl about, rapidly blurring its features into a shining green disk.

Alodar stared at the vision and he saw soft colors begin to form and undulate about on its surface. The rotation slowed and the hues changed from golds to pinks and reds as they randomly flowed and ebbed in shining patterns. Suddenly the motion stopped, and Alodar blinked at the metamorphosis. The dragon was gone; before him stood a stunning replica of the face of Vendora the queen.

"The starting point," he heard Kelric say. "But for each of you, an image of your own. Look at the beauty of the fair lady and it will transform into the object of your deepest desire."

Alodar felt his lips curve into a smile. Kelric was clever, he thought dimly. For most of the men present, the illusion would not change at all. He concentrated on the golden curls framing the finely chiseled face and tried to taste the feeling of success with his quest. But as he watched, the illusion subtly began to change. The hair shortened and mellowed from gold to amber. The eyes darkened and danced to life. In an instant Alodar saw, not the face of the queen, but a vision of lady Aeriel.

In surprise, Alodar blinked a second time and the image diffused away. The room again was in sharp focus, and Kelric stood huddled in the center as he had before.

A spatter of applause broke out once more from the crowd. "Well done, Kelric," Vendora exclaimed. "Your illusions as always show great creativity and finesse."

The sorcerer bowed with a sad smile; with a fumbling

hand, he grasped at the small bag that Basil tossed to him as he straightened. With head down, he turned and shuffled out the way he had come, the gathering making more room for his passage than had been done for the queen.

Alodar rubbed the side of his face and then shook his head. How real the sorcerer's illusions had been! There was none of the blurriness of a dream, or the known hallucination of a drug, but an experience accepted by all the senses. No wonder the glance of the sorcerer was shunned. The step from illusion to enchantment seemed to be a small one and, once entrapped, one would have no hint that his will was the slave to another.

The musicians struck up a tune, and the lords and ladies maneuvered for position to dance with the queen or her suitors. Alodar hardly noticed the proceedings and shouldered his way past the crowd as it filled the center of the room. As he went through the tall double doors, he saw Kelric's stooped form rounding a corner and he raced after.

"Master Kelric," he called, "a moment for consultation, if you will."

Kelric turned and frowned in irritation. "Were you one of the ladies with the low cut gowns, I might have time to listen. But for a lord's son, you have not enough gold to pay me for whatever you want."

"It is not for illusion or far-seeing," Alodar said as he drew abreast. "I seek edification and instruction and I think I have an object that will interest you greatly." He reached into the pouch at his side and withdrew the transparent sphere.

Kelric's eyebrows raised momentarily when he saw the orb, but he quickly pulled his face back into a harsh and unyielding expression. "It may well be a legendary sorcerer's eye," he said. "And if I were still in my youth, the power it represents would interest me greatly. But my vital force is nearly gone; I can feel how shallow is the reservoir that remains. And I value what days I have left far more than the thrill of thousands marching in sway to my enchantment. No, it is only minor illusion and prophecy of short range in which I will indulge, and then only after the greatest of persuasion. Take this thing and seek out one of the younger fools who choose to practice this accursed craft, one who does not yet understand the price he pays."

"But what of instruction?" Alodar asked. "Your name has become a legend throughout the kingdom. Surely you wish to pass on your mastery to another."

Kelric tipped back his head and laughed. "They ascribe to the sorcerer the most evil of motives," he said. "But even in my most vile moods, I would not think of inflicting my fate onto another." He leveled his head and looked with a penetrating stare into Alodar's eyes. "Now be off and irritate me no longer, or perhaps, after all, I will make the effort for more than a simple illusion."

Alodar remembered the images still fresh in his mind and almost instinctively turned his head and raised his arm across his face. Kelric laughed a second time, turned, and continued his slow shuffle down the passageway.

After a moment, Alodar lowered his head and replaced the sphere in its pouch. He smoothed down the front of his tunic and exhaled deeply. So that was the great Kelric, the master sorcerer of all of Procolon. He shook his head and began to pace slowly down the hallway, hands clasped behind his back. And now what course? Should he seek a sorcerer of less renown? Perhaps someone away from the court, one whose limits had not yet been tested.

Alodar looked down at his side. Such a search would take him away from the fair lady. And he had pledged to seek Aeriel's aid in unsheathing Cedric's sword for the queen's cause. Yes, Aeriel! For both the marines and dealing with Kelric, lady Aeriel would provide the aid.

Alodar slapped the hilt at his side and increased his pace. And there was still time enough to arrange an appointment before the end of the ball.

The guardsman coughed softly as he ushered Alodar into the small, plain chamber, and Aeriel's face brightened with recognition. "Why, what a coincidence! It is Alodar the thaumaturge. And I see by your garb that you ply your craft to much greater profit than when we last met."

Alodar looked intently at Aeriel as she rose to greet him. She clutched an old shawl around her bare shoulders, not seeming to care how out of place it looked, draped over the richness of her ballgown. Her lips curved in a broad smile, but he could see the fatigue that pulled at her eyes as well. Behind her on a simple table, between two teetering piles of parchment, was scattered an array of seals, colored candles, inkstands, and quills.

"My fortune does not extend from journeyman training, my lady," Alodar answered, "but it does provide the means by which I may consult with you for sage advice."

"Advice?" Aeriel asked. "You seemed quite sure of yourself in Iron Fist. Why now would you need my council?"

"The ways of the court are not so straightforward," Alodar said, "especially when they concern the opinions of the queen."

Aeriel stopped and visibly stiffened. "The opinions of the queen," she repeated slowly. "By that do you mean you still quest for the fair lady?"

Alodar saw her change in mood and darted his eyes to the side. He paused a moment, then looked back into her eyes. "So I have done since we parted," he said with difficulty, "although oftentimes my thoughts have . . ." He trailed off and took another breath. "Yes, I still seek for the hand of the fair lady, and your parting words led me to believe that you would not look with disfavor upon such a goal, if it were in the interest of the queen."

Aeriel was silent for a moment and then returned to her seat behind the table. "I encourage any endeavor that truly assists the crown," she said. "And such aid is now sorely needed." She rubbed her eyes and waved her hand at the documents on the table. "Writs for the armory, rum allocations for the crew, promotions and certifications of skill, they all must be decided before we sail. And despite the seriousness of the hour, no one else will take the responsibility, so much do they fear offending one of the suitors by their choice. Many beseech my favor in intercession with the queen, Alodar, but I have little time for such petty intrigues, especially now."

"But it is an audience with Kelric that I seek," Alodar said. "I will gain the favor of the fair lady on merit, not because of some arrangement with the nobles of the land."

"And why then do you desire audience with the sorcerer?" Aeriel asked. "He traffics in the frivolities of the court no more than I."

"Because I bring to the fair lady a gift that surely is the

equal to those offered by the others," Alodar said as he removed the orb from its pouch and held it forward. "I need only such meager instruction as is necessary to activate it properly and I am ready to pledge wholehearted service to the queen. Kelric mentioned the enchanting of thousands. Surely such an ability will be of great value when she has to face the armies of the south."

Aeriel touched the sphere, and her lips pursed in surprise at its coldness. She studied the delicate sculpture of the eye and then looked at Alodar in silence, frowning in thought. After a moment, she reached out tentatively for his arm but then quickly shook her head and withdrew her hand before he could respond.

"Your boldness is no less than I have judged, Alodar." She sighed. "And in the calm light of reason, I see you as worthy a suitor as the others. I have pledged my service to the queen. If you do likewise, then I must aid you as I can. Come, follow me to Kelric's quarters. I can persuade him better than most."

Without waiting for a reply, Aeriel quickly swept through the room and out into the hallway. Alodar followed her through the maze of passageways in the huge palace. Unlike the buildings at the Cycloid Guild, the royal residence was a one-story sprawl, a jumble of wings and annexes added over the centuries as the power of Procolon grew.

Aeriel whirled past guard stations without explanation; after several minutes of bewildering turns, she ducked into the low and open entryway of a softly lit chamber.

He looked about in the dimness, straining to distinguish form from shadow. In a feeble flicker in the center of the room, between two giant columns of smouldering incense, he saw Kelric sitting crosslegged, clad only in a simple loin cloth, with his chin slumped forward on his bony chest. A brazier hung on a tripod, its meager flame providing the only light. Against the far wall, a lady of the court, her hair hanging long in imitation of the queen's, stood tensely erect, watching the scene.

Alodar started to speak, but Aeriel put her finger to her lips as Kelric opened his eyes wide in a glazed stare and sluggishly extended clinched fists. He opened his left hand over a disk suspended above the brazier, dropping a fine sand onto its shiny surface. With his other hand, he struck the shallow bowl sharply, setting up a complex set of vibrations as it swung. Kelric stared at the dance of sand in silence, eyes unblinking and seemingly oblivious to his surroundings.

"I see the camp," he said in a voice as thin as a distant wind. "The fire burns low and the sentry slumps at his post. The one for which you care is not asleep. With his head propped by his elbow on the ground he talks softly to the one who rests next to him."

"What does he say, does he speak of me?" the lady asked. "Is my favor still bound on his arm?"

Kelric's other hand opened and a second load of sand hit the disk. He clanged it again just as the first vibrations began to subside. "My ears hear the voices," he said, "although they are soft and faint." Kelric closed his eyes and was silent for a full minute, swaying his body back and forth with the rhythm of the gently swinging disk.

"It is not only Bandor and the other leaders, I tell you," a voice, deep and youthful, broke frim Kelric's lips as he rocked. "Each commander leads his own troops as if he were possessed as well. They will not ask for quarter so long as one of them remains standing. This siege will far outlast the season."

"Yes, and there are so many imps darting about," a second voice came from the sorcerer. "The talk of the camp has it that the barrier between the worlds has been weakened, and stronger demons can pass through without being called. Do not look even into our simple campfire, I say. Who knows what lurks behind the flame to grab your will as well?"

"But what of me?" the lady interrupted. "What are his thoughts of me?"

Kelric opened his mouth to speak but then fell silent. Gradually the sand stopped its jumping, and his eyelids slowly opened. "It has faded, Umbriel," he said groggily. "Any more would be greater than fair trade for what you have offered." With a trembling hand, Kelric reached for a cup at his side and drained its contents. He shook his head violently from side to side and arched his back. Finally, he struck his face with a series of sharp slaps and grimaced at the shock. "And so a little more is gone," he muttered as he hesitantly got to his feet.

Umbriel saw his slow motions and started towards the

215

doorway. The sorcerer quickly sprang to life and jumped in the way. "And a payment promptly rendered reflects so nicely on the debtor," he said with a toothless smile. "Come forward, my dear, and linger as long as you like."

Umbriel sighed and shut her eyes. She took a single step and then hesitated. She pursed her lips and extended them forward briefly, brushing the sorcerer's cheek.

"That is a kiss one would give to a brother," Kelric grumbled. "Remember, in a fortnight you will wish to see again how fares your heartthrob on the battlefield. And before I perform, you must have a clear account for what you have learned tonight."

"But I found out nothing of what I wanted," Umbriel said. "I heard but a snatch of conversation and then you were done."

"You know that he is safe," Kelric replied. "That alone is worth the price."

Umbriel sighed a second time and took another step forward. Kelric reached out and swept her into his bony arms. He thrust his lips on hers. With surprising strength, he resisted her attempts to push away his chest. After a moment, he released his grip, and she staggered backwards, face flushed and panting deeply. "That is more to my liking," he cackled. "And perhaps in time you will learn to enjoy it as well."

"Never," Umbriel choked. "I was weak with worry because I have not heard. For no other reason would I seek your service or agree to what you demand for it."

"Never is a long time," Kelric said. "And you will come again, I know it." His eyes widened and he stared at the woman. "And perhaps the next time you will not find me so repugnant."

Umbriel shuddered and then bolted for the door. She raced between Aeriel and Alodar and was in the hallway before Kelric's raspy laugh echoed after.

"It is unkind to treat her so, Kelric," Aeriel said. "She has done you no harm."

"Nor has she shown any favor," the sorcerer snapped back. "We had a fair agreement, and she was obligated to hold to her end of it." He waved his arm in irritation. "She is like the rest, choosing to ignore me until the need is great, and then expecting my gracious acceptance of a mind-numbing task for a mere pittance of fee. If she does not show me a little tenderness, then our relation will be governed instead by fear."

Aeriel pulled her lips into a tight line. "The queen is judged by the court she keeps," she said. "There may come a day when shortcomings of your craft outweigh the advantages you provide to the crown."

Kelric laughed again. "You are in fine spirits tonight, Aeriel," he said. He ran his hand across his bare chest and leered at her figure. "But I am most happy that you choose to see me at this hour. It must mean only that you have come to surrender your virtue for the sake of my person only, not for some service that I would provide in trade."

"I come as always on the affairs of the fair lady," Aeriel said. "If you instruct Alodar here in the manner of your craft, then the safety of the queen will be greatly augmented."

Kelric turned to look at Alodar and wrinkled his brow in recognition. "I have dismissed him already, and the matter is closed. Come now, let me see at least some of what lies underneath that silken gown."

"Your talk is far worse than your deed, Kelric," Aeriel said. "My request has royal authority behind it; you cannot dismiss the matter so lightly."

"Then perhaps an illusion for just the three of us? The young man here would be as interested as I in how you might look unclothed."

"You have no basis on which to paint such an image," Aeriel said coldly. "It would not bother me if you did try."

Kelric stomped his foot in frustration and looked around the room for a robe to cover his bony frame. "Oh very well, Aeriel. This meeting will be for business, the same as always, but one of these times I will loose my control and then who can say what might happen?" He opened his eyes wide and stared at Aeriel as he had done at Umbriel, but Aeriel did not turn away.

Kelric sighed in final defeat and turned to some chairs stacked in the corner of the small chamber. As he arranged them for sitting, he continued the conversation over his shoulder. "It is a sorcerer's eye, Aeriel," he said. "Most rare and powerful, I do admit. I have heard of it only from others who long ago used the last of their vital forces in our craft. And they had heard from older ones

217

still. None of us have had the opportunity to see if what is reputed of it can actually be true."

He finished positioning the chairs to his satisfaction and motioned for Aeriel and Alodar to join him in the small circle. "Great enchantments, it is said, come from the holder of the eye. Nearly instantaneous and subtle, like the ones talked of in the sagas. But enchantments I risk no more, my lady. Even a single one would more than deplete what remains of my life force."

"You are far craftier than you lead us to believe," Aeriel said. "You bemoan the loss of your powers and that you must carefully husband what meager resources remain. Yet for a single embrace, you search all the way to the west for a lovesick maiden."

"It is true, nonetheless," Kelric protested. "And the few kisses and squeezes I receive for what remains are far more valuable than whatever pile of jewels the queen could heap upon me."

"You would not have to use the eye," Alodar interrupted. "I am willing to take whatever risk is involved. I want from you only the instruction that will make it possible for me to do so."

"But then, Vendora sails tomorrow across the sea," Kelric said. "There is too little time remaining for me to explain something as potent as this. Any execution must be built upon a firm foundation of well-learned fundamentals."

"With lady Aeriel's help, I can come as well," Alodar suggested. "You can teach me during the voyage."

"Then there is the matter of payment," Kelric said, his face brightening as he looked at Aeriel. "What do you offer me in exchange, my lady?"

"You know the peril which now threatens the queen," Aeriel replied. "And I know as well that, beneath the threats and leers, there is the man who still has loyalty to the crown. Loyalty for providing him with bed, food, and protection, regardless of the howls of the ones he had outraged by his actions. It is not a question of payment, Kelric, but one of duty."

Kelric sighed and lowered his head to his chest. For a long moment the room was silent. "Very well," he said at last. "We will begin instruction when we are out to sea and the routine of the voyage has been estabished."

Aeriel rose and kissed Kelric gently on the forehead. "And your secret is still safe with me." She laughed. "It would spoil your image if anyone knew that a sorcerer's heart was not constructed entirely of stone." She turned to Alodar and extended her hand. "Come," she said, "tell me if it is to Feston or Basil you would rather belong, and I will see that the arrangments are made."

Alodar stood and grasped her hand in his. "To neither. I want no more than to be a member of Quantos' marines."

Aeriel's smile broadened. "Quantos, of course," she said as she looked Alodar in the eye. "It is the right choice for one who is truly worthy."

CHAPTER FOURTEEN

The Power of the Eye

ALODAR steadied himself with a hand on the ship's rail as the deck rolled beneath his feet. The events of the past two days crowded together in a jumble. Along with the marines, sailors, clerks, heralds, and other functionaries of the court, he had been tumbled onto the giant flagship of state that now beat east in the middle of a royal fleet. The details of bunkspace, battlestation, and the protocols of life aboard ship had occupied all of his time, but soon enough he hoped to see the sorcerer and learn the secrets of the eye.

"An ill-tempered decision to be sure," muttered the leather-faced man on Alodar's left, as they leaned against the rail of the poop deck and squinted into the grayness which surrounded them. "A full complement of officers, rowers and marines stood at the ready for the queen's command. But before we embarked, the courtiers descended upon us, adding two to every one on board. And to what effect. Those silk-armed dandies will be of little value if indeed we do stumble across some privateer in this fog. And the galley and bunks are so crowded that we must take turns on deck in this miserable wetness, while others eat and sleep below."

Alodar grunted a reply as he idly ran his hand along the rail and looked up into the rigging. Yesterday the cold east wind had howled, but today, on both of the masts, the lateen sails were furled tightly against their yards, useless in the whisper of wind that barely stirred the fog. Over the side, he watched the lazy rhythm of the oars that maintained their headway. Unlike the sleek wargalleys with their multiple rows of synchronized sweeps, the broad-beamed barge depended primarily on the wind for its motive force. The meager complement of twenty oars to a side was used only in calms such as this or to aid in coming quickly about.

Looking forward, Alodar could barely see the gently heaving forecastle. The bowsprit, some three hundred feet away, was completely hidden by the mist. The main deck ran a full fifty feet beam to beam but was broken into many small areas by the masts, stays, capstans, chests, and hatches which led below. On the poop itself were stowed two longboats for use in shallow water, and a small deckhouse that sheltered the wheel stood near the ladders that descended to midship. All along the superstructure, nothing broke the silence of the calm sea except for the slow creaking groan that coursed down the great ship as each wave rolled under its hull.

"So you are a page to the lady Aeriel," the man continued. "Though I hear that you are also well watched by lord Basil of the bottomless purse."

"Yes, Quantos, that I am." Alodar laughed. "He and his followers at court do not wish me well. Nor, for that matter, does lord Feston—or Duncan, the practitioner in magic. But so long as the queen maintains the ban on confrontation between the factions, I think nothing will come of their desires.'

"So I understand," Quantos said. "The court cleaves itself asunder. The lot of them have no courage to stand on their own merit but seek instead to ingratiate themselves with one of the suitors. Depending on who seems to have the upper hand in the struggle for the fair lady's favor, they shift allegiances like the tide, ripping first

Feston's colors from their sleeves and then Basil's. Why even Duncan has a following, though he has been here less than a week. And look what distortion it brings to our order on deck. Feston's supporters are to man the starboard watch, Basil's the port; Duncan's cluster about the queen below deck. The rest of us spend our idle hours up here out of the way on the poop. Let us hope that the queen gives no new sign of favor. It will take a good day to reassign the stations once again."

"Why do you not speculate with the rest?" Alodar asked.

"I serve the queen, man," Quantos said with a thump of his bow to the deck. "I served her father in many a sea battle before. My men and I are marines for the crown of Procolon. We earn our pay by keenly sighted arrow and sharply swung blade, not by the foppish exchange of wit in the palace."

Several voices about Alodar grunted agreement but suddenly, before more could be said, a high whistle pierced the fog. Alodar turned to listen and heard a heavy splash off the starboard bow. He strained to catch the direction from which the noise came and heard the whine of two more projectiles hurling by.

"Catapults," he shouted as the memory from Iron Fist raced back. "Catapults. We are under attack!"

As he spoke, he saw, breaking through the mist, the flash of banked oars moving in unison and a low-riding hull gliding across the waves.

"A wargalley," Quantos added to the cry, "by the markings, from the south. Somehow it slipped past the rest of the fleet in the fog. And it is on collision course at the beam. Below decks quickly, Grengor! Sound the alarm."

One of the marines left Quantos' side and quickly ran down the ladder to the main deck and then into the hatchway to the levels below. Alodar watched in fascination as the sleek vessel cut the water with graceful ease, a small wave bubbling outwards from a two-pronged ram just beneath the waterline. Unlike their own giant, the trireme had some two hundred rowers crammed into a freeboard of no more than five feet. A hundred feet long but only fifteen across, it seemed like a dagger, rapidly closing to pierce the balloon that was the royal barge.

Another shot from the wargalley whistled through the air and then another. A third found the range and, with a splintering of wood, a heavy stone rattled across the decking between the masts and their stays. As the two ships closed, the hatchways of the barge suddenly discharged a volley of men, scrambling upwards to prepare for the attack. Two more missiles crashed down into their midst, and cries of pain mingled with the curses of confusion as the various contingents shouldered past one another to their stations on the deck.

Finally a deep voice boomed out above the rest. "Archers fire to starboard," Feston bellowed as he hurried up from below and saw the trireme approaching. "Rake their decks before they close. Oarsmen to port, back your oars; oarsmen to starboard, stroke at ram speed."

Two more stones plunged from the sky, striking the forecastle as Quantos' men nocked their shafts and fired. "Archers to your mark," Feston shouted in anger as arrows flew only from the stern. "Strafe their decks, I say."

He looked rapidly about as his men struggled to form at the starboard rail, and then vaulted across to the other side.

"Sweetbalm, Basil," he shouted in a rage as the next volley crashed into them. "You know that I have no bowmen in my contingent. Yet I am the commander still. Have your vassals arch their fire over our heads and aid in our defense.'

"Your men have the fortune to be the closest to the engagement," Basil answered over the growing din. "Use them as you see fit. We will aid in repulsing boarders when the moment is the most propitious."

Alodar saw Feston clench his fist in frustration and then leap back across the deck. In mid-stride, he grabbed for the main mast as the ship lurched from its smooth forward motion. The portside oars were stroking backwards and the huge ship began to lumber about, swinging out of the oncoming vessel's way. Alodar's eyes darted between the rapidly closing trireme, its ram kicking up foam, and the changing geometry of the gap as the royal barge slowly spun.

He heard the hum of arrows and ducked instinctively behind his shield, as did Quantos at his side.

"It is too late," the marine said as the flight of arrows from across the waves struck the deck and bulwarks around them. "We turn too slowly to avoid the ram. Brace yourself for the blow."

With a shocking jolt, the ships collided, and the air was filled with the shrieking protest of ripping wood and metal.

"A sound hit," Quantos shouted as he sprang from the bulwark. "And guided no doubt by a sorcerer's vision far keener than Kelric's. Lively, lads. We must grapple on before they reverse oars and strike again."

Alodar saw the trireme's oars come to a stop and then reverse in synchronism so that their pull backed the smaller ship away from the hole it had made. Following the examples around him, he picked up one of the coils of rope at his feet and flung the attached iron hook across and down to the wargalley's deck. He glanced forward and saw Feston's men doing the same amidship. The enemy crew abandoned the catapult and hacked away at the grapnel lines as they came and stuck.

The compact sleekness of the trireme left little room for other than the rowers, however, and the hooks were being cast faster than they could be cut away. Two launched from the poop lodged firmly, high on the sternboard, out of the deckhand's immediate reach. In an instant, Quantos and his men had the lines firmly secured to anchor capstans near the stern of the barge. With a precision that was the product of years of drill, the crew bent to the crossarms and began to crank the two ships closer together.

"The angle of contact becomes too shallow for them to ram again," Quantos shouted as he watched the slack being taken up. "If our port side rows vigorously enough, we can get the ships alongside and then have a chance."

Alodar looked down towards the bow and saw the closing gap. The men aboard the trireme abandoned their attempt to cut free and, except for a few archers still harassing the queen's men in the stern, most of them converged on the beam opposite Feston's forces.

The ropes flew faster as Feston's followers sensed success in their endeavor. Then, as the last few feet closed and the two vessels hit with a dull thud, Alodar saw at least a dozen grappling hooks strike out and pull the bond fast.

"Forward and at them," Feston called above the yell of success and he sprang up on the rails with his sword flying. He leaped without hesitation to the lower deck alongside. With a mighty slash, he hacked at the first man who opposed him, tumbling him back onto the galley's deck. Feston's momentum carried him forward into the middle of the other vessel and his men on either side began to follow. But Alodar saw the reluctance increase up and down the line on either side of Feston until no man moved in the bow and near the stern. Across on the port, Basil and his men stood silent, awaiting the outcome.

The fighters on the trireme converged on the small party that had boarded, attacking at the flank and pushing to cut off the bulge of Feston's line at the rail.

"We must storm the poop and aid from behind," Quantos shouted. "Come, my lads, drop your bows and draw your blades. Across the guardrail we go."

Quantos drew his sword; with his banner in the other hand, he placed his foot up on the rail to wave his men on. His troops prepared to follow. But just as the first of them drew up to the rail, a fresh shower of arrows hailed into their midst. Two men fell to their knees, screaming in pain, feathers fluttering from shoulder and arm. Quantos let out a weak croak and then tumbled in a heap, a single shaft transfixing his throat, its bloody point sticking out the back of his neck.

Alodar looked across the decks and saw one of Feston's men fall and then another. The trireme fighters pressed their attack vigorously at those who had boarded. Alodar hesitated a second longer, clutching Cedric's sword. Then, with a full intake of breath, he stepped to Quantos' slumping form and grabbed his banner. Standing over the fallen marine, he waved it aloft. "For the queen!" he shouted. "For revenge and victory! Attack!"

Another round of arrows came and two splintered off Alodar's shield. With a fierce yell, he sprang over the bulwark and fell into the midst of the archers who faced them. He dropped the banner, drew his sword and hacked at the head of the one who stood dumbfounded nearby. "For Quantos," he yelled.

Then, in a massive wave, the marines responded. They swarmed over the gap and began swinging at the archers, who retreated towards middeck.

The men pressing Feston turned and glanced at the commotion, hesitating in their own attack. Alodar waved his sword overhead and led the marines onto their rear. The others on the royal barge saw the men of the trireme drop back in confusion, trying to protect their suddenly exposed flank. Now sensing victory, Feston's full contingent stormed over the rails. Basil gave the command and his men also followed. The oars of the trireme stopped and the rowers began to pour onto the deck from two hatches to aid their beleaguered comrades.

The deck of the wargalley became a mad swirl of sword and shield, without pattern, as the two forces engaged. Alodar jabbed point first at the man on his right, while hastily raising his shield to the left to ward off an axe swinging down from a seeming giant. The blow numbed his arm, but he instinctively stepped forward to pass beyond the thrust of his foes as his own followers closed to engage them. The man on his left screamed and fell, spouting blood from neck and arm, as Quantos' marines pressed on the attack. The trained fighters drew together and formed a line about Alodar. With him as the center, they began slashing forward to midship.

Alodar's mind slid into the intensity of concentration that Cedric had taught him, fear blotted out, eyes alert for an opening or a surprise thrust, and arm darting out to give pain. He swung his sword in a swift horizontal arc and felt the sharp blade bite into flesh as his adversary raised both arms high to crash downward an instant too late. With a cry already hoarse, he egged on the men who lagged on the left and closed up the right when the roll of the ship or blow of the foeman created a hole in their line. He moved his troop steadily forward, mindless of stinging cuts and slashes. Almost in a daze, he called halt when he recognized that only armbands with Feston's red plume faced them. The wargalley was theirs and Alodar had had a taste of battle.

Alodar leaned against the railing, still clutching Quantos' banner, as he watched the transfer of prisoners from the trireme to the barge. He glanced about the deck

225

to see that the thaumaturgical wax he had used on the more serious wounds was safely stored away. The larger vessel now rode quite low in the water and even listed slightly to the side. A steady procession of divers dropped over the rail, each one adding another nail to fix a makeshift patch over the ragged hole ripped by the wargalley. The fog had lifted with the beginning of a gentle breeze, but it would be many hours more before the repair was tight, the water bailed from the bilge, and the barge again underway.

One by one, the followers of Feston and Basil emerged from the trireme's hold, carrying back what meager plunder there was aboard. Then amidst a general murmur from both decks, a knot of closely linked figures emerged, all save one with arms across their faces, nearly stumbling as they groped forward to the gangplank.

"The sorcerer from the trireme," Alodar heard Grengor say at his side. "Only an enchanted vision could have guided that ship undetected in the fog through the surrounding fleet and so unerringly into the barge's side. Had we not more than twice the normal crew, they well might have ripped us from stem to stern before we could have grappled her. The kingdoms to the south sorely press the fair lady on land and nearly cut off her aid as well.'"

In the middle of the block of men that stumbled forward, Alodar saw a mane of unruly hair shake free, and then a face contorted with rage, surrounding deep-set and burning eyes. Almost instinctively, Alodar flung his hand in the way of the glare, menacing even at a distance.

"A sorcerer who has been thwarted makes a most dangerous captive," he said. "The guard we place around him better be both careful and complete. But his presence reminds me of why I am here. I must go below and seek out the sorcerer of the queen."

"And your instruction during your absence, master?" Grengor asked. "Are we to remain on station here in the stern, transfer to the trireme as part of the queen's crew when it takes station with the rest of the fleet, or can we go below, since the watch bells have long since sounded?"

Alodar turned in puzzlement to face the sergeant. He saw a round face set on a stocky form, wide-set green eyes, large and trusting, and a plain mouth between jaws of crushing strength. "Why do you ask me, Grengor? Why not ask the one who commands in Quantos' place?"

"I beg your pardon, sir," Grengor said. "Our band is small, now not even a dozen, but we have fought together for many years under Quantos' banner. In our grief, I—we all feel that none of us has the wit to lead the others. But rather than disperse to follow the banner of one of the lords, we would rather answer to you, wherever you may lead us. Indeed you are no Quantos, but you showed much spirit in what happened today. We have decided among ourselves that this is as he would have had it."

Alodar's jaw dropped in surprise, but before he could answer, a page wearing the same colors as he bounded up the ladder to the deck.

"Attend to our lady," the newcomer said. "She is accompanied by the sorcerer Kelric in her cabin at this moment."

"On station until I return," Alodar said hastily. He turned and followed the other page down the ladder, his mind aswirl with what the sergeant had said.

"Alodar, you are safe," Aeriel cried as he entered her cabin a few minutes later. "I heard that Quantos was felled and members of his troop as well. I did not know if you were among them."

"There are losses enough for which to grieve," Alodar said, "and we are lucky to be still afloat." He looked at Kelric, slumped on a small stool in the corner. "The power of sorcery was great indeed."

Kelric tipped back his head and laughed. "Sorcery!" he cackled. "The power of sorcery. It reads so easy in the sagas. Pressed on land from the west and south, and on the sea, as well. And when all seems blackest, a simple charm saves them all so they may live in contentment thereafter."

Alodar looked around the plain cabin and saw it was no larger than his own. Aeriel sat on the bunk, dressed in men's breeches and tunic. To her left, on a small chest, was a pile of documents and the quills and seals. There were no other chairs and Alodar stood facing the two, leaning against the wall.

"But a single charm might activate the eye, and then it will be as the sagas say," he replied.

"It is not so easy," Kelric said. "The charm for what

you have is most complex. You cannot learn it unless you are proficient and, more importantly, are confident in many a charm of lesser power. Without the basis to build upon, a sorcerer's eye will be forever useless to you.'"

"But why is that?" Alodar asked. "Certainly in thaumaturgy, alchemy, and even magic, each spell is entire unto itself. Even if learned by rote, it has no bearing on the others."

"The difference, lad," Kelric said, "is that each of those arts manipulates the physical objects and forces about us. Sorcery deals instead with a matter much more elusive, our minds. You cannot see or touch the medium with which you work. And the subtle and intricate will be totally missed, unless you become familiar with the rough outlines first."

"The words are different, but the message is the same as with the other crafts." Alodar sighed. He shook his head and looked back at Kelric. "No matter, regardless of the effort, I am ready."

"Well then, let us start at the beginning," Kelric said. "There are five types of charms in sorcery. A charm of prophecy or far-seeing is a cantrip; a charm of illusion is a glamour; a charm of fate is a curse; dominance of one's will by the sorcerer is enchantment; and transfer of consciousness from one animate object to another is ensorcellment. To take effect, charms are recited three times or, as the Rule of Three states, 'thrice spoken, once fulfilled.'"

"I noted at the royal ball that you cast your glamour in that repetitious way. Each word seemed to follow the next in a pattern but somehow with a logic that I could not follow."

"Yes, the chanting of the charm is all. Great skill and practice are necessary to say all of the words with the proper rhythm and intonation for success. The slightest falter produces hallucinations and head pains that can last for weeks. In my own practice, I have misspun a charm but twice and the memories still give me a shudder. Not only are even the most simple charms difficult, but they must be mastered before a more complex one can be attempted. As one proceeds towards completion, each word somehow becomes more difficult to slide off the tongue, harder to remember. Indeed, the more complex and powerful spells create back pressures that cannot be comprehended by one who has not tried his mettle on hurdles more easily surmounted. And the greater the charm, the greater is the sickness and agony for failure. It takes a stout heart to attempt such castings, knowing the difficulty and the consequences of error. If anything is the mark of the sorcerer, it is possession of enormous bravery."

"Then why not carry a grimoire as does the alchemist?" Alodar asked. "Or have a library, like the magician guilds. Reading from a correct text to reduce the risks would seem easy enough."

"Because," Kelric responded, "no written language or special symbology yet evolved can convey the precise nuances of tone which are essential for a successful charm. They are passed by word of mouth from unwilling teacher to foolish pupil, from generation to generation. It is the only way that the lore of sorcery is preserved. And far better it would be if the craft sank into decay, as has the practice of wizardry."

Alodar frowned. "Why do you always deprecate your craft, master Kelric?"

"Why? You ask why?" Kelric snorted. "Is it not obvious? Oh, I was like you once, young and eager, lured by the promise of power, the respect of all with whom I dealt, the ability to control and mold the thoughts of others to my will."

Kelric paused and closed his eyes for a moment, pulling the memories to the surface of his thoughts. "And I succeeded," he said, again looking Alodar in the eye. "I learned quickly and discovered many new charms known to no others. I acquired the fame of masters many years my senior. But at the same time I lost what every sorcerer looses and can never regain . . . Today's battle is over. When you leave you will share a slap on the back and a few tall stories with your comrades in arms. You will relax in each other's presence, feeling warm in the glow of friendship and trust. But it would not be so if you were a sorcerer. What man then would talk with you over a cup of rum, or bet the bill on who is first to pinch the barmaid? And what woman would come willingly into your arms and look trustingly into your eyes as you murmured sweet nothings? You would be shunned by all and dealt with only by necessity. Only by spilling some of your vital forces would you see an occasional glimpse of soft thigh and at that you would judge yourself lucky. It takes bravery to be a sorcerer, I have said, and far more than what is required to cast the charms."

The cabin was silent for a minute and Alodar looked at Aeriel, then darted his eyes away. "My quest is for the hand of the queen," he said. "The embrace does not matter."

He nodded slowly and touched the pouch with the sphere at his side. "Let us return to the matter of instruction," he said. "If sorcery is taught by oral means only, how then do new charms ever come about? It would seem that the number would gradually diminish away as masters met untimely ends before they could pass on their heritage."

"New charms are always in the making," Kelric replied. "The trances you see me slip into to aid my concentration in matters of prophecy are not only a crutch for an old man. No indeed, the trance is primarily the means by which the master frees his mind of the encumbrances of this existence. With it he opens up his inner self and seeks out the states where the cadences of charms roll like thunder and the words flash in strokes of lightning before the eyes. Upon return to the here and now, often the mind is exploding with the power of a new charm hitherto unknown to man."

"Then why not effect such a state often," Aeriel asked, "and bring back great powers that can only accumulate with time?"

"Alas, my lady," Kelric replied, "it is as I have often said. Each charm enacted, even the trance of seeking, subtracts something of vital presence from the sorcerer who uses it. Each of us is born with a fixed supply of whatever is his for life; once we have used it all, we perish. And the leeching of inner power depends on the strength of the charm. I restrict myself now only to illusions for the court or simple prophecies of short range and even for those I need the aid of sand, fire, or cards. I dare not try to enchant a single person, no matter how shallow his mind, for fear of consuming all that remains."

"Then why do you not have more interest in the eye?" Alodar interrupted. "You said that it can amplify the powers that a sorcerer naturally possesses."

"No, my pulse does not quicken as I think of the sphere," Kelric said. "I am so small a shadow of my prime that I dare not use such a device. It means nothing to me, though in the hands of a young man, a fool with no thought of the morrow, such an eye indeed increases the charm of enchantment a thousand fold.

"You see, despite the fear in which sorcerers are held, despite the way arms are flung over eyes when we approach, enchantment is not easily achieved. Remember that the charm must be recited thrice and eye-to-eye contact must be maintained throughout the third recital. It is not easily accomplished if the intended victim is on guard. And the more insidious enchantments are the hardest of all to effect. The complete extinction of consciousness is the easiest by far. You become the automaton of the sorcerer and think your own thoughts no more.

"But the more subtle enchantments in which some or most of your own free will and thoughts remain are very difficult. The charms are long, the restive forces great, and the drain on the vitality greater still. Yet, how sublime is that charm that gives you the heart of a lady and changes nothing else! She feels she acts of her own free will but the grip of enchantment binds her to you. It is this power which makes the sorcerer so feared.

"And such is the strength of the eye that it can give the master the potency the sagas ascribe to him. Gaze on it but an instant and you are undone. From the crushing of all free thought to the gentlest suggestion, it will be as the sorcerer wills it. And more besides; when the lid is open, the eye reaches out and compels, drawing you to look, tempting you, forcing you, conjuring you for just one little glance and then you are trapped forever.

"But enough for now," Kelric concluded. "It depresses me to think of it further. Tomorrow, if you still are steadfast in your foolishness, we will start with the cantrip for the tossed die."

"I will be at your cabin door," Alodar said. "Your words have not dissuaded me."

Kelric scowled and then looked at Aeriel. "And now my lady, what are your plans for the next hour?"

"I must readjust some of the berth assignments," Aeriel replied, waving to the littered chesttop, "and then confer with the cooks to reaffirm that we are well enough provisioned."

"Then I suppose the chance of your changing into something less practical while I am here is slight?" He leered.

"Oh, begone, Kelric," Aeriel said, "and try your persuasive manner on one of the other women of the court."

"As my lady wishes." With shoulders stooped the sorcerer shuffled out of the room.

Aeriel and Alodar remained in silence pondering Kelric's words for several minutes longer. Then she arose and turned up the wick of the single lamp hung on the cabin wall.

"You show great trust in me, Aeriel," Alodar said, "and I pledge to show it is well placed. When I can control the eye, I will use it most certainly to benefit the queen."

Aeriel turned to look back at Alodar with a small smile. "You have demonstrated your worth already, Alodar. Else I would not have striven to aid you when you petitioned in Ambrosia. I ask only that you serve her with your head as well as your heart. The latter is too frail an organ to use in affairs of state."

"My motives are indeed from the heart," Alodar admitted, "although not in the way that you might think. But what of you? What draws you to such service of the queen?"

"It is apparent, is it not," Aeriel replied, "that Vendora never can be truly certain of counsel given her by any man? She has great need for someone to see through the emotion to the truth that lies underneath."

"Then what is your reward for the service that you provide to the crown?" Alodar asked.

Aeriel rubbed her eyes and looked at the pile of documents. "There are times indeed when I wonder why I travel the path I do. But my father served Vendora's as minister of most grave counsel. Alas, I was an only child. But I have tried to aid the crown of Procolon in the tradition of my family nonetheless. As for the drones who buzz about Vendora, enough of them seek her favor first through me that I have few idle hours in Ambrosia. Fortunately I am keen enough to see through their interests, so that I have not been greatly disappointed. And those who are not so dull, those who indeed might . . ."

Aeriel broke off and lowered her head with a touch of color in her cheeks.

"I tell too much," she said. "The petitioners who beset the fair lady concern me not at all. I am no longer Vendora's companion in whispered schoolgirl romances. She is now the queen and I her counselor. Such petty concerns are from long ago."

"Shall you then spend the rest of your days in Vendora's shadow, passing into spinsterhood as the reward for your dedication?"

"I said, Alodar, that I have not been disappointed in my dealings with the men of the court, nor have I been a recluse. As for the course of my life, it will depend upon the man the fair lady settles upon as her consort. If he is strong enough to rule Procolon through her, then perhaps I will no longer be needed and can then seek my own destiny."

"For my own part, I thank the random factors that no such decision has yet been made," Alodar said. "Though obviously Vendora does not lack ardent and able suitors."

"Ardent yes, but able, only perhaps, Alodar. The man who fills the needs of the queen and the kingdom has yet to prove himself. And be forewarned in your own quest that more than chance affects the queen's moods. She is strong willed and can be influenced only by subtle pressures.

"Feston struts about the court in jingling mail, but then must show his empty pockets. Basil gives great strength to Vendora's coffers, but must apologize when one of his band refuses to draw sword. And Duncan will find that he is called upon to do far more than merely throw his sphere about the queen.

"And if you prove as incomplete as the rest, Alodar, repeated opportunities to lose face will present themselves to you as well. My task is to give Vendora the man who is the best for Procolon, and I work diversely at my craft."

"Then you have been my unknown ally all the while," Alodar exclaimed. "While I toiled in the alchemist shop and the magician's Guild, I despaired of returning in time. But through your machinations, I dare say none of them can show himself supreme."

"Take care at what I say, Alodar," Aeriel replied. "Vendora makes the final decision still. Feston and the rest have already established their claim to be suitors. I strive to delay Vendora's choice, not for you, but for the best, whoever that may be."

"And if the hero for Procolon does come forth and you are then free of your charge," Alodar asked, "what sort of man then would you seek for yourself?"

Aeriel laughed. "In truth, I have no answer." She paused and then after a moment continued softly. "Suffice it to say that the man in my dream knows full well how to judge the relative worth of two women."

Aeriel slowly swept her hands back to rest on the chest behind her and looked deeply into Alodar's eyes. Her face was framed with twin cascades of amber, falling upon shoulders that beckoned in the lamplight. Her eyes sparkled with the deepness of jet, and her lips, though turned in a small smile, were taut with resolution and challenge.

Alodar took a step towards her, then another. She said nothing; her eyes held his and there was no change in her expression. He stopped and with slow deliberateness surveyed her body. He locked his eyes back on hers and advanced another step forward. Aeriel, still silent, flicked a curl from the cascade behind to fall over her shoulder.

Alodar stopped and blinked, trying to understand the intensity of the feeling suddenly rushing over him. His loins tightened and the image of Vendora, this time only days old would not come. He saw only Aeriel, proud Aeriel, warm Aeriel, challenging him in his resolve.

He struggled to hold on to his quest, but in a flood of emotion, it was swept away. "At the ball, I saw the object of my deepest desires," he said simply, "and it was you."

He swept her into his arms, half expecting a haughty laugh at his weakness, but he did not care. He thrust his lips on hers and pulled her body to him, pressing the breath from her lungs.

Aeriel did not resist, but clasped her hands behind him

and grasped as savagely as did he. After a long moment he pulled his head back slightly, but Aeriel pursued and reattached her mouth to his. Some time later, how long Alodar could not tell, their crushing grips relaxed, and he led her to sit on the bunk behind them.

"When I saw you again in the palace," Aeriel said as she recovered her breath, "I remarked on the coincidence. That was because the vision that I saw in Kelric's illusion was you."

"My thoughts are a jumble," Alodar said, shaking his head. "For nearly a year I have pursued the queen. I turned away the favor you showed me at Iron Fist for the quest of her hand. But somehow, Aeriel, I have seen too much of the woman you are, and the strength to resist is now far harder to find."

Aeriel smiled at Alodar and then looked down to his side. She squeezed his hand and gently touched the pouch that held the sorcerer's eye. "You have made my heart glad, Alodar," she said, "although by my selfish actions I do not deserve it."

She was silent a moment and then trembled with a deep sigh. She squeezed her hand into a fist until the knuckles showed white and looked back into his eyes. "Why do you quest for the fair lady," she asked, "if not for her beauty and power, like the rest?"

"It is for my heritage," Alodar replied. "I desire to recover my rightful peerage of the realm and the respect that goes with it. As consort to the fair lady, none could deny them to me." He stopped and thought of his dream of the hero's welcome in Ambrosia. "And for the touch of glory that goes with it as well," he said quietly.

"And I have pledged to serve the crown," Aeriel said. "To see that the best man stands at Vendora's side." She paused and lowered her head. "Continue with your quest, Alodar. The fair lady needs you far more than I."

"I have not quested in blind steadfastness," Alodar protested. "Along the way I have faltered and puzzled at the path I choose. And nothing has given me such pause as you, Aeriel. Can I truly throw my heart into pursuing a goal if you are not part of that success?"

"We are both tired, Alodar." Aeriel shook her head gently. "You from the battle and I from the work that

235

must go on. The fatigue weakens our judgment and makes us easier prey to our desires. I apologize for tempting you so. In the morning we will be refreshed and have reaffirmed our resolve to do what we must do."

Alodar frowned at her words, his head reeling from the emotions that swung back and forth as if at the end of a snapping whip. He tried to remember the forces that drove him on, and in the corner of his mind he finally saw a vision of Vendora, the queen. "Perhaps you are right," he said, "but I do not think a single night will unscramble my thoughts. I thunder after an abstract goal, Aeriel, but have no idea what I will do after it is achieved."

"It is a conundrum," Aeriel agreed. "But for now, Procolon is in peril, and you must learn how to use the sorcerer's eye."

Alodar nodded his head slowly and started to speak again, but suddenly two soft knocks echoed from the cabin door. "The queen's council assembles to plot the course for the morrow, my lady," a voice said from without. "Your presence is requested at once."

Aeriel's expression melted into one of annoyance and Alodar let out his breath as the tension oozed away. The mood was broken and Aeriel spoke as if nothing had happened as she waved him to the door. "I must prepare. Good luck, Alodar, good luck in your quest."

"My lady," he mumbled thickly and left with eyes averted.

CHAPTER FIFTEEN

The Sorcerer's Revenge

ALODAR steadied himself against the roll of the deck as he walked slowly towards the small hole in the corner of Kelric's cabin. Two weeks had given him sea legs. Holding his head and eyes steady, he concentrated on the two tiny sparkles of light which stared back at him. A bare three feet away, he lowered himself to his knees and began to undulate his hands in the outline of a pie-shaped wedge. A tiny nose poked out of the hole; long whiskers jutted hesitantly into the room.

Alodar rapidly ran through the glamour, his face contorting into a grimace as he labored to stutter past the last few words. As he finished, the rat extended its head from the hole and then its entire body. Torn between instinctive fear and unbelievable good fortune, the rodent moved slowly across the intervening space towards Alodar's hands.

As the rat advanced, Alodar felt the reaction, an uncomfortable tug that pulled from his toes and fingers up through his body and then spilled out into the air above his head. Like a nail against slate or bone against jagged bone, the feeling coursed through him, too much to ignore, yet somehow too undefined to merit the aversion it produced.

He shook his head in annoyance. The rat suddenly halted in midstride and looked nervously back to its hiding place. Alodar frowned with renewed concentration and slowly started the enchantment. He stared at the rat as he spoke, trying to bore past the gleaming eyes into the small mind behind. He completed the first recital and the rodent did not move; during the second it resumed its cautious tread forward.

237

Alodar began the third. Although his mouth seemed filled with cotton, and nausea bubbled up from his stomach, his pulse quickened when the barrier suddenly gave way. In a rush, he felt himself drawn into the small confusion of the rat's mind, tasted its hunger and felt the sharp edge of its fear. For a moment he paused, marveling at what he had done, but the growing discomfort forced him to continue his task. He frowned deeply and then carefully separated the pulsing emotions from his own. Like a potter at his wheel, he massaged the simple thoughts and reshaped them, rounded the corners of the apprehension to a smooth pebble and tickled the stomach to growl all the more.

Alodar unstuck the last word from his throat and the rat did not bolt away. With trusting eyes it sat placidly on the planking and curled its tail about its legs. The uneasy tug at Alodar's innards continued for a minute more but then began to fade. He sighed with relief, knowing that he had succeeded and the worst was over. He marched the rat, stiff-legged like a child's doll, towards the illusion of the cheese at his feet. When the twitching nose was within inches, he released control of the limbs and let the rodent pounce on the imagined feast of its own will. The rat showed no concern for Alodar's presence; with a vicious bite, it snapped its jaws on empty air. Alodar felt the upwelling of simple anticipation in the rodent's brain and carefully stimulated the tongue and stomach to make each gulp a savory delight. In a moment the phantom morsel was completely devoured, and the rat again curled its tail in contentment. Alodar watched for a second and then suddenly took away the cloak that sheltered the fear. The rodent started and quickly scampered back into its hole.

"You must maintain eye contact at all times, Alodar," Kelric said over his shoulder. "Had you not laced yesterday's bait with that sedative, the rat would have broken away when you faltered. And the discomfort you felt was nothing compared to what it would have been if the charm was not completed."

"I will gradually reduce the dose," Alodar said. "In a few days more, I will be able to enchant a rat as well as one who does not have the benefit of alchemy. And by working up gradually, I think I progress far faster than otherwise." He bent down and picked up the crumb of cheese he had dropped nearby. "It is the same with the illusions. By starting with a real sample, I can make them more realistic with far less effort. The drain of the vital force made me hesitate, but without the aid of thaumaturgy I would have been unable to get both the glamour and the enchantment finished together."

"Oh, you are progressing well enough without such aids," Kelric growled. "Your mind is quick and there is no reason not to proceed as I did in my youth."

"It is my training as a thaumaturge that provides the edge," Alodar said. "Without some measure of cunning, one cannot aspire to be a master."

"Yet sorcery is not learned by wit alone," Kelric warned. "It takes dedication as well." He paused and scratched his side. "Although I must admit, I find no fault with you there. You have labored hard and indeed are further along than I thought possible in such a time."

"The perseverance comes from alchemy," Alodar replied.

"And the precision with which you speak the charms?" Kelric continued in mild annoyance. "Do you have a craft for that as well?"

"Magic." Alodar laughed. "The rituals would not complete if not correctly performed."

Kelric shook his head and stroked his chin in thought. "The crafts have always been so separated," he muttered. "Perhaps there is some profit in intercourse between them."

"Regardless of that, my concentration is now totally on sorcery," Alodar said. "What next must I learn of the fundamental charms before I advance to ones more potent?"

"You have yet to show mastery of the simple illusions for dumb beasts without the fancy shortcuts," Kelric said. "And believe me, those must be second nature to you before you can profitably continue. You should rest and try again with the rodent tomorrow."

Alodar frowned and started to protest the delay but a last rumble of his stomach changed his mind. "You are right. I can tolerate no more, at least for today. I will go topside to clear my head."

Kelric nodded in agreement. "And I shall attend the queen in your absence," he called after Alodar. "Perhaps some lady of the court will lower her guard and let me look her in the eye."

Alodar slowly climbed the companionway to the main deck, pushing his thoughts of Kelric and sorcery aside. He pressed on the hatch and frowned as he had to shove with his shoulder to pry it open. With a forceful crash, it slammed shut as he let go. He reached for a line nearby to steady himself in the gusts that lashed the deck.

The motion of the barge as it plowed through the waves was even more apparent than it was below. High walls of spray rained over the bow. Ever so often the line between water and air seemed high above the tightly wrapped spars that tilted madly with the wind.

Alodar bowed his head and stomped purposefully to the rail amidship to join a soliatary figure that was peering out over the churning sea.

"A bit rough today," Alodar greeted Grengor as he reached his side.

"Yes, that it is, master Alodar," Grengor replied drawing his hood closer about the wide face and stubble of beard that protruded from it. "Everyone below is packed together like fortune cards but no one complains. Not even the ones who must guard the sorcerer from the south. The discomfort is far less, they judge, than enduring the wet and cold up here."

Alodar nodded and looked out over the rail across the water. "I cannot see any of the fleet in these waves and spray," he said.

"Long ago, each has furled sail and shipped oars to ride out the storm. We will be leagues apart when it blows over."

"And no nearer Arcadia either I wager," Alodar said. "This wind from the south blows us farther from king Elsinor with each minute."

"Perhaps so, master," Grengor said, "but the same wind batters any enemy wargalleys out here as well."

Alodar grunted in reply and then both men lapsed into silence, drawing their cloaks about them and exposing little save their eyes to the lash of wind and wave. As they watched, the broad bow nosed down under the wall of water which broke over it, and spray bounded across the deck to strike Alodar in the face. He and Grengor retreated aft as the bow sluggishly rose and the wave rolled underneath.

The ship plunged over the back of the wave and met the overtopping crest of the next one low in the water, shuddering as the shower pounded the deck. This time both Grengor and Alodar were pelted where they stood. The ship began to right itself with agonizing slowness, barely coming up to level as the wave slid past.

Alodar turned to Grengor with a question in his eye. By his small experience, the barge at first had seemed a city afloat, but the tremble and groan as the ship steadied for the next pitch upward put in perspective how small they were in the fury of the storm. He arched his eyebrows in surprise as Grengor returned his glance. He expected to see the condescending smile of the experienced sailor, but saw instead a set jaw and eyes alive with concern.

The next wave hit the barge and a cascade of water skittered the length of the deck, spiraling past their boots and drenching their cloaks to their knees. Again the water tumbled off in giant falls to the side, but Alodar held his breath as he waited for the bowsprit finally to break through to clean air.

He looked all about the deck, expecting to see that only he, Grengor and the helmsman were insane enough to be about. He saw instead a head emerging from a hatchway near the forecastle. In a moment, another figure was on deck and Alodar wrinkled his brow in puzzlement. The wind and water howled as before, but no cloak protected the newcomer and his pole axe of shining steel. With a somewhat halting step, he lumbered past, not even acknowledging the small nod that Alodar threw his way.

"One of Feston's men, no doubt," Grengor said. "Too disdainful to return even the slightest courtesy to someone not of his faction."

"It is of no importance, Grengor," Alodar said as he stared at the figure retreating past them and climbing the ladder to the poop deck. "Such slights might have angered me greatly a year ago, but now I give them no thought."

Alodar watched the man finally reach the level of the poop deck and then point himself in the direction of the deckhouse. He took one slow step and then another. Just like the gait of the rat on which he had demonstrated the charm, Alodar thought. So totally entrapped that every motion had to be directed by the enchanter.

"Grengor," Alodar cried, suddenly breaking out of his slow reverie. "What duty did you say that Feston's men performed today?"

"Why, let me see." Grengor said. "The oarsmen yesterday and again on the morrow. It must be the sorcerer then that they watch today."

"Then follow me quickly," Alodar yelled, springing across the deck and then immediately stumbling as the roll of the ship caught him in midstride. "To the helmsman! I fear he needs our aid."

Alodar and Grengor raced to the ladder as the figure ahead of them entered the small enclosure on the deck above. With a strong pull on the railing, Alodar jumped up onto the deck, just in time to see the axehead plunge into the unprotected chest of the helmsman. A feeble cry of surprise and pain was swept away by the wind. The assailant flailed his blade again at the bloody form as it fell.

Alodar and Grengor burst into the house with swords drawn. With near simultaneous thrusts, they jabbed their blades forward and felt the parting of flesh and jarring contact with bone. Alodar drew his sword out with a wrench and stepped back in anticipation of a swinging axe-blade in reply. The figure paid them no attention. With a face undistorted by apprehension or pain, he swung his next blow at the wheel, oblivious of the blood gushing from the two fresh wounds in his sides.

The wheel exploded from its post in a shower of splinters and careened across the deck. Grengor thrust out again, his sword biting deeply into an arm as it swung past, but the guardsman took no notice. Alodar watched in amazement as the axe rose high overhead and crashed it down on the post, splitting it asunder.

"Enchantment, master Alodar," Grengor called out. "Somehow the sorcerer from the south has made him a slave. I can dispatch him in a few strokes more, but I fear his damage is done. Get quickly below and alarm the rowers to bend their oars. Without the helm, we cannot long stay pointed into the wind. And the patch that was

242

placed over the hole ripped by the wargalley may not last long if we are wallowing in the troughs."

Alodar grasped what Grengor was saying. Without another word. he ran from the deckhouse to the ladder leading to midship. Another wave toppled over the bow and raced down the deck. As the water coursed by, he felt a slight lurch and then saw the runoff at his feet reverse direction and head for the port side. With a backstraining pull, he flung the hatch cover aside and bolted downward to the first deck. He ran for midship where the passageway opened wide on either side to the benches of the rowers. As he sprinted along, he could feel a noticeable tilt to port as the ship responded to each wave.

Up ahead, before he reached the benches, he heard the sound of a disturbance and saw several heads pop from cabins along the way. He pulled himself up as he passed the last cabin, ready to shout the alarm. But the sound died in his throat as he saw the reason for the commotion. Two more guards with Feston's arm bands were hacking at the oars along the benches, ignoring the blows raining down to stop them.

Another wave rolled under the ship, and Alodar grabbed for support as the deck tipped dizzily to the side. Through a port, he saw the choppy horizon shoot past skyward and then slowly return as the barge almost righted itself.

Reversing direction, he sprinted the length of the ship. On a dead run, he barrelled by the two guardsmen who stood with halberds at parade over a single entrance that led to cabins far aft. The men hesitated at Alodar's approach, not immediately dropping their weapons to block the way.

Alodar thundered past their indecision, yelling over his shoulder about an oversight as he passed. One turned to follow, then shrugged his shoulders and resumed his stance. Racing down the narrow passageway, Alodar pushed aside a curtain and exploded into a great cabin at the very stern of the ship. Only a few supporting posts interfered with a volume open from beam to beam, windowed on three sides with huge sheets of isinglass painted opaque by the bounding spray.

Vendora shrieked at Alodar's sudden entrance. Aeriel rose to her feet, eyes wide in surprise at the intrusion. Kelric sat numbly crosslegged before the two and responded not at all. "A full moon of pardons, my fair lady," Alodar gasped, "but I fear the ship is in great danger. We must sound a general alarm before it is too late."

"What is the peril, Alodar?" Aeriel asked as she picked up her cloak. "What besides the storm presents risk for the royal barge?"

"I am not a man of the sea," Alodar replied, "but we have lost our steerage and with the weakened hull we may founder."

"Then there is no time," Aeriel decided. "We must board the other vessels, those that can."

"The longboats are far smaller than the barge," Alodar said. "They could be easily swamped in the high waves. Our safety would be greater if we could get the great ship about."

"Then which is it?" Aeriel said. "If the hull does not hold, there may be little time to change our minds."

Alodar quickly thought of the enchanted guardsmen and the struggle amidst the oars. "If I were to decide, my choice would be for the longboats despite their meager size. But by no means can we provide for everyone aboard."

"Then we shall begin with the queen," Aeriel said waving her hand to the door.

Alodar nodded, grasped Vendora by the waist and began to push her down the corridor. Aeriel tugged Kelric to his feet and spun him to follow. The two guards turned questioning glances to the queen as she came to their station, but she waved them to silence as she passed.

The ship lurched violently as they reached the companionway to the main deck. Cabin doors along the corridor burst open in surprise. Vendora cried out as she reached for the railing and tumbled from her footing instead.

"What happens with the fair lady?" Feston shouted as he peered out of his doorway in the direction of the queen. Receiving no answer, he reached back inside his cabin and buckled on his sword to follow.

"Lord Feston races after the queen," a voice shouted from another of the open doorways. In an instant Basil and Duncan also scrambled forth.

Alodar pulled Vendora to her feet. As the ship righted, he pushed her up the ladder banging shins and ankles in his haste. They climbed but four rungs when the barge rolled again, this time heeling far over. Alodar grasped the rails with both hands and held Vendora against his chest as she fell backwards. Behind him he could hear Aeriel's frantic struggle with Kelric as their feet slid from under them and they grasped wildly for balance. Alodar gathered up his strength and, with one thrust, shoved the queen to the hatchway. Holding her firmly with one arm, he shouldered the hatch aside with the other and stepped into the fury of the quickening storm.

Grengor and the others of his band were there at the opening, extending arms to aid. He shoved Vendora forward and turned to pull Aeriel and Kelric up onto the deck. The wind now came at his side, stinging his cheek with the spray. The barge was wallowing in the troughs.

"The longboats," Alodar shouted. "We must get the fair lady safely over the side." He led Vendora across the heaving deck and the party streamed after. They climbed the ladders to the stern and ran to where the two boats were battened besides the wreckage of the deckhouse. Quickly, the canvas covering was ripped away. Alodar thrust Vendora and then Aeriel into one of the hulls as the barge lunged dizzily when another wave rolled underneath. Feston and the others exploded from the hatchway as Alodar's men cranked at the hoists and swung the boat over the side.

With great leaping strides, Feston bounded across the deck and up the ladder. He plunged into the marines, shouldering several aside, and jumped aboard next to the queen. "Followers of lord Feston," he bellowed above the wind, "assemble unto me and aid the fair lady."

The men scrambling on deck looked about hesitantly for a moment; then they shouted with alarm as they saw the activity at the stern. The boat began to lower, and they sloshed through the water, climbed up the ladders to the poop, and ran to the rail. A knot of men collected against the bulwark and, pushed from behind, Basil and Duncan tumbled aboard into the midst of Alodar's small crew. The barge listed heavily and several more sprang to the rail and jumped into the descending boat.

"Too many," Alodar shouted. "We will sink as surely as the barge. Cast off, cast off before more hurl aboard." Grengor and another of his men began to pay out rope more quickly and the sloop plunged away from the rolling deck.

"Followers of my banner," Feston shouted, "seize the second boat and after us."

"To my banner," Basil yelled as loud. "Prevent the others from taking what we must have, and then after me."

Alodar looked up to the deck as his own boat hit the waves. He could see the beginnings of a mêlée as the factions fought with drawn swords for possession of the other longboat. In the press of battle no one could focus his attention on the blocks, and the boat remained immobile on the deck. Alodar turned back to his own plight and quickly counted the men aboard. Of his own eight, he saw that all had made it safely. Vendora, Aeriel, Kelric, Feston, Basil and Duncan were accompanied by a tangle of six more men. Whose supporters they were, he could not tell.

"Man the oars," he commanded. "Get us clear of the barge before some wave dashes us back into her side. You there, make room for the queen. My fair lady, if you and lady Aeriel can move forward, you will find that the small shelter will protect two from the strength of this gale."

"I command the forces of the queen," Feston growled as he wriggled himself erect in the pile of men amidship. But before he could say more, a wave broke over them ending a deluge of water into the midst.

"The rest of you to the bailing," Alodar continued and several of the men about Feston began to look for buckets in the hatchway aft. Feston glowered at Alodar for a moment, and then a second wave washed over the rails. The men about him filled and dumped buskets furiously. When Basil thrust one into Feston's hands, he bent and started bailing with the rest.

Alodar turned to look back towards the barge and saw that the thrust of the wind had opened a wide gulf between them. The huge ship was crosswind. As she rolled, the leeward rail almost touched the waves.

"Grengor and you, Melab, in the rear," he shouted. "Let us assemble the mast and try to erect it now. If we are lucky and the wind slackens, we will be ready to hoist sail."

Alodar glanced about the boat. Except for Kelric still lying in a jumble, his face barely above water, every man was usefully employed. He shut out all thoughts of the precariousness of their position and bent his mind to the task of raising the mast.

Weary with cold and fatigue, Alodar steadied one leg on top of the small shelter and held the glass from the meager stores to his eye. The wind was dying beneath a placid moon, and the sea was growing calm. All about the boat, men slumped in the disarray of sleep. Alodar leaned against the mast, now holding aloft a sail unfurled to catch the breeze that remained from the storm. How soothing it would feel to collapse among the tangle of limbs at his feet and let consciousness slide away as it had from the rest. But he dared not relinquish the grip. So long as he stayed awake, threatening, cajoling, and pushing himself harder than any, the random collection of men who had jumped from the barge would act enough in consort to save their lives.

Twice again Feston had balked at the continual bailing, but Alodar had stared him down. One of his marines and Duncan's retainers squabbled over what constituted a fair share of the load, and he had pushed between them before their inattention let the boom run free and rake across the rear deck with a vicious sweep.

They somehow had bailed enough to keep afloat, mended the sail at least thrice, and tumbled in rough water throughout. To relax now and let chance determine which of Feston's, Basil's or Duncan's followers awoke first might throw away all they had struggled for in the past four days.

With only half-open eyes, Alodar slowly scanned the sea. The clouds were all but swept away, but the sliver of moon did not provide enough light to see to the horizon. They must find land soon, and drifting about aimlessly the few hours till dawn was a waste they could ill afford.

Alodar grimaced and collapsed the glass. He stepped down into the jumble of sleeping forms and gingerly picked his way to where Kelric was curled up in the stern. The sorcerer shivered in his sleep. His breath gurgled and wheezed as it struggled in and out of his lungs. His flesh was pale and hung limply on his scrawny frame. The exposure had been hard for all of them, but on the old man it had taken the greatest toll.

Alodar bent down and gently shook him awake. In the quietness of the night, Alodar explained what had to be done and then listened attentively as Kelric provided the detailed instructions. In an hour, he had memorized the cantrip and returned to the shelter amidship.

Alodar climbed wearily to the roof, made himself as comfortable as possible, and began the charm. Had he been fully alert, he would have spoken the words with great care, fighting the increasing resistance a measured step at a time. But both his mind and body were dulled. He rattled off the three repetitions like a schoolboy reciting his pledge to the queen. In an instant it was finished. He blinked in surprise at how mild was the internal reaction.

Alodar slowly scanned a full circle from where he sat and then closed his eyes against the scene. An image of what he had just seen sprang into sharp focus as if lighted by the noonday sun. He willed his thoughts forward and, like a great-winged bird, he seemed to spring from the boat. Soaring low over the water, his mind raced ahead of the bow, straining for the horizon and sight of ship or land. The miles sped by, but the scene remained an unbroken circle of water as far as he could see.

Gradually the rush of his thoughts began to slow; though he strained all the harder, the waves dissolved into an indistinct haze, and the sky dimmed. His pace slowed to a crawl and then, at the moment he seemed to stop, the scene blacked out from view. Instinctively Alodar realized he had reached the limits of his vision and brought his thoughts back to his inert body sitting on the shelter roof.

With his eyes still closed, he turned his head and sought to port, again sailing over the waves far faster than any ship could take him. He breathed deeply as he finally slowed, hoping to see a landfall of Arcadia before the scene faded away. But when the blackness came, the ocean looked as unchanging as it had from the bow, and Alodar returned a second time to begin the search anew.

He turned to starboard and saw over the horizon in a heartbeat. Before he even noticed any slowing, he saw a line of low hills pushing down to a sandy beach. Land, he dimly thought in his trance, land to the west and not far away.

He willed his thoughts to return so that he could break the spell and head for shore; but to his surprise, the rush in his mind continued onward. Up into the hills his sight took him, past smouldering campfires and huddles of sleeping figures. On and on his thoughts raced, to higher and rougher ground. The mountains were cleft and folded, fissured and cracked with jumbles of boulders strewn about. Alodar's attention wandered over the scene but then focused upon a slender spur of rock that soared before him. A monolith of cold granite, it stood like a giant spike thrust into the contours of the hills and seemed to challenge even the peaks beyond for height.

Alodar recognized the spire as the one he had seen when he tried to use the sorcerer's eye. As before, he felt himself drawn inside into a tomblike room. In the very center stood a stone coffin with a thick glass lid, and Alodar's thoughts rushed forward to peer inside. He saw a man of middle age, eyes peacefully closed, and mouth curled up in a haughty smile. The hands were folded across the chest over a robe sprinkled with many small, stylized logos of flame.

Alodar tried to look about the room, but the scene suddenly went black. He felt himself slowly pitching forward from the roof of the boat's shelter. He quickly blinked his eyes open and grabbed at the mast to steady himself. A moment of vertigo washed over him and then a hot fever that turned his limbs to rubber. Alodar clutched at the mast to gain support and gradually the feelings subsided, leaving him weak and lethargic.

Slowly Alodar climbed down into the hull and picked his way aft. For a moment, he puzzled at his vision but then pushed it aside, too weary to expend the effort when there were more important things to be done. The coast was not that far away; perhaps by late morning, they could be safely ashore.

Alodar nodded his head with decision, loosened the boom and cut hard on the tiller to aim the small craft landward. The wind hit the sail at a flatter angle. With gathering momentum, the boat began moving towards the shore. Alodar leaned against the after railing, holding the craft on course and staring into the darkness.

The hours passed, and gradually the sky brightened, until the boundary between sea and air could be discerned in all directions. Alodar watched the west. Finally a second hazy line appeared above the first. As the boat approached, it resolved into individual low hills that began to loom higher and higher on the horizon. Eventually the sound of breaking surf mingled with the whistling of the wind. Alodar saw a row of whitecaps racing up towards a sandy beach.

With more seamanship and alertness, he might be able to bring the boat smartly about and drop sail and anchor. But such detail was beyond what little energy remained. Holding his course, the craft sped directly onwards and, with a sudden lurch, ran aground.

The sleeping men scrambled awake with surprise. "You there," Alodar shouted, "to the shelter and rouse the queen. And you on the left, give aid to the sorcerer. He is too weak even to walk on his own."

The men sluggishly complied and, one by one, dropped overboard to head for shore. Water began to bubble in through the hull. The longboat sagged gently to one side as she slowly filled. Duncan arose from a position in the bow. With shaking legs, he staggered to the queen.

"At last, my chance to protect the fair lady," he croaked through lips cracked from the salt air. He withdrew his sphere from the small bag at his waist. After several moments, Alodar could see a shimmering bubble of translucence which engulfed Duncan and Vendora. His two followers rolled the bubble up on the bulwark and tossed it into the waves, tumbling Duncan and Vendora together in a confusion of cloak and gown. Obviously, from its motions, the bubble could not be used in any rough sea. Alodar watched as the attendants jumped in after and began pushing the two landward, untouched by the chilling water. He saw Aerial come back to join him, as the last two, they jumped overboard and waded to shore.

Watersoaked and fatigued as they were, simple foraging and lighting a fire took the rest of the day. Only Alodar's curt commands and steadfastness kept tempers in line and limbs moving until it was done. As darkness fell, the small band huddled in close about the flame, seeking at last dryness, warmth, and rest from their ordeal.

"Now that the emergency is over," Feston said, rubbing his hands together and then touching the hilt of his sword, "we can, I feel, revert to our original chain of command. And my first direction is that we should abandon this beach and quickly search out a cave in the hills, so that the night can be spent in some sort of shelter."

"There is no strength left for that, Feston," Alodar said. "We have already endured the elements for four full nights. Another will tax us less dearly than a search without light over the rough ground."

"I have given a directive," Feston growled. With a savage gesture, he withdrew six inches of blade from his scabbard. A sudden rumble of disapproval checked his action, and Feston looked quickly about at the men who circled the fire. "You there, by your insignia, you are royal marines. Follow the orders of your commander," he said.

"We serve the person of the fair lady," Grengor said quietly in reply. "Until she gives us direction otherwise, we will follow the command of master Alodar. You bail as well as any man among us, lord Feston, but it is lady Aeriel's page who has seen us safely through the storm."

"And that is the truth, Vendora," Aeriel cut in. "Just as at Iron Fist, the thaumaturge has proven his worth to the crown of Procolon. Let the deed and not the station be your guide, my fair lady."

"I am not so dim of sight or slow of mind as you sometimes make me, Aeriel," Vendora said, pulling erect and drawing her robe about her. She looked slowly about the ring of Alodar's marines, each grim-faced and with a hand on sword hilt. "I observed with care the events of the past days. Indeed, the man has acted well in behalf of the crown. But tell me, Alodar, how did you know, when none else did, that the barge would founder?"

"In truth, my fair lady," Alodar said, "I do not know that it did. The helm may have been repaired or the patches held. The barge still may be plying the seas, having ridden out the storm as well as we. Yet, to determine with certainty the seaworthiness of the vessel could well have been fatal. I made the decision that I felt I had to."

"And then, instead of possible comfort in my stateroom on board, where has your decision brought your liege?" Vendora said.

251

"To the uplands north of Bardina—north of the boundaries of Procolon itself—my fair lady," Grengor cut in. "I campaigned here in your father's time and recognize the black oak which creeps down from the hillside."

"My fair lady," Basil said, "perhaps this makeshift alchemist has served you well these past days, but we are by no means safe from major peril. Our voyage was for aid to stop the forces that threaten to overrun the kingdom. In the west we fight no less than demons, and our army makes no headway in dislodging the grip of their crazed servants from the land. And from the south march even more, to stab at the heart of Procolon."

He paused and looked about the landscape. "We cannot chance another voyage across a sorcerer-watched sea in such a little craft. And little time remains to return to Ambrosia for one more seaworthy. Our one hope now lies in recruiting to our cause the barbaric nomads who aimlessly roam these lands. And only by statesmanship and bribery can we bend their primitive passions to our will. Fortunately for you, my fair lady, watersoaked though this tunic is, it still safely protects many a jewel of great value. Appoint me leader, and I will see you safely home in triumph."

"If the danger is as black as you paint it," Duncan said, before Vendora could reply, "then a handful of jewels will be no guarantee against the treachery of these simple-minded ones. Permit me to be always at your side, my fair lady, and with my sphere and command of the others about me, no matter what happens, your safety can be assured."

"Enough, enough!" Vendora cried, with a hint of irritation in her voice. "We must deal first with the matter of Alodar's recompense for services duly rendered. I doubt that any of you would act with such decision, faced with the question of abandoning ship. Indeed you did not. Such boldness must not be stifled, but rather it should be encouraged. Tell me Alodar, what boon do you wish from your queen?"

Alodar breathed deeply and then replied with a rush. "You speak of boldness, my fair lady, and it encourages me to speak of my driving quest."

With a sweep of his hands, he turned and addressed

the entire assemblage as well as the queen. "You all know that lord Feston accompanied the fair lady from the confines of the siege at Iron Fist, and for his effort he was made no less than suitor for her hand in marriage. Then Basil the apothecary, armed with the treasures secured at great peril from the Fumus Mountains, earned like status for his aid to the power of the throne of Procolon. And finally, Duncan of the Cycloid Guild offered the fair lady protection most magical; and for this, he too is suitor for her hand. My fair lady, though my deed may in your mind not compare with these, my desire is yet no less. I too seek your most royal favor and your hand."

Vendora threw back her head in a peal of laughter. "Ah Alodar," she said at last. "You do lighten the weariness that hangs so heavily upon me. But stay, your words are well chosen, and by logic's laws you have saved and prospered the life of the queen as well as any. Stand forward by the fire so that I can note you better."

Alodar slowly rose and approached the queen, his heart pounding with the little energy that remained in him. He felt every impulse to glance away as she stared, but he held his gaze level, looking back at her squarely.

"You are comely looking enough," Vendora said, as she turned to face the others. "My good company, may I present Alodar, suitor for the hand of the queen of Procolon."

CHAPTER SIXTEEN

Alodar Enchanted

ALODAR stretched his legs and smiled. The weariness of their journey still hung over him, and the meager morning meal did little for his hunger, but he was content. He flexed his fingers in the coarse sand just inches away from Vendora's arm.

He looked about the camp. Only Grengor and a few of

his marines remained. The rest were away, scouting the surrounding hills for signs of the nomads. Down the beach, Aeriel stood alone, staring out to sea. Behind a nearby dune, Kelric had yet to stir from his slumber.

Alodar shot a sideways glance at Vendora while she idly scraped a bit of beach tar from her gown. He had come this far from the most humble beginnings, spurred on only by hopes and dreams. To rank finally above them all must be within his grasp, if becoming a suitor ever was. It was only a matter of seizing the opportunity.

Alodar looked to the north and saw the line of hills slowly converge upon the sea. The beach narrowed to a slender ribbon and then terminated abruptly against a rocky point that cut off the view. Back to the west, a sprinkle of vegetation dotted the slopes, chokecherry and spicebush still green beneath the bare branches of oaks and dogwoods that yielded to pines and cedars as the elevation climbed. At the limit of vision, a hint of snowy whiteness mingled with the hazy purples of the great mountains that thrust into the interior.

Alodar lazily scanned the panorama a second time. As he looked to the lower hills, he caught sight of one of the scouting parties that had left at dawn. He squinted into the morning light, trying to resolve some detail, and decided finally that the specks slowly bobbing his way must be Basil and his retainers. As they drew closer and confirmed his guess, he sat upright and then pointed at the approaching figures.

"Look, Grengor," he said. "Basil does not return empty handed. He left with two followers but there seem to be four men marching back to camp."

"And by the looks of the last," Grengor replied, "he journeys as a captive rather than a friend. It is not an auspicious beginning, if we are to convert all of these wild northmen to our cause."

Everyone turned to watch Basil's progress; several minutes later he puffed into the camp. "My fair lady," he said, as he rushed to the queen, "already I prove the great worth of my wealth to your crown. Behold, I bring forth your first new subject from the wastelands."

Basil paused to catch his breath, and Alodar looked at the captive. His hair was matted in snarls; even though no breeze was blowing, Alodar caught the pungent odor of his body. His chest and legs were bare. The muscles trembled in his arms as he strained against the cords which bound his hands together behind his back. He looked around the circle of armed men, and his expression stiffened into a mask of defiance when he returned Basil's stare.

"The barbarian's mouth dropped when I showed him a few samples of my gems," Basil continued. "Great treasures were back in his camp and a fair trade for a few of the jewels could surely be made, he claimed. And while he fingered them, it was simple enough for my followers to overpower him from behind and drag him here."

Basil stopped and looked at the dying embers of the fire. "And I think that there is sufficient means in camp to make him tell us the rest of what we must know." His eyes widened and he licked his lips as he pushed a coal aside with his boot. "Where the rest of his group is hiding and how many they may be. It can be found in a few hours, if you know how."

"But the gift of one of your pretty stones would have been simple enough," Grengor interrupted. "And far less trouble than torturing one who probably would have dealt in good faith. I do not care for how you have acted in behalf of the fair lady, apothecary, and even less for what you propose to do."

Basil turned and faced the marine. "The temporary success of your master has weakened your judgment, sergeant," he said. "As you apparently have forgotten, Procolon is in grave danger of being overrun. We do not have time to barter for days with each scattered tribe that we meet. We must convince them in haste to harken to our banner, using whatever tools prove most expedient. And the fair lady will reward the suitor who provides the army to save her crown, not the one who labors over some petty distinction for what is just." He stopped and looked back at the prisoner. "Besides, he is as likely to be a treacherous brigand as a simple wanderer. There is no other way in which we may proceed."

"What about enchantment?" Alodar said suddenly. "He could hold nothing back if under the charm of a sorcerer. If his tribe proves friendly, then he can be freed."

"Kelric would attempt no such feat when fully in health and in the comfort of Ambrosia." Basil waved the words aside. "He certainly will not try such an adventure now."

"I was not thinking of Kelric," Alodar replied coldly. "I have studied enough that I am willing to give the charm a try."

"An idle bluff," Basil shot back. "The fair lady will not be fooled by such blatant attempts to win further favor."

"It is not a bluff," Alodar said. "I have been successful with far-seeing. There is no reason why I cannot enchant as well."

Before Basil could reply, Vendora rose and extended her palm for silence. She looked at Alodar and smoothed a loose curl in place. "Kelric never wavered in expounding the difficulties of his craft," she said. "And even in his prime, his enchantments numbered less than a dozen. Can you really perform as you claim?"

Alodar looked back into Vendora's eyes. "I have never attempted it before, my fair lady," he said, "but my studies thus far have increased my confidence so that I feel there is a reasonable chance of success. If you would prefer touching the nomad's mind, rather than tearing his body, then I shall attempt it."

Vendora's eyes narrowed, and then she looked back at Basil. "If Alodar indeed can effect such enchantment, then it is a skill which I can employ well in my service," she said. "I thank you, Basil, for your efforts in my behalf, but I judge it is in my best interest if you turn the prisoner over to the aspiring sorcerer."

Basil's scowl deepened, and he stood silently for a long moment. Finally, with a wave of disgust, he spun and tromped off to the other side of the firepit. His followers pushed the barbarian forward, and the nomad pitched to his knees at Alodar's feet.

"Get Melab," Alodar said to Grengor, "and prepare to hold the prisoner steady. I will consult with Kelric and learn what I must know."

Alodar ran up the beach to the low ridge where Kelric slept. He touched the sorcerer's arm and gently rocked him back and forth. The flesh felt hot; as the eyes slowly opened, Alodar touched the bare forehead and frowned.

"Ah, my sugar plum," Kelric's voice wheezed. "Are you so impatient for more that you disturb my sleep?"

"It is only your student," Alodar said. "And I interrupt your rest on service to the queen."

Kelric started to reply but gagged instead and then coughed spasmodically for several minutes. He shook awake and widened his eyes as he recognized Alodar hovering over him. "Not more sorcery," he whispered at last. "You push too hard, Alodar, and will end in no better condition than I."

"I wish that Basil carried with him the substance of his trade, rather than the tokens of his wealth," Alodar said, ignoring the sorcerer's words. "With the proper ingredients, I could brew an alchemical potion to cool the fever and purge your sickness. But neither my thaumaturgy or Duncan's magic sphere can offer any aid."

Kelric shrugged and rattled out a deep sigh. "It is far less discomforting than if I attempted one charm too many," he said, "and the visions that swim before my eyes are as good as any I have had when in a trance. Let it be, Alodar. Even though a sorcerer can see the workings of fate, he cannot alter them."

Alodar looked back over his shoulder to the firepit. Grengor and Melab struggled to hold the captive in a sitting position, and Vendora stood with her hands on her hips, looking Alodar's way.

"I was successful with the cantrip last night," Alodar said. "Even the third repetition came without much difficulty. The queen now has need for an enchantment, and I feel I am ready to attempt it."

"No, Alodar," Kelric said weakly. "Do not be misled just because one charm seems to progress well. You were probably fatigued and your senses dull. If you tried the very same cantrip fully alert, you might find it beyond your power to complete it."

Kelric raised one shaky hand and motioned Alodar closer to his head. "And the enchantment of a mind as complex as a man's is too large a step," he continued softly. "I studied for two years before my mentor judged me proficient enough to try it. If you have seen afar for the first time less than a day ago, then you must rest instead, before pursuing anything more."

"But it is for the queen," Alodar said, "and the favor that I hope to find in her eyes because of it."

"Ah, the fair lady." Kelric choked out a laugh. "Even

I have not dared dream so high." His chest heaved with effort for several moments more, and then he slowly shook his head. "In my youth, it was always just one charm more," he said. "Just one more and my power would be great enough that men would bow their heads with respect and my choice of the ladies would be a pleasant confusion." He shook his head a second time. "You state that you do this for the queen, Alodar, but in the end I doubt that she will behave differently than any other."

He stopped and looked Alodar in the eye and saw the resolution. "But I recognize the fierceness that cannot be denied," he sighed at last. "And there will be little more that I will teach you. If you must know of enchantments, then listen to my words well."

Kelric whispered the charm, and Alodar concentrated intently to remember the strange pattern of words. It was only a third the length of the cantrip for far-seeing. After a short while, he returned to Vendora and the others. He looked about and raised his brows in surprise as they all stepped back and flung their arms over their eyes. He coiled into a crosslegged position and directed Grengor and Melab to set the captive before him. While the two marines held the nomad's head steady and pressed his eyelids open, Alodar began the charm.

The first recital went smoothly enough; but from the first word of the second repetition, Alodar felt the beginning of the resistance. Hee spoke half a dozen words correctly, then almost gagged as he attempted the next. He tried to force his tongue flat in the bottom of his mouth, but spasms of nausea forced his lips closed each time he pursed them into a circle. He braced himself, concentrated on the next three in succession and finally forced them out.

He licked his spray-chapped lips, and beads of perspiration broke out on his forehead. The rest of the charm faded away. Almost in panic, he mentally grabbed at the chain of words as they seemed to disappear down a hole in his memory. He focused on the next and brought it back into sharpness. By holding his breath, he kept his stomach calm. With excruciating slowness, he finished the second recital.

Alodar felt dizzy. A chilling numbness ran up and down

his legs. His tired body protested the abuse. The thought that the strain would only increase began to weigh heavily on his mind. He broke the starting word of the final repetition into syllables and concentrated on uttering the first correctly. But each time he opened his mouth, his lips trembled and he fought to force back the rumbles of his stomach. He gasped like a man choking and beat his fist into the sand to pop the sound free, but it would not come. For several minutes he struggled, his arms twitching and his eyes stinging with salty tears. A dull pain started to throb in the base of his neck and pulse upwards between his ears as the realization that he might not finish began to form.

In desperation Alodar flailed about and untied the pouch with the sphere from his side. He grasped the coldness and held it at eye level, hoping somehow to tap its reputed powers to aid in finishing the charm. He stared at the closed eye, but his thoughts crackled with tenseness. The strange feeling that poured over him outside of the Cycloid Guild would not come.

With a final effort he twisted his lips into the correct form and squeezed his sides. A raspy growl dribbled from his mouth and then his head seemed to explode in a flash of light, as if he had been struck by a well-aimed mace. A searing pain raced through his body. With a feeling of his skin being stripped away, he slid from consciousness.

"The queen explicitly left him in our custody," a voice shouted angrily.

"Then you did not discharge your duty with much competence," a second answered. "Well, we have what we need to know, and one barbarian life more or less does not matter.'"

Alodar blinked his eyes open and then quickly squeezed them shut again. He moved his head slowly to the side and felt a sudden throbbing that continued unabated for several minutes. He wrapped his arms about his stomach, but the pressure did not help, and he kept his lips firmly pressed together, trying to force back the queasiness. Kelric had been right; he had pushed too far and misspun the enchantment.

Alodar felt a gentle touch on his brow and cracked one

259

lid open to see Aeriel bending over him. "You have been in a swoon for over a day," she said. "And during the night, Basil carried out the rest of his plan."

Alodar propped himself up on one elbow, grimacing at the pounding the motion started in his head. "Then what did the apothecary learn?" he asked weakly. "I think my sorcery will not be the means by which we deal with the nomads."

"Their camp is to the north, beyond the rocky point," Aeriel said. "Their group is a small one; their men number no more than ours. They plunder as much as they hunt. On the morrow they will move southwards, looking for shipwrecked booty from the storm. We must either retreat before them or make the conditions of confrontation our own choosing. From the way the captive related their history, a civilized parlay is out of the question."

"Are they the only ones with whom we can deal?" Alodar asked.

"No, there are others scattered throughout the north. The larger tribes are in the hills to the west, seeking the game that winter drives down from the higher peaks. But enough of that. Let the other suitors carry forth the queen's banner for awhile. From the looks of your face, you need more rest. I can fetch you a meal, as well."

Alodar slowly shook his head. "Had I succeeded, there would have been no denying my primacy," he groaned. "As it is, now I must strive all the harder not to loose more ground."

"Kelric warned that it takes more than a week for a misspinning to fade," Aeriel replied. "Are you truly ready to contest again after a single day?"

Alodar tried to push himself to a sitting position, but his arm trembled with the effort, and he collapsed back to the ground. "Perhaps just a little while longer to gather my strength," he said.

"And the meal?" Aeriel asked.

Alodar clutched his stomach. "Food I can still do without." He looked into her face filled with concern. "But your presence would be a comfort indeed."

Aeriel smiled, sat down beside Alodar, and placed her hand lightly on his shoulder. Alodar managed to smile back and then turned his attention to the loud voices around the firepit.

"Sweetbalm on their prowess!" Feston said, pounding a fist into an open palm. "We still outnumber them by one or two. If we strike at dusk, surprise will carry the day. And it is only force that these barbarians respect. They will submit to us no other way."

"You speak with the imprecision of a neophyte," Duncan shot back. "Suppose we were to take their camp. What would we have when we were done? Half of our men slain and half of theirs. Our numbers would be no greater than what we have now. And we would have traded ten stout hearts for an equal number who will serve only with a sharp blade at their backs. Let us retreat south, I say, as best we can. Even if they catch up, my sphere will protect the queen from harm."

"A fight in their camp would not be as bad as all that," Basil said, "if we could fell the chieftain with one of the first blows. According to our captive, his hold on the group is slight. He bullied them to rob anyone who ventured this way, regardless of the profit in it. Why, their treasure he bragged of was no more than some alchemist's rotting samples they had plundered a week ago. You look with scorn at what I have done with a barbarian. But apparently that was nothing compared to what this chieftain delights in whenever a civilized man falls into his clutches. If we can kill the leader, then the rest just might lay down their arms and follow the victors."

"Such a blow will not be swung easily," Grengor said quietly. "These nomads are a suspicious lot. They would insist we drop our arms before entering camp. And if we rushed them, the leader would be in the center. We would have to hack through them all to approach him." He stopped and rubbed his chin. "It would take a berserker to slash through the defense—a berserker or perhaps someone like Feston's guard whom we saw on the royal barge. His own safety concerned him not. Indeed, he took more than one mortal wound without even flinching."

"More sorcery," Duncan sneered. "That plan is no better than any other." He looked at Kelric, propped up against a rock a little distance away, his arms sagging limply at his sides, and then over to Alodar, barely managing to hold his head off the ground. "One nearly dead and the other unable to complete an enchantment. I say that the key to our dilemma somehow involves the use of my sphere and that we should not act until we discover it."

"Then what is your proposal, Duncan?" Vendora asked. "If we cannot gain by arms or guile, how does your magic assemble the army that I need?"

Duncan looked back at the queen and then dipped his head in silence. For a long moment, Grengor and the suitors stood shuffling their feet in the sand, saying nothing. Finally Vendora turned to two other marines standing further back. "Bring me Kelric," she said.

The two men fetched the sorcerer. With a hand under each arm, they brought him to stand before the queen. Vendora looked at the sagging form and spoke softly. "Master Kelric," she said, "I am sorry that your loyalty to the court has brought you such distress. But with the conditions being as they are, can one final enchantment make any difference?"

"You are so tactful with your words, my fair lady," Kelric wheezed without bothering to raise his head from his chest. "Since my hours seem numbered and no one cares how many remain, why not one final gesture for the glory of Procolon, you say." He nodded his head back and forth. "There are not enough jewels in Basil's coffers to make me want to attempt it."

A flicker of irritation crossed Vendora's face, and then she pressed her lips in thought. After a long moment, she reached forward and touched Kelric's arm. Frowning with the effort, she bent over and brushed her mouth against his cheek. "I am not so removed from the gossip of the palace that I do not know for what reasons you ply your craft," she said. "We have ignored your plight since we landed, one and all, it is true. But if you perform this labor in my cause, then your nurse and comforter shall be none other than the queen of Procolon."

Kelric raised his head and looked at Vendora through half open eyes. "And if that comfort requires a caress or two or perhaps even a lack of haste to resmooth a gown blown above the knee by the wind?" he said.

"We shall see later what it entails. Perform for me what I require and you will be appropriately rewarded."

"You are no different from the lowest chambermaid," Kelric said. "Full of vague promises that must be wrenched out of you, once the deed is done."

Vendora drew erect and placed her hands on her hips. "There are two important differences, sorcerer. First, I am none less than the queen. And second, even if I were not . . ." She left the sentence unfinished and curved her lips into a slight smile.

Kelric's eyes widened as he drank in Vendora's beauty. "But, my fair lady," he said, "in refusing an enchantment before, my words have been true. With full health I would fail; now even if I desired it as nothing else, the result would be the same."

Alodar frowned in concentration as he sensed the opportunity. The suitor that resolved the course of action would gain, relative to the others. Despite how he felt, he must enter the discussion. He ignored the weakness and pushed himself up.

He looked to his side and saw the top of the sphere poking out of the sand from where he had dropped it. He scooped it up and slowly climbed to his feet, panting rapidly. For a moment he gently swayed back and forth, waiting for the throbbing to quiet and the flashes of light to clear from his eyes.

"But with the sorcerer's eye, would not the effort for enchantment of only one be greatly reduced?" he called out. "And with a willing subject, even less required."

All eyes turned to Alodar as he weaved across the beach and finally thrust the eye into Kelric's hand. "Use it," he said. "It will be some time before I will be of full service to the fair lady."

Kelric looked down at the translucent orb, up to Alodar, and then back to the queen. He ran his eyes over her a second time and then scratched his side. For a long moment, he was silent. "Oh, it just might work," he conceded at last. "Yes, with the help of the eye. I learned the charm in my youth and thought I never would have cause to use it. And for the attention of the fair lady against expiring alone, I may as well try."

"Then there remains only the matter of the subject," Vendora said, looking quickly around the circle. "Who among you will seize the opportunity for greater glory?"

Heads dropped as she scanned the group. As if she

263

were a sorceress herself, the circle of men avoided her eyes. A minute passed and no one moved.

"Men of great bravery and pledged to the fair lady!" Kelric laughed. "And not one as brave as an old man with insufficient strength to draw a sword."

"My life for the crown of Procolon I have always sworn," Grengor responded quietly. "I do so still. But that life I have pledged to give in honor in battle, not smothered and stolen away by the foulness of sorcery."

"But it seems the only way," Alodar said. "Without the enchantment, we will not bend this first small band to our side."

"Then let it be you, suitor and savior of the queen," Duncan sneered. "You have the righteous air of the pure hero of the saga. If you are indeed true to your ideals, then it is you who should do the deed."

Vendora turned to Alodar and her lips curved into a small smile. "It seems your boasts with sorcery far exceeded your craft, Alodar," she said. "How soon then will it be before you can swing a blade and carry an equal load with the rest?"

Alodar licked his lips and held himself steady as he returned the gaze of the queen. He heard Aeriel rush to his side but nodded before she could speak. "It is as Kelric states, my fair lady," he replied, "a question of bravery. When you weigh the virtues of your suitors, remember who spoke when all the others remained silent."

The first recitation had been long. Alodar sagged with weakness as he sat in front of Kelric, who still held the small sphere at eye level. He looked from the motionless old sorcerer, mumbling before him, to the ocean beyond. In the low afternoon sun, he could see the sail of the longboat still fluttering above high tide. He looked to the south, over the unending beach that finally blurred out in the distance. He studied the hills to the north that curved to the surf, cutting off his view.

Then with a sudden shock, Alodar felt his gaze wrenched in the direction of the sphere. Instinct took over; he tried to draw his head away or raise an arm, but his muscles would not respond. With great effort, he squinted his eyes to thin slits, resolved to catch only a glimpse of what Kelric held in his hand and then dart away. But he could only blink once, then stare directly into the globe.

A single eye, now fully open, glowed back at him, its pupil golden yellow and dilated with power. Around the white, perfectly spaced black lashes stood tensely erect, and tiny crackles of blue flame darted from one hair to the next. The eye floated free in the confines of the sphere, circled with but a hint of the palest flesh. In fascination, Alodar examined the orb which confronted him, feeling that he must let no part go unstudied or neglected. Even from the distance, he could somehow tell that the lashes curved inward in the same precise arcs; not a single vein marked the perfect whiteness in which the pupil swam.

With a last shudder, he stared straight at the pupil and felt a sudden dizziness as the world about him swept away. The sea, the hills, the men who stood with faces guarded, one by one they dimmed and were gone. Alodar lashed his mind out in blackness. He groped for the fabric of his existence but felt it dissolve. The other suitors, the craftmasters, Vendora, Aeriel—visions of them warped before him and slid away into the blackness. And Alodar, Alodar the suitor, the neophyte magician, the alchemist's apprentice, the journeyman thaumaturge, the one who quested for the fair lady—like the layers of an onion, his self-images were peeled off and crumbled away. Shell after shell faded into oblivion. As the innermost core was bared and dissolved with the rest, Alodar screamed in anguish and then was quiet.

Now there was only the eye and the eye was everything. The blackness was complete; he could not see. The silence was complete; he could not hear. He was composed of nothingness; he could not feel. But the eye was there. The eye would provide; the eye would guide him. What was proper for him to see, he would be shown. What was proper to hear, he would hear. What was proper for him to feel, he would feel.

Gradually and gently, he began to perceive. At first it was only a whisper and, because there was nothing else, he dwelt upon it; the murmur grew into a hiss of surf on sand. As it did, the darkness lifted; the sun shone behind him, lighting a gentle sea, broken only by a single mast standing above the tide. The sea ran upon a beach, a beach that stretched off in the distance to the south and butted against hard granite hills to the north.

He felt the wind course about him, heard the call of gulls above the beach. The scene before him shimmered for an instant. Then, where there had been no one, a tired old man was sitting in the sand. Without asking, Alolar knew the man was Kelric the sorcerer. He heard a cough behind. Without turning, he knew of the marines and the men of the court of Procolon.

He watched the sorcerer without feeling. And as he waited, he felt himself take form, felt the layers build upon the seed that sprang into being as he watched. He was Alodar, Alodar the journeyman thaumaturge, the alchemist's apprentice, and the neophyte magician. Feeling coursed through his limbs. He was Alodar the fighter and he felt a restlessness welling up in him, to take form and guide him to action. He felt a desire to strike, to bring forth blood, to hack until he could hack no more. And it felt right. He was Alodar and this was his purpose for being.

He rose to his feet, eyes still on the sorcerer who somehow held his attention. Behind the huddled form he saw a woman, looking away, walking slowly along the beach. She was beautiful, cheeks aglow, crimson hair flowing behind as the waves rolled up to touch her bare feet.

In a flash he was Alodar the suitor as well as the fighter. As he looked at the woman, something began to matter greatly. It bubbled up beside the desire to fight and it grew angular and sharp and sawed at his mind for attention. But the lust for blood flamed higher, and the edges of the other desire shrank beside it. The sharpness rounded and it subsided. She was only Aeriel, a lady of the court. He was Alodar the journeyman thaumaturge, the alchemist's apprentice, the neophyte magician—but most of all, Alodar the warrior.

The feeling exploded within him and he drew his sword with a mighty flourish and a piercing scream. Without waiting for the others, he turned and raced out of the camp, across the sand, and to the fight, to the blood that beckoned him from the hills to the north.

Like a machine of the thaumaturges, Alodar stomped forward with an even cadence up and over the low dunes, across the gullies that emptied to the sea, striding evenly, breathing evenly, not pausing to check his direction or how far he had gone.

He was aware of the others scurrying behind, trying to keep pace. Once, after an hour, two of the marines raced by, carrying the sorcerer between them on a makeshift stretcher. The old man raised himself shakily on one arm as they came alongside and looked Alodar deeply in the eyes. Alodar paid him no heed. After a moment, Kelric signaled that all was well. His bearers dropped back to join the throng behind.

The sun sank towards the west, casting the men's shadows before them as they finally climbed through a cut in the hills. At the narrow pass, Alodar felt a sudden compulsion to pause. He waited for the rest to draw up beside him and look down to a cove beyond.

They saw a narrow finger of the sea crook inland in the midst of a scattering of small campfires. Around each, two or three men sprawled in relaxation, talking, picking fleas from each other, and gnawing on the remains of the evening meal. Nearest the inlet, one roared with laughter, holding high a silver cup and wiping the back of his hand on a woolly vest. On the peninsula of land between the bay and the sea, women and children clustered about low-slung tents and hobbled ponies.

"It is as the captive painted it," Grengor said. "If we hurry we can take them as they eat."

"Then let us group at the outcropping over there," another man replied. "With master Alodar rushing out, and a bit of luck, he will have the chieftan down just as we show ourselves and charge."

Alodar heard grunts of agreement, and the desire to rest quickly passed. The bloodthirst rose again, and he jerked at the hilt of his sword. He struck out in the lead down the hillside, scrambling over the rocks and just barely remaining behind cover. The urgency boiled higher, and his nostrils flared in anticipation. The rest followed behind as he descended the irregular trail.

Halfway down, his view suddenly blurred. As he lurched around a large boulder, he did not see the cove, but more of the hills leading to higher mountains in the distance. In the very center, a monolith of cold granite soared into the sky. Alodar stopped and blinked in confusion. He was Alodar the bloodspiller, with a purpose soon to be fulfilled. There was no room in his existence for anything but his mission.

But the spire compelled, and he felt himself drawn forward. He seemed to skim over the rough ground. Like a tiny leaf blown by the wind, he hurled to the tower. At its base, his compulsion grew, and he launched himself up the side. Hand over hand, as rapidly as he seemed able, he climbed into the sky, drawing nearer to whatever called him. In an instant he neared the peak and stopped to stare at what was before his eyes. The stone was smooth, with no more grips to pull him higher; but directly in front, protruding from the rock, was the tarnished surface of an ancient bracelet.

As Alodar reached forward to pull it from the wall, the vision wavered and blurred. He felt the presence of the eye expand in his mind, growing, consuming, absorbing into blackness the sights about him. The scene flashed away and he looked down into a cove populated by a small tribe of barbarians. He blinked again, but the image remained firm.

He resumed his hurried descent, untroubled by what he had seen and intent only on what he was meant to do. Down the hillside the party went, until at last they stood poised at the outcropping, barely fifty yards from the small camp at the water's edge. With perfect calmness, Alodar marched out from the hiding place and headed straight for the barbarians, his hand on the hilt of his sword and his gaze steady.

The men in the camp spotted him almost immediately. Alodar heard an order barked from the water's edge as two men rose to meet him. He closed half the distance and scanned those still seated, marking for sure the one who commanded them.

"Drop your arms," the two guardsmen growled in unison as he approached. Alodar took but two more steps and felt the last restraint hurl away. The lust for blood billowed up. With a frenzy, he drew his sword. Swinging it high overhead, he ran at the two with a chilling yell.

The man on the right cleared his blade of the scabbard but did not have time to use it. Alodar's sword swung down into his shoulder with a bone-breaking thud. As the man sank, clutching spasmodically with his free hand at the wound, Alodar pulled his sword backwards and wrenched it free. The other nomad stood openmouthed, still not comprehending the folly of such a suicidal attack. Alodar thrust his dagger into the nomad's stomach with his left hand in a swiping zigzag that spilled the man to the ground.

The men behind all scrambled to their feet. The ones nearest instinctively drew their swords as Alodar thundered into their midst. They formed a shallow bowl around him, animal hide shields high and swords pointing out. Alodar looked beyond, down to the water's edge, where he saw the chieftain now on one knee, peering in puzzlement at the commotion.

Using sword and dagger together, Alodar lunged at the two immediately in front. As his blade skittered off their shields, he bolted around them. The man on his left slashed backwards, and Alodar felt the sharp edge of pain race through his left arm. He convulsively dropped his dagger and faltered for a step, his vision fogging from the blow. But the urge to run amok welled up even stronger and beat down the pain, hurling it away. With the arm dangling at his side spewing blood, he sprinted down the beach to his target.

The chieftain rose to his feet, barking new orders to the men scattered along the way. Behind Alodar, the original group pounded after, now out of sword reach but sealing off all retreat. Glancing quickly to the side, Alodar saw a bowman nock an arrow and began to track his progress across the sand. One arrow sailed by in front, and then a second fell inches behind.

He burst across the logs which defined the chieftan's campfire and closed upon the three men who still stood between him and his goal. With a savage yell, he hacked low underneath the falling shield on his right and hit just above the ankle, sweeping the man from his feet. The two on the left both slashed downward on his unprotected side but missed as Alodar dipped and scrambled forward.

The man nearest swung again, this time in a low horizontal arc. The point reached Alodar's calf, and his leg buckled. The leader and the two aides closed about him, each eager to deliver a mortal blow.

The pain coursed up through his leg and spine as Alodar struggled to stand and get past the chieftain's guard. Three blades were raised against him, but he concentrated only on one, trying to find an opening before they fell.

Suddenly beyond the periphery of the camp, a mighty yell arose and the marines and the rest of the royal party charged into view. The three swordsmen hesitated and turned to see the cause for the commotion. Alodar saw his chance. He swung his sword up into the air, reversing his grip, and plunged it daggerstyle at the face of the leader. The point caught the barbarian in the left eye and snapped his head backwards with the fury of the blow.

The other two nomads spun back to see their leader fall and then dropped their jaws as they saw Alodar standing with both arms at his side, staring vacantly. One took a step forward, sword still high, but then hesitated to look back at the wall of men racing his way.

Alodar felt the fury slowly subside and the pain from leg and arm return. As the delayed blow slashed down, his leg again buckled. The sword caught him in the flesh of the shoulder and deflected off and down into the sand. Without caring, he saw the nomads waver and then throw down their swords.

The world without fell away and the crescendo of the pain rose higher. In desperation Alodar sought out the eye, the eye which had comforted him, which had provided for him, which gave him his reason for being and protected him from pain.

But the presence was not there and the pain grew stronger, throbbing through limb and torso and beating on the fiber of his brain with ever-increasing strokes of lightning. Alodar groped for a touchstone, some reference point in the void to guide him to the eye, but none was there. Then, as he was on the edge of consciousness, a vision came of a granite crag, a bracelet embedded in its peak, and the sleeping form of a great wizard. As the pain finally overwhelmed him, Alodar clawed the air, reaching out to grasp at the strange force which beckoned him over the hills.

PART FIVE

The Wizard

CHAPTER SEVENTEEN

The Improbable Imp

"LOOK, Grengor, he stirs." Alodar heard the words filter through the numbness that permeated his entire body. He opened his eyes slowly and saw Aeriel's auburn curls cascading down about his face. He shifted the position of his head and felt her caress on his cheek. A dull throb pounded in his head.

"Gently, Alodar," she said softly. "My lap will serve as well as any cradle till you mend. There was some sweetbalm in the chieftain's plunder but it was far from freshly brewed. It closed the wounds and stimulated the regrowth, but it still will be some time before you are whole."

Alodar frowned as dim memories stirred. A bouncing ride, thin acorn gruel forced between his lips, Aeriel's soft words, sunlight and campfires swirled together in a blur. He looked out into the evening light and saw a dozen campfires scattered about the slopes of a wide-mouthed valley. The hills came together like cupped palms, and ferns and long-stemmed grasses clustered near the small stream that ran where they touched. On the slopes, the naked oaks were few, and stately pines soared over a hundred feet into the sky. Ponies whinnied in the distance, mixing their cries with the guttural accent of the northmen's voices. In the group nearby, two tangle-haired women served the queen, while one of the marines passed a waterskin back to a chieftain.

Alodar opened his mouth to speak, but Grengor cut him off. "Fear not, master. After your deed, not a man among us begrudges your weight. Your litter will be carried all the way back to the palace halls in Ambrosia if it need

272

be. Each bearer remembers that, because of your wounds, he did not receive any.

"And the barbarians regard you as some great hero from the sagas. We tell them that you sleep in peace, that if they do not heed your followers' commands, once again they will face your terrible wrath. Why, in the eight days that you drifted in and out of your swoon, the first tribe's terrified tale and Basil's beads have swollen our forces many fold. We are nearly a hundred now, moving southward for the queen."

"It is not quite so simple, Grengor," Aeriel said. "I have seen the petty quarrels and heard the whispered conversations among these hastily assembled allies. Basil's gems and Feston's promises for greater reward will not keep their attention forever. As the ranks swell, they will become much more difficult for the few of us to manage."

"I am as aware of the truth as you, my lady," Grengor assured her. "Under the circumstances, our present course seems the best. A hundred men will make no difference in Procolon's defense, but there is no time to build a large and disciplined army. We must move down the line of hills that parallels the coast as rapidly as we can, convincing whomever we find along the way to enlist in the cause of the fair lady. Each of us now directs six or seven of the nomads. With a bold front, perhaps we can command ten times that number. If we are lucky, we will cross the border with more than a thousand swords."

Alodar struggled to sit up. "Grengor," he said, "the crag, the wizard's tower to the west, where the snow dips to the hills. How many days for all of us on foot? We must go there."

"Be not alarmed, my lady," Grengor told Aeriel. "It is but a delirium. A small phantasm from having undergone the charm of the sorcerer. As the body mends, so will the mind."

Alodar still felt sick and dizzy from his miscast charm. The sweetbalm was no longer potent enough to blot out all of the pain. "Fetch Kelric, I say. He must interpret the vision. We cannot choose our course until it is settled."

"He alone of our troop has perished," Grengor said. "Even with the aid of the eye, he gave up the little power that remained within him to quell your pain and guide your final thrust into the cheiftain's brain. Indeed, had he not so passed from us, you still would be only what he chose to make of you."

Grengor paused and looked off into the distance. "But in the end, I think he judged his choice to be the right one. As he sank away, the queen pronounced him a suitor for his deed in her behalf. His last expression was a smile rather than a scowl."

Alodar was silent for a moment as the news sank in. But the feeling of urgency grew and pushed his reflection aside. "There is more to the eye than just a sorcerer's tool," he said at last. "I saw and felt far beyond what Kelric impressed upon me."

"And what if it is so, master?" Grengor persisted. "The deed of the eye is done, and we must soon return to Procolon with whatever forces we can muster. Aeriel even replaced the thing in your pouch as you slept; no one else coveted it. Leave thoughts of sorcery here in the uplands. What can they possibly matter to you now?"

Alodar leaned one hand back to steady himself and closed his eyes. The scene of the hills with the mountains behind sprang into his mind, almost as vivid as it had under enchantment. Mentally he soared over the terrain and unerringly sped to the one spot that had compelled him before. The giant spire was there and inside it was a tomb. A tomb to be opened. A wizard to be questioned. The answer to a riddle for which he could not even formulate the question.

He thought of his quest for the queen; but beside this great yearning, it did not seem to matter. He wrinkled his brow in puzzlement and reached out to stroke Aeriel's arm at his side. How could the spire connect with what he strove for? It must be an enchantment produced by the eye itself, independent of the wielder. Had he not looked, it would be no more than an idle thought to be consumed by the fires of his ambition. But the compulsion tugged and he knew he must respond.

Alodar opened his eyes and thought through what he would say. Waving aside Aeriel's restraining arm, he slowly rose to face the sergeant. He swayed for a moment and then drew in a deep breath and was steady.

"I know that it will take time as well as sweetbalm to mend my body, Grengor," he said in a slow, deliberate tone. "But my mind is clear, clear enough to know what we must do. If we continue directly south as we have, we will find only more of the smaller tribes in our path. But in my vision of far-seeing on the boat, I looked down on larger camps higher in the interior, larger tribes hunting where the game is more plentiful. It will take us longer to return to Procolon, but we must strike to the west so that we increase our chances of finding greater numbers."

"But, as lady Aeriel says," Grengor objected, "it would also mean greater risk of losing control of whatever forces we now command."

"I cannot ignore what I have seen under the spell of the eye, Grengor," Alodar said. "I must go west and seek out the answer. This beckoning I cannot explain, but the truth of it I do not doubt. If you will trust me as your leader, then I ask you to join me."

Grengor looked back at Alodar's face. "The other suitors will not be convinced easily. And if we argue in front of the barbarians, the feeble hold we have on them may vanish."

"I will go alone if I must," Alodar said, looking out over the campfires. "But if you marines and the nomads you command come, then the others will follow. We are the majority. As you say, the suitors will not risk a confrontation. They will reason that a few days detour is far better than proceeding southward with a small fraction of our party."

Grengor rubbed his chin. "The south or west; we do not know for certain the outcome of our fortunes either way," he mused.

"You followed me onto the wargalley's deck and into the longboat in a raging sea."

Grengor was silent for a moment. "And into the nomad's camp." He slapped his side at last. "Forgive my hesitation, master. If you command to the west, it is to the west we will go. Rest lightly while I pass the word. We will strike into the interior tomorrow."

Grengor went off, and Alodar felt Aeriel's touch on his shoulder. "There is still time for rest," she suggested. "Come, make yourself comfortable."

They settled to the ground and Alodar looked up into dark eyes that reflected the flickering glows of the campfires. "I still quest for the fair lady," he said. "I do not

275

know what we will discover in the west, but I hope that somehow it will aid in my cause."

"I understand that." Aeriel continued her gentle stroking. "Your charge into the camp redeemed your loss of face for the miscast sorcery. That is all in the past now. The queen's favor will shift to the one who can aid her best on the morrow."

For a long while Alodar thought of his thirst for glory, the granite spire, Vendora, and the foggy memory of Aeriel's nursing in the days past. Finally he reached out and grasped her hand in his. "But were it not for the quest . . ."

Aeriel smiled. "And I understand that as well," she said.

The huge fire crackled in the first light of dawn, and Alodar huddled close for its warmth. He tentatively stretched one of his legs forward and felt the stiffness in his calf. Idly, he fingered a chip of agate he had found on the trail and then tossed it among the clippings of herbs, twigs, rocks, and other thaumaturgical and alchemical gear he had scavenged along the way. He slapped at one of the fleas that he had acquired from the nomadic tribesmen.

"Despite its age, the sweetbalm has done its work well, Alodar," Aeriel said beside him. "Only twelve days of healing, and already you are nearly well."

"Yes I think I am ready to try some of the trail on my own feet," Alodar responded, rubbing his shoulder with his free hand as she leaned against him. And I will need to be far more supple when we finally reach the spire."

"It is well that you are so steadfast in your determination," she said. "You know full well that Duncan and the others accompany your marines against their will. They seek only the smallest opportunity to show you still bemused from Kelric's spell. Once even a hint of doubt creeps into your manner, they will try to exploit it to gain control."

Alodar nodded and looked down the trail. They were higher now, and the valley walls closed together. Rather than scattered on a broad floor, their troop snaked back in almost single file, the row of campfires strung like fiery beads on an invisible string. The trees crowded in close, taking turns eclipsing the sun as it rose into the sky. Long shafts of light filtered through the needles, bathing the dusty air in a golden glow. Alodar heard Feston's deep voice and Vendora's laugh in reply. He chafed at his self-imposed exile from her presence but, after his failure with sorcery, thought it best to resolve the mystery of the wizard's tower before approaching her again. He looked back at Aeriel and saw her staring silently into the flame.

After several minutes, Grengor walked into view from up the trail and playfully slapped his relief guard on the back as he passed. "By the spirits, a solemn lot," he cried as he approached Alodar and Aeriel. "Did not your training maids tell you, my lady, of the danger of staring with such intensity into the blaze?"

"Yes, that they did, Grengor," Aeriel said, shaking her head and looking up to the marine as he approached. "Many a time they warned me that the fascination of the flame was only the will of some demon in the world beyond. Reaching out and trying to bewitch me, just as the sorcerer does with his eye. And many times as a small girl I tested such old tales, too."

"You make much too light of it, my lady," Grengor said. "Your maids instructed you well. As the romances say, it is not only by the wizard's brazier that the realms are connected; innocent flame of whatever type might serve as the means also."

"But the sagas say that only the simplest and least powerful can come through of their own will," Aeriel protested. "Demons of true power can bridge the gap only by the intercession of a wizard. Unless he deliberately seeks to make the contact and provides the exotic ingredients for the flame, then there can be no transferral."

"Yes, my lady, it is probably as you say," Grengor replied as he moved across the campsite. "But I shun staring at the flame nonetheless."

Alodar rose stiffly from his sprawled position and tentatively stretched to his tiptoes. "Pause a few minutes while you can, Grengor," he said, "but we should break camp and begin the climb. I hope to be well up the mountainside and perhaps even at the base of the spire before nightfall."

Grengor grunted as he slumped down for a moment's rest at the edge of the fire. One of the other marines rose and sent the word down the line. One by one, the fires were snuffed out. Soon the valley walls echoed with the sounds of breaking camp and loading the ponies. In half an hour, the long string was ready to march, and they started up the trail.

The early going was easy, up a modest incline with little rock and debris to impede their progress. As the sun began to arch up to its zenith, the slope steepened and the smoothness underfoot gave way to bare rock, tumbled and cracked by the snow melts of spring.

Alodar panted near the lead, his lips pulled into a slight grimace as he tried his weight on his healing leg. With such a large party, the pace was slow enough; but he was tiring rapidly and wished that a good place to halt would soon appear.

"A moment, Alodar," Aeriel gasped. "I am beginning to feel the effects of the height. Should we not pause, even if we do not prepare a meal?"

"I petition with the lady," Grengor said as he struggled to join them. "I have an itch between my shoulders that has tormented me since we broke camp this morning."

Alodar smiled at Grengor's efforts to reach a spot high up in the center of his back. "Hold still for a moment," he said. "I will give you aid while Aeriel catches her breath."

Grengor turned his back, and Alodar briskly began to rake the area with his hand.

"Aieeee!" Grengor shouted and danced away. "Desist, master. Your scratch turns the itch into pain. I prefer the more gentle touch of the lady." He knelt down before Aeriel, and she cautiously laid her hand on his back.

"Why, there is something caught underneath your tunic, Grengor," she exclaimed. "I can feel the lump of it quite plainly against my palm."

Alodar stepped forward and ran his hand down the neck of the garment. After a few exploratory jabs, he withdrew a small, round, and barbed object. "It is an ivoryroot burr," he said. "I would not think that such a plant could grow so far north. No wonder you had discomfort this morning. Those spines would drive even the concentrating sorcerer to distraction."

Grengor rose to his feet, flexed his shoulders and grinned. "Many a wound have I borne in silence," he

278

said. "It seems this ivoryroot is more than a match for a marine."

He attempted to step forward to take the lead as the rest of the party began to bunch up behind. But with a flailing stagger, he pitched onto the rocky slope, breaking his fall only at the last instant. He turned and struggled to regain his feet as a marine and two barbarians nearby began to bellow with laughter at his plight. Alodar looked down, puzzled at his usually sure-footed sergeant, and saw the reason for his fall.

"Grengor," he said, "your bootlaces are tied together!"

Grengor scowled first at Alodar and then at Aeriel. "Such frivolity does little for discipline on the march. I am surprised that one of you two would act so out of character."

"But, Grengor," Aeriel protested, "in no way would I do such to you. Perhaps your laces entangled themselves when you stopped to have the burr removed."

"Unlikely that a double bucket knot could be made accidentally." Grengor retied his boots and turned to resume the climb. "Enough. I know better than to confront your denials. Just do not be surprised if I give your campfire a wider berth in the future."

Aeriel turned to Alodar and they exchanged questioning glances. Alodar shrugged and resumed the climb. Grengor worked out his heat as he attacked the ever-steepening mountain. Soon the entire party was again strung out in a long, thin line, clambering over the fallen rock and gasping for air.

They traveled for barely a quarter hour more when the monotony of heel on stone was broken by an angry shout back down the line.

"By the shields, I will have no more of this badgering." The voice carried up to where Alodar circled a large boulder in the way. "Draw your sword now, knave, and let us settle it."

Alodar quickly limped back down the line, shouldering marines and nomads aside. He reached the commotion just as blades clanked for the first time. "To your station," he commanded the marine. "Attend to your chieftain," he shouted at the nomad. The two men stopped and momentarily stepped backwards. "Enough," Alodar concluded as he halted between them. "You both know that the gain of all depends on each of us working together, not against each other. Now what brings on such folly?"

"He drew on me, for what cause I do not know, master," the marine said. "I unsheathed my own blade only to defend myself from his attack."

"Away with your smooth words," the other shot back. "Look at my head and shoulders. Do you think that I sweat so much in this dry air to drench me so? Ha, now look at this one's goatskin. Empty with not a drop left for its intended purpose.

Alodar looked back to the marine. His goatskin was flapping empty against his side. "Perhaps a leak, master," he mumbled. "And I swear I did not come near this man until he whirled about and accosted me."

Alodar eyed the evidence, trying to formulate a reprimand that would deter the rest of his troop from such conduct while not hampering their fighting spirit. As the marine's glance dropped to the ground under Alodar's penetrating stare, a startled cry from the head of the line shot down the mountainside.

"And now it is lady Aeriel," Alodar growled in irritation. He sighed and began to limp back up the trail. "I shall attend to your punishment later."

He passed two nomads, huddled beside the rough path, and saw them pull their garments about them in a sudden gust of wind. A fine mist billowed down the trail. Before Alodar could react, he was surrounded in dimness. He frowned and tried to brush the fog away with his hands as he continued upwards. He felt a tingling on his exposed skin as when he accidentally had spilled one of Saxton's acids. His eyes began to sting, and only with difficulty was he able to force them open.

He heard Aeriel call again, this time quite near. Through squinted eyelids, he could barely see her, a little distance ahead, huddled behind Grengor's bulk. Alodar joined them and Aeriel slipped from behind Grengor to his arms.

"It came up in an instant," she said. "From totally clear to this biting fog."

Alodar squinted out into the swirling mist, searching for an answer. Off to his right, he caught the dance of a feeble light. As he focused his attention, he heard a tiny malicious laugh. Aeriel and Grengor turned in the direction of the noise, and at that instant the breeze stopped.

The obscuring cloud dissolved and the light grew brighter, making small random motions in the air.

"Master," Grengor shouted. "By the flames, somehow a bottle has been broken nearby."

Alodar started to answer, but the air totally cleared. A tiny humanoid figure stared back at him out of the diffuse brightness. Scarcely a hand high, with long double-jointed limbs covered with coarse bristly hair, the creature hovered on long, transparent, veined wings that protruded from a misshapen knob in the center of its back. The small head sat oddly out of place before horny shoulder blades and shone with burning eyes above a gross caricature of human nose and mouth.

"Perhaps a broken bottle," Alodar said at last. "Or perhaps, Grengor, you indeed were prudent to avoid gazing at the flame these many years. We have an imp among us, no doubt about it."

Alodar looked into the glowing eyes. He felt a sudden pressure on his shoulders and a weakness in his knees. "Kneel and submit. Submit to your master." A thin, reedy voice floated through his mind. "Resistance is futile when you are so tired."

Alodar shook his head. "It speaks," he said aloud. "Like a sorcerer, it seeks my free will." He looked back at the small devil hovering inches in front of his face and tried to concentrate, as he had learned under Kelric's instruction.

"Lay down your defenses," the voice continued. "I will pester unceasingly until you do."

Alodar felt a prickly itching on his chest and back. The teeth in his lower jaw began to ache. He sensed the imp's presence in his mind, a hard and spiny ball that pulsed its message of supremacy. Like the ivoryroot burr, the sphere stabbed into his consciousness, each expansion blotting more of his free thought and increasing the distraction.

"You cannot conquer my will," the sprite doned on. "Therefore it must be yours that will falter."

Alodar's thoughts blurred in confusion. The itching spread to his limbs and the pain in his mouth sharpened.

281

He felt the impulse to do as the sprite said, to be done with the aggravation. But a deeper sense of preservation halted the reaction. He filled his lungs and focused on the throbbing irritation. To shy away from the confrontation would lead only to defeat. Mentally he formed a shell around the sphere and concentrated on expunging it from his mind. "Away, detestable irritation," he ordered. "Back whence you came and bother us no more."

The pulsing stopped for a moment, but then resumed with increasing frequency. "Submit, manthing. The itches, boils, and stings at my command will make your existence a torture. An infestation of a thousand fleas is nothing in comparison."

"Begone," Alodar yelled as he strained to crush the ball into nothingness. "Begone before I change my mind and choose instead to keep you in a bottle." He clinched his fists and increased the mental pressure.

The itching continued, and Alodar felt as if he were plunged in a vat of ravenous beetles. He squeezed his eyes shut. Imagining a great vice, he turned the shaft and closed the plates against the creature. For a second, nothing happened; but then, for the second time, the throbbing paused. Alodar detected a slight relaxation in the feelings which bedeviled him and pressed all the harder. The oscillations began again, but beat irregularly for only a few strokes more. With a gasp, he slammed the vice closed and felt the imp's presence pop from his mind.

Without warning, the dancing brightness suddenly exploded in front of Alodar's nose. With a loud bang, the imp disappeared from view. Alodar blinked twice in surprise and then rubbed his eyes, trying to wipe the after-images away. He looked quickly up and down the trail. All was quiet with no hint of a breeze.

"An exorcism as good as any in the sagas," Grengor said. "Have you managed somehow, master, to study the craft of the wizard as well?"

Alodar slowly shook his head. "My reaction was instinctive. Probably what any man would do if likewise confronted." He stopped and ran his hand over his cheek. "Perhaps my sorcery helped somewhat, although the sensations were remarkedly different. The imp did not have the irresistible tug of an enchanter. If I surrendered, it would have been because I gave my will to him, not because he took it. And for my own part, the sickness and reaction were not there. I just willed him away until he accepted the command."

"But a sprite nonetheless," Aeriel marveled. "Unheard of this far north. It was remarkable enough when some spontaneously appeared in the Fumus Mountains. But here there is no source of exotic flame to help them through. I do not like it, Alodar. Throughout our history, demons have shown little concern for the doings of mankind. But now in the cold north, the interior of smouldering mountains, and the rebelling west, they are everywhere—and in not one case because of the intercession of a wizard."

Alodar nodded and frowned in thought. He closed his eyes; instantly the vision of the spire sprang into view. "The wizard in the tomb," he said. "He will have the answer."

Alodar wearily climbed the rise and limped to look over the edge. Even his arms throbbed from the bounces of the trail. Quieting the nomads after the appearance of the imp had taken the better part of the day. Even without further incident their pace seemed to slow. Now at dusk, they would camp still a half day's march from his goal.

Alodar topped the crest and his eyes widened. A high meadow, like a giant platter, rested between peaks which circled on three sides. At the far edge, butting against one of the slopes, was another barbarian camp. He quickly counted the fires and knew that they had found one of the larger tribes. A show of force might not work this time. His force was outnumbered two to one.

Grengor and some of the others clambered to his side. "A display of peaceful intentions and quickly, too!" the marine said as he scanned the scene. "We must give them no excuse to draw their blades."

As the rest of their troop poured over the ridge, a small advance party rapidly was formed. Alodar, Grengor, the rest of the suitors, Vendora, and two of their chieftain allies broke apart from the rest and began marching across the intervening ground to the other camp. The

283

carcasses of two hares swung from an extended lance as an offering of friendship.

A group of similar size left the larger encampment; midway between the two, they met under the darkening sky. Alodar stood at the head of his party, flanked by the two chieftains, and surveyed the men who faced them. Five were simply dressed in loincloths and carried swords and hide-covered shields. Two otheres wore vests of matted wool, and leather belts circled their waists. The man in the center towered above the rest, as tall as Rendrac had been, but trim and lean, with skin pulled tight over rippling muscles. His hair was jet black, framing deep-set, smouldering eyes over a jaw clamped with determination. His lips were thin lines, ready to challenge or yell a warning; only with difficulty could one imagine them turned upwards in a smile. His vest was lined with leather, and iron bracelets hid each of his massive wrists.

He stood with his fists at his hips and looked in turn at each of the chieftains at Alodar's sides. "This year the game in these hills is too scarce to feed us all," he growled. "The tribesmen of Grak are as hungry as any. Begone back to the lower slopes and we will have no quarrel."

"We do not come to compete for food," Basil called over Alodar's shoulder. "Our direction is southward to acquire great treasure that will make concerns of the stomach a minor affair. We detour to the west only so that you have the opportunity to join and share in the good fortune to come."

Grak frowned and looked back to the chieftans. "It is as the lowlander speaks," one said. "Already he has showered us with jewels beyond even what you would dream. And mighty fighters will swing their swords among us as well. This one hacked his way through twenty men without the slightest frown of pain."

Grak looked down at Alodar and shook his head in puzzlement. "The words of a soft lowlander can be trusted only when a sword is at his throat," he said. "Besides this small one, with what other marvels do they widen your eyes?" He took a step forward and shouldered Alodar aside.

Alodar whirled and reached for his sword. Feston stepped in front of Vendora and Duncan began fumbling

284

for the pouch at his side. "Hold your arms," Vendora shouted as she saw the dark eyes stare down at her. "He comes only to look."

Grak took another step forward and Vendora, stepping from behind Feston's protection, drew herself erect. The nomad reached out and tipped her chin up, studying her face as he would appraise the booty from a battle. Vendora did not move but returned his stare unblinking. Grak touched her hair and ran a few strands through his fingers. "Like the sun," he muttered.

"Say the word, my fair lady," Feston growled. "I will make this barbarian pay for the indignity he shows your station."

Grak continued stroking Vendora's hair. Alodar tensed, darting his eyes back to Grak's companions and deciding where to make his first thrust. It had been foolish to bring her along to the parley, he thought. It would have been far better to ignore her command, even though she was the queen.

"He has no perception of my station," Vendora said at last, still looking Grak in the eye. She paused and then smiled. "And if you make it known, it will be to my displeasure."

Grak's frown returned and he looked back to Feston and the others. "Whose woman is she?" he asked. "Perhaps there is some basis on which we can barter."

"To the four of us collectively," Duncan blurted. "No single one does she call master."

Vendora threw back her head and laughed. "I am sure that many of our ways seem strange to you, Grak, but it is for me to decide who is to be my chieftain."

"In the north, a man takes what he wants," Grak said.

Vendora's face hardened. "The men of Procolon would make the price dear. You outnumber us, it is true, but many a warrior would feel the sting of our blades before it was through." She glared into Grak's eyes and then softened her expression with a smile. "And the prize is not nearly as sweet as when it is freely given."

Grak grunted and studied Vendora for a moment more. He turned and again faced the two chieftans. "And do you adopt other lowland ways as well?" he asked. "Is there none among you who leads the others?"

"We go to the west, another half day's journey," Alodar

285

said, "I lead the rest to the spire, and then we turn southwards."

"Demontooth." Grak spat. "It is folly to venture in that direction. The trees are gnarled. There is no game. And the devils give no rest to any who strive there. My father kept us well away and his father before him. How can you lead when you command your tribe so?"

"The barbarian speaks no less than the truth," Feston cut in. "It is time we abandon this trek to nowhere and proceed southwards while we still can."

Alodar looked at Grak, then at the doubt forming on the two chieftains' faces. He frowned and tried to weigh the chances of getting them all to continue.

"Here, chieftain," Basil broke the silence as he handed Grak a gem. "This is a mere token of what can be yours if you cooperate with what we wish to do. We seek little of your game. In a few days, we will be well away from these hills. At the very least, you can show us the courtesy to let us pass in peace. And if you join forces with ours, your rewards will be even greater."

Grak looked down at the jewel thrust into his hand. He idly rolled it around his palm. He stared back at Vendora and his eyes narrowed. "Camp here for two nights while we talk," he said. "I give you my permission."

"And the west?" Alodar persisted.

"As I have said," Grak replied, "there are demons there." He waved his arm at the two chieftains. "And after I have spoken with them, they will not go either. It is only the trip south that we will discuss."

"Then if it is to take two days," Alodar said, "there is time enough for me to make the journey alone. I will be safely returned before you are done."

Vendora looked at Alodar in surprise but quickly pushed her puzzlement aside. She studied Grak and then his campfires. "The strength of your tribe would aid me greatly," she said, "and as Basil has stated, if you join forces with ours, your reward could be even greater."

Grak stood in silence contemplating Vendora's words. "Perhaps our talk will touch on more than a trek south," he decided.

CHAPTER EIGHTEEN

Demontooth Tower

ALODAR glanced over his shoulder as he started down the other side of the pass. The meadow that held Grak's tribesmen disappeared from view. He looked ahead and visualized the contours of the trail. Rather than moving further upstream, it looked as if he must traverse two valleys to reach the spire. And even though foraging took the entire morning, he should reach the base of the tower by nightfall. He touched the small pack on his back and felt the reassuring lumps of his rations and the implements of his crafts.

From what Grak had said, he need not worry about blundering into another group of nomads along the way. And by leaving Grengor and the rest behind, the chance of losing control of the group was lessened. He flexed his fingers, stretching the tendons in his arm. The sweetbalm-accelerated healing had continued, and the soreness was less than the day before. He broke into a slow jog to test his muscles further. For over an hour he bounded along in silence. The descent reversed into a gentle rise and he climbed upwards towards the next pass.

When Alodar reached the saddlepoint and looked into the valley, his face broke into a smile. There on the other side, jutting up higher than the surrounding slopes, was the spire which had been such a persistent vision. He scanned the intervening terrain and then suddenly halted.

As the queen's party had climbed from the shore, the transition from woodlands to forest had been gradual, the short broadleafed trees slowly giving way to the ever-green conifers and firs. But here the change was abrupt and startling. The pines were stunted, some reaching only twenty feet above the ground. Green mixed with equal parts of brown and gray. No tree was without dead and naked branches. Bare and broken snags knifed into the sky. Under the sparse canopy of scraggly limbs, the ground was as sterile as the trail, dust and bare rock uncluttered with smaller plants or decaying mulch.

On the far slope, the trees thinned as they approached the monolith, until only a few gnarled dwarfs sparsely dotted the mountainside. Across the entire canyon, the air hung with a deathly quiet. No birds sang, no insects buzzed, no rodents chattered around the trunks. The strangeness of the scene, now that he finally saw it, tinged his elation with an unsettling apprehension. Cautiously he resumed his tread, darting his eyes into the thin forest on either side of the trail.

Another two hours passed, and Alodar reached the nadir of his traverse of the valley. He scrambled across boulders in a dry stream bed and noted that here and there an occasional low lying shrub broke the monotony of the uncovered ground. As he skirted a big rock directly in his path, he heard a sudden rustling in a nearby bush. Many small lizards had scampered away as he pounded along the trail in the preceding valley, but this noise was louder and hinted at something of much larger size.

He felt a gentle prickling in his mind that reminded him of the sprite he had exorcised the day before. He drew his sword and stepped forward. Where the undergrowth was thickest he jabbed with his blade.

"There is no need, there is no need." A form roughly the size of a small pig leaped into the air. "I will provide for you delights undreamed and without the use of force. All you have to do is ask."

Alodar blinked and looked at the figure suddenly hovering before him. The smooth skin shimmered in an irridescent purple and, except for the face, was covered by a bristly stubble of black hairs. The eyes were owl-like, golden and seeming to glow from small lights within. A pointed nose twice the length of a man's sat on top of a small puckered mouth. Unlike the sprite, no wings sprouted from the spindly back; thin, rubbery limbs curled tightly around the bulbous torso. The demon floated with no visible means of support.

"Begone, whence you came," Alodar said. "I dispatched your impish brother and have no need for you."

"Do not judge so rashly," the devil said. "I am no mere sprite whose only powers are to distract and irritate with feeble rashes and common pranks." The small mouth pulled into a deep smile that spread the rubbery face from ear to ear. "The sun is hot and there is no breeze. Would not a sip of water from melted snow provide a refreshment that the hot waterskin at your side could not equal?"

Before Alodar could reply, the devil waved a slender hand and produced a flask filled with ice. "Here," it said as it decanted a gurgling stream into a clear cup. "This is but a small token of what can be yours."

Alodar watched the water bubble in the cup. He ran his tongue across his suddenly dry lips. "Why do you submit so easily?" he asked. "I would think that you would contest my will even more strongly than the sprite."

"Submission, surrender, putting aside resistance? It is a detail that need not concern us now." The demon shrugged and pushed the container forward. "Refresh your throat, and then we can progress to more intense desires."

Alodar frowned and knocked the cup aside with a flick of his blade. "The sagas speak of no gift from demonkind that does not ultimately bear a price," he said.

"A shrewd bargainer, I see," the demon replied without breaking his smile. "Then perhaps the satisfaction of a more sophisticated urge will change your mind."

The air crackled and Alodar suddenly felt a gentle brush across the nape of his neck. He whirled about, sword still extended, and looked into the face of a darkskinned dancing girl, silently gyrating to an unheard rhythm. Her dark eyes beckoned; with a playful snap, she flicked one of her scarves at Alodar's blade. A long swath of cloth was looped around her neck, over her breasts, and tucked into the top of diaphanous pantaloons. The afternoon sun silhouetted her nimble legs. Her bare arms fluttered with the motions of the dance.

"And this is no mortal sorcerer's illusion that is in your mind's eye," the demon said over Alodar's shoulder. "Step forward and discover that she is a delight to the touch as well."

The dancer gracefully advanced and flowed past Alodar's guard. She reached up and ran her fingertips down his cheek and then pressed her body to him.

"Just place your trust in my hands," the devil continued. "Delegate your cares of this world to my attention. I will see that all is taken care of, and your petty concerns will trouble you no more."

The dancer clasped her hands behind Alodar's neck. Rubbing herself against his chest, she stretched on her tiptoes and bent back her head. Alodar shook his head. With his free hand he reached behind his neck and gently pushed the girl away. "The lass will avail you no better than the water," he said.

The dancer suddenly vanished, and the demon streaked from behind to face Alodar again. "Then to the crux of the matter. Perhaps you would prefer pleasure undistorted by the infidelity of your feeble senses."

Before Alodar could speak, a gentle prickling moved in his mind and seemed to brush against a sensitive nodule buried deep in his consciousness. The pressure expanded with a burst of energy, and a sudden wave of pleasure radiated through his body: the drowsy comfort of falling asleep; the exhilaration of a last-second victory; the breaking of a three day fast; the softness of a woman's body; the spice of the newly mastered craft. The delights mixed together in a jumble that made Alodar gasp. With tears in his eyes he slipped to his knees and let his sword fall from his grasp.

He tried to focus on his peril. Before the thought could be half formed, a second pulse triggered the reaction and he pitched forward to the ground, drowned by the ecstasy that flowed over him. He rolled over onto his back and sprawled on the ground, breathing shallow gulps of air as the feeling slowly faded away.

"It is yours for the asking, continual and everlasting," the devil said as he floated over Alodar's chest and peered down. "Merely surrender your will to mine and you will have strokes of bliss that come in an unending procession.

Alodar slowly rose to sitting and looked at the grotesque smile. "You will never, by your own devices, experience a pleasure so intense," the demon said. "And if you do not agree, then what you have felt will be but a distant memory."

Alodar clamped his teeth and stared at the demon. "Begone," he said weakly.

"Such power in your words." The devil laughed. "I think one more sample should seal the bargain."

Alodar tensed, trying to rally a defense against the next onslaught, but at the same time savoring the anticipation. How could anyone resist such an overpowering feeling? He banged his fist against the ground in frustration as he realized what his next answer would be. A pulse of dull pain ran down his arm from a wound not yet completely healed, and he blinked as an idea struck him.

"But a moment," he said to the devil as he fumbled in his pack. "I think what I construct here will help me decide." He withdrew a small forked branch from a fallen tree and then rapidly coiled a hair from his head around the stem. "You see, with imagination," he said, holding the figure forward for inspection, "one can construe this as a simple model of a mortal man. And the most critical element is the piece of wire from a discarded pack clamp I bind to one of the arms, not unlike the fiber that carried sensory messages to the brain. Finally, for the energy, my body heat should be enough."

Without pause, Alodar raced into a spellbinding. Before the devil could react, the connection was complete. The demon flapped one of his hands on a rubbery wrist. "Enough stalling," he ordered. "Drink again of my sweet nectar and tell me if you can then forsake it ever more."

Alodar felt the touch of the devil's presence. As the rapture spread through his head, he grabbed a sharp rock and pressed it savagely against the wire. A numbing shock exploded in his arm and he screamed with pain. A ripping sting ran up into his head, mingling with the feeling of pleasure before it could completely form. The diluted ecstasy soaked through his body, but the raw intensity was not so great as before. Gasping for breath, Alodar rose to his feet, dangling, his limp arm at his side. "Begone, I command you," he whispered hoarsely.

Rows of wrinkles undulated across the devil's forehead. "A strong resistance," he said, "but surely you cannot withstand one more."

As the next pulse came, Alodar planted his foot over the simulacrum and ground his heel against the wire. His knees buckled and his vision blurred. He felt as if a red hot saw were slicing his flesh and reopening the wound. The bubble of pleasure grew for an instant but then burst into nothingness. The searing hurt swept it away in a torrent of agony. All feelings were blanked. Alodar struggled to remain conscious in the maelstrom of pain. He gulped for air and tried to focus on the purple demon hovering before him.

The devil backed away a few feet, and then his face sagged into a comic frown. "What is your wish, master?" he asked. "Do you desire a woman of a different type, or perhaps to tempt an enemy into the bliss from which he cannot escape?"

Alodar broke the thaumaturgical connection and the pain disappeared. "I command you to depart this world," he panted. "I have no use for your powers until I understand how to use them well." He stopped and regained his breath. "And I care not to have the temptation of your presence to distract me as I struggle to my goal. Back to the world of demons from which you came."

"But it has taken centuries for me to bridge the gap, master. And my duty is to ensure that no one passes. My punishment will not be light if I return with a tale of failure. If you have no need, them let me wrestle with another for his will."

"Depart," Alodar said.

The sad expression twisted into a scowl. "Very well, master, since it is your command. But know that when I return, I will tell others. You proceed to a far greater doom than what I so generously offered."

Alodar retrieved his sword and waved it in irritation. The purple skin of the devil suddenly glowed into incandescence and then disappeared from view. The air popped as it rushed to fill the void where he had been.

Alodar slowly sheathed his blade and scanned the valley floor. He listened for another rustling but heard instead only the oppressive silence. His arm throbbed, and the thought of immediately plunging ahead was suddenly distasteful. He struggled to recapture the feeling of bliss but the last hint decayed away. With a shudder, he sagged to the ground for a short rest.

Alodar pulled his cloak about him. All along the final

upgrade to the base of the tower, the breeze had intensified. Now as he topped the last rise, he squinted to keep the swirling dust out of his eyes. The mountains further west hid the descending sun. The heat of the day was gone, but dustdevils danced along the trail.

A level clearing surrounded the base of the spire, three times as wide as the monolith itself. Around the perimeter, stunted bushes and gnarled trees huddled close to the ground, their branches twisted sideways and leaves tattered and torn. The tower flung itself into the sky, steep, sharp and angular, defying the elements to pull it down. It was cold and unyielding, one huge rock without fissure, a subtle pink flecked with shiny black, totally unlike the surrounding hills which crumbled under his heels.

Alodar ran his hand over the surface. It was a plane extending twenty feet in either direction, straight and flat as if cut by a giant knife. He moved to the side where a second plane intersected the first. They met in a shallow angle and the boundary, sharp as a crystal's, soared into the sky. Like an irregular polyhedron thrust into the ground, all angles, lines, and planes, the spire stood in jarring contrast to its surroundings.

A dike of firm granite, Alodar thought, gradually exposed as the softer rock about it weathered away. He looked up the sheer wall towards the apex, trying to see the tarnished ring of his vision in the failing light. But the peak retreated into the soft shadows. All he could discern were a few possible handholds, barely fingertip wide, strung along the rock. He felt the urge to fling down his pack and race up the side. But it would be safer to wait till morning, when there was enough light to climb safely.

Alodar stepped back a pace, and the wind snapped at his cloak. Puzzled, he approached the tower again and the air fell quiet. He turned his back to the spire and extended his hand outward into the clearing. The breeze rippled through his fingers as if he had thrust them out of the window of a rapidly moving coach. Some sort of barrier kept out the gusts, he mused. He twisted sideways and knelt to the ground. Unfortunately, it was too narrow to make a shelter for his campfire.

Alodar walked back into the quickening breeze. He chopped a few limbs from one of the larger trees and built a small square ring of shelter on the ground. In the middle, he piled smaller branches, twigs, and dried grasses and struck his flint hopefully. To his surprise, the spark caught and held. In a few moments he had a small fire that somehow defied the wind.

Alodar ate slowly. When the sky turned black, he spread his cloak and curled around the fire. A gibbous moon rose over the crestline in the east and cast long, cold shadows on his simple camp. For several hours, he shivered with the cold and his anticipation of what the morning would bring. He knew he needed the sleep but it would not come.

Restlessly he sat up on one elbow and stared at the last flickers of his fire. Only a few wisps of flame lapped up from the glowing embers. He watched one of the flamelets suddenly die with a final puff of smoke. The kindling which had fed it slowly turned from a brilliant yellow to a dull red. Idly he turned to another spark and saw it dance along a log, lighting first one end and then another. A second glow appeared by the first; they skittered to and fro in unison.

Alodar sat up and squinted at the campfire as a third dancing ball joined the others. Cautiously, he reached for his scabbard. As he touched it, a tiny laugh cut through the silence of the night.

Alodar sprang to his feet and danced backwards, drawing his sword. The three dots jumped into the air; two flew high and the third arched over, diving for his head. He swung and missed. Peals of shrill laughter rang through the air.

He thought to knock apart the pile of wood. Before he could act, it suddenly blossomed in yellow flame. Openmouthed, he watched as the few charred sticks sent tendrils of gold into the sky, far higher and more intense than the fire he had set at dusk. The heat burned painfully at his face. Throwing his forearm up, he retreated towards the spire.

The three sprites converged over the fire, hovered for an instant, and then dropped what looked to Alodar like the branches from one of the scrubby plants which grew nearby. The foliage fell and instantly disappeared from sight, totally consumed. The yellow turned deep emerald and then starlight blue. The heat pushed outward like Duncan's expanding sphere, and Alodar took a step irresistibly backwards.

The flickering flames took on structure. From a rounded outline grew two small, earlike flaps, long-lobed and filled with coarse hair. Over a low, slanting brow, deep-sunk eyes darted back and forth behind pockmarked lids. A high and crooked nose sat above a long, thin mouth that turned down in a malevolent sneer. The head rose with the flame; as it did, a body filled in underneath, hunchbacked and spindly, naked and tufted with hair on a scaly skin that flaked off into the fire.

"By the laws, a djinn," Alodar cried aloud. He looked up to see the imps assemble and drop more foliage into the blaze. The demon, already formed, stepped from the fire and another head began to form in his place.

The fire had to be quenched quickly, before more could pass through the gate! Wincing from the heat, Alodar lunged forward, stabbing at the demon that stood in his way.

The djinn's eyes flared open at Alodar's advance. A deep rumble spilled out from his lips. He waved his taloned hand sideways, and a sudden blast of air caught Alodar in the chest. Unlike the wind of evening which had gusted and pushed, the blow pounded like a hammer. Alodar gasped for breath as his lungs emptied from the shock. He staggered forward one step. A second blow hit, spinning him backwards and knocking him to the ground. As he fell, the flame behind the djinn danced skywards, coalescing into a second demon.

Alodar rose to one knee. The djinn formed a pulse of air that caught him on the chin and made him reach for the ground for balance. Alodar looked up into the eyes of the figure towering over him. Its penetrating stare reminded him too much of the eye that Kelric had awakened in the sorcerer's sphere. He felt a trickle of fear race down his spine. Instinctively, he grabbed the pouch at his side and felt the smoothness of the orb.

The demon's thick brows shot upwards into his wrinkled forehead as he saw the motion. He walked forward and extended his hand. Alodar drew his sword, but a furnace blast skittered it away. Still clutching the sphere in his left hand, he reached for his dagger with the other. The demon opened his mouth to speak and Alodar wrinkled his nose at the sudden foul stench of decay.

"An item of some interest, I surmise," the djinn said

with the hint of some unplaceable accent. "It is well that I have chosen here and now to walk again among you mortals."

Alodar held his breath and said nothing as he watched the djinn approach. With lazy contempt, the demon held out a calloused palm and beckon with his knobby fingers. "The pouch, if you will," he said. "You fear already what my power can do to you. Do not chance my wrath in addition."

Alodar stared back at the distorted face. The blazing eyes bored into him, but he suppressed the impulse to flinch. He felt the prickly presence in his head, this time radiating a numbing terror rather than annoyance or pleasure. "The pouch," the demon repeated. "It is so much easier if you do not resist."

Alodar hesitated, then nodded and offered the bag temptingly. Then, as the piercing eyes flicked down to watch the transfer, he thrust out with the dagger and slashed at the demon's outstretched palm.

Thick greenish ichor oozed from the slit, and the demon leapt quickly backward with an unearthly howl of pain. "You dare to trifle so with one of my kind," he raged as he pressed his good hand about the wrist and attempted to staunch the flow. "Thus do I deal with such puny beings as you." He gestured with his injured hand and another blast of air slammed into Alodar's kneeling form.

The blow sent Alodar sprawling backwards and he tried to flatten out for the one to follow. But the current of wind curled under him and lifted him from the ground. In a frantic swirl of arms and legs, he tried to regain his balance, but the gust propelled him higher.

"I can smash you against the rock," the djinn yelled above the howl of the wind. "You will be no more than shattered bone and jellied flesh. Submit your will to mine. Even your wildest fears are but a small hint of what I can do."

The gust abruptly stopped and Alodar crashed to the ground. Groggily he climbed to his feet, trying to grasp what he must do. He was no match physically for the djinn. He could not stand his ground as he had done with the others. If he resisted, he would be bludgeoned into submission.

The last flurries of the blast fluttered around his legs,

dying away almost to the stillness he had felt against the tower.

He stopped before he was fully erect and tried to remember the feeling next to the rock wall. The breeze was not merely less, he pondered. The air was still, perfectly still, as if controlled through the workings of magic. He sucked in his breath with sudden hope. And if it were magic, then even the demon blasts might be turned aside.

Alodar pushed aside speculation on the djinn's reaction if he were wrong and quickly whirled towards the tower. The wind increased and the dust danced about his feet, but with one quick lunge he pounded against the cold stone. He saw the demon's face contort with rage, and the campground exploded in a fury. Sword, the pack, logs, leaves, and branches swirled into a cyclone of dust and then hurled in Alodar's direction with a shriek of groaning air.

Alodar flung his arms in front of his face and hunched in anticipation. He heard a sharp crack; then what sounded like a giant bell reverberated in the night. He put down his hands and saw a pile of debris massed a few inches from his feet and the glow of the fire still dimly visible in a cloud of swirling dirt and dust. The djinn stepped forward, eyes blazing hate and talons extended. He ran his claws down the invisible barrier between them. Alodar winced from the grating screech.

"You cannot stay there forever," the djinn growled. "The hunger and thirst will only add to your fear. When you are ready to submit on bended knee, you will plead for my mercy and hope for a gentle touch."

Before Alodar could reply, the demon turned his back and walked through the settling dust to the fire, now quiescently flickering low to the ground. Two other demons, colored and featured like the first, stood clear of the blaze, awaiting his return. They exchanged deep and guttural sounds for an instant, then stopped. Each turned his back on the other and radiated outwards from the fire, stopping and surveying the ground. Alodar watched with his back and arms pressed firmly against the spire, not daring to venture from the safety of the shield.

After several minutes, the first returned and tossed a load of pebbles and small stones into the blaze. Just as before, when fed by the sprites, the flames roared upward, this time a deep purple that blended into the blackness of the sky. The second demon reappeared, holding two head-sized blocks, and tossed them after the small rocks. The third waddled back soon after, hands cupped around a boulder easily as big around as the demon was tall. With a grunt, he added it to the blaze and stepped back to watch the flames dart out from under it.

From his vantage point, Alodar saw another shape begin to form in the fire, another head, many times human size with outlines that suggested a grotesque countenance. Alodar's eyes widened as he grasped what was happening. The imps had somehow made it possible for the three djinns to span the worlds and, powerful in mortal terms though they might be, they were bridging the gap for yet more potent demons to come.

He spun about and sprang for the first handhold above his head. He pulled one leg up to a resting place and then the other. He felt sudden pain in his arms but he shoved it aside. Without waiting, he reached for a new grip and scrambled up the face of the rock. The purchases were few and treacherous, but he did not care. Seconds seemed vital now. He could hope to succeed only if he took every risk.

Up he scrambled, not looking to see how far he had come or to judge the remaining distance. Like the enchanted fighting machine he once had been, he ignored the protests of unhealed muscles and bursting lungs. Hand over hand, in a hypnotic reverie, he drove himself toward the summit. The column narrowed and the rock on which he pressed offered fewer grips, but he did not notice. With a rush, he clambered onto the upshoot which bent to the final pinnacle.

The thickness of rock narrowed to thrice a man's breadth, and Alodar stopped and ran his hands over the stony surface. In an instant he found what he sought, the tarnished bracelet set in the stone. He pulled it. With astounding ease, a great slab parted from the monolith, swung out horizontally, and revealed stairs leading down into the tower. Alodar glanced back down the dizzying distance to the ground and caught one glimpse of a huge demon taking final form. With a last catch of breath, he plunged into the passageway.

The way was dark, and the entrance slab cut off all

light from the fire below. With one hand on a wall and the other in front, Alodar spiraled down the stairs as fast as he could without stumbling. Around one circle he went, and then another. His sense of direction became lost, but he continued onwards. Suddenly he hit a level floor and staggered. The stairs had ended, and he was in a room.

Alodar fumbled at his waist for flint and steel and started a small match to glow in the darkness. The tiny flame burned dimly, but he saw what he knew was there. A stone sarcophagus carved from solid granite lay at the far end of a vault. On the wall behind hung an embrace of oil like those in the dungeon of Iron Fist. Alodar moved forward, shielding his match with a cupped hand. He tossed the last sputtering embers of his splinter into the pool, and the room burst into light.

Staring down at the stone coffin, Alodar saw a thick sheet of glass shielding the occupant from the musty air that hung in the chamber. He placed his feet against the wall and began pushing the slab from its resting place. At first, the heavy covering did not move but then, as he strained and knotted the muscles of his back and arms, it slid an inch across the stone with a grating rumble. Alodar breathed deeply and pressed the smooth edge into his palms. The glass slipped further, opening a gap between it and the stone rectangle it covered. A strange, sweet smell rose from the coffin to fill his nostrils, but he ignored it and shoved again. The slab jerked and then gathered momentum. With a final thrust, he propelled it across the opposite side and down onto the stone floor in a loud shatter of broken glass.

"Water," a voice, soft and dry, whispered up at him. "On the wall as you came in—a door to a second room."

Alodar raced around to the other side of the vault and spied a small bracelet, like the one on the outside of the tower. He pulled it open and saw another chamber the same size as the first, but filled with braziers, kindling, piles of dried plants, capped cylinders, liquids, and small, tightly bound chests. Just like Saxton's shop, he thought, as he spotted a flask tightly sealed with a metal cap. He struck off the neck against the wall and hurried back to the wizard, who was sitting up in his stone bed and stretching arms and fingers with a chorus of pops and cracks.

The wizard tilted his head backwards. Alodar poured the water down into the eager mouth, spilling some onto a robe of deepest jet, set with the logo of the flame. Although the musty vault suggested a sleep of centuries, the features were those of middle age. Short ringlets of light brown hair covered his head and cascaded over his ears to merge with a well trimmed goatee. Brown eyes flanked a high thin nose, delicately enscribed with tiny blue veins. The face was gaunt and pale, the hands smooth and uncalloused. The wizard was a man of vault and contemplation rather than sun and physical labor.

"Enough, enough," Alodar heard him sputter at last. "You have awakened none less than Handar, the great wizard. That I stretch and stir again is of itself a tale for the sagas."

Handar paused and stared at Alodar. "Stand closer to the light so that I can look at you better," he commanded. "But a lad, I see. Who of the others would have thought it?"

"Demons," Alodar cut him off. "Many of them below. I came for help. How you can aid I do not know, but it seemed what I must do."

"They would be the thickest here, of course," Handar said. "But the shield will keep the imps away, no matter how many."

"Not only sprites," Alodar persisted, "but djinns of power as well. And they work to bring forth even greater ones of their own volition. It was only by the smallest of margins that they did not prevent me from reaching you safely."

Handar studied Alodar intently for a moment and then shook his head. "In numbers already," he said. "Then we have cut the margin exceedingly fine." He swung one leg over the coffin wall. "Quickly, the brazier of gold and the skin of oil beside it. There is wizard's work to be done."

Alodar hastened back to the storeroom and dragged forth the requested equipment. He set a tripod midway in the room and filled the brazier that swung beneath its apex with oil from a skin hard and brittle with age.

"And now the chalk and the woods," Handar said. "Then we can begin."

Alodar fetched the gear from the storeroom. When he returned, a small fire was flickering from the now-steady pan. The wizard was standing ready with no signs of stiffness or sleep. He reached into the chalk box and rapidly sorted through the pieces; a small cloud of colored dust rose from his haste. At last he withdrew one piece and turned his attention to the bundle of wood.

Handar deftly untied the knot, sending the small sticks swirling across the floor. "Let me see," he muttered, holding up the rods one by one and occasionally rubbing or smelling their smooth surfaces. "Ah, ironwood and myrtle. The very ones for him I seek."

Handar turned quickly and cast the ingredients into the blaze. "Come forth, Balthazar, I command you. Awake from your idle reverie and sloth. Your master decrees after these many years a new task for his bonded servant and slave."

Alodar looked from the flame that arched between them and then into the eyes of the man he had awakened. He saw the brow wrinkled in concentration and eyes fixed unswerving on the fire. Bony arms extended forward, beckoning to the flame.

"What is happening?" Alodar asked.

"Silence," Handar ordered. "We have no time to trifle with idle curiosity. I must stretch to my limits and call up the most powerful that I dare. Do not distract me to our peril."

As Alodar returned to silence, he saw the beginnings of an outline in the center of the blaze. An orange head, eyes and ears blended with the flames, rose above a massive trunk of huge scales and thighs the girth of barrels. Up into the room it towered, cloven hooves and tail dancing in the small fire from which it sprang. Alodar looked up at the head, which now touched the top of the chamber, and shuddered. The ears were large, covering the sides of the elongated head and ending in sharp points that soared above a bald crown. The eyes were small glistening beads of black, deep sunk beneath a jutting forehead that formed a permanent frown. With each breath, tiny nostrils flared from a small bump of a nose.

A mouth shaped like an inverted U cut deeply into the chin.

"So Handar, you again choose to settle your fate in rash manner after all of these mortal years. It is well that you have not practiced your art in so long a time. It will make the submission all the quicker."

"Silence, Balthazar, silence," the wizard shot back. "I have had the will of two of your kind since I toddled from my father's knee. The passage of time does not weaken my steadfastness but gives me all the more experience and confidence to handle your feeble puffs of will. If you do not believe it, look into me and see what you find there."

The demon sneered from bristly jowl to jowl. His luminescent eyes bore down on the wizard. For several minutes there was silence. Neither moved. Alodar saw beads of sweat break out on Handar's forehead. He saw the demon's tail begin to twitch slowly, first to the left, then to the right. Finally a spasm ran up the entire length to the large plates which covered his back.

"And so, Balthazar," Handar said. "say again who is master and who is the slave."

"I am at your bidding and service," the demon mumbled.

"I cannot discern your usually wonderful diction, Balthazar," Handar continued. "Speak louder for my companion here."

"I am at your bidding and service," Balthazar boomed. "What task will you give me so that I may have it done?"

"Know then, Balthazar," Handar said, with a tinge of smugness in his voice, "that below this very pinnacle several of your kindred have forced their way into the mortal world without being called here by one of my craft. Plunge downward and dispatch them to whence they came. Rend them limb from limb and distribute the essence of their being to the farthest corners of their natural realm, so that eons may pass before they coalesce again."

Balthazar glanced groundward and stared through the rock. "But they are indeed of my closest kindred," he said. "Spawned from the same clutch in which I was laid. I see they only frolic about, and about them are none of your kind to be harmed. Such action does not deserve unjust wrath from one with your mighty will, master."

"As I have said, Balthazar," Handar commanded, "dispatch your obligation and whine no more about it."

The tail twitched twice more above the tripod. Then suddenly the demon was gone. The chamber was still, with only the small flicker of flame and a hint of a foul odor to mark his presence.

"Up to the entrance," Handar said. "We can see how well Balthazar strives after such a long rest."

Alodar sprang for the spiral passageway, and the wizard marched after at a more stately pace. In a moment Alodar reached the slab, which was still cantilevered from the steep sides of the pinnacle. Racing out onto it, he looked below.

The campfire flamed in a rainbow of colors. The original three sprites had grown to a swarm of lights that dove and climbed among perhaps a dozen of the smaller djinns. In the center of all towered a giant, from the distance seemingly as tall as Balthazar, hands on bony hips and head tipped back in a fiendish yell as the smaller devils danced about him.

Suddenly lightning flashed. Deafening thunder cracked through the air. As Handar reached Alodar's side, a small cloudlet formed over the blaze. A second flash struck the earth in the midst of the demons. As they scrambled away, a staccato burst of rain fell and doused the fire. In a ball of orange flame, Balthazar appeared in the middle of the smouldering rocks and branches. Without warning, he snatched up two of the small demons, one in each hand, and dashed their heads together in a spray of greenish pulp. With seeming nonchalance, he tore limb from lifeless limb and scattered them airwards to vanish in puffs of smoke and flame.

The demon confronting Balthazar roared in challenge and waved his arms in warning. A giant globule of ice suddenly appeared between his hands; with a snap of his long arms he hurled it at his opponent. Balthazar dropped the remains of his smaller brothers, turned, and caught the missile against his scaled shoulder. It burst into a thousand tiny shards and dashed to the ground, hissing into steam when it touched the still glowing embers. Before the other demon could attack again, Balthazar stomped the ground. A fissure opened at his feet. It raced across the clearing from one fighter to the other. From a small crack, it grew wider till it spanned a full six feet and caused even the pinnacle to rock as the shockwaves spread from the disturbance.

Balthazar's opponent danced to one side and then the other as the jagged crack approached, but it sped unerringly to him. With a guttural yell, he fell into the abyss that opened under his feet. Balthazar stomped the ground again; the earth closed as rapidly as it had split asunder. No trace was left of the demon, except for a few bubbles of green which oozed upwards from the crack that marked the fissure's path.

The smaller demons and imps that had watched the battle suddenly began to scatter, but Balthazar pursued each with relentless precision. He dispatched the sprites with a clap of his hands. In a few moments it was over and Balthazar streaked skywards to stand before Handar on the slab.

"It is done, Balthazar," Handar said. "Transport us gently below and then return whence you came."

In a rush, Alodar felt himself scooped up in a pillow of air and hurled down to the campground with breathtaking speed. Just when he thought that the demon planned some revenge upon his master, they came to a gut-wrenching halt and stood on the firm ground.

"Use the embers," Handar said. "It is enough to give you passageway back." Balthazar said not another word but moved to the glowing remains of the drenched fire and wrapped his tail about him. He stepped upon one of the coals, still red-yellow, and vanished from sight.

Alodar looked at Handar with a stunned expression on his face. The events he had just witnessed were so far removed from anything he had experienced that it was hard to believe they had happened. The raw power of Balthazar pushed his own strivings into insignificance. He felt like a small child, bewildered by the complex world of adults manipulating their surroundings in a way he could never hope to master.

"It is cold," Handar said, as if nothing out of the ordinary had happened. "And I am hungry. Repair your camp, and then we will talk."

CHAPTER NINETEEN

Possession by Design

ALODAR warmed his hands in front of the fire. The events of the past hour were slowly ebbing away. He closed his eyes, but the vision no longer came. He was free of the enchantment which had drawn him to the spire.

He shook his head and looked across the flame at Handar, who was complacently pulling the remains of the meal out of his beard with a small comb. "Why was I drawn here?" he asked at last. "For what purpose did you sleep in the tomb? How can demons of such great power cross unbidden into our world?"

"It all will be explained in good time and proper fashion," Handar said, raising his hand to stop the rush of questions. "But first I must know more of your journey. How is it that you and no other broke the seal that awakened me? And besides the demons here, how does our world fare elsewhere in interaction with them?"

Alodar frowned with impatience, then sighed when he saw Handar tilt up his chin and close his eyes to mere slits. "I am Alodar, suitor to the queen of Procolon," he said. "And I am here as a result of my quest for her hand." He paused and let his thoughts tumble back into order. "From the dungeons of Iron Fist, to the depths of the Fumus Mountains, to the inner sanctums of the Cycloid Guild, through the enchantment of the sorcerer's eye, I have striven to aid her cause better than any other."

"For a mere queen?" Handar asked.

"For the respect of all men, for a parade of triumph through the streets of Ambrosia, for the glory of the sagas, for a reason for existing." Alodar flushed as the feelings flooded back through him. He breathed deeply, savoring the taste of his goal. "But each step along the way led only to the next, the promise of some greater marvel to turn the eyes of the fair lady. Now armies from the south and west sweep into the heart of Procolon. If only I could find the means to swell the ranks of the nomads around her banner and defeat the demon-led hordes which oppose her!"

Alodar stopped and blinked. "Balthazar," he exclaimed. "With his might and the others you could muster, we could rid the warriors who oppose the queen of the fiendish influence which drives them. Or more easily convince Grak and the other chieftains to join in the fair lady's cause. My quest goes onward. It was right to divert our trek southwards so that I could visit this tower. A powerful wizard is just what the fair lady needs in the struggle for her kingdom."

Alodar halted again and looked at Handar through narrowed eyes. "But I must admit I view the prospect with mixed feelings," he said at last. "My efforts before have benefited others as much as they have aided me. Vendora would look to reward the wizard who did the deed rather than the messenger who brought him."

"Then do you wish to turn aside what aid I might offer," Handar asked, "and continue your petty struggle on your own?"

Alodar was silent for a moment more. He thought of the sprite with its boils and rashes, of the pleasures he was able to resist only with intense pain, of the raw power of Balthazar and the other djinns. Already he had seen and experienced too much of what demonkind could do. He nodded slowly with decision and looked Handar in the eye. "The demons must be exorcised from our world. No matter who gets the credit."

Handar returned Alodar's stare. He lightly touched his fingertips together in front of his chest. "It is well that you answered as you did," he said, "for any other would have meant that your quest was for naught."

Alodar raised his eyebrows with surprise but Handar continued. "It would be my doom if I summoned Balthazar to satisfy my every whim. Each time we contest, he learns more of my will, of my weaknesses and petty failings, my irritations, desires, and fears. If I persisted one time too many, it is he who would be the master and I the slave. It well may be that I must call upon him again before the struggle is finished, but it will be only when he is desperately needed and not before.

Nor will I appear before this queen of yours juggling imps in my hands like some jester. I am a wizard and know better than to dissipate foolishly the power of my craft. You need not fear for the effect of my art on the heart of this lady. It was for a much graver reason that I was laid to rest."

Handar collapsed his palms together and brought his thumbs up to his chin. "You mention building an army," he said, "and using wizardry to aid in persuasion. I think that it would be a good enough first test. Listen well and I will instruct you on the workings of my craft."

"You offer to teach me how to deal with djinns such as Balthazar?" Alodar asked.

"One as mighty as he will come later," Handar said. "For the moment, summoning a sprite or two should suffice to build your confidence and probably impress this queen as well."'

"But why?" Alodar asked. "You pile one mystery on top of another."

"Why?" Handar echoed, stiffening into an erect posture. "It is not for a wizard to answer why. He does as he chooses, as he wills things to be. I elect to tell you of my craft now. More will come when I judge you worthy to receive it."

Alodar shrugged and settled into a comfortable position. Handar waited several moments more in silence and then rose.

"What you saw transpire in this clearing tonight was an exercise in one of the fundamental laws of wizardry," he said. "The law of ubiquity. Or stated in simple terms, 'fire permeates all.' It is by fire and fire alone that a bridge or gateway is formed between the demon world and ours. It is through fire that they come to us. The simple blaze of a fallen log is enough to furnish passage for the most feeble among them, such as tiny imps and will-o'-the-wisps. Their presence is harmless, even though an annoyance and surrounded by much folklore and baseless superstition. Any man with a whit of courage can bend them to his will and make them behave. The powerful demons require more exotic means of access. Fire of a natural kind will not do. Exotic plants, woods, and even rarer substances such as rock must burn to make the conditions right."

"Then what I surmised was true," Alodar said. "The less powerful opened the way for the greater djinns to pass through."

"Yes," Handar agreed. "But if it were as simple as that, then long ago this world would have been overrun with demonkind. There would not be wizards enough to wrestle with all that might appear. But in the scheme of things, although flame is necessary, it is not sufficient. Except for an irritating imp or two, none of the demons have free access, even though a path may be open. The flame makes a channel where there was none before, but all resistance is not overcome. The greater the demon's power, the greater in proportion is the barrier which impedes him. A sprite, devil or djinn of any strength must make contact with a human mind and be pulled across the friction that remains. Indeed, all of the so-called craft of wizardry is concerned with just one thing, the establishing of a link between the two worlds, of making the contact of minds that allows the demon to come forth. Once the connection has been made, the resistance vanishes and what happens next is governed by the second law, the law of dichotomy."

"But there were no wizards pulling the sprites and djinns through," Alodar objected. "Once the flame was established, they came of their own will."

"Of that I will speak later," Handar said. "But first the law of dichotomy, or simply stated, 'dominance or submission.' There is no middle ground. Once the demon has been called forth, then who controls whom is determined solely by a contest of wills. If the wizard is strong enough, he will dominate and the demon, at least for the particular conjuring, will be his to command. If the man falters and the demon wrests mastery from him, then he becomes the pawn of the other world, a warlock, a mere toy to strut and twist about as it suits their eerie amusement."

Handar suddenly raised his palms and stopped. "And that is all there is to the craft," he said.

"No words of power, formulas, rituals or chants handed down from master to pupil?" Alodar asked.

"Only which flames are appropriate for which demon," Handar replied. "And that is just so that the foolish do not attempt beyond what they are capable. But such knowledge is peripheral to mastery of the craft. The essence is the will to resist, to remain free, to preserve one's spirit. And this central core of wizardry cannot be taught, only experienced."

"But the power I saw your creature unleash," Alodar said. "With such as he to aid you, no kingdom could resist."

"It is as I have said," Handar replied. "The more powerful the demon, the stronger is his will and the greater risk there is of submission rather than domination. And there is somehow a flaw in those who seek skill in wizardry and perhaps in most men as well. A flaw that leads us to temptation almost without fail. As we practice our art and summon again and again the lesser demons which we can easily bend to our will, we grow tired of their supplications, their flattery, their bemoaning of the small tasks that are placed upon them. We reach out and try to bring forth a devil of more power, to test our strength against him and to measure our accomplishments against our peers who strive as well. And as the sagas show, one by one, the daring craftsmen of wizardry eventually attempt what is beyond their reach and pass from free men to be the tools of those whom they wished to control. To be a wizard is no casual undertaking, though the preparation for it is small. And to be a great one requires character as strong as any hero in the sagas, a will unbending to the temptations that demonkind will offer along the way."

"And you, Handar?" Alodar asked.

"If I were strong enough, if wizardry alone were great enough, then there would have been no need for my long sleep of waiting for someone to come."

Alodar trudged up the pass in silence, the stiffness of his wounds almost completely gone. Except for more detail on how to probe through the flame, Handar stubbornly chose to say no more about his background or any of the other puzzling questions. Most of the morning had passed while Alodar gave an account of his adventures starting with the siege of Iron Fist over a year ago. All along the trail back to the meadow, the wizard's only comments had been an occasional grunt or introspective smile.

Alodar looked down from the pass and saw that little

had changed since his departure the day before. The goat-skin huts of Grak's tribesmen still clustered near the base of the mountain. Further out in the grasses, the collection of nomads who were pledged to Vendora's banner huddled around a scattering of small fires, preparing a midday meal. Between the two camps, one isolated group stood apart from all the rest. Alodar squinted at a pole thrust into the ground there and saw a crude banner with the colors of the queen.

"They still parley," Alodar said over his shoulder as Handar climbed the last few paces to his side. Handar nodded wordlessly and started down the slope. In a quarter of an hour they walked into the small camp.

Alodar could tell as he looked into the dozen or so faces staring his way that conversation had stopped several minutes before their final approach. Grak, other chieftains, the suitors, Grengor, and Aeriel sat in an informal circle around a single fire. Alodar sought the face of the queen and shouted his greeting. "I bring powerful resources and fresh hope for the fair lady. The wizard Handar, and great are the demons at his command."

A buzz of conversation started around the group. Grak conferred with two of his nomads sitting nearby and the other suitors exchanged glances among themselves. "You return at a most propitious time, master," Grengor said. "Three of Grak's subchieftains have experienced enough of Basil's show of gems and Feston's words of plunder to want to join our cause. If you can aid in convincing the fourth, the one with the long unruly mane, then I am sure that chieftain will follow."

"We talk in terms of carats of ruby and ounces of soft gold," Basil said. "A tale from these highlands, even a wizard's, carries no weight compared to these. Return your hermit to wherever you found him and let his imps scavenge his existence as before."

Handar turned to face Basil. His eyes sparked and the muscles in his face hardened. His stare bored into the apothecary. Basil hesitated for a moment. Before he could speak again, Handar looked away and scanned the rest of the group.

"I am a true wizard," he announced slowly, "not some carnival attraction. A wizard from the time of the sagas, when even kings would walk behind. And I have heard of Bandor's possession, of the sprites deep within the fissures of the Fumus Mountains, and of the djinns who stunt the trees, kill the game, and make the winds howl around the spire to the east. It is not by chance that all of these events crowd together. No, they are deeply related. Shall I return to my hermitage, as you call it, or do you wish to hear instead of the doom which hovers over you like a block of granite suspended from a cotton thread?"

"If you speak of Demontooth, then we will hear your words," Grak said. "It is but a half day away, unlike all the battles of glory many weeks march to the south."

The nomads grunted their acquiescence and all of the others were silent. Handar's lips curved into a smile. "Perhaps not the pomp and circumstance to which I am accustomed," he said, "but until you know better it will suffice."

He paused, then continued. "Despite the decay which has apparently rotted my craft, you must all know at least a glimmer of how it works, of the flame that is necessary to form the pathway between the worlds, of the resistance which prevents the most powerful demons from appearing here of their own choice. But do you know as well that with each passage into our world, the resistance is slightly lowered? Less effort is required to bring the next demon of the same strength across. When one returns, the barrier increases by a like amount. If the contacts are sporadic in space and time, the situation remains relatively static and no great harm is done. But concerted effort to flood us with demonkind could cause the barriers to fall, so that more powerful djinns could reach out and touch our minds with simpler flames. And as more come forth, the hurdle becomes lower still."

Aeriel frowned. "But such a process is unstable," she said. "Eventually, demons of inconceivable might could vent their great power as they willed."

"The potential has been present from man's distant memories," Handar agreed, nodding his head. "But so long as demonkind viewed our intrusions and summons as a minor irritation from another world, then it did not matter. The mighty devils soon tire of—and destroy—the few foolish men who challenge them. But if for some reason, by logic that only their fiendish minds could follow, a demon prince came to covet our world and the hearts and minds that dwelled within it, then our peril would be great indeed. And if a prince did desire such a conquest, how would he proceed?"

Handar paused and noted with satisfaction the up-turned faces and backs hunched forward. "We cannot know for sure, of course, but it is plausible he would act as follows. First he would wait until in the random course of human events the craft of wizardry sagged into a nadir of petty exhibitions and traveling entertainments. Without great wizards to interpret what was happening, his designs would proceed undiscovered and unchecked for far longer than otherwise possible. He would direct his minions to act towards a common goal, once they succeeded in dominating the fools who dared too much. Rather than strutting these warlocks as comic puppets to be used and then discarded, the djinns would force their actions to be like normal men. And then, as these slaves moved among us unsuspected, there would come a time when a group of them would be alone with a man with some military power, perhaps an outland baron with few guards to subdue. After a hearty meal in front of a roaring hearth to keep out the cold, they would seize him and hold his head toward the flame and force his eyelids open until they had another subjugation. Or perhaps in a dungeon without food or hope until the will to resist weakened. I do not know the details; they are unimportant."

"Bandor," Aeriel interjected. "From the beginning his possession was most puzzling."

"From what Alodar has explained, he was probably the first of the ones who did not dabble," Handar replied. "With his peerage, the demons had control of the beginnings of an army. Far more important, it meant that there was opportunity for trusting lieutenants, neighboring barons, and captured opponents to be tricked and forced into submissions as well. And with each look into the flame and transferral, the resistance weakened, so that more could come. More demons to direct the growing chaos of war, to conquer greater fiefdoms, to bring still more into bondage. Under the guise of a mortal struggle, the demon power would grow from baronies to kingdoms and eventually the whole world."

"But how do you know?" Duncan protested. "It is a pretty theory and nothing more."

"Yes," Feston joined in. "Except for the talk of the sorcerers, we would not even suspect that the revolt in the west is more than the well-understood actions of ambitious men."

"A rebellion that swelled from a single barony to ally the entire west?" Handar replied. "And one that fights with such ferocity that you cannot put it down? Kingdoms to the south who have squabbled among themselves for centuries suddenly uniting and thrusting at Procolon together? A resistance so weak that not only sprites but djinns of true power appear unsummoned about the base of the spire? These events are not random chance. We are faced with possession by design. There is more than the fate of the ruling class of Procolon at stake."

"But if what you say is true," Aeriel asked, rising to her feet, "what can we possibly do against such power?"

Handar patted his fingertips together. "We can at least hope to defeat them in battle. Not all of the men are demon-possessed, only the leaders. If we can crush the forces which march against Procolon and either slay or free the ones possessed, the resistance will return to its former values. Then it will be only imps with which we will have to deal. Once on our guard, we may be able to resist until the prince behind the attack loses interest and turns his attention to other worlds."

"But that is no less than what we already strive for," Basil cried. "We hope to convince enough of these rough barbarians to the fair lady's cause so that we can crush the insurrection, as you say. Procolon's regular army battles Bandor in the west. With enough additional swords, we will also halt the thrust from the south. Demon plot or none, our course of action is the same."

"If you could imagine the fate which will be ours if we fail," Handar said, "then you would not be so glib about what it is for which we will fight. Now they control only a few, but in the end it would be each and every one of us a slave. And for what perverted delights we would be the pawns, I cannot say. To shear off our own fingers and toes one by one, to labor for years to pound our towers and walls into fine sand, to float for eternities with no sight, touch or sound, to hack loved ones into pulp. The horrors they press upon the poor warlocks when they are bored can be only a small glimmer of what would be."

Handar halted and a heavy silence fell on them all. Alodar saw Grengor and Duncan squirm as they imagined their own private hells. Aeriel bit her lip in pensive thought. Vendora stared at the slowly heaving chest of Grak the barbarian.

Grak broke the silence as he rose. "It is well enough for you lowlanders to be so clear as to what you must do. But for my tribesmen, we have heard first a day of soft promises and now words of fear. We have had the devils among us for ages and they have given us no bother, so long as we stay clear."

"The demons will seek you out," Handar promised. "They will concentrate first on the lowlands where there are more to possess, true. But eventually there will be no place in these mountains in which you can hide."

Grak stared down at Handar for a long time in silence. "You claim to be a great wizard," he said at last. "Show me some of your craft so that I may verify the truth of what you say."

Handar returned Grak's stare with his chin extended. "I have said I am a wizard," he replied, "and that is sufficient. As to the power of my craft, Alodar can demonstrate enough to make you tremble."

Grak's nostrils flared. "I have seen imps enough in my time not to fear their irritations. Work your spell, and we will see if I judge it to be great wizardry."

Alodar looked quickly at the scowling face of the barbarian. Handar's manner had given Grak an insult that could not be put aside easily. And it would be uncertain that this first effort in conjuring would be startling enough to impress the proud nomad. Another tack was called for if he was to be convinced. Alodar looked at the subchief scratching his head to Grak's left. Without thinking, he reached down and rubbed the latest flea bite on his leg; then his eyes brightened with an idea.

"There are more products from the labor of wizardry than just fear," Alodar said. "Rest easy while I provide something that should benefit your tribe far more."

Alodar knelt to the ground and rummaged through his pack. He withdrew a few clusters of pine needles and the roots from a painted daisy. He placed them in a rough stone bowl by the fire. From the carcass of a freshly killed hare he dripped the fats and juices until the plants were covered. Into a wicker basket he scooped some ashes from the smouldering fire.

"All of this is unnecessary," Handar objected. "For a simple imp, you need only common flame."

"I am ready now," Alodar said. "The rest is for what will come after." He looked once more at Grak, breathed deeply, and turned his attention to the fire. As Handar had instructed, he let his eyes decouple and drift out of focus.

The yellow and gold blurred together. Wide-eyed, Alodar felt the fascination of the dancing flame tendrils, the lure to probe the mysteries that lay beyond. He clinched his fists and willed his presence forward, past the incandescent sheen, into the very heart of the blaze.

Alodar stared and his sense of time melted away. Unlike the effort of sorcery he felt no discomfort, no pain and gagging nausea to overcome. He envisioned the pathway as a great pipe connecting one world with the other, a vertical shaft with a tough, translucent membrane stretched across its throat, preventing transfer. He concentrated on building his will, making it stronger, constructing a huge weight, pressing against the barrier to break the resistance and allow passage. The membrane twisted, sagged and stretched out of shape so that it finally ripped and failed.

He concentrated upon wishing the tattered remains of the barrier away. For a moment, nothing happened; then his mind exploded with the feeling of a dozen gentle pricklings. In a rush, he sensed a dozen more. Boiling balls of consciousness whirled in confusion, each one subtly distinctive, diving at his thoughts and snatching them away. "Gladril," he thundered aloud, as the identity of one sprang to mind. "I have work for you, sprite of the water. Until I am done, your will is mine."

The presence of the other imps immediately winked away. Alodar felt only one skittering around in his head. His conversations with Handar and the experience with the sprite on the trail gave him confidence, and he projected resolve as hard as steel. "Come forth, Gladril," he said. "I command you to my bidding."

Instantly the air above the fire fissured with a sharp

crack. In a tiny cloud of steamy vapor, Alodar saw thick, horny wings and the ends of spindly and hairy legs. He heard gasps and grunts of surprise in those about him but he ignored the distraction.

"You have chosen an imp of no mean power," a voice squeaked from the mist. "Either submit or let me return. You interact further at your peril."

"Silence," Alodar ordered. "There is no time for you to exercise your feeble desires. I fell the pulsing of your will and know I can crush it to nothingness in an instant." He grabbed the wicker basket and held it above the stone bowl. "Quickly now, hot water to leach the ashes."

Without further protest, the cloud zoomed to hover above Alodar's outstretched hand. With a brief flash of light and a tiny pop of thunder, steamy rain fell into the basket and then trickled through to the bowl below.

"Enough," Alodar said after a few moments. "Now to the bowl and boil the brew together. Use your wings to beat the ingredients into a fine emulsion."

"But the mess will stick to my hairs. I will be a mortal year in cleaning it all off."

"To the deed," Alodar growled.

Like a dense fog the imp settled into the bowl. Almost instantly, the container filled to the brim with an oily water. Bubbles formed around the edges, and then a violent frothing churned in the middle. Above the bubbling, Alodar heard the high pitched buzz of the sprite's wings as the imp stirred the mixture together.

"And now cool the broth and dump it on the sub-chieftain's head," Alodar said as he pointed to the one with the shaggy mane. "And when you are done, rinse it clean with clear cold water."

"A task more to my liking." The imp laughed as he shook himself free of the lather. Grasping the bowl with all four limbs he chuckled as he bore it into the air and poured the contents on the barbarian's head.

"Now the rinse," Alodar said, "and then I command you to be gone."

A second rainfall washed the lather free. Without another word, the imp popped from view.

"A petty trick," the subchieftain growled. "Is this what you call the great power of wizardry?"

"As I said," Alodar replied, "the value of the craft lies

not only in fear. With the aid of the sprite, I brewed a lotion of alchemy. You head should be free of fleas for at least a fortnight."

The nomad started and then cautiously raised a hand to his head. He ran his fingers through his hair. "There is no more itch," he said slowly.

Vendora rose and walked to Grak's side. "It has a nice scent," she said. "There are others among you who could benefit from it as well."

"Sweetbalm, my lady, there is no time to worry about the control of vermin," Feston grumbled. "We must get on with the task of assembling an army for the south."

Vendora turned to the warrior, frowning in irritation. "Yes, yes, I know, Feston. And through it all I unfailingly must continue to play the part of the queen." She looked at Grak, standing silently with his face an unreadable mask, and then turned to Alodar. "And so you prove your worth once again. No doubt, with these imps we can scout ahead to see what other tribes lie in our path. And produce more gifts of enticement. With your help we may then cross the border with perhaps even two thousand fighters."

"It is as the fair lady says," Alodar replied. At Iron Fist and the shore of the sea, his spirits had soared when she gave him her attention, but this time her manner made him uneasy. He studied her beauty, still dazzlingly apparent through unkempt hair and soiled gown. He glanced at Aeriel and then back to the queen. Yet the logic of what she said was firm enough.

"Then the only issue remaining is the decision of Grak the chieftain," Vendora continued, turning her attention away. She ran the back of her hand down the nomad's arm. "We have tarried a day and offered you much. Do not the rewards of journeying with us outweigh the risks?"

Grak glanced back at his subordinate. He stooped down and rubbed some of the soap between his fingers. He stood again and faced the queen. "And you journey to the cities of the south with these halfmen of yours?"

"I do."

Grak held the soap to his nose, then cast it aside with a grunt. He looked deeply into her eyes. "And also with the tribesmen of Grak," he said at last.

CHAPTER TWENTY

The Second Quest

ALODAR nudged his mount forward in a slow walk down the dusty street. Aeriel and Handar followed on either side. Grak reined a huge gelding with his right hand and guided Vendora's pony with his left. Grengor and the other suitors brought up the rear.

"I hope that Bardina is large enough to house a decent bath or two," Aeriel said. "The fair lady is not the only one who has become rather testy from such a long journey."

Grengor rubbed at the dirt caked to his stubble of beard. "Yes, to that I fully agree. The barbarian horde may prefer to camp outside the wall, but my back has had enough of sleeping on the hard ground."

"We can stay but a short while," Grak said, looking uncomfortably at the building fronts which pressed in from either side. "The farmlands around will not long provide meat for nearly two thousand mouths, and my people have little taste for your grains."

Vendora ran a hand down the length of her gown. "There is time enough for a change of clothes and to have my tresses properly done," she decided. "After all, if a proud chieftain finally agrees to soap himself, it is a fair return."

"And now that we are back across the border into your realm," Basil said, "we will learn as well how fare our forces to the south."

"More important than that," Handar added, "we will see firsthand how low the barrier between the worlds has become. Even if we are far from the battles where possession is forced, there will be changes that we cannot help but notice. It is like a rock dropped onto a tightly

318

stretched blanket. The maximum depression is where it falls, but the effect is felt even at the edges."

Alodar did not join in the conversation. In silence, he mulled over the events of the past weeks. The recruiting had gone according to his expectations. With a cloud of speedy imps, they had found all the tribes within a reasonable distance of their southward trek. Between Basil's gems, Feston's promise of steel weapons from the slain, Grak's endorsements, and his own healing salves, all had been won to the cause. Along with the tale of the enchanted warrior, the nomads now whispered of his great wizardry, of how imps had blown the mosquitoes and gnats away, fused broken stoneware together, and pressed streambed mud into hard slate.

Alodar watched the activity of the street as they moved along, and the contrast with his mental image jogged him out of his reverie. The low buildings on either side crowded close, leaving passage barely a coach wide. Though it was midday, few of the townspeople journeyed outdoors and those marked their passage with sullen jowls and squinting eyes.

Vendora's troops reined up in the town square, scarcely wider than the road on which they had come. It was deserted. Alodar cupped his hands to his mouth to shout out their arrival. "Attend onto the fair lady. The queen of Procolon honors Bardina. Attend her and receive her regal presence."

His words echoed off the walls. For a long moment, no one stirred. Then gradually, in twos and threes, the townspeople began to appear in the doorways of the buildings and narrow alleys between. They shuffled into the square in silence, forming a thin line that surrounded the royal party. Alodar looked rapidly about at the faces which confronted him. In some were apprehension and even a hint of fear, in others hate glowered out of piercing eyes. In none was the excitement that should accompany a visit of the queen.

The square filled, pressing in on them. "The fair lady," someone cried out. "She has come to deliver us at last."

"It cannot be she," another yelled. "This handful of men matters for little. It is more like another witch sent to torment us further."

"My fair lady, set free my daughter. Possessed she is

319

not." An old woman in coarse tatters pressed against Duncan with arms outstretched to the queen. The magician pushed her back and the crowd responded with a buzz of anger.

"They are demons. Deal with them now before they can infest our townfolk further." More shouts hurled upward and the agitation grew. Three figures in an alleyway struggled with a fourth. With a final shove, they pushed him to fall through the crowd to the horses' feet.

"Another of your kind," a gruff voice called out as the group joined the rear of the throng. "Take him when you depart. Bardina is his home no more."

The man staggered to his feet and absently ran one hand down the side of a tattered cloak, caked with mud and decay. He squinted through swollen eyes past a tangle of long black hair that streaked across a nearly bald crown. Bits of moldy food clotted a mangy beard. Slack jowls hung from what once must have been a full and fleshy face.

Vendora leaned forward in her saddle, instinctively smoothing her own hair into place. "And what manner of visitation is this?" she asked in annoyance. "An official delegation to apologize for the treatment thus far accorded my presence? Speak ruffian, what message have you for us?"

The man did not heed the queen but stood with hands stiffly at his sides and eyes staring straight ahead. "Sandacar," he mumbled at last. "Sandacar, my master Sandacar, will provide for me."

"Periac!" Alodar exclaimed in sudden recognition.

Handar dismounted, walked forward, and gently placed his palm under Periac's chin, looking him deeply in the eyes. "His will, his being, his essence, they are gone," he said. "This empty hulk is animate only when his demon master abides among us."

Vendora watched as Periac spasmodically thrust a hand to his face and pulled free a tangle of mud and hair. The queen shuddered and turned in her saddle. "Tell them to take him away. Such display is most unfit for my presence."

The rumbling increased. Feston stood in his stirrups, arms outstretched and motioned for silence. "You speak most rashly," he shouted. "Know that it is the fair lady,

320

indeed. Only her forgiving spirit stands between you and the swift vengeance of our swords. Do her the proper honor or suffer the just consequences."

More shouts of anger hurled from the crowd. In a confusion of arms, they jostled one another for room in the crowded square. One man stumbled and fell. The others quickly trampled over him, raising clenched fists.

"Honor to the fair lady," Feston blasted again as he tried to keep his balance while his mount banged against its skitterish comrades. Before he could say more, a rock whizzed overhead and the tumult increased.

Alodar looked again at the swaying thaumaturge. He scanned the crowd that was slowly creeping closer to Aeriel and the queen. He grimaced and made his decision.

"Enough of this mob, Grengor. We will have to attend to Periac later. Let us move to safer ground," he commanded as he started his horse forward.

Suddenly the townsmen exploded in hatred. Two more rocks hurled by and then a third crashed painfully into Alodar's shoulder. With a piercing shout, the mob converged, pushing the ones in front under the horses' hooves and scrambling upon their backs to pull the riders down.

Arms from all sides reached up to grab at Alodar's reins. He heard Vendora scream behind him and turned to see Basil's horse rear and toss him to the ground. Grak pulled his sword and slashed at two who leaped upwards. Duncan jostled about on his saddle as he tried to activate his sphere. Grengor and Feston kneed their mounts forward into the crowd, making room to draw and defend themselves.

Alodar turned his horse to the side, out of the clutches of the men on the left; immediately three from the right surged forward to attack with bare hands. The tallest sprang upwards and grabbed Alodar about the waist. As he grappled to disengage, he felt his leg pulled free from the stirrup and painfully wrenched by another. With a crash, he fell to the street, barely ducking his head to avoid the nervous stomp of Aeriel's riderless horse.

Two of Alodar's assailants fell on top, pinning him to the pavement. A third raked his nails across Alodar's cheek. Alodar arched his back, freeing his left arm, and drove an elbow sharply into the groin of the one astride his chest. The man rolled off and Alodar brought his knees suddenly upward, lifting the second from the ground. As the townsman fought for balance on one leg, Alodar kicked savagely and propelled him into the forest of horse legs tromping whatever was underfoot.

Alodar rolled aside, missing a kick by the third attacker. Grabbing at an empty stirrup, he pulled himself to his feet. He glanced about quickly, just barely able to see over the rise and fall of the horses' backs as they reared. Everyone was down in the confusion of the square.

"Handar," he called, "assist the fair lady." He danced aside from his antagonists as they stumbled forward, pushed from behind by others trying to join the fray. He ducked beneath a horse's neck and stepped over a body which lay sprawled in his way.

Alodar shouldered past a knot of intertwined men, each trying to bring the others to the ground. He elbowed a man with an upraised rock on the left and drove a hard blow into the face of another. He vaulted up onto a horse's back and then down on the other side, stumbling over a black-robed figure as he landed.

"Handar!" he shouted as he struggled to turn the wizard over. "We need a devil to aid our cause. Suggest one I should seek."

The wizard's eyes rolled in his head but then locked on Alodar's face. "No, you must not," he said thickly. "You must deal with the townsmen instead. In my sleeve —the small candles. Toss them skyward one at a time but do not look as you do so."

Alodar puzzled at the commands but did as he was instructed. He groped in Handar's clothing and retrieved a flint and three small tapers, dimly glistening in the sunlight and strangely heavy to the touch. The first instantly ignited from a small spark. Alodar hurled it high in the air.

He ducked his head and shut his eyes. Suddenly, even through closed lids, everything flashed painfully white. The random hubbub of the mob ceased, replaced by shrieks of surprise. Alodar felt the crowd give way around him. He lofted the second candle, this time burying his head in his arms. A yell more piercing than the first accompanied the flash, and Alodar could hear footfalls

322

stumbling away from the periphery of the square. He threw the third candle. The retreat turned into a stampede. More rapidly than they had rushed forward, the townsmen trampled one another as they sped away, yelling about demons who tormented them still.

"It is what we call sunfire," Handar yelled over the screams of the departing mob. "We use it to summon certain fire sprites when simpler flames will not do. Your sight will return in a moment. Rest patiently and all will be well."

Alodar stood up slowly and soothed one of the horses. He saw Aeriel staggering to her feet. She bore a few scratches and some torn clothing but was apparently unhurt. Vendora and the rest were either sitting or struggling upwards. Except for the party of the queen, the square was deserted. Even Periac was not to be seen.

"The townsmen were quite startled by the fireworks," Handar said. "It probably will be some while before they gather sufficient courage to try us again."

"But what caused them to act so?" Duncan asked. "It is no less than treason against the queen."

"And Periac, a master thaumaturge," Alodar wondered. "He would know better than to traffic with such great risks."

"No less is to be expected when demons freely walk the land," Handar said. "When only will-o'-the-wisps could come of their own volition and wizards sought the rest, there was some measure of control. But with a sprite in every bush, the perils and temptations are too great. Either the common craftsman is possessed by his encounter or, if he achieves domination, he cannot resist using the power for his own petty ends. And if the concentration of demons is as strong as I now fear, then we have little enough time to prevent the complete disaster." He stopped and looked into one of the alleyways. "With what Grengor has caught, we will get the confirmation."

Alodar turned in the direction Handar indicated and saw the marine dragging a screaming youth by the scruff of his neck back to the feet of the wizard.

"I never doubted the identity of the fair lady," the boy sobbed. "I never doubted it. Let me go to join my brothers. Let me go. I hurl no rocks into your midst."

"Control yourself so that you speak properly to a wizard," Handar ordered. "We seek information about what has transpired in Bardina and the rest of Procolon."

As Grengor released his grip, the youth nodded and shifted to one knee to bow to the queen. "My fair lady," he stammered. Aeriel nodded encouragement and the boy started again with a rush.

"It was barely a month ago that all this began. Kellic's daughter had a spat with another lass down the road and woke the next morning with her comely face covered with pox blisters that would not heal. The cows in the herds nearest the east went dry and the hens would lay no longer. The peddlers who trudged from Bardina to Graymill and back would disappear for weeks. When they returned, they had eyes of madmen and tongues that none could understand. And then in this very square, one of the merchant wives ripped the shawl from another to expose a little imp riding near the base of the neck and working his mischief on whomever he passed.

" 'You witch!' the first exclaimed. 'So this is how my Hentor's eye is made to wander. Well it is only just that you are dealt with in kind.' And the next morning the second was struck dumb within the confines of her own well-guarded house. It did not take long for the curse to be full upon us after that. The smallest slight was dealt with in most cruel fashion; revenge answered revenge as more and more trafficked with demonkind.

"And those who did not lash out, those in fear of what was happening around them, they became unreasoning avengers seeing evil wherever they looked. On the slightest pretext, many were trapped and slain, some protesting their innocence to the end. All commerce stopped and we became no more than roving bands, suspicious of one another and always tempted to use demonpower to protect us from each other. And we have no news from the south. No one ventures anymore from Bardina and no one dares step foot within the city walls.

"My mother, even she . . ." The boy shuddered and then shut his eyes. His voice trailed off and he said no more.

"It will be the same in every town and hamlet of the kingdom," Handar told the queen. "Part of the citizenry possessed, part temporarily dominating sprites until their

324

wills falter as well, and the rest guided only by suspicion and terror. As more and more are coerced in the battles with Bandor, far wider does the influence of demonkind spread throughout the land."

The wizard shook his head. "It is even worse than I feared, although our first efforts must be the same. First to the south to defeat the forces of the petty kingdoms and exorcise those demons that we can. And then to the west to add to the forces trying to route Bandor from his strongholds. But from what I have seen and can infer, even ten times our number may not be enough."

Alodar released the cinch and removed the saddle from the horse's back. He looked into Aeriel's eyes and read the same weary resignation. For the last two days the meaning of Bardina had slowly sunk in and weighed them down.

At the very least, they had all looked forward to a rest from the trail, a return to familiar and comfortable surroundings, decent food after a month of rabbit meat.

But Handar had said that all of the towns would be the same. Wherever there was a concentration of mankind, the demons would also be. The queen's party had to continue as before, foraging from the countryside, taking all livestock from each farm they chanced upon, trying to ignore the sullen faces, driving like exiles rather than the royal party of a queen in her own realm.

And behind the loss of comforts, the depressing isolation, the hostility of the plundered subjects, the bickering of the free-spirited nomads, was the true meaning of what they had seen. A quarter of the population was demon-possessed; the rest had turned into snarling mobs. Periac, a master thaumaturge, rotted away in some hidden hole, undiscovered despite Alodar's careful search. And with each day, more demons poured across the bridge between the two worlds.

A sudden commotion behind Alodar spun him around and he looked up the slope. They were encamping on a gentle rise, with the nomads scattered into rough groups of fifty. The ridgeline to the south cut off their view. Now over the crest appeared two of the marines, whipping their flagging ponies.

They raced across the inclines, splattering foam from their mounts. With a swirl of dust, they savagely reined to halt in the middle of the camp and called for the queen.

Alodar crowded around with the rest and heard the gasping report. "Banners of Procolon, no more than an hour's march away. But hotly pursued by a far larger force. They are in retreat and sundown will find them in our midst."

Alodar ran to the ridge and looked across the broad valley on the other side. The land dipped to the bed of a small, meandering stream and then rose to a crestline slightly higher than the one on which he stood. Long-stemmed grass rippled in a gentle breeze. Here and there domes of bare rock poked through the cover. An occasional glint of sunlight reflected off the stream as it sluggishly trickled to the east.

The opposing ridgeline was silent and bare. Except for the stubble of grass nothing moved. Alodar sank to the ground as Vendora and her followers arrived and clustered about. Her crude banner was thrust into the soft earth and fluttered in the quickening afternoon breeze.

Eventually a small cluster on horseback came into sight, followed by precisely formed squares of men on foot. As they splashed across the stream, additional groups appeared, more ragged than the first—partially filled squares, wavering oblongs and chaotic clusters that seemed to stagger and lurch rather than hold to a definite direction. Finally in the rear, craftsmen whipped horses pulling overloaded wagons, and men with backs piled high with family possessions tugged at the gowns of women staggering under the load of small children. Isolated individuals zigzagged back and forth in a daze. In a ragged wave they tumbled down the slope, straining to keep up with the warriors in front.

As the last stragglers forded the stream, the horsemen trotted up to where Alodar stood. With an arm dangling at his side, the leader slowly dismounted and threw back his casque. The face was gaunt and deeply lined, and the eyes glistened with pain, but Alodar recognized the bristly moustache and bulky frame.

"Cedric!" he cried, "Cedric, what luck to see you here and in service to the fair lady!"

The warmaster nodded back to Alodar and stiffly approached the queen. He grabbed the offered banner from the man behind and placed it at her feet.

"The volunteers of Ambrosia," he announced. "And a few units of the army of the west as well."

Alodar looked at the men who formed a line a respectable pace behind. His eyes widened as he saw white-haired men and spindly youths far younger than he was. Another two thousand—but they looked ready to drop.

"Your fame is still remembered, warmaster," Vendora said. "And no doubt it aided you well in recruiting a militia to my cause." She paused and looked at the haggard faces staring back. "But why a forced march northwards? You could have aided in the siege or waited in Ambrosia until we arrived for our offensive to the south."

"There is no longer a siege to conduct in the west," Cedric answered. "Bandor burst through the lines which tried to hold him."

"Impossible!" Feston shouted above the sudden chorus of voices. "Bandor and his allies were in a vice-like grip. He was to be crushed for his impudent rebellion—not our efforts against him abandoned."

"Abandoned they were not," Cedric replied. "But with each day, Bandor grew stronger, sending forth more sallies, wrecking the engines of war, capturing more of the disheartened besiegers. Whole companies of men, nobles and warriors alike, changed their allegiances, joining the force which seemed to burst out of the west with demonic power. The three squares which marched with me are all that are left. Even those I had to persuade back into formation as they fled in panic before the very gates of Ambrosia."

"And the kingdoms to the south?" Basil asked. "How deeply have they penetrated into our heartland? How many leagues between them and the royal palace?"

"The armies have linked," Cedric answered. "Bandor and the others pursue us together."

"But if you are so far north," Duncan asked, "what of the defense of Ambrosia?"

"There is no Ambrosia to defend," Cedric said wearily. "Procolon has fallen, my fair lady. Your forces and mine are all that remain." He stopped and looked at the setting sun. "They are at our heels and we no longer have the strength to run. Tomorrow there will be a final battle and it will be here."

With a wave of his good arm, Cedric pointed back across the valley. As if on a playmaster's cue, a line of men appeared on the other crest, their energetic step in ominous unison. The vanguard halted on the ridgeline and spread out into the distance on either side. As Alodar and the others watched, more and more climbed to join them, filling in the gaps and piling up behind. In the quickening darkness, they merged into a solid wall, shoulder to shoulder and many rows deep.

In the very center of the line, huge stones were dropped from a wagon and shaped into a ring. A small fire sprang to life, and a dim, blue-green flame twinkled in the twilight. Drums began to sound, leading an unearthly chant. The warriors jabbed their swords into the sky. Mindlessly they gestured and roared, flaunting their freshness at the end of the day.

Alodar looked up and down the line as it stretched before him, uniformly thick and extending farther than he cared to imagine. He looked back over the royal forces and tried to visualize them strung out thinly to meet the next day's charge.

He and the others were silent with shock as they watched the scene fade into the night. The line of men dissolved into the darkness, but dancing lights marked where they stood. An occasional beat of luminescent wings fluttered in their midst, and soft but spinetingling laughter wafted across the valley.

Alodar recalled his longing for battle before entering Bardina and felt it dash to splinters against the hard strength of what he had seen. He followed the flittering of imp glow and smiled ruefully at his hopes of tipping the balance with the control of a single demon.

He shuddered as the final reality hit him. Tomorrow, outnumbered, by how many he could not tell, they must defeat those demon-driven, screaming hordes, or it would all be over. There would be no fair lady, no Procolon, no Ambrosia. All would be swept away and replace by horrors that even Handar had difficulty describing.

Vendora stood speechless, her face a tight mask and her fists clenched at her sides. Grak placed a hand on her shoulder. "So this is the battle for which we will receive our great rewards," he growled. "It is more likely that our women will see few of us again."

Vendora blinked and her eyes widened as she looked up at the nomad.

"No, I will not abandon you," Grak promised. "It is not for the pretty rocks or shields of shiny steel that I have pledged my sword to your aid. We will see tomorrow through, no matter what the consequences."

"And after a meal for my weary men, we will plan," Cedric said. "They will attack at dawn and we must be deployed as best we can."

Handar looked at Alodar in the darkness, his eyes glowing. He sighed. "I wish that there had been more time. We might have had a better chance."

Alodar raised his eyebrows as Aeriel approached and she laughed self-consciously. "Vendora has decreed that our council tonight be held as a proper court," she said. "So after a hurried meal I did what I could to clean my tunic and wash my hair." She whirled for his inspection and patted a hand to her hip. "Yes, even the magic dagger. Somehow Basil managed to carry two with him throughout the entire trek. He presented one to the queen, and she insisted that I display mine."

Alodar nodded and accompanied her to the fire pit where the advisors were assembling. The moon was nearly gone, and the yellow flames silhouetted the closest figures in harsh shadows. He looked around the group and saw Cedric resting comfortably, the lines of pain in his face softened into creases of fatigue. The vat of sweetbalm Alodar had brewed with ingredients scavenged from the refugees was not the best; but there was enough so that each of the warmaster's men received some share. He saw Cedric nod his head slowly as he listened to Grak explaining the numbers and weapons of his men. While he talked the nomad pulled uncomfortably at a silken shirt embroidered with metallic threads that sparkled in the firelight. Clearly more than willowbark had been requisitioned from the fleeing subjects of the queen.

"The fair lady," Grengor announced, rising to his feet and pointing to the periphery of illumination. Out of the shadows Vendora slowly approached, walking in synchronization to a silent promenade. She wore a gown of gold, and her hair was pushed high, held in place by jeweled combs. She smiled as she slowly sat in a chair roughly constructed from a wagon's planking. She motioned the assemblage to rest as well.

"The hours till dawn are few enough," Feston muttered. "I hope, my fair lady, that you do not intend to start with the ritual proclamations."

"I am still the queen of Procolon, if only for one more night," Vendora said. "All shall be conducted with the proper decorum."

Feston frowned but said no more. For a moment a heavy silence hung on them all. "There is very little to discuss," Cedric said at last. "We are too few to have many options. My men with mail will take the center and Grak and his nomads will form on either side. The horses we have must guard both flanks and try to prevent an envelopment."

"And while you hold them at bay, there may be time to slip away," Basil suggested. "We should be able to bribe enough silence for a safe hiding place."

"With my sphere, the number accompanying need not be large," Duncan added. "Consider carefully, my fair lady, the choices you have left."

"We are pledged to fight for this woman, one and all," Grak growled. "To slink away is to cast aside one's honor."

"Do not be swayed, my fair lady, by the folly of the sagas," Basil said. "The fate of most of those assembled here may be determined, it is true. But for one with personal resources, the result need not be so clear."

"The sphere wards off demons as well as mortal blows," Duncan reminded the queen.

"Duncan, you are not the only suitor to whom I can turn for aid," Vendora said. "In fact I have decided today to increase my options further." She stopped and swept her arm across the circle. "Stand up, Grak, and receive the congratulations of your peers."

The nomad rose stiffly and placed his hands behind his back, glowering at the looks cast his way.

"For what deed this time?" Aeriel asked. "Are not four suitors enough to play one against the other?"

"I could justify it as a reward for assembling my barbarian army," Vendora replied.

"But that is favoritism even more blatant than at Iron Fist," Aeriel said. "It is not because of his aid alone that we have gathered as many as we have."

"I could say for assembling my army," Vendora repeated, "but I will not. It is because I want it so, and that is reason enough."

A rash of whispers shot around the circle but Vendora ignored them and continued. "You cannot fault the role of queen that I have played. My father taught me in fine detail how to balance the competing factions and to win independent power to my cause. But I am a woman as well as a queen. Not all of my choices will be made because they suit the purposes of the state."

"But your beauty is renowned throughout the kingdom, my fair lady," Duncan protested. "We suitors pursue you as well as the dignity of the crown."

"Oh I know you would eye me even if I were a wench in a tavern." Vendora smiled. "But without the glitter of the throne, how many gems or magic spheres would you offer my way? Grak pledged to Vendora the woman, and for that he would have the same reward if he alone came to my banner. After tomorrow it may no longer matter; you will not suffer for the one night he is your equal."

"Our fate cannot be as certain as all that," Aeriel cried. "Surely fight or flight are not all that we can consider. Handar, I do not believe you slept only to warn us of what we would finally discover of our own accord. What else can we do besides stand firm and wave our swords until we are swept away?"

"Yes, there is another hope," Handar said as he rose slowly and stepped to the center of the circle near the fire. "Another chance, less direct but one that we must take as well."

He looked around the group and saw everyone waiting for him to continue. "Years ago when it was decided that one day what we see about us indeed could come to pass. the great wizards planned what must be our defense. Our hope would not lie in struggling with the mischievous imps, the devils of power, or even the great demons. No, we must strike instead at the capstone. We must subjugate the very prince who plots against us and bend him to our will to trouble us no more. Only with one such as he working for our good fortune rather than against it could we ensure that our peril was gone. Directed by his human master to turn his attention elsewhere, he would bring his minions home and look to other worlds to satisfy his lust for conquest. And even though the barriers subsequently might fall again, he would be bound to prevent any free transfer."

"But a demon prince, one more powerful than Balthazar," Alodar protested. "Has any wizard ever tried to undertake such a task?"

"No, such a conjuring has never been attempted," Handar replied. "And for two compelling reasons. The first is the flame; the prince can be summoned only by the burning of a metal extracted and purified from many substances which are nearly its twin. From no common earth does it come. And as far as I know, only one quantity of sufficient size has been refined by the most painstaking alchemist's art."

"Then where is it now?" Alodar asked. "Back in your spire?"

"No." Handar smiled. "Much nearer than that. Here, Alodar, let me see the sorcerer's eye."

Alodar reached into his pouch and handed the wizard the nearly forgotten orb. His eyes widened with surprise as Handar suddenly snatched it away and hurled it to the ground. The sphere hit a rock with a crash and shattered into a myriad of tiny jagged pieces. The eye was gone and Handar stooped and picked up a single crystal of shining metal hidden in its interior.

For a moment Alodar was silent, studying first the remains of the sphere he had struggled so hard to obtain and then the gleaming beauty Handar held between thumb and forefinger. "But if you knew that it was there all along, why wait until now to bring it forth? When I awakened you at the tower, why did you not summon the demon prince at once and be done with it?"

"As I have said," Handar continued, "No such conjuring has ever been attempted. I am among the best of my craft, but Balthazar is the limit of what I can hope to master. For one such as the demon prince, no mortal wizard would have the strength to impress his domination upon him."

"Then what is this hope of which you speak?" Grengor asked. "If none can subdue this mighty demon, then we are left with nothing but to struggle with blade and shield."

"No wizard, I said," Handar replied. "One armed only with the powers of my craft, no matter how skillful, would have no chance to succeed. Therefore we consulted with masters of the other arts, an event most unheard of. But thaumaturge, alchemist, magician, sorcerer—they all agreed that none of their arts singly applied could fare any better than mine. The one to confront the demon prince would need proficiencies far greater, far more encompassing than any of those in a single craft. He would need to be an archimage, the master of all the arts."

"But even if such a wonder existed," Grengor persisted, "would even he be enough?"

"I do not know," Handar said. "But by logic, there is nothing more potent that a mortal could try. We know that knowledge of one of the arts is insufficient. But yet this one spark of hope is there. Even though each art would fail by itself, perhaps, if used together by someone versed in them all, the effect of the whole might be greater than the sum of the parts."

Handar stuffed the crystal into a pocket and then touched his fingertips together and rested his thumbs on his chest. "And so we, the great wizards, made our plan on this premise. We began by building Iron Fist, the fortress of the far west. Great effort was spent in raising its long, smooth walls. Much thought was given to the design of its passageways and mighty keep. Many demons were pressed into the labor of its construction. When the trigger was complete, we set them upon themselves until they all were destroyed."

"The trigger?" Feston interrupted. "I was at the fall of Iron Fist but saw nothing of what you speak."

"The trigger was the castle itself," Handar said. "After we had finished the other tasks of our plan we went to sleep in the tower to the north. And so long as the interaction with demonkind was random, we would slumber on. Awakening—my awakening—was not to come until precipitated by the desires of the demon prince for our world. When the prince finally directed his attention to us, his first act would be to attack our tower. He could not penetrate our protective shield so he acted instead to ensure that no mortal would awaken us either.

"And after the passage of time had sealed us away from other men with taboo and superstition, his interest then naturally focused on the structure for which we had lavished so much care, the mighty fortress built by the wizards he was unable to reach. He could not but think that some great secret of our craft lay somewhere hidden within its protective walls. And so, after isolating us in the north, he directed the sack of Iron Fist to learn what we must have hidden there. That attack started the sequence of events that resulted in my awakening and the culmination of our defense as well."

"None could fathom why Bandor chose to raze the castle rather than fortify it for his own." Feston nodded his head. "But you speak of a man of great skill to lead the defense. Ask and you will hear of my prowess in that fall, how I saved the queen from a dire fate and became suitor for her hand."

"Ah, skill in arms. Most commendable," Handar said. "But was it by that skill that you made your escape with the treasures that were hidden there?"

"Why no, it was not so," Aeriel interjected before Feston could speak again. "It was Alodar who solved the riddle of the column and the well. It was he who found the passage that let us reach the cool air of the hills beyond."

"Most clever for you to solve the riddle, Alodar." Handar smiled. "But then, cunning is the mark of the master thaumaturge."

He patted his fingertips together and then put his hands behind his back. Like a lecturer before a group of apprentices, he slowly circled the fire with his chin bent down to his chest. "But there was more buried in Iron Fist than just a means of escape. As we returned from my tower, Alodar told me that he carried away a scrap of paper with a single formula, most arcane. A formula that was used to probe the secrets of the Fumus Mountains."

"And not by the novice alone," Basil interrupted. "My minion Rendrac pitted his great bulk against the heat of those furnaces. He brought forth a treasure the likes of which man has not hitherto seen. It was pledged to the queen to provide the means by which she might finance her struggles." He drew his dagger and waved it about. "And for my great generosity I am her suitor as much as any nobleborn."

"I have heard of Rendrac's fate," Handar continued. "With ointment applied thickly, he braved the mountains, only to die a suffocating death in the end. And with no ointment, the treasure could not be reached. Only by pushing onward against great pain could one hope to return with both orbs of magic and his life. But then, perseverance is the touchstone of the master alchemist."

"It may have been wizardry which placed the spheres in the mountains," Duncan said. "But it was my magic which completed the sphere of protection, proof against man and demon alike. What greater gift could one give a queen in exchange for marriage vows."

"Yes, magic and wizardry mixed," Handar admitted. "A source of heat, lasting forever, to keep the lava bubbling in its basin of solid rock. And the two incomplete spheres placed by a fire demon in the bowels of the mountain. Two spheres, not one, and subtly different. When completed by tradition the results are the same. With a different ritual performed with precision, however, one becomes instead a sorcerer's eye." Handar shrugged. "But then, precision is the essence of the master magician. It was the eye that led Alodar to me and completed the chain for which Iron Fist was the trigger."

"Kelric showed great bravery in unlocking its power," Grengor said. "Even though he died with the badge of a suitor, he knew that he willed his own death by attempting to use it."

"Great courage indeed." Handar nodded. "But which was greater? Who among you submitted to look into the eye when it opened? It is one thing to resign yourself to death but quite another to accept an uncertain fate which may be even worse. But then, bravery is the heart of the master sorcerer. And through it all, who ran the entire gauntlet of tests, refusing to succumb to the events which threatened to dominate him?"

Handar stopped and turned to face Alodar. "But then, strength of will is the quintessence of the master wizard.

Yes, our plan encompassed more than the mechanism for our awakening. They included as well the means by which we would find and test the one who possessed the inherent capabilities to master all the arts. The lid of my coffin was not pushed aside by a random messenger. It was done by the one whom we sought."

Alodar blinked. For a moment, he was speechless. "I have faced these trials as you say," he said at last. "But I do not know of what you speak. I sought only the hand of the queen."

"Yes, my lad," Handar replied. "Most certainly you moved forward from endeavor to endeavor with some other goal in mind. But the first quest is but the shadow of the second. It is for more than a single kingdom that you are here. All else is the pettiness of dull history and not the fabric of the sages."

"But I could have faltered along the way," Alodar protested. "Had I not acted correctly at each step, what then of your plan to save us?"

"To defeat the demon prince, the need is for the archimage," Handar said. "No less will do. Not one who claims to know all the crafts, not one who is willing to learn them. But one who possesses the attributes that make a great master of them all. We had to take the risk that someone capable of being the complete master would be present at Iron Fist when it fell."

"But in no craft am I master, let alone five," Alodar protested. "I studied thaumaturgy for a few years, alchemy for half of one more. With each art my knowledge and experience is less than the one before. I have controlled a few simple imps and exorcised one or two more. Yet I would fear Balthazar or the tower demons, let alone their master."

"It is not their power on which you should dwell," Handar said. "That is as they would wish. It is their will that must be your focus, independent of how they manipulate the natural elements at their disposal. Such is the way with Balthazar and with the prince as well."

The wizard paused and then continued slowly. "I understand some of what you feel, but events have proceeded all too quickly. I could wish to see you develop more fully in my craft, to build the confidence needed before you were distracted by the task for which you were groomed. But tomorrow precludes such an option. And master in the arts or not, we have no other candidate. You are the best that mortal men at this junction can offer."

Alodar looked around the circle, his mouth suddenly dry. He saw all eyes staring his way awaiting his decision. He felt a touch on his arm and turned his head to see Aeriel at his side. Numb with the weight of what was asked of him, he looked at Vendora and thought of how hard he had struggled for the prize of possessing her. He ran his tongue across his lips and visualized his dream of the triumphant march of the hero. He brushed his hand by his side and then suddenly looked across at Cedric.

The warmaster returned his stare, cool and steady. "I said to wear the sword so that it did honor to us both," Cedric said. "I have no cause to wish it back."

Alodar glanced at Aeriel standing quietly beside him, only dimly aware of the pain her grip sent through his arm. He looked back at the wizard and read the truth of all that Handar had said.

"Is it so certain that I alone have walked this path for you?" Alodar asked.

Handar nodded silently.

Alodar filled his lungs with a rush of air. "It is not for this that I have quested," he said. "But I have offered my life once already and that was merely for a queen. How can I sacrifice less for what you ask?"

"It is as I knew you would say." Handar tossed Alodar the crystal of metal.

"But when and how should I use it?" Alodar asked. "Now, just before the attack, during the battle, or only if all seems irretrievably lost?"

Handar slowly shook his head. "That is for the archimage to decide," he said softly.

PART SIX

The Archimage

CHAPTER TWENTY-ONE

Master Times Five

"THAT should be enough curing," Alodar said as he dropped the formula-laden scrap to the ground. The potter grunted and slowed the spin of his wheel to a halt. Alodar peered into the large barrel. Guided by overhead torchlight, he scooped out the last of the small, dripping pumicestones. He felt the rubbery coating that had been flung against the inner walls of the barrel and nodded with satisfaction at its dryness.

Pressing all that goldenrod for the milky sap had taken time, and he had been forced to try four times for the desiccation to activate properly twice. But otherwise these crude potato barrels would not be watertight.

"Put it on the wagon with the other," he said, "and take them down to the stream to be filled. Grengor has a party building a dam and will sound alarm if anything stirs on the other crest."

The potter waved his understanding, and Alodar pushed the details from his mind. His thoughts raced forward to the next task to be performed in the little time remaining before dawn. After the council had broken up, he had talked with Handar for another hour about what to expect when he tried to conjure the demon prince. Each question had led to two more; when the wizard finally broke off, Alodar was no more sure of his course of action than when he began. But he could not tolerate the frustration of waiting and plunged into a whirlwind of activities, manipulating the things that he could understand, seeking ways to combine the virtues of the five arts, to scrape together the meager resources at hand into potent weapons for the battle. The bog illusion was prepared and the demon for the barrels must wait until the proper time. What next could be done with the bits of board and metal that remained in the camp?

"I did not expect to find you still about." Handar's voice cut through Alodar's reverie. "Let the thaumaturges and alchemists among the refugees handle these tasks. If anyone is to get his rest tonight, it should be you."

"I cannot stand idly by while others rush forward for our cause armed only with their swords," Alodar protested. "I have spent the evening formulating a means by which we can match the length of their line to ours." He waved at the departing potter. "And something to halt the ones that might break through."

"I also have been busy," the wizard said. "On the wings of djinns, I returned to the tower. I awoke two sleeping comrades from tombs like my own. Their power is not as great as mine but it will be used tomorrow. More than Balthazar will be wrenched from his study of other worlds to struggle against his brethren."

"These other places?" Alodar asked. "Several times you have mentioned them. What have they to do with us?"

"Though I have never seen one," Handar answered, "the demons speak of many worlds parallel to theirs, some in fact inhabited by men like ourselves. And on some of these the crafts by which men lifted themselves from savagery are different from those we use here. There the five arts have fallen into disrepute, their principles forgotten or distorted, their place taken by other skills similar in nature but guided by different laws. The truth of thaumaturgy remain only in a few imperfectly remembered spells; instead, a huge edifice of complex postulates has been erected to explain the nature of space and time. Impatient with the uncertain success of alchemy, they replaced it with another art. The beautiful symmetries of magic became a thing unto themselves, symbols to be manipulated and arrayed, their underlying significance lost. The skill of the sorcerer to enchant fell away, and the practitioners concentrated instead on small changes in character of those with whom they dealt. And whole populations cope with devils and imps by turning their backs on them and dismissing their existence as primitive superstition. Places such as these are not threatened by demonkind, or if so, care little for the consequences of the interaction. And perhaps this indifference is what

341

draws the prince's attention to us. I do not know. I only can hope that you will find the means to turn it in another direction."

"There will be little time for another meal tomorrow," a second voice, brittle with strain, interrupted the conversation. Alodar turned to see Aeriel approach from up the slope. She thrust a still-steaming piece of fowl into his hand. Her face was tight, and she avoided his glance and lowered her head. Alodar frowned and gently placed his fingertip under her chin. He raised her face to his and saw tears sparkling in the corners of her eyes.

The wizard cleared his throat. "I will attend to the others of my craft," he mumbled and disappeared into the darkness.

"Do not grieve yet," Alodar said after a moment. "Handar and the others will aid our cause. And when the time comes I will also be ready."

Aeriel opened her mouth to speak but then stopped and sighed uncertainly. "My tears are not for what may happen at the worst," she told him softly. "If that is to be our fate, then we will share it. It is the possibility of victory on which I ponder. And I am troubled about how I truly feel about it."

"But if we win the battle, it will mean the war as well," Alodar assured her. "All demons gone, and the ones they control restored to their former dispositions."

"Yes, I understand the aftermath either way," Aeriel said. "Just as I knew how you would respond when Handar presented you with the decision. I admire you for that, Alodar, and wish you to find the same strength in me."

Alodar blinked and tried to understand the meaning of her words. "Admiration is too tame a description for what I feel for you, Aeriel. And the support you have given the queen is second to no other."

"But do you not see?" Aeriel cried. "If you finish the second quest, you succeed in the first also. You will have saved Procolon, you alone, and no one can deny it. Vendora can have no other choice but to select you above all the others. Craftsman and peer alike will demand it. There will be no more need to play one against the other for momentary gain. And so, either way, I will be the loser. What follows defeat I do not wish upon anyone, and yet, if we win, the result for me will be no different."

Alodar sucked in his breath. Part of his mind wanted to pull away and deny Aeriel's logic, the logic he knew had also deeply troubled his own thoughts. He looked into her tear-filled eyes, and his throat grew tight. "Your boldness exceeds even my own," he whispered.

Aeriel paused and then continued more slowly. "On the royal barge I stated that my goal was to serve the queen, to see that she finally selected the mate that would make her kingdom secure. And so I have done, acting unselfishly to advance your banner because you seemed the most worthy. But through it all, my own feelings became harder and harder to push aside."

Aeriel again ducked her head. "In the mountains to the north you expressed what your feelings would be if you did not quest for the queen. And so long as the pursuit continued and did not reach for its climax, it was enough. But the events have compressed too quickly. They transcend the struggle for a single kingdom. Now there can no uncertainty about Procolon's future if you pass one final test. And so, even though everyone else makes their individual sacrifices to aid our common cause, mine I cannot give freely. Here am I, a lady of the royal court, proud of my record of putting state before self. One who looked with disdain at those who maneuvered to protect their own petty interests. But when I face my own test, when I am called upon to part with something that truly matters, I find that I fall short of my image of myself. I hesitate; I falter. Other feelings are there and I cannot deny them. If one were to ask if I truly prefer a victory tomorrow, a victory that allows you finally to choose Vendora over all others . . ."

Alodar's thoughts exploded. Perhaps it was the fatigue, the uncertainty of what lay ahead, the pressure of keeping so many thoughts hidden, Aeriel's presence, the openness with which she revealed herself to him. But regardless of the reasons he could suppress his feelings for her no longer. With all the rest, like a sprite's dustdevil, they whirled in his mind.

It was her companionship he had enjoyed in all the wanderings to the north. If ever there was a fair lady worthy of the quest of any of the heroes of the sagas, he thought, it was Aeriel and no other. But the pursuit of Vendora, the battle, the confrontation with a prince of

343

demons, they all crowded in and tumbled together. He could not sort his feelings out and speak with decision. But after tonight, he might never see her again, he thought dimly above the confusion. They could not part until he told her something of what he felt.

He drew his free arm around her and pulled her to him. "I know the fair lady for what she is," he said softly. "It was not for her that I quested so much as for what she represented. And I understand as well the conflict that brings your tears. It can be no less stormy than my own. Many times in my quest, I thought of you and what in the end success would mean. And each time, like a timid magician, I would not complete the ritual and drive my thoughts to their conclusion. Instead I bound them up and stuffed them away, selfishly taking all the warmth and comfort of your attention and deferring to later what the consequences might be."

He paused and squeezed her tightly. "The sands have been cast, and the events of tomorrow will thunder to their resolution, regardless of our longings. But no matter what happens, Aeriel, I want you to know this. You are not the only one who will lose from either outcome."

Aeriel sobbed once and then smiled through her tears. Hungrily her lips sought his. Alodar stopped his mental struggle and let his thoughts slide away in the heat of their passion. Time passed, but he did not care. Finally they stood apart, looking deeply into each other's eyes.

After a moment Alodar glanced away and then with a smile held up the piece of chicken that was still tightly clutched in his hand. Aeriel laughed, and the mood suddenly was broken. The ventilated emotions evaporated away into the gloom. Aeriel licked her lips and then accepted the offered bite. Without saying more, they took turns shredding away pieces of meat from the bone.

"I am glad you came with the meal," Alodar said when they were done.

"And I," Aeriel replied as she pulled the wishbone apart from the rest. "A superstition that plays no part in your crafts, I know. But certainly a wish for good fortune could do us no harm."

Alodar nodded, and they snapped the bone. "I will carry the favor into battle," he said as they carefully put the pieces away into their pockets. He looked to the east and again drew her gently to him. In silence they stood together, waiting for the first rays of dawn.

Alodar's heart pounded to the beat of the drums. He looked quickly at the half circle of the sun and then at the warriors already on the march towards them. Under the brightening sky the final contingents of the queen moved into position. Because of Grengor's dam, the meandering stream had swollen into a long, shallow lake. On the side nearest, Alodar saw the glint of sunlight from Cedric's militia. Shoulder to shoulder, they stood behind a row of long pikes thrust into the soft shoreline. Five rows deep, the warriors marked a contour of the valley, a spiny serpent of steel, a thousand feet long, silent and waiting.

Grak and his kinsmen spread out on both sides to extend the defense farther. Much less densely packed, the nomads formed narrow strings of leather, each man refusing to hide behind another. Tucked just behind the last in line on the left, a small cavalry, led by Feston, pawed the ground. Of the twenty horses, only a dozen wore mail, another five were mere ponies. Their nervous snorts fogged the cold morning air. Directly behind Cedric and in front of the knoll on which Alodar stood, a score of archers finished stringing their bows and slowly testing the tensions. A little to their left, Handar paced with two other black-robed wizards.

Alodar looked hastily about to ensure that all his preparations were ready. His marines stood on guard around a small semicircle pulled bare of grass and shrubbery. A cauldron of wax bubbled at the center. A supply of molds crudely pounded from pots and plates lay near the thaumaturge standing nearby. Two of the refugees, too old to swing a sword, but understanding well the futility of further flight, beat a pile of willowbark into powder for the next batch of sweetbalm.

Near Alodar's feet, a row of bottles, apparently empty but all tightly corked, stood in a row. The one on the left dangled above a fire in a pit, and the next was piled on all sides with glowing coals. Down the line, the intensity of the applied heat declined until the bottle on the farthest right bobbed in a bucket of water from the icy stream. At the end was a glove with the wrist tied around the snout of a bellows and the tips of the thumb and little finger neatly clipped off. Farther away stood the wagon with the two barrels of water. Seven hobbled horses, the worst of Vendora's scavenged lot, munched on the grass nearby.

Alodar looked to the crest behind and saw all the rest gathered in small clumps to watch the outcome. The sun reflected brightly off Vendora's gown. At her side he could see Duncan squeezing the pouch that contained his sphere. Basil kept looking over his shoulder as if he hoped to find a refuge he had missed before. At the last moment, Alodar had sent Aeriel away to join them; as he watched, she reluctantly faded into the throng.

Alodar turned back to face in the direction of the drums. The cadence was slow and booming. Each throb seemed to intensify with hypnotic incessancy. On every beat, the troops of the rebellion took another synchronized step down the incline. The slow march was deliberate, Alodar knew. The final yell and haphazard rush would come only after Vendora's defenders had been given ample time to contemplate the might arrayed against them.

They marched in rectangles three men deep and thirty wide, each one marked by a long banner hanging limply from a lance that poked skyward. Only narrow gaps separated groups one from another. But when Alodar looked to the left and right, he saw the air shimmer and the approaching men seem to fade from view. Except for a narrow portion of the line about the same length as that of the royal forces, no more of the huge army that had reached the crest the night before was visible.

"Even though we are outnumbered," Grengor said at Alodar's side, "if they do not choose to use their superior forces to envelop us, we still have a chance. The center will hold, and the savagery of Grak's kinsmen will be more than a match for minds that are demon-doped."

"They all move against us," Alodar replied. "You see but part of the illusion that I am casting in order to nullify some of the advantage. Last night Cedric and Grak agreed that it would be folly to stretch our line to match their length. Densely clustered, we would stand no chance against a sweep of the flanks. They said that they needed to defend a pass rather than a plain. So with the arts, I have attempted to form one."

Grengor wrinkled his brow and Alodar continued.

"They came too late yesterday to get a clear view of the land between us. If we can convince them that deep bogs lie on either side, they will compress into the middle and trip over themselves as they try to jockey forward. The imp Gladril carried water-filled jugs into the sky. He periodically dumped them as he rose, thereby replacing their contents with the vapors of the various layers. Upon return to earth, each jug was then subjected to fire and cold as you see at my feet, and the sky above now bends the rays of light as I choose. The warriors coming down the hill do not see the empty plain to our right and left but a far wetter marsh we skirted in the north."

"But shimmering air alone will not bend them from their instructed course," Grengor objected.

"And so the camphor was used to make the solvent, imperfect as it was," Alodar said. "Delivered by the sprites into the path of the march, it has eaten at the grasses and rock for long enough that more than one boghole will result. For the rest, though you cannot hear them, no less than a dozen sirens caress their ears as they approach. And this time their song is not a meaningless wail but the word of sorcery as I have instructed them to say. Visions of cattails, rushes, sedge, and milkweed will mix with the flickering air. By themselves, each part of the effect would be insufficient, but together they will do what they must."

Alodar smiled as he saw a block of men emerge from the haze and move behind the line that marched without deflection down the center. Another group appeared and then another. "If I had had a magic sound box for the croak of the frog and buzz of the fly I could have used it as well. But no matter, it seems to be working with what I have already done. We still have to face them all, but at least not at the same time."

Suddenly the drums stopped. With a yell, Bandor's warriors flashed their swords and raced down the remaining portion of the hill. Screaming unearthly warcries, they dashed into the water, tromping up a fine spray with their passage. Some lost their balance and fell, but the ones behind ran over them, eyes gleaming. The precisely formed rectangles pulled apart into ragged lines and then disintegrated entirely. In twos and threes, they staggered to dry land and flung themselves at Vendora's defense.

Alodar caught his breath with the first clang of sword on shield. He saw a nomad nimbly sidestep an awkward thrust and then slash downward on the exposed neck and shoulder that tumbled after. More warriors reached the line. With a shout of their own, Cedric's center and Grak's barbarians met the attack. The noise of contact popped and groaned all along the line into the morning air.

Alodar saw the mailed militia momentarily fall backwards from the shock but then stand firm and cut down the first who reached them. The nomads whirled their swords in great swinging arcs and leaped forward to meet their foes knee deep in the water. The attackers fell like wheat before a scythe.

Before the nomads advanced farther, hastily barked commands pulled them back into a more disciplined line. With taunting swords, they awaited the next rush, which came with far more caution. Bandor's troops reconsolidated into a wall, and the first row waded across to meet the defenders. More blocks squeezed in behind but hesitated at the far side of the lake, unwilling to stand in the cold water behind those who fought in front. Farther up the hill, other groups ducked behind their shields as they came within range of the hail of arrows. Alodar quickly surveyed the entire line. For the moment they had held the first charge.

Alodar let his breath out and then snapped his attention back to his own duties. "Quickly, Grengor," he ordered. "Untether the horses that pull the wagon and get two men alongside the barrels. I will tell you in a moment where we will best need them."

"Our proper place is down on the line with the rest, master," Grengor shot back. "I do not like this meaningless guard duty. The wounded who can walk will find this place well enough and the thaumaturge and alchemists can tend to the mending as well as you."

"We cannot hold this position, forever," Alodar said. "We must be ready for the breakthroughs wherever they may come. Do as I say. Your utility will be far greater."

Alodar did not wait for a reply but swung his eyes to the small fire under the bottle on the left. In an instant, he willed his presence through the flame. A sparkle of light. no bigger than a firefly, danced before him.

"You make a great error, master," a tiny voice whined.

"Even the most immature imp has powers which are great compared to mine. Why, since my hatching, only the wizard Maxwell on another world has even bothered with my summoning."

"Into the glove," Alodar ordered. "There is no time for wordy quibble." He picked up the bellows and ran to the wagon. As he climbed aboard, the spark of light followed and disappeared into the interior of the contraption in his hand.

"To what position?" Grengor asked, slapping the reins against the horses' backs. "I would think that the nomads on the east will most need whatever help we can offer."

"Cedric says that stopping the first penetration, no matter where it occurs, is most important," Alodar replied. "No one can aggressively hold a line if he feels his backside threatened. And if the enemy is halted once, they will be less bold a second time. Now silence, I must concentrate on where it will be."

Alodar looked back at the line. The battle surged forward and back. In the center, as men fell on either side, those behind moved up to fill in the gap. Cedric's forces buckled and bowed, alternately retreating among the pikes or pushing the attackers back into the lake. The struggles of the barbarians gradually diffused into an unstructured mêlée, each nomad fighting alone, whipping his sword in all directions in vengeance for his fallen comrades. With each passing minute, they thinned and weakened, but the confusion they caused on the other side was as great as their own, and no advantage immediately could be taken.

For an instant Alodar grimaced with distaste at what he would feel next, but then plunged into the charm. The prophecy would be for this place and only for moments away; it should not be a severe undertaking. He spoke the words quickly, too intent on what he must do to notice greatly the discomfort. In a moment it was done. With unblinking eyes, he scanned the future of the tumult.

The swirl of fighting blurred and then jerked back into focus. The turbulence looked the same on the left In the center, Cedric held firm, although his line was far more shallow. Alodar slewed past the center but then halted and looked again. There on the boundary, between Cedric's mail and Grak's barbarians on the right, the line suddenly ruptured and a mass of yelling warriors streamed through.

Alodar blinked back to the present. "To the west," he shouted, "and use the whip!" A wave of nausea rose from his stomach as the wagon lurched forward, but he paid no attention. Steadying himself with one hand, he reached for a deep-bowled ladle bouncing on the wagonbed.

"Use the barrel in the rear first," he said to Melab, who rocked along at his side. "Insert the hose and prepare the plunger so we will be ready when we arrive."

The marine put the round wooden lid with the wide rubber flange into the mouth of the barrel and inserted one end of a hose into a small hole near the center. He pressed tentatively on the surface and a spray of water shot from the other end of the hose.

"One more burst so I can fill the ladle," Alodar said, bending forward to catch the last of the stream. When the spoon was full, he flung the hose aside and cradled the sloshing bowl. They raced past the archers nocking the last of their arrows and the wizards observing without apparent emotion. He looked back to the line and yelled for Grengor to stop. The last oscillations of the wagon had barely faded away when, just as he had envisioned, four men fell side by side in near unison, and the attackers surged through.

"Wet them all," Alodar yelled. Melab quickly bent his back to the barrel cover, and another marine with the hose arched a geyser into the leading edge of the warriors rushing their way. Alodar looked quickly at the distance to be covered and then at the apparatus he still held in his hand. While the marines washed the spray back and forth over the fighters as they charged, he carefully set the ladle of water on the wagonbed. Then, inserting the thumb of the glove into the bowl, he bound the metal wheelrims as a heat sink and began to pump the bellows.

Alodar saw the glove expand into a balloon and felt the jet of air escaping from the fingerhole of his crude tee-junction strike his cheek. He cocked his head to the side to intercept the rush from the other airstream, burbling up through the water in the ladle. He looked up at the warriors thundering towards them, swords held high and eyes wide with blood lust. "Only the coldest to the thumbhole," he yelled. "I do not care how warm the other side becomes."

"As you wish, master," the voice inside the glove squeaked, and the bubbling stream turned icy cold. Alodar looked at the marines and saw the strain on their faces as they watched the approach. The fastest of the intruders sprinted forward and, with a yell of glee, locked his eyes on where Alodar's unprotected form huddled on the wagon.

Alodar's legs strained to bolt away, but he held himself firm and pumped all the harder. He cringed in anticipation of the downward swinging blow but, as he did, felt a sudden resistance to his inward squeeze.

Alodar glanced up and ducked to the side as the warrior pitched forward into the wagon, his arm locked and his face in a puzzled stare. He looked back at the others who followed and saw them fall to the ground one by one, mimicking the grotesque statues of the children's game. He examined the glove and found the finger frozen solid in the small block of ice that had formed in the ladle.

"A simple matter of thaumaturgy," he explained to Melab as he rose. "And a demon who could separate the hot air from the cold in order to freeze the small quantity that once was a part of a larger whole." He looked for a final time at what he had done. "The circles of mail are just the right size to hold the water until it freezes into a solid coat. I witnessed the effect once before, although it was with a caloric ointment rather than common ice."

The squad of archers came rushing up, and Alodar turned away, not caring to watch how they ensured that the downed warriors would bother them no more. He breathed deeply and tried to prepare himself to recast the prophetic enchantment. But before he could act, a sudden shout from the west caught his attention. At the very limit of Alodar's illusion, a troop of horsemen forded the stream and turned towards the battle. With a trumpeteer's charge, they kicked their mounts into a run and bore down on the flank. As Alodar watched, Feston wheeled his cavalry to meet the attack.

For the better part of a minute, the horsemen raced over the tall grass. Feston surged to the front and, with his sword over his head, waved on the stragglers. The troops rushed together with the sharp report of steel on steel. Great jets of mud and uprooted grass exploded sky-ward from the impact. The cries of men and horses in pain replaced the dull rumble of the charge. The thin lines broke and dissolved into small swirls of energy, ringing sword on shield and riders tumbling to the ground.

"They circled around the illusion on the far side," Alodar said. "And if on one flank, then why not the other?" He whirled to the east and saw four horsemen crossing the stream downstream of Grengor's dam. Alodar looked back. Feston's troop was fully engaged, the archers busy with their grueling task, and the line of warriors still pressed from the south. He thought of the impact of even four swords cutting into their thinly held flank. "They will move too fast for this to work again," he shouted to Grengor as he flung the bellows aside. "Enough of the fancy craftwork. Back to our post and the few horses that we have. There is no one else to stop them."

The wagon turned a slow circle and then bounced back to the clearing. Alodar sprang from the bed and ran for one of the horses. He scooped up and sheathed his sword and then jumped into the saddle. Wrenching around the reins, he kneed his mount into a gallop. The remaining marines abandoned their guard duty and followed.

Bandor's horsemen saw his troop coming and veered from bearing down on the nomads to meet the charge. Both men and horses were heavily draped in mail. The morning sun flashed angry reflections from the polished surfaces of helms caped with billowy blue plumes. A long standard decorated with Bandor's arms fluttered from a staff on the lead horseman's saddle. Although the heavily muscled mounts raced rapidly forward, the men sat stiffly erect as if walking in a procession.

As they approached, each of the four reached to his side and spun a spiny balled mace into the air. Alodar drew his sword in response. Closing for the collision, he tried to recall Cedric's instructions on how best to deal with the whirling weapon. He frowned as he studied their orbits above the warrior's heads. They rotated so slowly that he could see the dodecahedral symmetry of the spikes.

He blinked and pulled back on the reins. "Magic weapons!" he shouted. "Maces of crystal resonance. I read of them in the library of the Guild. It is no wonder they come with only four. Our metal will do us no good."

He slowed to a trot, but two of his followers sped past and converged on the leader from both sides.

The marines swung their swords high simultaneously, aiming at the warrior's exposed side and his hand stiffly holding the reins. With a sudden jerk, the mace wrenched out of its flat trajectory and smashed into the blades, one after the other. Sparks flew at the contact and metal shrieked in protest as the surfaces grated together. One sword snapped at the hilt and sprang skyward. The other broke nearer the middle, sending both halves spinning to the ground. Before either man could recover, the mace dipped lower on its second revolution, crashing into one marine's jaw and hitting the other in the chest. With what sounded like the bursting of a bag of coins, the ringlets of mail tinkled to the ground.

"Stop the swing. It is the only way," Alodar shouted. "Hanging limply, they have no power; but so long as they whirl we have no weapon to stand against them." He looked quickly about as the rest of the marines sped forward to engage the others. He saw one immediately knocked to the ground and heard again the shriek of breaking metal.

The leader did not turn to continue his attack on the marines as they rode past. He sighted on Alodar and kneed his horse forward. The banner on the mast at the rear of his saddle snapped stiffly with the increased speed. Alodar's eyes flicked to the standard, and he saw what he must try. Gathering his resolution, he grabbed his reins with his teeth. Sheathing his sword, he loosened a small shield hung from his saddle and held it stiffly with both hands. Biting down on the leather, he hunched behind his protection and aimed for the slowly revolving ball.

At the last instant before they collided, Alodar tilted the top of his shield backwards and ducked even lower underneath its layers of hide and steel. With a jolt that shocked his arms numb, the ball hit the flat surface, crumbling metal and ricocheting up and over his sheltered form. His horse stumbled, dropping one knee to the ground and then the other. Alodar pushed from his stirrups as he fell, tossing the pieces of shield skyward.

With one arm he reached across the warrior's waist, pivoting himself up behind on the horse's back. He ducked beneath the mace as it swung overhead. With his other hand, he ripped the banner from its mast. He flung the tangle of cloth upwards into the path of the ball just as it came around a second time.

The sharp spikes ripped the fabric, but Alodar tugged and crashed the weapon down to his side. The horseman pulled on the chain, but before he could wrench it free, Alodar's two marines circled back alongside and grabbed his arms. Alodar linked his hands around the helm. With a back-straining tug, he rolled off the horse. One marine pulled with the thrust and the second pushed from the other side. The warrior tipped and then slid from the saddle.

Alodar scrambled free and spun about in time to see one of Bandor's men lean low and dip his mace as he raced by. Alodar dived for the ground, feeling the weapon whistle past his ear. He looked up to see another of his marines charge from the left, his surcoat outstretched in imitation of what he had just seen. The second mace snagged as the two men collided. They tumbled to the ground in a heap with the rest.

Alodar got to his feet and saw the last two of his troop staying just beyond the range of Bandor's remaining warriors, tauntingly holding forth scraps of cloth rather than gleaming swords. Alodar exhaled slowly, bracing himself to return to the wagon and prepare for the next breakthrough.

Before he could act, he heard the beginning of a high-pitched buzz above the clash of battle. The men still remaining on horseback obscured his view, but there was no mistaking the direction from which it came. Along the line, the fighting momentarily stopped. Even Bandor's men looked over their shoulders for the source of the noise. Then suddenly the sound grew into an ear-ringing crescendo. From the south, a streak of black darkened the sky and descended onto the battlefield.

The plunging shaft broke against the line of Cedric's mail. Like a wave against a shallow shore, it rolled down its length to the last combatants at either end. With cries of pain and alarm, the rearmost line bolted from their formation, madly flailing arms and beating at mailed chests and backs. Despite his losses, Cedric had stood three deep against his foes; but now he thinned to two, and in some places a single defender opposed the wall massed against him.

"Imps, a swarm of imps," Grengor exclaimed as he rode closer, dragging one of Bandor's ensnared followers along the ground. "They are stinging through the ringlets of mail. No man can swing a decent blow with such distraction from a dozen directions at once."

Alodar grabbed his glass to see if the flanks escaped the enraged buzzing which hovered over the center. But his attention was pulled upwards as he saw a spray of fiery arcs bending down out of the sky towards Grak's nomads. Oil-soaked rags attached to long-vaned arrows descended in formation and followed precise trajectories to land in the barbarians' rear. As each hit the ground, it exploded in a shower of flame that flashed in a display of eye-paining brilliance. Alodar shielded his face from the bursts. As he blinked his eyes back into focus, he saw that where each arrow had struck stood a small, scaly, grotesque form, a miniature of the demons which had confronted him at the foot of Handar's tower.

Without delay, the lobster-red devils opened their mouths into wide ovals; from each belched forth balls of fire that energized the air into incandescence as they passed. The first hit two of Grak's men squarely on their leather-covered backs. With screams of surprise and showers of glowing embers, they immediately crumpled to the ground and were still. Bandor's men rushed forward into the gap.

Alodar swung his glass back to where he had last seen the wizards. He saw Handar coming his way, pulling the long hems of his robe high from the ground. To the east, another wizard hastily extended the telescoped legs of a portable tripod he had swung from his back. With practiced precision, he lit a fire in the wildly swinging brazier. A demonic form appeared, hovering in the air overhead. The wizard gestured once, and the djinn leaped skyward, deforming like a scarf of sheerest silk and creating a howling wind with his passage.

The wind buffeted at the fireballs as they sped on their deadly trajectories, and small wisps of flame tore away from the glowing spheres. Then whole balls blew out, leaving dark, carbon black cores bare and cool. With a

355

dull thump, they struck leather backs and fell harmlessly to the ground.

The wizard remaining in the center completed his conjuring, and Alodar saw more of the fire devils spring into existence. These bellowed globules of flame like the ones their cousins lofted from the crestline to the south but they rode on the air with the slow beat of thick pockmarked wings. Great, gaping holes tore through the swarm of imps, leaving small amorphous smears of crackling ooze, slowly sinking to the ground. The flight from the line halted, but the defenders wavered, still fearful of the attacks which came from the rear and uncertain of the aid which had come to help them.

Suddenly a series of flashes and explosions erupted from the stone firepit on the southern crest. Sparkles of light soared skyward, and from each sprang a djinn to join in the fray. A form like a salamander, purple skin glistening with wetness, soared above the rest, his body-length tail slowly uncoiling to reveal rows of stiletto-sharp stingers attached at either side. In immediate answer, three smaller djinns streaked from the north, gliding with undulating membranes stretched between outflung arms and legs. From small knobs on their heads, bolts of lightning cracked through the air, converging on the purple one with a web of forked energy. But before the accompanying thunder could reach the ground, the salamander flicked his tail forward, drawing the strike onto his stingers and cascading the energy down to the tip of his tail, which began to glow with an expanding ball of crackling blueness.

More unearthly forms sped across the valley, and each was met by a demon conjured by the wizards on the northern slopes. Streaks of energy pulsed through the air, and Alodar was forced to turn his eyes away from the intense flashes. Up and down the ragged battleline, strokes of pink and orange and bolts of deep magenta ripped through the sky. While men below stood dumbfounded, a second battle formed above, fire, wind, and water hurling with awesome force between the foes. Moving too fast for the eye to follow, the demons darted past one another, blasting forth their weapons, dodging behind defenses that men could not comprehend and drowning all the shouts below with their raspy cries.

Minutes passed as the battle raged and Alodar saw a second swarm of imps swoop down to replace the first roasted out of the sky. More volleys of fire devils zoomed overhead and began to project their balls of flame. Alodar looked to the two wizards, surrounded by concentric rings of exotic flames, gesticulating wildly, and trying to direct all the demons under their control. He searched for Handar and saw him only some ten yards away, raising his hands upwards before the beginnings of an outline in the center of a high-leaping flame. Alodar ran forward to the wizard as the orange head and massive form slowly took form. The cloven hooves and tail flickered into existence as he reached Handar's side.

"So, Handar, the battle goes not quite so well as you had hoped," Balthazar's voice rasped out at them. "For no long stretch of time did your meager forces hold at bay Bandor and his minions. Too soon did you call forth those lesser devils over which you have some sway. It is time, is it not, to let down your waning resistance and let me assume control of what is rightfully mine."

"Silence." Handar ordered. "Such speculation is not for your slothful meditation, so long as you are mine. There is work to be done. Rise and dispatch those who oppose us."

"Can you truly force me yet another time?" Balthazar shot back, his deep set eyes boiling down on the wizard standing before him.

Handar did not reply. With lips set firmly and fists clenched, he returned the demon's stare with an unflinching one of his own. As in the tower, Alodar saw the veins in Handar's forehead bulge with the effort.

"Go and do my bidding," Handar gasped in a dry wheeze at last, shaking with effort as he spoke. "The line here on the west. Rid them of the devils which bombard their backs with fire."

"I go to slay a few," Balthazar growled. "But if there is more to be done, then I will return, and you must reinstruct me."

With a rush of air, Balthazar streaked away, soaring high over the battlefield and then plummeting to earth with hands outstretched as he darted into the fire devils, smashing them out of existence with sharp claps of power.

"Handar, what is the matter?" Alodar asked as the demon departed. "It is not as it was in the tower."

357

The wizard sank slowly to the ground and pressed one fist to his sagging head. "So many, there are so many," he moaned. "Who of the council would have thought that they would come across with so many? It is not only Balthazar on whom I must concentrate but the minor djinns as well."

Before Alodar could speak again, Balthazar screamed across the slope to hover above them. "I rid you of four," he said. "Do you wish to try to direct me to another task?"

Handar climbed to his feet and stared again at the demon above him. With glowering menace, Balthazar hunched his huge scaly shoulders and looked back at his master.

Minutes passed and Handar trembled from the exertion to impress his will as he had done before. Suddenly he brought both clenched fists to his forehead and screamed in pain. "I cannot hold," he yelled. "He is too strong and I cannot hold."

Balthazar rasped a stomach-curdling laugh. "On your knees and salute your master," the demon cried. "It has taken many a summoning, but the final victory is mine."

Alodar looked rapidly about. The defending demons were fewer in number and huddled as shields around the two wizards on the ground. Like great hawks, the djinns from the south dove and blasted those that remained from the sky. Additional clouds of imps appeared from the south, and no devils rose to challenge them. More fireballs slammed into the rear of the nomads, leaving gaps too wide for a single blade to guard. The salient on the west expanded, and the line of barbarians tumbled backwards, letting them pass. Cedric's forces sagged in the center. More and more left the line to slap away at the darting imps. For a moment, Cedric's booming commands held the formation, but then columns of Bandor's men blasted through in two places. To the east, more fire devils flew through the sky, and the smell of burning flesh and leather drifted along the line. At the far end of the other flank, Alodar saw some of the horsemen thunder past Feston's few remaining defenders and swerve to the north, heading for the clumps of onlookers on the crest.

In ones and twos, men began to fling down their weapons and run from those who chased them. Then, like a dam crumbling from an overwhelming flood, Cedric's line collapsed from end to end, and a solid wall of Bandor's forces charged forth, waving their swords and shouting victory. Here and there, isolated clumps of men stood their ground, flicking swords outwards at the warriors who swelled to surround them on all sides. But, except for them, the entire defense dissolved in confusion.

Alodar stood rooted in position, watching the cavalry charge up the hill. He took one last look at the havoc as Bandor's army hacked its way forward. His marines still struggled with Bandor's horsemen on the ground. He looked across the other crest and saw it clear of men and the huge stone firepit silent and dimly glowing. He touched the pocket containing the wire he had beaten from the rare metal. He knew that he could forestall his task no longer.

"I shall use the portal the prince has erected to send his minions to us," he said aloud. "Perhaps the gesture will symbolize more strength than we have."

Alodar shook his head and sprinted to the west, hoping to duck into the shimmering air before any of Bandor's men turned to cut him down.

CHAPTER TWENTY-TWO

The Final Battle

ALODAR panted up to the deserted firepit. Screams echoed across the valley, but he turned his back so that he could concentrate. He lit a fire and thrust the end of the exotic wire into the heat. Impatiently he waited for ignition.

Several minutes passed but, although the coil grew painfully hot, the silvery-gray luster did not change. "I expected as much," Alodar muttered to himself. "Despite his great prowess, Handar never worked with any substance that required more than an open flame. He did not consider that kindling the gateway to a demon prince would take a bit more effort."

He dropped the wire and quickly pushed some of the larger bricks, still warm to the touch, into the form of a crude anthanor. He stuffed kindling in its base, started a second blaze, and blew air through the chamber with a piece of hose until the stones glowed cherry red. Cautiously he inserted the end of the coil. Almost instantly, it ignited. Squinting at the intense spot of flame as it raced around the loops, he willed his adversary to come forth.

For an instant, nothing happened. Then the ground shook in a great spasm that crashed together the stones of the pit. The wind howled, and the sky grew suddenly dark. The air above his head exploded in a shower of imp light, and hundreds of shrieking voices bombarded his ears with sound. More devils burst forth with sizes and shapes that spanned the descriptions of the sagas. Spitting fire, roaring the wind, throwing sheets of hail and ice, and quaking the ground they shredded the elements.

Finaly, with a flash of blinding light and a clap of thunder, a last figure stepped forth from the fire. Then all was quiet. Alodar stared with surprise. The form confronting him was not a stooped djinn or a towering hulk such as Balthazar. Barely his own height and with straw-pale hair pulled back over a smooth brow flecked with gold, the demon prince glowered through eyes half closed under long curving lashes. His face was thin and delicate with an upturned nose, thin lips, and ears barely pointed. Rather than the coarse and hairy nakedness of his kindred, he wore a flowing gown of deepest sea green which covered all his slender body except for the tips of his fingers. A prince of demonkind, Alodar thought, but without a close look he would pass for the ruler of some exotic and far-away realm of men.

"So you seek a prince of my kind," a voice tinkled from slightly parted lips. "Your folly only makes possible a little sooner what would be my pleasure in a short time to come." He waved one draped arm across the valley. "The end of the battle is but minutes away, and soon an entire mortal kingdom will be mine. With the name of Elezar on every being's lips, enough of my minions will come forth that the resistance to passage will vanish. Any of my kind then will journey freely between the realms."

Alodar braced himself as he tried to hold in focus the plan he had constructed the night before. He felt his face tighten into a grim mask, hiding the small kernel of self-doubt he harbored inside.

"Submit," he commanded with a throat suddenly dry. "Submit to him who ordered you forth."

Elezar threw back his head in a human gesture and his laugh jingled skyward. "Such impertinence and bluster! You mortals think that because the browbeating of a hapless imp or simple devil is successful, you are more than a match for any of our realm. Look at me. How closely do I resemble the lesser ones over which I hold sway? The ratio of their power to mine is no greater than that of a toad to yours."

"The relative strengths of our wills cannot be decided by words alone," Alodar said, "no matter how glibly spoken." He paused and then continued with a rush. "I have been chosen as the one to bring you to submission. Show me the reason that this is not so."

Elezar's finely pencilled brows raised slightly. "The question is not who is the stronger. Only the means by which I will demonstrate it to you." He studied Alodar for a moment in silence. "No doubt you have met the mild annoyances of the lesser sprites. Tell me, if you can, how what they do compares to this?"

Three of Elezar's long fingers undulated in a complex gesture. Suddenly Alodar felt an itching rash break out on his back and spread over his limbs. Involuntarily he raked one hand across his thigh and reached frantically between his shoulder blades with the other. Down the small of his back he gouged, along both legs and across his chest. Wherever he touched, the itch seemed to increase with maddening intensity, driving his uncontrolled flailing into a frenzy.

For over two minutes, he spun about on the ground in a tight ball, kicking up dust. Then, just as suddenly as it had begun, the feeling slipped away.

"Or perhaps you have dealt with demons of fear," Elezar continued.

Alodar felt a paralyzing chill race down his spine. His chest muscles cramped and he gasped for breath. He looked up wide-eyed at Elezar and threw his hands across his face. Thoughts of searing thirst, smashed bone, and

361

ragged lungs ripped from his chest flashed through his mind. Nothing mattered but escape. His intent, his reason for being there, his plan to cope, all vanished with a brain-numbing jolt. He tried to rise on wobbly legs, but the trembling muscles would not respond.

"And the strong emotions manipulated by my lesser minions are not the only ones for which I am your master." Elezar shrugged. "I can crumble you as well with ones more subtle, with gut-burning rushes of anxiety, the muscle-knotting barriers of frustration, the will-sapping blanket of despair."

Alodar tried to stop the swirl of his thoughts and bring them back under his control. Unlike the projections of the other imps and devils, the brutal force of Elezar's onslaught had raced through his mind undiminished by any feeble resistence he could offer. Like a scrap of paper in a storm, his will was blown about with no volition of its own. There was no way he or any other wizard could hope to stand for more than an instant against a prince of demons. It was foolish even to try. Alodar felt his spirits sag. With a trembling lip he choked out a sob.

It was a problem without solution, a task that could not be done. Alodar's head throbbed with the impossibility and the muscles of his neck strained in painful contractions. His left cheek began to twitch and his hand shook uncontrollably.

Alodar's stomach churned and his thoughts cut through his mind like a spray of stinging acid. Submission seemed a minor price to pay if it would end the uncertainty and give him even a moment of peace. Alodar lifted his eyes upwards and opened his mouth to speak.

The demon cut him off. "Even with those, it is hatchling's play. I choose to use instead the means that will give me the most satisfaction." He gestured a final time and Alodar felt the intense feelings evaporate away.

"You have tasted my might," Elezar continued, "and now know well what easily can be your lot if I choose to inflict it."

He stopped and parted his thin lips in a twisted smile. "I want your submission as a gift, freely given. Under no duress, with your thoughts completely your own. You mortals pride yourself on your logic, on how you can sort through the facts and conditions to the conclusion that

362

is inescapable. In the end you will be mine, if you choose to resist or not. Is it not better to minimize the discomfort if the final result is the same? I will give you a few moments. I want your decision based on the cold light of your clearest reason. Contemplate it in the pavilion I erect for you here. In the meantime I will amuse myself with reports of the battle."

A momentary burst of light dazzled Alodar's eyes. When he could see again he found himself in a domelike cage. Iridescent struts crisscrossed and joined in a complex web that rose from the ground on all sides and met in a point over his head. He looked for Elezar and found him standing some five feet away, conversing in rasping tones with two hovering devils.

Alodar slumped to the ground. For a moment he sat in stunned silence. The validity of the demon's logic was overwhelming. There was no way for a wizard to struggle against him. Despite his slight form, Elezar could not be resisted.

Alodar blinked and sat upright. He pulled into focus dim outlines splattered about in his mind. He breathed deeply to steady himself and remembered the sketchy plan that the demon had so viciously dashed away.

Alodar grabbed at the two bars nearest and felt them yield to his touch, stretching like rubber away from his body. He changed his grip and forced the bars apart; but as he did, two adjacent ones contracted closer together. He could not enlarge the opening. He rose to a crouch and felt the pressure of the webbing on his back. Straining with his legs, he forced himself to a standing position, but no spar ripped or parted.

He withdrew a small knife from one of his pockets and vigorously sawed at the strut nearest. His eyes widened with surprise as the blade grated across a surface suddenly hard and unyielding. Even though it retained a soft and maleable texture under his hand, the line of contact with his knife seemed like the strongest steel.

Alodar turned slowly to examine the intricately woven net, frowning as he caught hints of a subtle symmetry. He pushed again with his knife and met inflexible resistance. When he extended a finger, the bar bowed gently to his touch. With his shoulder and head, he forced a deep bulge that crept back into place when he released the pressure. He turned the knifeblade on its side. Surprisingly, the flat edge caused the greatest indentation of all. Somehow the blunter the object, the more effect it had. But what could be flatter than a plane of steel?

Suddenly, like the ingredients of a complicated formula, all of the elements of what he must do coalesced together. He would have only one try, he thought excitedly, but nothing else offered even a glimmer of hope. He glanced at Elezar, still occupied with the demons. His pulse quickened as one of the hovering devils darted away. Hastily he patted at the many pockets of his tunic, throwing out vials, matches, string, a mirror, pebbles, twigs, scissors, and the other contents as he searched for what he needed.

Finally he found the piece of Aeriel's wishbone and formed the binding. Goosebumps raced along his arms and legs as he felt his body heat provide the energy for the connection. Slowly he removed the bone from his pocket and placed it on the ground. He looked across the valley at the swirling confusion on the slopes and Bandor's waving banners already on the opposite crestline. For a moment, he thought of Aeriel racing away from warriors in hot pursuit, or already thrust to the ground, but he pushed the possibility aside. He grabbed the bone like a knife and, with bold slashes, drew a summoning message in the soft ground. Across the valley, the other part of the bone would also be scratching the earth, copying his motions stroke for stroke. Twice he looked over his shoulder at Elezar's back and increased the speed with which he inscribed the words that explained what she must bring.

When he was done, Alodar studied the webbing carefully one final time. He found the junction he wanted and settled on his knees before it, trying to burn the position of the vertex into his mind. He closed his eyes and practiced hitting the exact spot with no clues to aid him. Over and over, with methodical repetition, he conditioned himself to perform the precise stroke. With each fleeting moment, the chance of finishing his preparations before having to face Elezar's awesome power diminished, but there was no other course to try.

Finally he heard a commotion down the slope and turned his head to see Aeriel struggling up the hill, batting away a small swarm of imps. Her clothing was torn and her face and arms swollen with many angry welts. She hobbled barefoot over the rough ground, the remnant of a boot top still tied about one leg and the last drops of bog solvent dripping into smoking rivulets on her skin.

Gasping for breath, Aeriel struggled upwards to the far edge of the firepit. One small devil flew from Elezar and yanked at her hair. She stumbled with exhaustion and fell. The prince turned to watch as she shakily propped herself on one arm. With a final effort, she tossed her dagger into Alodar's cage, collapsing a second time.

"A common blade will avail you nothing." Elezar said, drawing his attention back to Alodar. "The sharper the edge, the greater will be the resistance of my pavilion to it. And even if you were to break free, your legs could not propel you away so fast that my power could not follow. Now tell me of your decision. Am I not your master, the master of your will freely given? Or must I take it in exchange for pain and suffering?"

Alodar grabbed the dagger and it instantly molded itself into the contours of his hand. He ran his finger along the blade edge and felt the magically perfect flatness. Elezar raised his eyebrows expectantly, but Alodar ignored the question. Making sure he was back in position he began the charm.

"Answer me not with gibberish," Elezar snapped. "And do not trifle with my patience."

Alodar raced on through the three recitals, pushing aside the nausea and not contemplating the consequences. With a rush, he completed the last word and looked at himself in the small mirror at his side.

Instantly the world vanished. He was in total darkness and without sound. The sickness in his stomach, the residual aches from Elezar's bombardment, even the tactile sensation of kneeling on the ground, all were gone. As when Kelric had enchanted him with the eye, he was totally cut off from any stimulation from the outside.

Mentally Alodar sighed with relief. He had not been sure he could complete another enchantment, but the resistance was far less with himself rather than someone else as the subject. Apparently he still had his consciousness, even though he knew nothing of what went on around him.

He jerked his attention back to his task and visualized

raising his hand to cut at the cage with the magic dagger. He felt nothing and had no way of knowing if he had hit the vertex at the precise spot but he had to assume that he did.

Next he imagined himself jumping upwards and crashing into Elezar. Mentally he wrapped his arms around the demon as they fell. Straining muscles that he could not feel, he crushed his arms towards his chest. At Handar's tower, even a demon had felt physical pain when cut. Now to see if a demon prince could also feel it. With unwavering persistence, Alodar focused on a picture of Elezar encased in his arms, with spindly ribs cracking one by one.

For a moment, nothing happened. Then Alodar felt a sudden stabbing thrust into his bubble of blackness. Somehow, in a way he could not describe, his barrier thinned and retreated before a probing pressure. A portion of his wall paled from black to gray, and the beginnings of pain trickled inwards.

Alodar concentrated on controlling his senses. He increased the intensity with which he blocked them out. Pushing against the indentation, he halted the rush and forced it backwards. With a shove, he slammed it into the smooth wall of nothingness which surrounded him.

Another thrust followed and then another. Like an inverted sea urchin, the spines poked inward from all directions. Alodar felt the seed of doubt, the kernel of fear, the germ of indecision take root in his mind. For a moment, he faltered. Then he focused on the first and repelled it away. One by one, he expelled them all and reinforced the thickness of his protection.

Finally Alodar felt a uniform pressure on all sides. There was no hint of pain or distress, but instead a subtle discomfort, as if he were surrounded in a growing crowd. He braced himself against the squeeze and exerted his will to keep Elezar's influence away. But the pressure increased. With a shudder, his barrier constricted closer to his innermost being.

Alodar felt his pride pushed on top of his curiosity, his anger mingled with his need to succeed. His drives tumbled among his doubts and fears. The wrinkles of his personality collided as they were pressed by the uniform smoothness. He strained to expand the bubble, but the pressure waxed greater. The sphere contracted with a jerk, once and then twice again. The forces gathered momentum, hurling inward, imploding him towards a featureless smooth mind and then non-existence.

Alodar reached for intense feelings to counteract the thrust. He thought of Aeriel's blistered face and torn hair. He remembered Periac's mindless stare in Bardina's town square. He saw Quantos fall on the deck of the royal barge, the warriors on the walls of Iron Fist, and all the others who resisted the demonic forces which swept from the west and south.

The inrushing walls slowed their acceleration but still continued collapsing. His thoughts merged together and distorted into incomprehensible babbles. In desperation he recalled the events of his own quest, the humiliation with which it started, the pain, fatigue and frustrations he had borne along the way. He tasted again the decision to shoulder the burden that Handar gave him, the trap for his relationship with Aeriel no matter what the outcome. All of these feelings squeezed out of the recesses of his mind and flowed into the determination with which he strained. Mentally he gritted his teeth. With a wrench, he tightened his grip about Elezar. As his horizon of consciousness closed in, he willed his knees up onto the demon's chest and gouged them into Elezar's stomach.

One by one, the efforts added to his defenses. And with each thought, each memory purged from its hiding place, the onslaught slowed. But onward it came, shredding memories, flattening the essence of his being. Alodar felt parts of himself distort and then fade away. But as he shrank, he tenaciously locked onto one thought and held it precisely. He pictured his vice-like grip and the breaking of Elezar's body.

As the last hint of consciousness flickered, Alodar screamed his defiance, willing all his muscles to aid in a back-cracking snap. Like an arrow shot skyward, reaching the zenith of its trajectory, the inrushing forces decelerated against the dense kernel they labored to crack. At the very limit of Alodar's existence they coasted to a halt.

For a long time, nothing more happened. Compressed to near madness but holding to his one thought, Alodar resisted the weight which would crush him and strained his arms towards his chest.

Finally, after how long he could not tell, he felt a slight lessening of pressure. Then, with a sudden rush, the blackness ballooned to its original size. As quickly as it had vanished, his personality inflated to its former shape and size. He waited for another attack, but the limit of his bubble was quiet and still. He hesitated a while longer and then decided to act. Cautiously he opened a pinprick in the blanket, a tiny tunnel by which a whisper could reach him from the outside. For a moment there was silence. Then, in perfect clarity, a thought seeped through his screen.

"Please master, unhand me so that I may serve you," Elezar begged. "My body is broken and it will need repair."

Alodar struggled up on one arm, but Handar gently pushed him back down on the pallet. "Rest," the wizard said. "It all proceeds as you have commanded it. The lesser demons are being tracked by the greater and dispatched back whence they came. Your servant will ensure that they do not threaten us in like fashion again. And those subjugated, men and wizards alike are being restored to their former state. There is much confusion throughout the land, but I and the other freed wizards are spreading the word about what has happened. And the fair lady and the rest have survived it all, with no more than minor scratches and wounds."

Alodar nodded in understanding and slipped back into his painful and exhausted slumber.

"You recovered far faster from your wounds after Kelric's enchantment," Grengor said irritably as they slowly bumped along. "A month's lingering in the north while Vendora and the rest marched in triumph back into Ambrosia! You should know by now not to trust what she and the other suitors might do in your absence."

Alodar did not immediately reply, deep in his own thoughts. Like waves lashed by a storm, they crashed against the rocks of his innermost self. He looked at Handar, now freed from Balthazar's dominance, and across at Aeriel riding a pony at his side. She dropped her eyes and did not return his glance. He touched the proclamation which had come at last, fingering the thick seal and lines of signatures from the grateful subjects far and wide. He thought of his satisfaction in solving the riddles of Iron Fist and the Cycloid Guild, the self-esteem from having braved the Fumus Mountains and the sorcerer's eye, the pride in having Cedric's respect. He puzzeled over how empty the glory seemed now that it was won.

"The summons explicitly stated that I was to travel when I felt ready," Alodar said. "And we broke camp as soon as the wizard's council was concluded. I am sure the fair lady had enough to keep her occupied in my absence."

"Without the persuasive presence of the archimage, I doubt if our agreement could have been forged in a year, let alone a month," Handar told Grengor. "Alodar properly saw his duty to serve his craft before the whim of a queen."

The wizard nodded and continued. "And the accordance was a good one. Elezar has agreed only to halt voluntary and coordinated transfer between the worlds. He cannot stop a summons by humankind, even if he wished to. As long as we possess the knowledge and means to reach through flame across the gulf which separates us, even without the ambitions of a prince, there will always be risk and potential for great peril.

"To submit to periodic examination by one's peers is a difficult step for men of my craft to take, but it gives us a chance to detect something amiss before it gets out of hand. It was Alodar's persistence and vivid retelling of how vast were Elezar's powers compared to our own that finally convinced us to establish the testing procedures. And with my awakened comrades and the most powerful who practice today in agreement, the lesser will follow. After these ceremonies in Ambrosia, whatever they may be, I will cross the isthmus to the south and carry the word further."

Grengor did not reply, and the four turned their horses from the muddy side street onto the cobblestoned avenue. Mentally Alodar pictured the screaming crowds, swirling streamers, and slow procession to the palace gates. He tried to recapture the exhilarating taste of so long ago: the vision of the royal guardsmen clearing the way; the brave lads darting from the side to touch the horse that bore him; the young girls batting their eyes as he passed; the

369

chant that echoed from the walls in a deafening crescendo. Alodar the hero, Alodar the savior of the fair lady, Alodar of Procolon!

Alodar licked his lips and frowned at the dryness in his mouth. The image was as vivid as before, but the excitement which should accompany it was gone. As they approached the main boulevard, he reached across his saddle and squeezed Aeriel's hand.

They turned the corner, and the empty street rang with the clop of their horses' hooves. Alodar reined to a halt and looked about with puzzlement. He scanned the line of rooftops to the palace in the distance. Both skylines were deserted, as silent as the walkways underneath. Ambrosia was as unmoving as the quiet and open sea.

For several minutes, the three halted in silence. Then they heard the sound of horses other than their own, and Alodar saw four riders coming their way.

"Lord Festil, Feston, Basil, Duncan," Grengor exclaimed as the riders drew near. "Where is anyone else? Did not Melab's message of our coming reach the queen? Is not the reception and wedding ceremony prepared?"

"A wedding ceremony there was, indeed," Festil announced as he stopped before them. "But it was for that unclean nomad from the north. She rushed it through as soon as she felt she could. Only after it was done did Vendora send the summons demanded by her subjects. For three days now the entire city has wined on the palace grounds in celebration."

"Then my summons is for an empty honor and no more," Alodar said. He turned to Aeriel and smiled. "I am no longer honor bound. Grak is destined to be the victorious suitor, after all."

"You do well to cover your anger," Festil replied. "With low cunning, she conspired to satisfy a personal whim at the expense of the state. And the barbarian! Already his outland ways offend many who have upheld Procolon's proud tradition."

"Land for his kinsmen as reward for their defense of the fair lady," Feston growled. "Land held for centuries by the oldest of our noble houses and ripped away less than an hour after the crown of consort was on his head."

"Talk of new taxes," Basil muttered, "and hints of confiscation of my jewels as a national treasure. Every

370

merchant on the street laments about how an outsider tramples on the delicate balance of factions which has supported the queen. And that stiff-necked Cedric has been made grand marshall of arms."

"He demands magic swords and shields in exchange for the right of the guilds to keep their gates sealed," Duncan cut in. "And room in the royal chambers for the objects, but not for those who would wield them. None of the magicians will stand for it long. With the right one to lead us, the barbarian soon will be deposed."

"Yes, the orbholder speaks truthfully," Festil agreed as he dismounted. Feston and the others followed. As Alodar watched, they knelt and placed their swords at his feet.

"There is doubt and suspicion still," Festil said. "Vendora's grip on the throne is little better than before. The demons have left us all untrusting. Only one stands out from the rest. Only one has the unblemished standard and reputation around which all can rally. Take up the banner, Alodar, and the peerage will follow."

"And the merchants also," Basil continued. "With my fortune and the promise of a return to the way things were, none on the streets will dare oppose you."

"The weapons of the guilds which Grak craves so," Duncan said. "They will be for our warriors instead. Lead us forth, Alodar. Take the last small step to finish what you have started."

"There is no other," Feston concluded. "With you at the lead, the rebellion will be short and swift. Even with Cedric and Grak to defend her, it can hardly last more than another year. And when we are done, you will be king and not consort. You can do with Vendora what you will."

Alodar sighed at the news. Wearily he looked down at the figures kneeling before him. He saw part of his dream, if not the whole. And with one more effort, the rest could be his. One more struggle. The humiliation of his father erased, the cheers of all lords and craftsmen, and bows and flattery any time he wanted them. He paused and glanced to the side. He could even choose Aeriel as his queen.

Alodar slowly exhaled and shook his head. What would he have when he was done? With the homage of a Festil, would there also be the offered sword of a Cedric? With a chest of Basil's jewels to bribe away resistance, would there also be the pride of a struggle hard fought and won? With Duncan's sphere to shield from assassins, what would he see in Aeriel's eyes?

The pomp of tradition, the intrigues of state, the fear of the shadow behind the next column—was it for these that he had cast aside the cape of the thaumaturge?

Alodar ran over the reasons for his quest but found they had melted away. Instead he tasted the excitement of the rising air car, the smell of freshly ground duckweed, the beauty of a six-fold symmetry, the mystery of an out-reaching tendril of the mind, the wonder of what lay beyond the flame. He stared at the men awaiting his answer.

No, by the laws, it was not for this that he was meant, his thoughts thundered suddenly with determination. The quests were done; they were completed. There was no remaining adventure that now cried for a finish.

"Vendora's decision frees me of any further service," he shouted aloud. "I need pursue her no further. What concerns the lord and craftsman is no longer an affair of mine." He turned to Aeriel and spoke with rising excitement. "The consort has been chosen and your obligation is done," he said. "Aeriel, Aeriel, we have not lost the final battle after all. The way is clear for us to plot our future together. There are no more gauntlets to be run."

Aeriel started to smile back but then caught herself in mid-expression. Her brow wrinkled and she stiffened in the saddle. "It is well enough for you to exercise a second option, once the first is denied you. But despite how I may feel, the man who possesses my spirit will be the one who chooses me freely over all others, no matter how exalted they may be."

Alodar raised his eyebrows in surprise and then for a long moment was silent. He glanced at the kneeling men and back to Aeriel. "I pursued the queen to find the glory and honor it would bring," he said slowly. "And Handar stated that the first trek was but the shadow of another. But through it all, I was on a third quest as well, Aeriel, the one that all of us take, the quest to find oneself."

Alodar stopped and looked at each of those who faced him. "The man that I have found is not the one that you seek," he told them at last.

He turned to Grengor with a sad smile and gave him a salute. "Neither am I a warrior. You and the other marines have served me well, Grengor, but a far better future will be yours if you seek our Cedric, the grand marshall and place your trust under a proper master."

He turned to the wizard. "Continue your journey southward, Handar. Your task is far more important than any pomp and circumstance here."

Alodar looked back at Aeriel. "Through the random factors of fate, I am the makings of an archimage, the master of all five of the arts. Who knows what will happen when I am as proficient as Handar and the others intended me to be? And the answer to that riddle is my destiny.

"I still have the option, Aeriel. I believe what Festil and the others say. One more campaign and it would finally be over. But I choose to turn away from the queen, step aside from all the paths that I could follow to pursue what she represents. I elect to seek instead teachers of the arts. I will study with them all until I can rightfully call myself master. The beginning will be thaumaturgy under Periac in the north as quickly as I can find him." He stopped and breathed deeply. "And more than anything else, Aeriel, my choice is to have you at my side."

Aeriel's face softened but her eyes kept a hint of fire. "I have been a counselor of state, a molder of a kingdom's destiny," she said. "I do not intend to replace it with stoking dinner fires and beating clean the laundry."

"Come with me," Alodar said softly, "and we will journey on your quests as well as mine."

Aeriel finally smiled. She headed her horse around the way they had come. Alodar nodded and turned his mount to follow. Without looking back, they galloped away into the pages of the sagas.

About the Author

LYN HARDY became interested in fantasy while wandering through the fringes of fandom as an undergraduate at Caltech. In addition to reading and writing, he has sporadic bursts of enthusiasm for collecting stamps, comics, astronaut patches and playing cards. He currently lives with his wife and two daughters in Torrance, California.